THE BLUE AND THE GRAY UNDERCOVER

THE BLUE AND THE GRAY UNDERCOVER

EDITED BY ED GORMAN

A TOM DOHERTY ASSOCIATES BOOK
NEW YORK

THE BLUE AND THE GRAY UNDERCOVER

Copyright © 2001 by Tekno Books and Ed Gorman

Edited by James Frenkel

A Forge Book
Published by Tom Doherty Associates, LLC
175 Fifth Avenue
New York, NY 10010

www.tor.com

Forge® is a registered trademark of Tom Doherty Associates, LLC.

Library of Congress Cataloging-in-Publication Data

The blue and the gray undercover / edited by Ed Gorman.
        p. cm.
    ISBN 0-312-87487-1 (hc)
    ISBN 0-312-87537-1 (pbk)
        1. United States—History—Civil War, 1861–1865—Secret service—Fiction.
    2. Undercover operations—Fiction. 3. Secret service—Fiction. 4. War stories,
    American. 5. Spy stories, American. I. Gorman, Edward.

    PS648.C54 B57 2001
    813'.0108358—dc21   2001040486

First Hardcover Edition: November 2001
First Trade Paperback Edition: October 2002

Printed in the United States of America

0 9 8 7 6 5 4 3 2 1

CONTENTS

INTRODUCTION • *Ed Gorman*   9

HOBSON'S CHOICE • *John Lutz*   13

THE MEASURE • *Gary Phillips*   29

THE COUNTERFEIT COPPERHEAD • *Edward D. Hoch*   41

THE DEAD LINE • *Kristine Kathryn Rusch*   55

SOUTH GEORGIA CROSSING • *Loren D. Estleman*   83

THE INVISIBLE SPY • *Brendan DuBois*   91

MONICA VAN TELFLIN AND THE PROPER APPLICATION OF

PRESSURE • *James H. Cobb*   111

WORTH A THOUSAND WORDS • *Aileen Schumacher*   133

BELLE BOYD, THE REBEL SPY • *Bill Crider*   147

THE KNIGHTS OF LIBERTY • *Robert J. Randisi*   163

PORT TOBACCO • *Jane Haddam*   175

THE SWAN • *Ray Vukcevich*   193

THE COURTSHIP OF CAPTAIN SWENK • *P. G. Nagle*   211

THE ROAD TO STONY CREEK • *Jane Lindskold*   227

OTHER . . . . 1 • *Janet Berliner*   249

THE TURNCOAT • *Doug Allyn*   265

A SMALL AND PRIVATE WAR • *Ed Gorman*   283

SLITHER • *Marie Jakober*   301

INTRODUCTION

Harnett T. Kane wrote a masterly overview of Civil War spying, noting that what the spies lacked in acumen they more than made up for in enthusiasm. But for all the books that have been written on the subject, including *Secret Missions of the Civil War* by Philip Van Doren Stern, or *Spies and Spy Masters of the Civil War* by Donald E. Markle, the vast array of undercover missions and spy networks that sprang up on both sides of the Civil War will never be completely known.

For although the documents regarding espionage during the war collected by the U.S. Government became available to the public in 1953, the rows of crumbling, faded files are just a small fraction of the secret correspondence during the War between the States. The vast majority of reports and secret messages were carried verbally, so vital information would not fall into the wrong hands. Also, thousands of documents, both secret and public, were destroyed during the burning of Atlanta, Richmond, and other cities during the war. Who knows what secret missions of patriotic men and women, who risked their lives on a daily basis to bring a scrap of information to their leaders, have been forever lost in the annals of history?

When the Civil War began, both the North and the South were woefully unprepared for espionage activities. Although they played catch-up fast, the Confederacy did not have any official kind of secret service bureau until November, 1864. By then both armies had ciphers and codes, daring heroes and heroines, but most of the spying activity during the conflict was done by a cadre of amateurs from both sides, who were able to gather information with relative ease, though in many instances at great peril to their lives.

Take the newspapers, for example. Neither the blue nor the gray censored the press, so papers frequently ran extensive coverage of military plans in advance of battles. This practice was so common that Robert E. Lee appointed people to do nothing but collect and study Northern newspapers. Both sides quickly got smart and started planting false information in such stories. Lee himself spent many hours sifting through the major papers from the North, separating wheat from chaff.

Women played a significant role in spying. Charm, seduction, and overall cleverness got them many of the secrets they needed. One such female spy was Elizabeth C. Howland. Trained in medicine by her father, she used her skills as a cover while spying for the Confederacy. In one instance, she smuggled documents with Northern fortifications marked on them past enemy lines in a ham bone carried by her own children.

One of the more famous spies was Elizabeth Van Lew, who carried on a nerve-racking spy operation in Richmond, the capital of the Confederacy. Her eccentric behavior caused many of her neighbors to dismiss her as harmless, enabling her to gather information more easily. When Richmond fell, she entertained Union generals at her home, causing the city's aristocracy to denounce her as a traitor.

Perhaps the most daring female spy was Sarah Emma Edmonds, a Canadian who not only brought back valuable information from the Confederate garrison at Fort Monroe, but painted her skin black and wore a rough wig to impersonate a slave to do it.

Toward the end of the war, blue and gray alike had formal intelligence operations. In large part, these operations stuck to large enemy cities, and points where troops were massing—or were about to mass (newspapers frequently carried this information, too).

As for sabotage, there were two prime targets—railroads and munitions plants. The former inspired great rage in both the Union and the Confederacy; a lot of young men died when a troop train was blown up or derailed. Fire was a great asset to the saboteur. In 1864 a plot by a small group of saboteurs to burn New York City was uncovered by Union detectives. The plan failed when the "Greek fire" brought in by the Confederates failed to incinerate the building as the chemist who had sold it to them had described, and the fires were easily put out.

Historians today are struck by how easily one side slipped into the camp of the other. As Kane and Stern both pointed out, this was easy to do. Troops of both sides looked pretty much alike and—except for thick Southern accents—sounded pretty much alike. In fact, Union cavalrymen under the command of General Philip H. Sheridan's chief of scouts, Harry H. Young, often donned rebel uniforms and entered the enemy lines to gather information. Northerners working to hinder the Union were called Copperheads. Any number of well-known spies not only infiltrated the enemy camp but, in some cases, became popular members of it . . . all while conducting their surveillance.

However amusing some aspects of Civil War spying was, it was still a deadly business. Spies were regularly found out and hanged. And some of the espionage was so crafty and immoral—did Lincoln, for instance, unwittingly appoint a Confederate spy to his cabinet?—that thousands of young men's lives were lost due to revealed information and misinformation. In this age of James Bond and post–Cold War espionage, we sometimes forget that spying has terrible consequences. For both sides.

This, then, is a collection of original stories about that time and that occupation. The writers have used various aspects of the war as dramatic backdrops to their fiction. From Gary Phillips's gritty story of a black man doing whatever he had to do just to survive the war, to Bill Crider's fictionalized account of one of the most famous spies in all of the war, Belle Boyd, these eighteen stories re-create the days when American espionage was in its infancy, and, even worse, when it pitted countryman against countryman. Obviously, as in all fiction, liberties were taken with some of the facts, but this is a collection meant to entertain, not to instruct.

I hope you enjoy reading this book as much as I enjoyed editing it.

—ED GORMAN

John Lutz is one of the most skilled mystery writers working today. His settings and descriptions always have the ring of authenticity, whether he's writing about the blues scene in New Orleans or the relationships between men and women. His series characters are also in a class by themselves, whether it be the hapless Alo Nudger or the more traditional detective Fred Carver. A favorite contributor to both *Ellery Queen's Mystery Magazine* and *Alfred Hitchcock's Mystery Magazine*, his work has also appeared in numerous anthologies, most recently *Irreconcilable Differences*. In "Hobson's Choice," a unit of wounded Rebel soldiers comes upon a Southern woman doing her best to survive the depredations of the North, and find more than simple shelter on her abandoned plantation.

Hobson's Choice

❖

John Lutz

Eighteen sixty-four. Sherman had been here.

The fields were dark but for scatterings of green shoots and white and purple wildflowers that had fought their way through the ashes of the dry summer crops. Blackened corpses of farm animals lay grotesquely alongside the road or piled where they'd crowded panicked against fences in their attempt to escape the flames. The distant sight of the skeletal remains of farmhouses and outbuildings, where once prosperous and happy families had lived, tightened Jedediah Logan's guts as he sat astride his mount on the road south. The horse whinnied and stomped, so he had to pat its neck and calm it. Like him, it could feel and smell death all around them, the scent of decay instead of flowers, the taste of ashes instead of the clean moist air of open land. Even animals knew of the general's passing through their country.

Sherman.

Captain Jed Logan was the surviving ranking officer of the Tennessee Ninth Volunteer Cavalry. Riding slumped in their saddles behind him were his remaining men, all twelve of them.

On a scouting mission they had blundered across a contingent of Yanks prying the timbers from beneath a rail line into Atlanta, only ten men. Colonel Shivers had called a charge.

It had been a trap.

A larger body of Yanks had risen from where they were hidden in the high brush and opened fire with what seemed like everything in the Northern arsenal, even with light artillery that was concealed among trees on a nearby hill.

The Tennessee Ninth had stopped in midcharge, caught in a crossfire as well as frontal fire from the Yanks on the rails. Horses and men screamed and fell as they fought their way back the way they'd come, seeking shelter from the withering barrage.

But there was no shelter. Not for quarter of a mile. It was a dash that only thirteen survived. A dozen and Jed Logan, with a bit of grapeshot in his right thigh.

They kept going, pushing their horses full out, listening to the gunshots and screams and shouting become fainter behind them. It was like riding out of a nightmare.

Out of range at last, they regrouped, gritted their teeth when they assessed the damage, and turned south. Always they turned south now after such a whipping at the hands of the Yanks. It had become instinct for them. Retreat was set deep in their bones, even if fight was in their blood.

The noise behind them faded but for a few high-pitched screams. Yanks crowing over a victory, mimicking the Confederate Rebel yell. It was a sound Logan had come to hate.

He heard hoofbeats hard on his left and saw a shadow on the road. Sergeant Billy Matoon had spurred his horse so he would be alongside Logan's.

Matoon, a big blond man from Murfreesboro, wiped his sweaty and grimy broad face with his gray shirtsleeve and looked over at Logan. "How could the Yanks have set the bait for us? No way they coulda known we'd be along."

"Luck," Logan said. "They were ripping up some rail, and one of their outlying scouts saw us and rode ahead to report."

"Could have happened that way, sir," Matoon said. He didn't sound as if he believed it.

Logan knew what he was thinking. The Yankee spy Hobson—if that was his real name—was rumored to be in the area. Hobson, who seemed to have been in the area before and after every major battle of the war. Logan wasn't so sure there really was a Hobson. He was certainly a convenient way for officers to explain their failings when battle plans didn't work as intended. Hobson's fault. Perhaps every war had its Hobson.

"Country in Georgia sure ain't as pretty as back home," Matoon said. He held the reins lightly as he rode, his elbows out, one of the Ninth's most skilled horsemen.

"Wouldn't be too sure," Logan told him. "We haven't seen home for a while." As he spoke he realized home, Tennessee, was north of them, surely a saddening thought.

"Far, far from home," Matoon said, thinking the same as Logan. Then he glanced around. "At least Satan's son didn't torch the woods."

On the road's right, sparsely spaced trees had become closer together, so that now the area was thickly wooded.

"Only because the woods are too green to burn," Logan said. Then he raised his right hand and reined in his horse. Behind him, what was left of the Ninth came to a halt.

Everyone was silent now. The sudden quiet after the relentless thudding of horses' hooves seemed eerie. Not the slightest sound emanated from the woods. This was a spot Logan himself might have chosen for an ambush, in case a Yankee patrol came along the road. He liked the situation not at all.

Without speaking, he pointed to Jensen and Roache, two men not wounded back at the rail line. Silently he signaled them to ride ahead, then he waved the men off the road so if need be they could goad their horses east toward burned-out fields where there was little cover for ambush.

Ten minutes later Jensen and Roache returned. From the sound of their horses' hoofbeats Logan knew they were riding at military canter, so he guessed they'd encountered no danger.

Both men reined in their mounts next to Logan and Matoon.

"No sign of the enemy, sir," Jensen, a boy of sixteen from Morgan Springs, said. "But what we found us was a road."

"More like a path, sir," the older, sad-faced Roache said. He spat off to the side. "Mostly grown-over, and it looked like maybe somebody'd arranged some branches to make it less noticeable from the main road."

Logan knew that many of the large farm- or plantation-houses were set far away from roads, in the middle of vast fields, and ringed as they were by trees, escaped detection by Sherman's men. Or, if a house was grand enough, it was used as shelter by the Yanks, and it might be spared while the fields around it were destroyed.

"Let's have a look at this path."

"Road, sir," Jensen said. "I seen wagon ruts. Deep ones."

Logan gave a hand signal, and the Ninth urged their weary horses forward.

Roache was right. The branch off the main road didn't look like much more than a path. It was overgrown with grass and some hickory saplings where it met the road, and a few felled tree limbs looked as if they'd been dragged across it strategically for concealment.

And Jensen was right. There were wagon-wheel ruts, deep but old.

Logan looked at the cloudless sky still bright with afternoon sun. He knew the Ninth was testing its luck, pushing on though beaten and exhausted. His plan was to lead his troops south until they might meet up with and join a larger force commanded by General Wheeler. They weren't on a timetable. And they certainly could use some rest and water and—God willing—some food beyond what was left of their meager rations.

He looked at Matoon, and both men nodded simultaneously.

Logan sat straighter in the saddle and motioned Jensen and Roache ahead to scout. He gave them a few minutes, then waved the rest of the men on and spurred his horse lightly.

The trail led through woods that were thick at first, making the going slow. Oak and locust trees close on either side lent shade. Then the trail widened, and the wagon ruts were quite visible. Some of them appeared fresh.

When they were clear of the trees they saw the house.

Jensen and Roache sat mounted off to the side, waiting. There was nothing to scout here, only a dark, level plane of burned field and beyond it a white plantation house. The house was almost large enough to be called a mansion, with seven columns across the front of a wide gallery porch.

Logan smiled. This looked safe enough, but who could know for sure? The massacre at the rail line was still bitter in his stomach and poison to his heart. He smiled grimly and nodded to Jensen and Roache. "You two ride ahead and skirt the woods, then approach the house from the rear."

"We'll do 'er," Jensen said, as the two men tugged right on the reins and their horses set off at an angle.

Logan knew Jensen wouldn't have talked so casually to the colonel, but he didn't figure it mattered.

When his scouts hadn't signaled immediately for them to approach the house, Logan wasn't surprised. Danger was everywhere now, and the rail-line massacre was still vivid in his mind. The screams of dying men would echo for a long time, maybe forever.

Coming across this place was a touch of fortune, though. The Ninth would have concealment and shelter. But Logan doubted if they would find food in the house, and the well would surely be poisoned. It was possible that despite the pure white of the structure from a distance, the interior had been burned out.

"Nobody there, sir," Roache said, when the scouts had returned. "Inside of the place ain't been torched, but it sure don't look lived in."

"Not for a good while, anyways," Jensen said. "Dust over everything thick as peach fuzz. And spiderwebs and those white cloths over the furniture. Looks like it's haunted."

"We can be sure it is," Logan said, thinking of what must have happened to the inhabitants. The crops had been burned, so the Yanks who'd first passed this direction had known about the house.

"We go in," he said, and led the way.

The great house looked even larger, but much more decrepit, as they got closer. There were fine cracks in the white facade. Some of the shutters were hanging slightly crooked or were missing.

Logan dismounted, testing his weight on his wounded leg. It would do for a while.

He limped up onto the wide porch and toward the tall oak doors, noticing that several of the floor planks were rotted through. Ivy had found its way through one of the openings.

Above the twin doors with their imposing brass handles was a fan window with some of the glass missing from its leaded frame.

Logan knocked loudly on one of the doors.

Matoon glanced at him.

Logan shrugged and tried the door handle, then stepped ahead of Matoon into the dimness.

The inside of the house was as Roache and young Jensen had described it. Cobwebs, covered furniture, layers of dust. Add to that the scent of rot and mildew.

"Looks like whoever lived here was run out long time ago," Matoon observed.

"Looks like," Logan agreed. He walked about with his heavy limp, his leg aching, his cavalry boots thumping loudly on the wood floor.

The faint but unmistakable sound of glass breaking in an adjoining room made him stop and stand still.

He and Matoon exchanged looks, then drew their Colt revolvers and moved toward the arched doorway to the room where the sound had originated.

Logan motioned Matoon to stand back, then edged around the corner of the doorframe, Colt at the ready.

It was a spacious room, and much brighter light streamed through tall windows. The furniture was covered but for a large, plushly upholstered chair and a grand piano with a raised lid. An ornate wood music stand was in a corner near the windows. Bookcases lined one wall, containing stacked and leaning books and sheet music as well as busts of the great classical composers. Obviously the music room, thought Logan, who himself played the banjo and sang.

"I do seem to have dropped a glass," said a woman's voice in a rich Georgia drawl.

Logan wheeled to see a tall woman with long dark hair. She'd been standing out of sight at the near wall, next to a massive mahogany sideboard. She was holding a crystal wine goblet, and at her feet broken glass glittered with diamond brilliance in the stream of sunlight.

She seemed to glitter herself, with her flawless complexion and large dark eyes, her slender waist and pristine white dress with its draped lace and wide hoop skirt. The dress had a low neckline that allowed a glimpse of ample bosom beneath a lace modesty shawl. The brilliant light that another woman might have found harsh and revealing was her friend.

Logan holstered his revolver and was aware of Matoon entering the room behind him.

"I was about to partake of some wine the Yanks overlooked," the woman said with an easy, lustrous smile. "I was not aware that I had guests." She turned toward the sideboard. "There are more glasses. You must join me."

Logan bowed stiffly at the waist. "Captain Jedediah Logan of the Tennessee Ninth Cavalry, ma'am. And this is my adjunct Sergeant William Matoon."

"It is a pleasure, Captain," came the honeylike words through the perfect smile. "And Sergeant. I am Mrs. Amanda Lucinda LeGrande. Mrs. Gerald LeGrande until six months ago, when I heard of my husband's death in battle last year at Gettysburg."

"We are truly sorry for your loss," Logan said. He felt ill at ease in the face of such beauty, as he'd seen only ugliness and death for the past months.

The woman acknowledged his condolences with a sad smile and a nod, then turned to get down more glasses from the sideboard.

"You, uh, don't seem surprised to see us," Logan said.

Amanda LeGrande smiled. "You are not the first Rebs to come here. Ours is the same cause. Several times in the past month men have stayed here, some of them wounded. We've treated their wounds as best we could, and bid them stay. But they never stayed long, knowing they endangered our lives."

" '*Our* lives'?" Matoon asked, before Logan could speak.

"My servant Hampton and myself." She shrugged. "Everyone else is gone or dead. I stay on, as does Hampton because he refuses to leave his master's wife. His own dear wife, rest her soul, was treated vilely by the Yanks and died some months ago."

Matoon cleared his throat. "Why is it, ma'am, you appear to be dressed for a ball?"

Her laugh was clear as the breaking crystal. "I am not that gaily adorned, Sergeant. But I do dress for what passes for dinner now. To keep up appearances as well as my spirit."

Logan stared at her. " 'Appearances'?"

She melted him with a smile. "Why, in case unexpected guests might come calling. As indeed they have."

Logan returned her smile. "I'll have Sergeant Matoon instruct the men to bivouac outside, then he and I would be honored and pleased to join you for a glass of wine." He turned toward Matoon. "And Sergeant, do see if you can find some spare salt pork and hardtack to make something of a meal."

"Your men and yourselves are more than welcome to stay indoors," Amanda said.

"Only if the weather turns inclement," Logan said. "We'll all be safer if a force is outside and pickets have been posted. Sherman has passed through here, and Yankee patrols still roam the area."

"Roam it like packs of wolves." Amanda said, shuddering. "I will not soon forget Sherman's army. They were not gentlemen."

Logan drew himself to full height. "They abused you?"

"Not in the way they might have. But there were women of lesser standing who did not fare so well." She shrugged her dainty shoulders again beneath white lace. "Men are men, and war is war."

"Men do not have to be brutes," Logan said, "even in war."

"Unfortunately, Captain, that is not true."

"I meant in regard to women, ma'am."

"There, Captain Logan, we agree."

Matoon returned from outside, and Amanda, carrying the delicate stemmed crystal, led the way into a spacious dining room with a beamed ceiling.

Near the head of the table, she turned and motioned for them to be seated.

And frowned for the first time since Logan had laid eyes on her. "Why, you are wounded yourself," she said in a distraught voice.

"Some grapeshot in my thigh," Logan said. "Not serious. Some of my men are more gravely injured. One is carrying a bullet or minié ball in his shoulder. And we're without a doctor."

"I have some meager but useful skills in that regard," Amanda said. "As does Hampton."

As if at the sound of his name, a middle-aged, broad Negro of medium height entered the dining room. Beneath his shabby white serving uniform his shoulders were bunched and muscular, his stomach flat. Only the gray at his temples prevented him from passing as a much younger man.

"Hampton," Amanda said, "do take this food and put it in a proper serving dish, then please pour the wine."

Hampton muttered a "yes'm" and did as instructed. It was obvious from his actions that he was fond of Amanda and felt honored by his position.

"He has always been a house slave," Amanda explained, as Hampton adroitly arranged their humble food and drink before them.

The largest portions, Logan noticed with approval, went to Amanda.

After the surprisingly good meal, with his men outside and guards posted, Logan sat in an uncovered chair in the music room and sipped port wine that Hampton served in etched crystal. He glanced about him at the sweeping staircase to the second floor, the marble floors, and arched windows. Taste and elegance as well as onetime wealth. This would all be gone soon and forever if the war was lost. All this graciousness and tradition. The Southern way was something the Yanks held in disdain because they couldn't understand it.

For hours that seemed minutes, Logan and Amanda talked about the South before the Yanks had invaded, the long, hot afternoons, the endless tobacco and cotton fields, the sunlight bright on magnolia leaves so green as to be black at a glance. A lazy, beautiful, and safe world. Gone.

"I noticed after our meal that your limp was worsening," Amanda said. "Do bring in your man with the shoulder wound, and we will tend to him and then to your leg."

Logan was hesitant, but he knew his wounded trooper Clay Banning might soon be taken by infection. And he might lose his own leg to the rot. To let even a minor wound go days without treatment often ended in only one option other than death—the amputation of the limb.

"I was a volunteer nurse," Amanda assured him, smiling over the rim of her glass.

The smile made up Logan's mind for him. He rose and limped from the room and to the front doors that were open to the night breeze.

"Sergeant Matoon!" he called out. "Bring Banning here. Along with a bottle of whiskey."

Five minutes later Matoon, with Clay Banning, who was nineteen and afraid, were upstairs in what was once a library but would serve as a makeshift operating and sickroom.

Banning knew what was going to happen and gladly took what fortification and pain-deadener there was available.

When the whiskey bottle was near empty and the young trooper had finally passed out, Logan watched as Amanda, aided by Hampton, set to work. Hampton fitted a piece of leather tack in Banning's mouth to bite on so he wouldn't break his teeth clenching his jaws from the pain. Then Amanda, with instruments from a doctor's bag, parted the wound and probed for the bullet. Hampton deftly sopped blood with a folded cloth while she bent intently to her task. Logan watched her face, the beautiful sympathy and passion he'd seen only in likenesses of great European paintings.

What seemed five minutes passed before she drew the bullet from Banning's shoulder. Banning moaned, as did Amanda. She sat back and used a delicate wrist to wipe perspiration from her forehead. Hampton poured what remained of the whiskey over the wound, and Banning cried out, the toothmarked leather dropping from his mouth.

Amanda held his hand. "That was necessary. We're sorry. It is as much pain as you will feel. The worst is behind you and it is time for you to heal."

Banning couldn't have heard her, but he relaxed and his features became peaceful but for his eyelids fluttering.

Amanda looked at Logan. "We will move him to a room downstairs with good ventilation, where we can watch him easily and tend to his recovery."

"We can't be in this place long," Logan said. "The war."

"Yes, the war," she said bitterly. "In the morning we can tend to your own wound, Captain Logan. It seems minor enough that you'll be able to travel soon afterward."

"Tonight would be better, to save time," Logan said. "We can leave Banning here until he's well enough to ride south by himself."

"If you are game for such a thing so soon after watching," Amanda said, "we can attend you." She glanced to her left. "Hampton, go downstairs and fetch a bottle of good bourbon from my husband's private stock."

Hampton seemed surprised by the instruction. Then he shrugged his broad shoulders. "The master won't mind now," he said sadly.

After Banning was carried downstairs on a furniture cover used as a stretcher, Logan lay down on his back on the bed. The bourbon was a brand he'd never heard of, but one taste and he knew it was made for sipping, not guzzling as he was doing. He guzzled nonetheless.

Hampton refilled his glass from time to time, while Amanda sat next to him, holding his hand. She was talking to him softly and caringly, almost crooning. It didn't matter that he couldn't make out what she was saying.

Maybe this is all worth it, Logan thought, as the liquor took him. He vaguely recalled seeing Hampton use a large knife to cut off another few inches of leather strap. At the same time the strap was wedged between his teeth, Logan felt Amanda's hand slip gently from his. There was a distant sound, material being cut then ripped. His pants leg.

The numbness in his leg was almost immediately replaced by a sharp pain. He passed in and out of consciousness as the pain came and went.

"The wound is more serious than I thought," he heard Amanda say.

"Poor man needs more bourbon, ma'am." Hampton's deep voice.

The strap was removed from Logan's jaws as liquid trickled down his throat. He coughed, then began to swallow. The strap was not replaced.

And it was morning.

A bird was singing. Logan opened his eyes. Sunlight lay in a warm rectangle over the same bed he had lain in the night before. When he tried to move his right leg, a jolt of pain made him gasp.

"I would recommend at least a day of rest," Amanda said from behind his head. "The grapeshot went deeper than we thought." She came into view, holding in her hand the black, jagged iron that had penetrated Logan's flesh.

"There isn't time to rest," Logan said. There was a terrible taste in his mouth, and when he tried to sit up his head pulsed with pain. He fell back.

"You must find time. Your weakened condition is obvious."

"I am only in the condition of men who've drunk too much the night before," he told Amanda.

"In the condition of men with battle wounds in their legs," she said. She moved closer to him and sat on the edge of the bed, then rested a gentle hand on his shoulder. "You need care, Captain Logan. I want to care for you." And she bent low and kissed him on the forehead. On his cool flesh her lips were like fire. "I would like you to survive," she said. She seemed about to cry. "A gentleman could hardly refuse such a request."

He reached up and ran the backs of his knuckles along her soft cheek. "I'll stay."

She smiled and kissed him again, this time lightly on the lips.

He reached for her but she stood up. "Sleep, Captain. You need rest."

Logan closed his eyes, enjoying the scent of her and the rustle of her skirts as she stood and walked toward the door. She was a woman whose presence remained in a room long after she had left it.

When he awoke, the room was dim. A form was standing over him.

Sergeant Matoon.

"How's the leg, sir?" Matoon asked.

"Better. Where's Amanda?"

"Downstairs in the music room. I wanted to talk to you alone."

Logan struggled on the bed so that he was supported on his elbows, half-way sitting up. His leg still hurt badly. His head ached, but not so severely. The bitter taste still lay along the edges of his tongue. He didn't like the expression on Matoon's broad, sunbaked face. "What is it, Sergeant? Has something happened to Amanda?"

"No. It's Hampton, sir. Late last night one of the men saw him saddle a horse from a stall behind the house, then ride hell-for-leather away to the north."

"Hampton?"

"Roache and I mounted up and followed him along the main road," Matoon said. "Hampton didn't see us. We saw him meet with three Union officers. They talked awhile, and Hampton handed the Yanks a folded sheet of paper, accepted a drink from them, then got back on his horse and returned to the plantation."

Logan blinked and shook his head, trying to clear his mind and grasp what he was hearing. He recalled the leather being removed from his mouth as more liquor was poured down his throat. What might he have babbled in his drunken stupor as Amanda was removing the grapeshot and Hampton was listening?

"The men think he's Hobson the spy, sir," Matoon said. "I do, too."

Logan managed to sit up all the way on the edge of the sagging bed and place both bare feet on the floor. "Where is Hampton now?"

"Outside in a grove of elms, sir. We arrested him as a spy."

Hobson the spy, a slave? A Negro? Maybe it shouldn't be so unbelievable. Why wouldn't he be a Yankee sympathizer? It was possible. Logan had learned that almost anything was possible.

"My God! Does Amanda know?"

"She does, sir. She's distressed."

Logan swallowed. Sighed. The war . . . duty . . .

His voice was jagged with pain and weariness. "Hand me my boots, Sergeant."

Amanda insisted on coming with them to the elm grove. She walked silently, well off to the side by herself.

Hampton stood beneath the largest of the elms, his wrists bound behind his back. A rope had been tossed over one of the tree's branches. On the end of the rope was a noose, looped loosely around Hampton's neck. His head was high, his gaze fixed above the dozen men surrounding him, as if he might be staring at something off in the distance. Amanda stood nearby, leaning with one hand against a tree trunk for support. She looked at Logan, then away.

Logan stood before Hampton, the man who the night before had tended his wounds, and spoke softly. "Is what I heard true, Hampton?"

The slave glanced over at Amanda, who was looking at him with a stricken expression, her dark eyes moist.

"Hampton," Logan said, "you understand the situation, what happens to spies in this war. But I need to know from you if it's true."

Hampton's chest heaved as he took a deep breath. "True, Captain Logan."

Logan heard Amanda give a faint cry and turned to see young Jensen catch her arm and prevent her from dropping to the ground.

"We got no choice in what we have to do, sir," Matoon said beside Logan.

Logan didn't answer. He was looking at Amanda, who'd gained her balance and was standing firmly. Her graceful hands were at her sides now, balled into fists.

"Amanda . . ." Logan said helplessly.

She regarded him coldly. Then she walked over to look at Hampton. They stared at each other, their faces grim.

"It's true, ma'am," Hampton said.

Amanda nodded, looking ten years older. Her gaze remained fixed on her old friend and servant though she spoke to Logan. "It's a hard war, Captain Logan."

"It surely is that, ma'am."

"Do what you must."

She looked away from Hampton and strode toward the house.

Logan nodded and walked after her, limping on his wounded leg. Behind him Hampton gasped harshly as the noose tightened and he was raised off the ground.

On the wide, pillared porch Logan caught up with Amanda. "I am truly sorry."

"I know you are, Captain Logan. You have your duty, as we all do."

"I know Hampton was with you for a long time."

"Forever."

"Can you forgive me?" he asked.

She looked up at him with her newly old eyes.

"In my mind," she said, "but never in my heart."

Logan never hated the war more than at that moment.

When the Tennessee Ninth rode from the plantation fields, Logan raised a hand to signal a halt when they reached the main road. He had three of the men brush the dry earth and move branches back over the mouth of the path to the house. It wasn't unlikely that Yankees might favor Amanda with a visit. Hampton could hardly protect her now, buried as he was among the elms.

They'd ridden ten miles down the road, toward Aimesville, when Logan saw a shack next to a small creek. He told Matoon to have the men rest by the creek but not to drink from it or refresh the horses until they could judge whether the water was safe. The Yanks had a habit of killing livestock and staking the rotting corpses in creeks or small rivers upstream from where the water might be drunk.

An old man with a white beard came out of the shack and stood with his fists on his hips. He was wearing overalls and a straw hat with the wide brim bent up in front.

Logan motioned for Matoon to come with him, then tugged on the reins and veered his mount toward the man.

When he got closer, he saw that beneath the hat and gray beard the man looked about sixty. He was bent but he looked fit, and most of the fingers were missing from his left hand. His eyes were the brightest blue Logan had ever seen.

"That creek water safe to drink?" Logan asked, reining in his horse a few feet from the old-timer.

"Yanks ain't poisoned it," the man said in a raspy voice. "Use it for cookin' an' bathin', an' I'm still here."

Logan wasn't so sure about the bathing part. But he smiled and told Matoon, beside him, to ride to the creek and make sure they could agree with the old man.

Matoon clucked at his horse and flicked it with the end of the rein.

"You met up with any Yanks of late?" the man asked, as he and Logan watched Matoon ride toward the knot of men and horses at the creek.

"North of here, on the rail line. They were waiting for us."

"They're still thick here an' about, even though Sherman's moved on. Burned everythin' that'd take a spark in these parts."

Logan's leg pained him then, and he asked, "Know folks named LeGrande around here?"

"Sure. 'Bout ten miles back from the way you came. Fine people. Been wonderin' how they fared."

"Mr. LeGrande was killed at Gettysburg. Amanda LeGrande is still there."

"Damned shame about Gerald LeGrande. Fine man, that. But it's good to hear the wife's all right. That big buck Hampton lookin' after her?"

"Not anymore," Logan said. "We had to hang him."

The old man's eyes widened and seemed to take in all the blue of the sky. "Hampton? Why'd you have to do that?"

"Turned out he was spying for the Yanks," Logan said.

"You real sure of that?"

"I'd be sure before I ordered a man hanged," Logan said. "Slave or no slave."

"Poor Amanda was fond of that slave," the old man said. "I don't like to think of those pretty blue eyes filled with tears, what with all the rest she's been through these past few years."

"She's strong as well as beauti—" Logan bit off his words and stared at the old man. "Blue eyes? The Amanda LeGrande I met had brown eyes. Dark hair to her waist. Tall woman. Of fine breeding and bearing."

The old man shook his head. "That weren't Amanda LeGrande. Woman you described'd be Hampton's wife Lizzy. Lucinda. I could see how you'd take her for a gentlewoman, though, light-skinned as she is. And she speaks well 'cause she helped out at the school in Aimesville for a while, even taught herself to read and write some. Only slave in these parts can do that. But that was before the LeGrandes bought her from the Hobsons so she could be permanent with Hampton."

Logan remembered Matoon's words: *Hampton handed the Yanks a folded sheet of paper* . . . He knew he should have thought of that, how unlikely it would be that Hampton could write. Logan knew who had questioned and listened to a drunken, half-conscious Confederate officer with a wound in his leg, then put whatever useful information she'd gleaned in writing for the Yanks. Hampton had merely been the messenger. And back there in the elm grove . . . the way they had looked at each other . . .

Logan's heart went cold.

"You feelin' poorly?" the old man was asking. "You're lookin' white as bone."

Logan drew a deep breath. "I feel as well as can be expected. We thank you for your hospitality." And he wheeled his horse sharply and galloped toward the creek.

"You see them Yanks, you give 'em hell fer me!" the old man called after him.

For a brief instant Logan thought of turning his troops to the north, going back the way they had come.

But he knew he couldn't make himself do that.

Regrouped on the road to Aimesville, the thirst of men and horses quenched, Logan took his position in the lead, raised his right hand, and signaled for the ride south.

After a hundred yards, he didn't know why, but he spurred his horse on, stood high in the stirrups and let out the shrill Rebel yell that froze Yank blood. The rest of the men caught his spirit. As he rode he could hear the hurried, eager beat of the horses' hoofs pounding dry earth. He could feel the grit of dust as he clenched his teeth.

It was his last Rebel yell of the war.

Gary Phillips is a hands-on political man and a wise observer of the socio-political scene on the west coast. He's written several crime and mystery novels, including *The Jook*, all of them original and explosive. Over the years he has also watched every movie Anthony Mann, Sam Peckinpah, Sergio Leone, Richard Brooks, and Budd Boetticher made—some of them more than once. Recent releases include a novella about the unsavory "sport" of pit bull fighting out with its own rap CD soundtrack, and *Shooter's Point*, the second Martha Chainey crime novel. Robert Smalls, the main character of his story, was a real soldier and boatman during the Civil War, did not actually perform the heroics attributed to him in the following story. However, he did serve the Union in several distinguished government posts after the war.

THE MEASURE

Gary Phillips

That was a lot of money. More money than he'd ever see in his lifetime—he knew that for sure as his muscular stevedore arms cut into the frigid waters of the Stono River. Fortunately the half-dime of a moon was tallow-colored and barely cast light upon the ink Robert Smalls swam through. His body was cold, but his senses were alert to everything around him. He gained steadily on his destination, this escaped slave most wanted by the Confederacy.

One of the five slave catchers who'd tried to kidnap him in Beaufort had said he was the nigra he was going to become fat on. Another said happily, as Smalls ducked the flat of the man's short ax, that they would whore and drink away the $4,000 offered for his capture. Four thousand dollars, that was plenty for any man's head. And it signified the depths of hatred Brigadier General Roswell Ripley must have for him. And they wanted him back alive, thus a tortured end awaited him should the general get a hold of the bold coon.

After all, here he was a slave, sent to work the docks of Charleston by his master John McKee. He'd been a lamplighter, then waiter then apprenticed to John Simmons's boatyard. From there he became a docker and worked his way up to foreman. There were plenty of men, black and white, bigger than his five feet five. But that only meant he had to work harder and longer to show his measure. Yes, he had to send his wages back to his master, but as even the soldiers around the docks joked, he had it pretty good for a slave.

When Simmons didn't have work for him, Smalls signed on to the various boats ferrying supplies and men up and down the waterways of South Carolina. Robert Smalls had only been given the name Robert to balance the last, which he had added as a tip of his cap to his size. "For a runt he sure hauls like a full grown man," they'd rib. And he was quite familiar with the coastline's geography when the war broke out. And the longing that had been in him since he didn't know when got to fill him more and more on those nights he'd be resting on a pier, looking out across the black carpet of sea.

Smalls felt the ghostly brush of a jellyfish against one of his legs and this brought him back to his mission. Cole's Island was looming larger, and he kept stroking toward her. The island lay not too many miles off Charleston, and had once been a cannon and arms compound.

As the Union erected blockades at several intervals out from the coastline, the island had been abandoned by the Confederates. Or so the Northern forces had been led to believe. But as Smalls was piloting the *Planter* three days ago on a, what was the word Captain DuPont used, re-con-e-sant run, he'd spotted something the other troops hadn't given much mind.

"Yes, sir, Captain, sir, I'm'a sure of it," Smalls had insisted when they'd returned to headquarters at Port Royal. "I seen, I mean I saw, it through the spyglass I borrowed from Sergeant Matthews." His wife had been helping him with his book learnin'.

"You see this, Matthews?" DuPont bit off the end of his cigar and spat the chunk into the spittoon next to his desk.

"Well, sir," Matthews began, "I did see a schooner flying Confederate colors, yes sir." Matthews, Smalls knew from association, had laid out a career for himself in the Army. He wasn't about to side too much with a darky.

"Was this ship departing from the island?" DuPont struck a match with his thumbnail and lit his cigar. He kept his stone gray eyes on both men as they sweated in the humidity outside his tent. As was customary, he was seated behind his field table.

"I couldn't say that sir. But she was heading in a direction away from Cole's Island sure enough. But," he quickly added, "that don't mean she was at the island, sir."

DuPont rubbed blunt fingers in his beard's brown whiskers.

"But you say Smalls you recognized this particular schooner."

"That's right sir. I been on the *Jena* more than once sir. She's got a hold made to carry heavy guns and rifle racks along her insides. She wouldn't be out lessin' they's usin' her for that reason, naw sir." He didn't like to sound so, so accommodating, his wife Hannah would say. His life as a slave had been different than working sunup to sundown in the fields, an overseer always quick with the lash. But white men were white men, and you best step lightly 'round their feelings.

DuPont smoked and pondered then stated, "We have to make sure. As you men know, we're preparing to take our ships and men through the back door Ripley has left unguarded by removing the light garrison that had been on Cole's. Information we confirmed from our balloonists and you, Smalls." He quickly waved with the lit end of his cigar at the smallish black man with the wide torso.

"Yet," DuPont continued, "Ripley knows you are with us and he knows you know the rivers and back washes like he does." DuPont laughed and it made Smalls nervous. "Of course he being a fine Southern gentlemen and planter, he cain't take too much stock that you, a slave, actually have put that knowledge to useful purposes with us."

Smalls noted that DuPont hadn't said "former" slave, but what could he do about this man, or Matthews, or any of the other blue-bellies and how they saw him? He was determined to maintain his freedom, and that of his wife and two children.

Matthews couldn't hide his sly grin. "So we go forward as ordered, sir?"

The captain blew gray fumes across his kerosene lamp. "We send you, Smalls, and an oarsman to find out for sure. There is too much at stake for any kind of setback, Sergeant. Too much. We, like them, are strained to capacity and cain't afford unnecessary losses."

"You mean me and him——" Matthews began, a protest forming on his lips.

"Are to sneak out in a rowboat from one of our light ships anchored away from Cole's Island," DuPont finished. "You will conduct a reconnaissance of the island and thereafter report your findings. This will commence," he consulted his pocket watch which was open on the table, "at approximately 2100 hours this evening, Sergeant." He stood and puffed. "You have your orders."

Both men saluted though Smalls as of yet had not been given any official rank. Truth was, his position with the Union wasn't formal at all. Though he did know that when he'd first piloted the *Planter*, the ship he'd commandeered, into Union waters, and told of what he knew, DuPont had sent a letter to the Secretary of the Navy, Gideon Wells. The letter, it was rumored, had praised his observation skills and his daring. And fair enough, he'd been paid as a pilot for the joint Army and Navel command, so that was something. But it had only occurred to him now, standing next to these men in their uniforms, dirty and fraying though they may be, that he still wasn't truly part of their fight. And hadn't the Union soldiers helped him fight off the slave catchers? Obviously he was of some worth to them.

Smalls swirled fresh water in his mouth, the liquid bracing him as he drew close to the leeward side of the island. It was merely a slag of land, though there was a small hill upon which he remembered seeing kegs of gunpowder and cannonballs stocked once. He entered shallow water and his toes slid into mud. He'd tied his boots around his neck, as he didn't want to be squeaking around in wet shoes. Smalls did his best to minimize splashing and hunched over as he got onto land.

Quickly he shoved his feet into his boots and got his bearings. If the Rebels were encamped again on the island, they'd be by the hill. It blocked a view, and the cannons had been stored in the one cave in the hillside. The officer's tents and bedrolls had been spread around this. He'd had to bring hardtack and salt pork, by himself, up from the shore that time. All the while the Rebs were calling him names and threatening to shoot him should he drop any of the sacks or crates. But his back was broad for a man his size and nary a provision fell to the earth, even though several of the soldiers tried to trip him.

Smalls stuffed those slights away. Anything less than getting his foot chopped off by a slaver or getting lynched for sport by a mob, he considered rice and red-eyed gravy. The first thing he noticed as he crouched in a thicket was a dark mound set back from the beach. He waited and heard nothing except the rustling of lizards in the brush and croaks of frogs.

Cautiously, feeling fully exposed in the open space, he dashed to the mound.

The compact man was shivering but he had a job to do. Heading toward Cole's Island, Smalls knew something was up when Matthews had been the only one to come with him in the rowboat from the *Planter*. And the sergeant had made him row. They got within rifle range and Matthews ordered him to swim the rest of the way. When he questioned this, his position was made clear.

"Look, boy, you may have impressed DuPont, but that don't mean chicken dinner to me. Jus' 'cause you memorized what you'd seen and heard good as a white man jus' means you bein' on the docks all that time somethin' was bound to sink in that thick skull of yours."

Smalls was stuck. He knew Matthews had seen him reading a months-old newspaper he'd found. The sergeant had snatched the paper out of his hands and said he'd never wanted to see him pretending like that again. The sergeant, he was sure, couldn't read. It wasn't unusual that he couldn't, but it stuck out more so when it was a black that could.

"Now git your black ass in that river and over ta that island."

"Alright," he'd muttered, barely keeping his temper down.

"All right?"

"I mean yes, sir, Sergeant Matthews."

"That's better . . . Smalls."

Now, digging into the thin layer of sand he felt the scratchy surface of burlap. He tugged on the cloth and revealed part of the cold cast iron of a cannon barrel. In the weak light and by feel, Smalls assessed the armament was what the soldiers had called a ten-pounder, referring to the size of the cannonball the weapon shot.

Creeping about, he found several other areas where cannons, Napoleons, and even a few Union Parrott's were hidden. So that was it. The Confederates had correctly concluded that the Union knew about their previous withdrawal from the island and other defenses along the Sonto River. And also knowing that the Union was looking for a way to seize Charleston, Ripley had snuck back and assembled an ambush force. When the Union ships came steaming along the river, thinking they'd sneak in the rear, then the back door would be shut on them. And blue blood would flow into the waters.

Smalls did his best to count the secreted cannons, since this was the kind of information the captain would want. Though he had a feeling that Matthews would take the credit, as if he had dared get on the island, with Smalls sitting sniffling and praying to de Lawd in the rowboat.

"Is that you, Remmy?"

Hell, he swore to himself. He'd been easing up the rise, as it would be a good spot for heavy cannons—like the thirty-pounders he'd heard about. That's when he also smelled the dying smoke and chicory. "Yes, uh yeah," he said, trying to sound like a white man who was a fellow soldier.

"What the hell you doin'?" the voice challenged, feet crunching closer.

"Nothin'," Smalls said, standing up fully.

"Remmy?" The soldier asked again, his rifle held guard duty fashion.

Smalls leaped and the two tumbled down the hill. The Confederate was taller than him but his limbs were skinnier. They wound up along the side, the spy on top.

"A nigra," his opponent gasped. "You're a—"

Smalls silenced him with a punch to the mouth and another one to the side of the man's head. He lay still and Smalls scrambled up, running for the shore. That bastard Matthews should be there, should have rowed in to see what was happening. But no, he'd be nice and dry 300 or 400 hundred yards out. He was probably worrying about the girl he left behind, humming a tune.

Anger got his legs lifting higher and his heart racing faster. The crack of a rifle shot made that same pounding heart stop as if ice had suddenly formed around it.

"The next one takes that pointed head of yours clean off, mister. You better turn around."

Smalls did as the soldier demanded. There was two of them, and it was gloomy enough not to see that he was black.

"Hey, Remmy," a third one shouted, "McMahon has been cold-cocked."

"Well, well," Remmy said, moving forward. " 'Pears we got us a sneak of some kind. But is he a thief or is he a blue-belly?"

"They wouldn't jest send one," another man offered. "What kind of scout party would that be?"

"A quiet one," Remmy answered. He'd advanced far enough to get a good look at Smalls. It was just that the image refused to register with him. "Where's your master, boy?" he said querulously.

"I was jus' returnin' Massa Simmons raf, boss," Smalls replied, slipping into slave talk and dipping his head. At that moment, he was powerful glad he wasn't in a Union uniform.

"Massa Simmons," Remmy questioned. He violently thrust the barrel of his Sharps carbine into the other man's nostrils, causing blood to discharge. "What in the hell you talkin' about, darkie? John Simmons would no sooner let you have one of his rafts out than General Lee would let you shave him."

"I swears, thas so," Smalls embellished, hoping his act would buy him time. Goddamn Matthews must be wondering what was keeping him.

"Kill the nigger," the third one who'd discovered McMahon said. "He attacked a white man, didn't he?"

"But he ain't here by accident," the third one announced cogently. "He must be with the Union. I've heard tell they's drafting colored soldiers."

"With weapons?" the second one asked in utter dismay.

"Shut up," Remmy, a sergeant, ordered his men. The rifle was still thrust into Smalls face. "You been sent to snoop on us, nigger?"

"Naw suh."

"Uh-huh." With that, Remmy butted him with the other end of the rifle and Smalls reeled back. His first instinct was to strike out, but he knew that would earn him a bullet in his brainpan. He stood, watching and waiting, his fingers touching the wetness around his mouth.

"He ain't that big, but that buck sho cain take it," the second one said. He crowded closer to Smalls too.

"Come on," Remmy announced. "This is too important to make a mistake now. We gonna find out what this coon knows and what he's doing here. Neville, you and Sykes git him over to tha platform."

"Okay," one of them replied.

The two men roughly grabbed Smalls and started to take him back toward the hill. Desperate, he broke free from one of the men and swung on the other. He connected and sent this one back more in shock than hurt.

"This nigger's a wild animal," the man he hit blurted.

Smalls had nothing to lose, as he knew death was close on his neck. He started to run for it again but the third man was quick and landed on him. He clubbed him twice with the butt of his Leech & Rigdow .36.

Disoriented, the Johnny Rebs hauled Smalls between them to their encampment. He couldn't see well and realized it was from being hit in the head and blood trickling into his eyes. He felt himself being lashed against a pole, his wet shirt torn from his body. A widow's veil descended on his head and there was nothing but bliss. He stirred awake after water was thrown into his face.

"Time for some answers, nigger." Remmy lowered the wooden bucket he'd used.

Smalls looked around him. The other two plus the man he'd originally fought, McMahon, were staring at him. Each had a hungry look in their eyes. That is except the one who'd said he was here for a reason. That one looked sorry for Smalls. He was roped against a pole that was part of a platform upon which were barrels of black powder covered in tarpaulin. The Rebs had made it that way to no doubt keep the powder dry and off the sand.

"Over here, boy." Remmy stood with a dull pig sticker in his hand. "Git a fire going, McMahon."

"Yes, sir," the man replied with glee, as he set about his task.

"You got something to tell us?" Remmy jabbed the point of the Bowie knife into Smalls's belly. The thrust was enough to prick but not go in deep.

His head was exploding but all he could do was grit his teeth and wish he was in Hannah's arms. The worse was yet to be.

"Ain't had no dark meat in some time," one of them joked.

"Remmy, this ain't right," the only one to show concern said. "General Ripley will want to question this man."

"We gonna soften this hard case up for him, Sykes, don't you get your petticoats ruffled about it, here?"

"But—" the other man stammered.

"But nothing," McMahon interrupted, "this here nigger acts like a white man. He's got to be shown it's jus' plain wrong."

The fire crackled beside the man as he knelt near its flames, warming his hands. "It's ready." A canine fierceness lit his eyes from within.

Remmy heated the deadly steel at the apex of the fire. No one said anything, anticipation or dread had locked their vocal chords. The sergeant turned and paced methodically toward Smalls.

"What you got to say, boy?" The tip of the knife was releasing steam.

Smalls couldn't speak for fear he'd bust out praying. He'd be damned to two hells if he was going to give these crackers the satisfaction.

The white hot blade was laid against the skin of his chest and he cried out in pain. Again the side of the blade was applied and Smalls was on the verge of passing out.

"Throw water on him," Remmy said.

The one called Sykes did so.

Then Remmy asked, taunting, "Well, nigger man?"

"I'll show you," he gasped, his mouth hanging open as if broken.

"What?" Remmy dipped his head closer.

"I'll show you tha papers, boss, tha repot massa DuPont is spose to git."

The Rebs knew who DuPont was. "What papers is this?" Remmy asked excitedly.

"The one I's buried at tha beach. Tha one that they's orders from that Grant fella."

All the Confederates looked puzzled as he hoped they would. "How'd you get these papers, nigra?" McMahon piped up. They certainly didn't think he had the intelligence to concoct such a tale.

"Sergeant Matthews, suh," Smalls fibbed. "I was a rowin' his boat, and he was lookin' at your island here through one of them, ah, I don't know wha you call 'em, suh."

"Telescope," Remmy said disgustedly. "And then what?"

"Well, suh," Smalls added, making it up fast, "somehow the boat got tangled up on sumptin'. Next thing I knows, we tips over and well, suh, that fine young sergeant done drown."

McMahon laughed uproariously. "This nigger cain't walk straight, let alone guide a boat. He got panicky and got that Northerner drowned, probably flailing all about just to save his black soul."

"Sumptin' like that," Smalls muttered.

Remmy took a swipe with the knife, making a diagonal scar across Smalls's stomach. "And he left you with these papers?"

"He, he prayed to Jesus for me to get 'em to DuPont, yes suh." The sharp but brief pain from that last injury actually cleared some of Smalls's head. It was like getting slapped to wake someone from sleep.

"Where are these papers?" Remmy said.

"I got to show y'all, I cain't describe it correc'ly wit words, naw suh."

"He's lying," the Reb called Neville said.

Remmy scratched the side of his nose with the tip of his blade. "We got to check. The general trusts us to watch things here till he gets the men in place t'morrow. We got to check in case those Union boys is on to us." He grinned devilishly at Smalls. "Sides, this boy is all through. What can he do 'gainst four of us? Even if one is weak-livered Sykes."

The other two laughed.

Sykes got Smalls untied, who slumped. The young soldier helped him stand. For a moment their eyes met, and then the Confederate broke contact.

Smalls said, "It's over where you fount me. I knows 'zactly."

"Come on." Remmy stood beside him as Sykes stood opposite. McMahon was behind and Neville was in front.

"Hurry up, boy," McMahon declared, shoving Smalls. "We got us some skinnin' ta do."

"Yes, suh, boss, I sure hopes ya don't—" and he whipped to his left, where Remmy was. He got a hand around the man's wrist and summoned the strength that had made him foreman on the docks. In a wink he toppled over with Remmy as the others reached for him. The sergeant hit him in his seared flesh but Smalls, gnashing his teeth, couldn't let up. He bore down and there was a snap.

"My wrist, he broke my—"

Smalls had the knife and came around and up with the steel. The thing went into McMahon's soft gut and his breath, smelling of corn whiskey, rushed from his lungs. Sykes and Remmy jumped on Smalls. Neville had his gun out, but couldn't get a clean shot.

"Git him up, git him up," the man with the pistol repeated.

"Oh God, oh God," McMahon wheezed, writhing on the ground.

"You're dead, nigger, dead and gone," Remmy promised, grabbing with his one good hand.

Smalls broke free from Sykes who had his arms around his upper body. That was where he was strongest. He poured everything he had left into an attack on the sergeant. Being black and telling white men what to do on the docks, Smalls had had his share of bare-knuckled contests. He pummeled Remmy into the dirt, his fists striking every open area they could find.

Breathing raggedly, he turned, the barrel of the repeater filling his vision. He saw his mother toiling in the sorghum field, his father taking a lashing for talking back to the master.

"Smalls, Smalls," Matthews suddenly called from the beach. "Where are you?"

The man with the pistol looked at Sykes then toward the beach. That was his chance. Smalls dove and using that stevedore arm of his, scooped up sandy earth and threw it. A shot came through the cloud but he was already up again and hurtling at the gunman.

The two bodies collided as Smalls heard feet pounding toward them. Cold steel was against his rib cage and a shot was let off, just as he twisted aside. The bullet creased him and he yelped, but he couldn't let up.

"You black demon," the gunman swore. Frustrated, he bit the other man on the bicep.

This enraged Smalls and in a red fury, he beat at the other man until hands pulled him off his victim.

"That's enough, enough," Matthews said.

The river pilot was groggy, his whole body alive with hurt. It was an effort to breath, and something was blocking his left eyesight. It was blood.

"Good Lord, man," Matthews looked around. McMahon was on his back, his arms outstretched, gazing vacantly at the heavens. The knife was like a growth in his chest. Remmy was on one knee, groaning, his hand holding his wrist. Neville was at Smalls's feet, curled up, his form inert as if resting peaceably.

"Let's get back . . . Mr. Smalls," Matthews said. Vaguely, he waved his Colt at Sykes. "Tie your men up," the Union sergeant ordered his prisoner.

Later, Smalls rested in a rowboat, his head lying against the edge. He longed to see his wife and children.

A month later, mostly healed, he was summoned to DuPont's tent at Port Royal.

"Smalls," the man said, a cigar rolling back and forth in his mouth. He stood and came around his desk.

"Sir," the escaped slave replied.

DuPont regarded the shorter man for several moments, and then a hint of a smile creased his beard. "You certainly proved your measure on Cole's Island, Smalls. I understand General Hunter is requesting Secretary of War Stanton to immediately raise five thousand negro troops."

"So I heard, sir."

"Raw recruits. Some of them free born and some, like you, who tore their way to freedom. But as long as the South has an army, they won't be truly free, will they?"

"I suppose so sir."

"Well," he finally drawled, "that's all for now, Smalls."

"All right, Captain." He turned to go.

"Oh," DuPont said, "these new soldiers will need men to train and lead them, wouldn't you say, Smalls?"

"Of course." He started to walk off.

"Stop by the quartermaster and pick up your uniform, Smalls," DuPont called out. "And your sergeant's stripes."

He turned around, a smile on his face now. "Yes, sir." This time when he turned, he pivoted soldier fashion.

After the war, the real Robert Smalls served as a delegate to South Carolina's constitutional convention in 1868, and was in both houses of the state legislature from '68 to 1875. He also served two terms in the U.S. House of Representatives. In 1889, he was appointed by President Benjamin Harrison collector of the port of Beaufort. He held that post for the most part until 1913. He died on February 23, 1915.

Edward D. Hoch makes his living as a writer in a way that very few other people can attest to—he works almost entirely in short fiction. With hundreds of published stories primarily in the mystery and suspense genres, he has created such notable characters as Simon Ark, the 2,000-year-old detective, and Nick Velvet, the professional thief who steals only worthless objects, to the calculating Inspector Leopold, whose appearance in the short story "The Oblong Room" won his creator the Edgar Award for best short story. He lives and writes in Rochester, New York.

Much of the espionage done during the Civil War was by Northerners and Southerners working against their own people. "Copperhead" was a term for a Northerner who worked against his own people, and the "copperhead" in this story is no less tricky.

THE COUNTERFEIT COPPERHEAD

Edward D. Hoch

Cranston first met Maggie Little in a sailors' bar near the Toronto waterfront in August of 1864. The bar had an upstairs room that often served as a meeting place for American radicals of one sort or another. Some said it had even been a terminus for the Underground Railroad in those prewar years when escaped slaves made their way north by a devious route to freedom.

Now in this fourth year of the American Civil War, the room was being used for other purposes. A motley assemblage of two dozen men, and a few women, had come to hear Colonel Jacob Thompson, a middle-aged man with a short graying beard who bore the vague title of Special Commissioner of the Confederate States Government in Canada. He stood now at the front of the room, speaking with one of his aides before the start of the evening's program.

When he entered the room Cranston removed his hat and chose a seat next to a comely dark-haired woman in a slender black dress. The room was stuffy and she was cooling herself with a lacy French fan decorated with letters of the alphabet. "Are you a Copperhead?" she asked as they sat waiting for Colonel Thompson's appearance.

"I am, and proud of it," he replied. "The only way to end this insanity is to restore the Union to its prewar condition with continued slavery in the South. Too many lives have been sacrificed already."

"My name is Maggie Little," she responded, holding out her hand in a distinctly male gesture. "It's a pleasure to meet someone who shares my views."

He could detect a trace of the Old South in her manner of speaking.

"William Cranston," he said, gently accepting her hand. "Are you from the South?"

"Kentucky. A border state, but many of us side with the Confederacy."

Their conversation was interrupted by a call for silence. A man brought in a flag, the familiar stars and bars of the Confederate States of America, and a woman at a piano struck up "Dixie," the Southern anthem, while the spectators rose to sing. Maggie Little joined in with a full voice, covering Cranston's uncertainty with the lyrics.

"I was never much of a singer," he confided to her as they sat down.

"I could tell that," she replied with a bit of a grin.

A stocky man with a deep Southern accent introduced Colonel Thompson, who spoke with the quick, clipped tones of a military man trained to give orders. "As you know, the appalling casualties of Grant's campaign against Richmond and Petersburg have left both sides looking for a way out of this terrible war. We greatly appreciate the work of the Copperheads who are trying to restore the Union to its previous grandeur. For those who say you cannot turn back the clock, I say that is preferred to smashing it with a sledgehammer."

Thompson paced like an experienced politician as he spoke, ranging across the front of the crowded room so that all might see and hear him. "He's good!" Maggie Little whispered to Cranston. "This is the first time I've heard him."

"Next week the Democratic convention opens in Chicago," the colonel went on. "There are many within the party who want this war ended at any cost, which means defeating Mr. Lincoln at the polls in November. The Confederacy has assembled a large number of operatives here in Toronto, under my leadership. I have a personal letter of instructions from Jefferson Davis that I intend to carry out. Our Copperhead friends in this room can do us great service, especially in those states where your secret action arm, the Sons of Liberty, is strongest. I want to introduce you now to Captain Hines, who will tell you a bit about our plans for Chicago."

Hines was younger and physically smaller than Thompson, slim and dark-haired with lips that turned sinister when he attempted a smile. He explained in a careful voice that he had sixty men in Chicago, all wearing civilian clothes and carrying revolvers. Meetings had been held with the Illinois chapter of the Sons of Liberty, looking toward joint action during the Democratic convention. "What sort of action?" a man in the first row asked.

"That's not for me to say in an open meeting."

There was more general discussion of Chicago, and it became clear that several of those attending the meeting would be going there by train. When the meeting broke up Cranston followed Maggie Little outside and asked her about it. "Are you going to Chicago?"

"Of course. Something big is going to happen and I want to be there."

"Just who are these Sons of Liberty?"

She eyed him curiously. "Aren't you a Copperhead?"

"Of course."

"Then you should know about the Sons. They're a semi-secret society, the action arm of our organization. They operate in the North, doing what they can to support the Confederate cause."

"Terrorists."

"Not at all." She studied him in the flickering light from the gas lamps. "You're not a Copperhead at all, are you?"

It was his turn to grin. "I'm a spy."

"How did you get into the meeting?"

"I walked in behind someone else. The guard at the door thought we were together."

"But what are you doing here?"

"There'll be plenty of time to tell you on the train to Chicago."

All Copperhead members traveling to Chicago for the Democratic convention were given money for expenses. Captain Hines met them personally at the railroad station with an envelope for each one. When he was on the train, seated next to Maggie, Cranston opened his envelope and counted through the bills, in denominations of twenty and fifty dollars each.

"There's three hundred American dollars here," she told him, opening her own envelope. "What are we supposed to do to earn it?"

"I'm sure we'll find out in Chicago."

There was a slender man named Valland on the train with them, and it developed that he was a close friend of Maggie's. He was younger than Cranston, in his early twenties, and clean-shaven. A Yankee from New York City, he'd taken part in the draft riots the previous year and fled to Canada.

"What about you?" he asked Cranston at about the midpoint of their journey. "Where are you from?"

"Philadelphia," Cranston answered. "I worked for a printer there."

"And you're opposed to abolition?"

"I'm opposed to the war."

Young Valland seemed to know a great deal about the Chicago plans. The night before the train arrived there, after they'd all been drinking from his bottle of gin, he told them, "We're just a diversion, you know. They want us to disrupt the convention enough to draw federal troops there, while the Sons of Liberty attack two nearby prison camps and free twelve thousand Confederate soldiers."

"Is that true?" Maggie asked, wide-eyed.

"Of course. I overheard Hines and Colonel Thompson talking after the meeting in Toronto."

The scenario seemed unlikely, but Cranston knew the South was growing desperate. Twelve thousand Confederates freed from prison camps in the Chicago area would certainly cause a major disruption. If arrangements had been made to arm them, they could become a serious threat behind the Union lines.

When the train reached Chicago, the trio split up at the station and went their separate ways, arranging to meet at the convention site that evening. Cranston didn't know what to expect, but when he arrived there was only a scattering of demonstrators. He had no trouble finding Maggie Little observing events from a park across the street.

"I expected more people," she said. "We're almost outnumbered by the abolitionists."

"If Valland is correct, all the action might be at the prison camps."

But by the convention's end they knew the truth. The Sons of Liberty would not fight against superior Union troops that had been dispatched to the prison camps, and the Southern infiltrators could do nothing without them. As for the convention, the Democrats adopted a strong peace plank in their platform, but then nominated a Union hero, General George McClellan, who felt he had a mandate to carry the war to victory.

The following evening the three met at Cranston's hotel room and he agreed to travel south with Maggie and Valland. "Do you really think you can reach the Confederate lines?" he asked.

"There are regular steamboats up and down the Mississippi," Maggie told him.

"The entire river is now in Union hands."

"I'm sure we can reach the Confederate lines somehow," she argued.

"But why should we?" Valland asked.

"They gave us three hundred dollars each when we left Toronto," Maggie reminded them. "We owe them something for that money."

"We don't owe them much," Cranston said, taking one of the fifties from his pocket. "These bills are counterfeit."

They finally agreed to journey by train to St. Louis and board a steamboat named the *Paul Jones*, bound for New Orleans. Once Maggie thought she saw one of Captain Hines's men and feared they were being followed, but when Cranston strolled among the other passengers he saw no one familiar. With the Mississippi in the hands of the Union, the docks were crowded with militiamen, many in uniforms that were obviously homemade. Cranston could see that Maggie Little was nervous about paying for the journey with counterfeit greenbacks, but no one questioned it and they were soon safely on the river.

It was young Valland, once they were on board the *Paul Jones* and heading south, who took one of the bills from his pocket and asked Cranston, "How do you know these are counterfeit?"

The older man smiled like a teacher instructing his class. "There was no national paper currency before this Civil War. Various states and banks issued their own notes. These early Union greenbacks can be produced by anyone with a good printing press, and both North and South easily counterfeit them. These are a bit better than usual, and I would guess they were done by an engraver in Columbia, South Carolina, who also prints currency for the Confederacy."

"You know a lot about it," Valland remarked.

"I worked for a time with a printer named Sam Upham in Philadelphia."

"Counterfeiting greenbacks?" Maggie asked.

"And bluebacks, Confederate money, too. When the *Philadelphia Inquirer* ran engraved pictures of Confederate money, Upham bought the plates from them and used colored ink and heavier paper stock to turn out large quantities of counterfeit Southern currency. The Confederate constitution allows individual states as well as the central government to print their own money, which only adds to the currency confusion and drives up the inflation rate."

Later, when Valland had retired to his stateroom, Cranston and Maggie went out on deck, watching the moon's reflection on the water as the steamboat glided past the marshy shoreline. She stood fanning herself by the rail and he told her, "I thought you'd be spending the night with him."

"With Valland? He's little more than a child. We're only friends. I thought he showed very poor judgment on the train to Chicago when he told us about the Confederate plans to free those prisoners. Either one of us could be a Union spy."

Cranston thought about that. "Or Valland could be a spy, trying to spread the news so the mission might fail or be canceled. It certainly seems as if someone tipped off the Union troops."

"You told me that night in Toronto you were a spy," she reminded him.

"Do real spies ever announce the fact?"

"They do if they're clever enough."

A steamboat had run aground ahead of them on the river, and in the morning the captain announced they'd be docking at Memphis until the way was clear. The Mississippi was lower than usual for early September, and they needed a more experienced pilot to guide them.

It was Valland who suggested they leave the boat and move on. Much of western Tennessee was Union territory following Grant's victory at Chattanooga, and the young man was anxious to go east. "I want to reach the other side," he told Maggie and Cranston. "We all do, don't we?"

"Are you still worried about your part in the draft riots?" she asked. "They won't come after you for that."

"They might," he answered glumly. "I killed a militiaman during the fighting. I didn't mean to, but he's dead. They're probably hunting me for it."

"You're right, then," Maggie agreed. "We should move east."

"It seems safest right now," Cranston said. "We'll stay tonight at a hotel and leave early in the morning."

Maggie saw a problem. "We still have some of the counterfeit money left, but what good will greenbacks do us in the South?"

Cranston did not answer immediately. Instead he removed his coat and cut some of the threads holding the lining in place. His hand emerged with a packet of currency. "I have two thousand dollars in Confederate notes here. That should be more than enough."

"Counterfeit?" Valland asked.

"Of course, but they'll pass casual inspection. I took them along when I left my Philadelphia job."

"You stole them?"

"Not exactly. Mr. Upham sold them to me for fifty cents." He smiled at the memory. "I should have purchased more but I didn't know I'd be this far south."

They bought a horse and buggy in Memphis, loaded the carpetbags with their few possessions into the buggy, and set out in the morning toward the east. "Didn't you have two bags on the boat?" Maggie asked Cranston.

"I checked one at the hotel," he told her. "I expect to come back this way, sooner or later."

For the most part they traveled the back roads, hoping to encounter Confederate troops. Again Maggie had the feeling they were being followed, and from a high ridge they spotted a small band of horsemen who might have been on their trail. "What should we do?" she asked Cranston.

"Keep going. They don't seem to be in uniform." But he knew that meant very little in this war.

Before they'd traveled another ten miles the horsemen had overtaken them. In their lead was Captain Hines himself, the small, dark-haired man with a smile like a serpent's. "You are under arrest by order of the Confederate States of America," he shouted, pointing a long-barreled army revolver at them.

"What's the meaning of this?" Cranston asked indignantly. "You have no right—"

"We've been on your trail since Chicago," Hines replied. "One or all of you are Union spies!"

There were five men riding with Hines. They quickly dismounted and overpowered Cranston and his companions before they could resist. Their hands were tied and one of the horsemen took over the reins of the buggy. "We are in Union territory," Maggie protested.

"You are in no-man's-land," Hines corrected. "And you will soon be behind Confederate lines."

"That's just where we want to go," young Valland told them. "We're Copperheads, from up north. You must remember us from Toronto. We were at that meeting with Colonel Thompson."

"I remember you."

"Then you know we're not spies."

"We'll talk about that when we reach camp."

They rode through the afternoon and into the dusk before reaching a glen where campfires burned outside of tents. The Confederate flag was still flying as they were helped down from the buggy and brought into a large tent. Their hands were untied but two grizzled soldiers with rifles stood guard over them. Cranston estimated there were a hundred or more men in the encampment, and most seemed to be Tennessee volunteers. It was hot in the tent and Maggie fanned herself while they waited for whatever was to come.

Finally Captain Hines entered with another officer to question them. "Do you intend to hold us here long?" Cranston asked.

"As long as necessary."

"On what charges?"

"The Union forces were warned in advance that an attempt would be made to free Confederate prisoners in the Chicago area. A telegram in cipher was sent from the Chicago railway station just after you three arrived by train from Toronto."

"Which proves nothing," Cranston said.

"All of you were observed near the telegraph office."

"We separated there and went our own ways," Maggie told him.

"You pretend to be Copperheads, but at least one of you is a Union spy. We will search your belongings for code books or a key to the substitution cipher we believe was used. Unless we can determine which of you is the spy, you will all be hanged in the morning."

Cranston saw the fear on his companions' faces. "I'd like to speak with you in private," he told the captain.

Hines eyed him for a moment and then said, "That could be arranged."

They left the tent together. One guard remained with Maggie and Valland while the other followed along. Dusk had given way to darkness, and the Confederate flag no longer flew over the camp. "You're very close to the Union lines here," Cranston remarked.

"Too close. As soon as you people are dealt with I'll be on my way back to Toronto."

"How much would it cost to buy our freedom?"

Captain Hines snorted. "More than you possess."

"I could offer five hundred Confederate dollars for each of us."

"You have it with you?"

"Yes."

The small man snorted. "I must remember to remove it from your body after we hang you."

"That wouldn't be wise. The bills are counterfeit, like the Union currency you supplied to us in Toronto."

"Show me!" Hines commanded.

"May I reach into my pocket without being shot by your guard?" Hines nodded and Cranston showed him one of the twenty-dollar bills.

"These are good quality," the captain agreed after lighting a match to study it more closely. "Do you have more?"

"Some. And I can arrange for a larger quantity, as much as fifty thousand dollars."

"What are you charging?"

"Twenty cents on the dollar. A low price for currency of this quality."

"I believe we can work out a deal," Hines said. "Where is it right now?"

"In a carpetbag at a Memphis hotel. They're holding it for me."

"We can return there tomorrow."

"If you have ten thousand dollars. Payment must be in Union greenbacks, and none of your counterfeits. After the currency is delivered to you, we will all be set free."

"Of course. I can raise the money in Memphis once I show people the quality of your counterfeit."

"Then it's agreed."

Hines took out a thin black cigar and lit it, turning to squint at his prisoner. "You are a complex man, Mr. Cranston. I wonder which of us is really the captor and which the prisoner."

In the morning they were awakened by the sound of rifles firing in an irregular pattern some distance away over the next hill. Already the small encampment was assembling to join in the battle. Captain Hines appeared with two of his own men, ordering the overnight guards to rejoin their unit. "There's fighting nearby," he told them. "We must go back the way we came. Can all of you ride horses?"

"I can't ride in this dress," Maggie Little told him.

Valland, who was slim-waisted, volunteered a pair of his pants. "They're clean, and they should fit pretty well. You can try my spare boots, too."

The pants were a bit long but she managed to tuck them into the boots, which fit quite well. "I'm ready," she said finally, emerging from the tent.

Three of Hines's men were left behind so their horses could be used. Hines and the other two accompanied Cranston's party as they rode back to the west, the way they had come. "We'll ride at a gallop for the first hour," Hines ordered. "I want to put as much distance between us and the Yankees as possible."

Cranston assumed they would camp for the night, but it soon became obvious that Captain Hines was anxious to reach the relative safety of Memphis. Once they were stopped by a Union patrol, but Hines presented forged documents and they were allowed to proceed. By nightfall the gaslights of the city came into view.

"We'll settle our business in the morning," the captain said. "Meanwhile I need more samples of your counterfeit Confederate bills to raise the money for you."

Cranston handed over a few twenties and fifties. "Where will I find you tomorrow?"

Captain Hines smiled his serpent's smile. "I'll find you, in your room. One of my men will be spending the night with you."

"Not with Miss Little, he won't. She'll need a separate room."

"All right. I'll have my man in the hallway, on a chair between the rooms."

Once they were alone, Maggie said, "It shouldn't be hard to get away from him here in Memphis. We're safe in Union territory."

"I have no intention of getting away from him. We'll be closing a business deal in the morning."

"I saw you give him some counterfeit bills just now."

"And I'm going to sell him a great many more."

When they reached their rooms, the first thing Maggie did was to shed young Valland's pants and boots and return them to him. Back into her own dress and shoes, fluttering her French fan, she was Cranston's ideal of utter femininity and perhaps she knew it.

He sent down for the carpetbag he'd checked when they first arrived in the city, and when the bellboy brought it up Cranston set to work on its contents. Valland, sharing the room with him, looked on spellbound. "Is that real money?" he asked.

"Some of it is and some of it isn't."

"What are you going to do with it?"

"We'll see."

The young man eyed him curiously. "You're a counterfeiter, aren't you? That's what this is all about."

"No," Cranston answered with a smile. "Actually, I'm not."

When he finished with the carpetbag he slid it under his bed and turned in for the night. With Hines's guard outside the door he didn't have to worry about Valland stealing the money.

In the morning Captain Hines came to their room. While Valland went downstairs with the guard for breakfast, Cranston completed his business with the officer. He opened the carpetbag and revealed the packages of Confederate money wrapped in brown paper. Handing one to Hines, he told him to examine it.

Hines ripped open the package and fanned the bills. "Looks good to me," he said after counting the twenties. "One hundred. That's two thousand dollars."

"And there are twenty-five packages here. Fifty thousand dollars, as we agreed."

The Counterfeit Copperhead ✠ 51

The captain tore open the end of each package to be certain it contained currency, then returned it to the carpetbag. When he was satisfied he closed the bag and snapped it shut. "It sounds as if there are troops in the street," Cranston said suddenly.

Captain Hines hurried to take a look. "I see nothing."

"I must have been mistaken. Will you be heading north from here?"

"I go where they send me." He picked up the carpetbag.

"Aren't you forgetting my ten thousand dollars?"

"Of course." Hines reached into an inner pocket and brought out a thick packet of Union currency. "I think you'll find it in order."

The money was all in fifty-dollar bills. There were two hundred of them. "It's been a pleasure doing business with you, Captain."

Hines was almost out the door when he turned, as if with a suddenly remembered thought. "My spy investigation is ended. The guilty party was executed within the last fifteen minutes."

Cranston froze where he stood. "What?"

"It was young Valland. He sent the enciphered message in Chicago. The substitution cipher was in the cuff of his pants."

"Executed?"

"I ordered it, my men carried it out. There was no way to transport him back to Confederate lines with the fighting raging."

"You're a hard man, Captain."

"We have a war to win."

Cranston and Maggie caught the next steamboat north, which sailed within the hour. "What did it cost you to get us free?" she asked him as the boat pulled away from the dock.

"I think you did that," he told her, "and the cost was young Valland's life."

"They found his body in an alley back of the hotel. I had no way of knowing—"

"You went to Hines's room last night, didn't you? And told him that the cipher was hidden in the cuff of Valland's pants. You knew you were signing his death warrant."

Her face was impassive against his attack. "Valland admitted killing a militiaman during the draft riots. You haven't forgotten that, have you?"

"So you were his judge. And executioner, too, in a way."

"We're two of a kind, Cranston. You're a counterfeiter and I'm a schemer."

"I'm no counterfeiter." He opened the carpetbag he still carried and showed her the packages of money inside. "I suppose it would be more accurate to call me a confidence man. I showed Hines some real Confederate money and convinced him the bills were perfect counterfeits. Then I sold him fifty thousand dollars' worth for ten thousand."

"That's all real money?"

"Only the top bills. The rest are poor counterfeits. It didn't matter because I switched carpetbags on the captain while he was looking out the window for a second. This went under the bed and he took a duplicate full of my dirty clothes. I had two, you'll remember. I'd left one at the hotel and taken the other with us in the buggy."

"A confidence man?" she asked. "Then what does that make me?"

"A Union spy," he answered simply. "You planted that cipher in the cuff of Valland's pants when you borrowed them for the ride back to Memphis. The real cipher system you kept in plain view all the time, but no one realized it. One of the ciphers used by the North has a fanlike system of wooden tablets, each with a different ciphertext alphabet on it, with a keyword for choosing the proper alphabet. I noticed the alphabet letters on your fan the first time we met, but I didn't realize I was looking at the cipher system you used."

"What are you going to do about it?" she asked with the hint of a smile.

"It's a long trip back to Chicago," Cranston told her. "I'll think of something."

Kristine Kathryn Rusch won the Locus Award for best short fiction for her novella, *The Gallery of His Dreams*. Her body of fiction work won her the John W. Campbell Award for best new SF writer. She has been nominated for several dozen fiction awards, and her short work has been reprinted in six *Year's Best* collections. She has published twenty novels under her own name, and has sold forty-one total, including pseudonymous books. Her novels have been published in seven languages. She has written a number of *Star Trek* novels with her husband, Dean Wesley Smith, including a book in the Section 31 series called *Shadow*. She is the former editor of *The Magazine of Fantasy and Science Fiction*, winning a Hugo for her work there. Before that, she and Smith started and ran Pulphouse Publishing, a science fiction and mystery press in Eugene, Oregon. She lives and works on the Oregon Coast.

Here, in a tale based on the lives of real people, she reveals how betrayals during the Civil War could extract a terrible price years, even lifetimes, later.

THE DEAD LINE

∷

Kristine Kathryn Rusch

JUNE 17, 1911

Nathaniel Garrison gripped the silver handle on his walking stick and cursed the unsteadiness of his legs. After three days, he should have had his sea legs. The *Olympic* was the largest ship ever built and, as a result, was steadier in the water than most. He had spent a fair number of years on ships—both before and after the war—and he had never had so much trouble walking on a deck.

Of course, in those days he hadn't been recovering from a bout of pleurisy that had nearly taken his life. He hadn't been this thin since those horrible years in Andersonville, years he was still amazed he had survived.

The afternoon weather was balmy and he couldn't stay confined to his stateroom. He was supposed to remain indoors—all that outdoor air was supposed to be bad for him, not that he cared. He had not made it seventy-four years by believing everything other people told him. His body craved light and air and exercise. By gum, he'd have them.

The Boat Deck was filled with people. Many were sitting in lounge chairs, blankets at their feet, staring across the railing at the surprisingly calm Atlantic. Others were gathered at tables, having animated conversations. Rich people, of which he was one. Captains of industry, their wives, children, and mistresses. People he did not socialize with unless necessity forced him into it.

He supposed he would find a great deal of entertainment among the luminaries on this ship. It was the *Olympic*'s maiden voyage and, as a result, he found himself in a floating party. The party was a big do, complete with reporters hired by the White Star Line to capture the grandeur, and allowed access to all the first-class berths, so long as they did not bother the passengers.

Sometimes he wondered how difficult that was. In addition to him—a man who never gave interviews because he despised the influence of the scandal sheets—there were several other well-known men, including J. P. Morgan, who was here, of course, to monitor his investment. Several members of the British peerage were on board as well, many on vacation and some, like Lord Reginald Seton, to do business in New York.

If Garrison had been a reporter, he would have interviewed them all. What would the crew have done, after all? Thrown him off for violating his agreement? He suspected a number of journalists were taking notes, and the very thought of it kept him away from the public areas most of the time.

He rested his arms on the deck's wooden railing and stared at the gray Atlantic which stretched as far as the eye could see. The sky above it was bluer than the ocean but they still blurred at the horizon. Out in the middle of nowhere, going somewhere fast.

He looked down. Even though he'd been on the *Olympic* for three days, he still couldn't believe the size of her. Here, on the Boat Deck—"A Deck," as the brochures called it—he was as high as he could get: seemingly miles above the frothing water, as if he were watching from the balcony of one of London's tall buildings overlooking the Thames instead of from the deck of a ship. A floating palace, the ads had called it, and that was probably true.

A floating palace filled with the usual sycophantic and self-absorbed courtiers, all of whom thought they were more important than they were.

Behind him, a woman laughed. The laugh was fluted, trilling up and down the vocal register like a diva's playful attempt at a scale. The hair rose on the back of his neck.

He hadn't heard that laugh in nearly fifty years.

Surely he was mistaken. He was short of breath and just getting over being ill. He had spent too much time alone, and whenever he did that, he thought of the war.

He thought too much of the war.

Then he heard the laugh again, closed his eyes, and saw her, just as he had that first night.

She had taken his breath away then.

Much as she was doing now.

JUNE 17, 1861

Lieutenant Nathaniel Garrison placed his cap under his arm and nodded crisply to the Negro butler who opened the massive oak door. The man before him had to be at least eighty; his dark skin was lined with wrinkles, his curly hair a pure white. The man took his hat and his card and issued him inside.

Garrison had an odd feeling that he had suddenly stepped across the Mason-Dixon line. But he knew that wasn't so. It wasn't legal to own slaves up here. The butler had to be a free man.

But it still made Garrison uncomfortable. Despite Lincoln's denials that this was a war fought over slavery, slavery was the issue that had caused the South to secede. Even the appearance of it here, in the nation's capital, made him more uncomfortable than he dared say.

The air was cool inside, despite the awful heat. The entry was large and mostly made of oak. A wide staircase led to the upper stories. On the banister, an iron gas lamp rose, carved in the shape of Cupid.

Garrison had never been inside the Cunliffe house before, and had no real idea how to act. It was his first society party and he was here only because he was on General Scott's staff, not because he was important in his own right.

His summer dress uniform was still too hot for the heat and humidity of official Washington. A trickle of sweat ran down his back despite the coolness of the entry.

The butler had hung his cap somewhere and was opening the pocket doors that led into the main part of the house. "This way, sir," he said, bowing before Garrison.

Now Garrison could hear voices and the soft music of a string quartet playing Mozart. The sound wafted in from the verandah, but there were people in the drawing room as well, holding glasses filled with champagne and plates covered with hors d'oeuvres.

He caught snatches of conversation as he moved into the room.

". . . when Tennessee seceded . . ."

". . . President Lincoln isn't acting as if we're in a war . . ."

". . . General Scott isn't just old. He's senile. We're—"

That last conversation stopped as the speaker, a young man who wore a cream-colored summer suit, saw Garrison. Garrison took a flute of champagne from a tray offered him by a Negro waiter, and walked toward the verandah.

President Lincoln wasn't the only one who wasn't acting as if there were a war. Half of Washington's military was here, eating finger foods and discussing secession as if it were a parlor game.

Garrison didn't want to be here himself. He had a lot of work ahead of him drilling the ninety-day militia units and trying to form the new three-year volunteer units into a coherent army. None of them had had any real training. Many were simply young men who wanted to fight. And even though

Washington was now ringed by military camps, organized units and fancy uniforms did not make an effective fighting force.

Lieutenant General Winfield Scott, who was general-in-chief, had planned to spend the first year of the war preparing. Even if the plan hadn't leaked, Garrison thought it wouldn't have worked. The cries that started with the firing on Fort Sumter had risen in May when Richmond had been chosen as the capital of the Confederacy, and were now hitting a fever pitch.

Richmond wasn't that far from Washington, after all, and most people thought the war would be over quickly if only the United States quashed the Rebels in their capital. Garrison was worried that the Rebels might try to do the same to Washington—a fear he shared with General Scott. Either way, the war would escalate from small skirmishes to a large battle soon enough. The only question was when.

The champagne flute was made of crystal and he had to hold it delicately as he made his way to the verandah. Here, even more people stood. The air smelled of the small smoke-fires burning in bowls at the rim of the property to keep the mosquitoes away. Several more servants, holding large fans, waved them up and down so that the thick air moved.

It wasn't yet twilight, though that hour wasn't far away. The longest day of the year was fast approaching and sometimes it seemed to Garrison that the days would never be long enough.

Across the yard, he finally saw his hostess, Mrs. Evangeline Cunliffe. Mrs. Cunliffe was a widow whose husband had died of a fever several summers ago. She was known for holding the most important society functions in all of official Washington.

When General Scott heard Garrison complain about the invitation, Scott pushed him to go. Old Fuss-and-Feathers was never one to turn down an important social function. His political nature was too honed—perhaps from the days when he was the Whig candidate for president, days he rarely talked about, since he had lost so badly to Franklin Pierce.

Garrison was not a social man. He would thank his hostess, mingle for a few moments after that, and then disappear into the house. Without making his apologies, he would be on the road back to camp within the hour.

Behind him, a woman laughed. The laugh was fluted, trilling up and down the vocal register like a dancehall girl's playful attempt at a scale. In the days before his father had forced him to go to West Point, Garrison had fancied himself a musician. His father had sent him away precisely to destroy that ambition and had succeeded, for the most part.

Except when something caught his ear, as this laugh did now. He turned, looking for the source of it. Women in wide hooped skirts stood on the lawn, their shoulders bared, revealing cleavage, and their hair in ringlets that seemed too girlish for most of them.

The laugh came again, and he turned again, finally catching the last note of it. The woman who made the sound was wearing pink, but on her the color seemed natural. She had black hair and eyes equally as dark, against skin the color of alabaster. The pink dress had no ornamentation—no lace, no frothy ruffles designed to enhance the bosom. Even though the woman was petite, her features small and foxlike, she filled out the dress nicely, naturally, as if the style had been created just for her.

She wore diamonds around her neck—or what appeared to be diamonds—small ones that caught the light. They added radiance to her face, but he was already captivated. He had never seen such delicate beauty before, delicate beauty that added to, and did not try to hide, strength.

The cloying scent of perfume overwhelmed him, and he suppressed the urge to sneeze. A hand slid through his bent arm and gripped it tightly.

"Lieutenant Garrison."

He looked down at Mrs. Cunliffe. Her long black hair had been pulled to the back of her head and was held in a snood. She still wore black even though her husband had been dead for years, but the dress whispered as she moved. Silk, and from the look of it, expensive silk at that.

"Mrs. Cunliffe. I was just coming to pay my respects." His voice sounded foreign to him, stiff, formal, and unnatural, in a way it usually never was.

Her smile brightened her face. She lacked the beauty of the woman he had been watching, but she made up for it in personality. Even he could understand why so many men in Washington discussed her with such open admiration—and he was at least fifteen years younger than she.

"Come now, Lieutenant." Her voice had a soft Virginia accent that somehow made her seem even more feminine. "We both know you were not looking at me."

To his surprise, he felt a flush rising in his neck. He was not a man who blushed—but then, he was not a man who usually got caught unawares.

"If I had been looking at you, ma'am," he said, "I would have been more welcoming as you approached."

She laughed, deep-throated and rich, a woman who no longer had need of feminine games. "You are as charming as they say, Lieutenant."

"Who says?" he asked.

She shrugged and gestured with her free hand. "All of Washington. You're one of the city's most eligible bachelors, you know. Rumor has it that you're going to whip old Fuss-and-Feathers's troops into shape long before he realizes there's a war going on."

To hear Scott's nickname come from a civilian startled him almost more than her disrespect had. "General Scott is aware of the war," Garrison said quietly. "He simply believes we must prepare for it."

"Admirable," she said, "if we were going to fight a prolonged war."

He wasn't going to get into a political discussion with his hostess. He'd been raised in the country, but even in the hinterlands he'd learned enough about decorum to know that politics and parties did not mix.

She took his champagne flute and set it on the flat top of the wooden railing. Then she led him off the verandah and down the stairs to the lawn. "What, Lieutenant? No opinion? Or would you rather seem loyal to your commander by keeping your silence?"

He smiled. She was good. "I'm merely a lieutenant, ma'am," he said. "My opinions do not matter."

"I suspect that as a lieutenant who is out in the field every day—"

"If you call the perimeter of the city a 'field,' ma'am."

"—your opinions are probably more accurate than those of General Scott. I hear he's not as sharp as he used to be. Is that true?"

He was sharp enough to order me to this damn thing, Garrison thought, but did not say. "General Scott has a long history of military leadership in our country. That he is old and that the press has ridiculed his preparations does not mean that he has diminished capacity."

Even though Garrison had seen evidence of it. The shaking hands, the sometimes befuddled look in Scott's blue eyes. Occasionally the man forgot he had given an order, or forgot which day of the week it was. Other times he was so quick that Garrison felt he could never outthink the old man. It varied from day to day, and in degree and measure.

"You're one of the few to deny it," Mrs. Cunliffe said, her tone musing. "Of course, your carefully chosen words were not an exact denial, were they? More of a way of avoiding the question."

That flush still warmed his neck. The woman was smarter than he expected, and not nearly as retiring as most women of his acquaintance. Of course, most women of his acquaintance were matrons who were concerned with their broods, or girls who had just reached their majority and were interested in becoming an officer's wife.

"Such a shy man," Mrs. Cunliffe said. "Who would have thought such a big strong strapping fellow like you would be shy?"

He wasn't shy, just focused. But he would let her take his actions any way she wanted. It was easier that way.

She led him across the yard directly toward the beauty he had been admiring moments ago.

"Shoo," Mrs. Cunliffe said as they got close, waving her arm at the men who were surrounding the younger woman. "I have an introduction to make."

To Garrison's surprise, the men left, several with backward glances at the beauty as if they had expected her to defend them. She said nothing, merely watched Mrs. Cunliffe with a polite and curious smile on her foxlike face.

"Serena," Mrs. Cunliffe said, "I would like you to meet one of Washington's most eligible bachelors. That we even have him here is a rare treat. Lieutenant Nathaniel Garrison, Serena Freneau."

Miss Freneau offered her hand, small, delicate, and white, and he took it by the fingers, then bent over it, not quite kissing it. Her fingers were warm and smooth in his own.

"A pleasure, miss," he said.

This time, her smile was all for him. "The pleasure's mine."

"I'll leave you both," Mrs. Cunliffe said. "And remember, Lieutenant. This is a party. No need to be so very serious."

He looked after her, watching her black skirts sway as she walked away from him. A party, and he was too serious. Of course he was serious. There was a war going on, a war no one seemed to understand except him.

"Perhaps the city's most eligible bachelor is interested in the city's most famous widow." Serena Freneau's voice was soft and teasing, with a bit of a bite to it.

He looked back at her, unable to believe his lack of manners. He hadn't let go of her fingers yet, and didn't dare now. It would make him look even ruder than if he continued to hold them.

"I'm sorry," he said. "It was just that that was our first conversation. I had no idea she even knew who I was."

Miss Freneau's eyes were a shade of brown that matched her hair. They twinkled at him. "You're at her party, aren't you? Of course she knows who you are."

That flush—why was he cursed with it on this night?—rose again. A trickle of sweat followed the drying path along his back, tickling as it traced his spine. "I meant—"

"I know what you meant." Slowly she looked down at his hand, still holding hers. "Aunt Evangeline always surprises people with her knowledge. Perhaps it is because men think knowledge is unusual in females."

He almost felt trapped by those fingers in his, the way that she wasn't protesting what was becoming a faux pas. "I don't find knowledge unusual in females," he said. "I'm just surprised that as important a personage as Mrs. Cunliffe would know who I am."

"A member of General Scott's staff? The only one, it's said, who knows that a short war is what the country needs? Of course she knows who you are."

And apparently Miss Freneau did as well. "I didn't realize that Mrs. Cunliffe was your aunt."

Miss Freneau smiled at him, this one soft and rather indulgent. How many different versions of a smile did this woman have?

"You don't have time to keep track of social conventions." Her fingers squeezed his in acknowledgment of their touch, and then she broke the contact. "It's simply nice to know our fair city is being kept safe by men such as you."

"Our fair city is under no immediate danger."

"That's not what they say." Miss Freneau leaned toward him. "I've heard that the Rebels want nothing more than to destroy the capital. What sort of disgrace is that?"

"It's war, miss," he said, and wished he hadn't. When had he gotten so prim around women?

"Are you saying we should take their capital as well?"

"As your aunt just reminded me," he said gently, "this is a party. There's no need to be so serious."

Miss Freneau's eyes widened and then she laughed—that same musical sound he had heard before. It was entrancing, almost seductive, and he felt a small thrill of pride that he had caused it.

"Of course," she said, taking his arm just as her aunt had. "I'm the one being rude. I'm asking you to discuss work, and this gathering is supposed to make you forget about work, relax, and enjoy yourself."

He placed a hand over hers, noting the looks he got from the men who had been gathered around her before. He remembered how she hadn't touched any of them, but she had touched him. Again, that small pride ran through him.

"Would you like some punch, Miss Freneau?"

"I thought you would never ask," she said, leading him to the outdoor table covered with punch and various cakes.

Her skirts brushed his legs. She wore a light perfume, so unique that it took him a moment to realize it was lilac water mixed with her own scent.

When they reached the table, he slipped out of her grasp and took the cut-glass punch cup an elderly female servant offered him, then handed it to Miss Freneau. He took another glass for himself. He was going to ask if she wanted cakes, when she leaned forward.

"There will be dancing later, Lieutenant," she said. "My aunt has given permission for at least two waltzes. We're being informal—no dance cards—but I would hope you save one waltz for me."

This time he smiled. The waltz was a brazen dance not often allowed at social functions, especially social functions of this caliber. "Have you ever waltzed before, Miss Freneau?"

"Only with my dance instructor," she said, "and only because I forced him to teach me."

Garrison could see that. The woman had a strength about her that could not be denied. "To dance it might compromise your reputation."

Her eyes twinkled and this time her smile was wide. " 'Reputation'? Lieutenant, we're at war. In six months' time, who will care about reputations?"

"If we do this right," he said, "you won't even notice the war."

She tossed her ringlets back and sighed. "And here I was hoping for a measure of freedom."

"That seems to be," he said, "what everyone is hoping for these days."

JUNE 17, 1911

Garrison turned, the remembered scent of lilac water still in his nose. The waltz had been the highlight of his life until that point, Serena Freneau's small body moving with his in a sweeping motion, her skirts flaring behind her, his hand pressed against the small of her back, her bright eyes holding his as if there were no one else in the room—indeed, no one else in the world.

It had been the beginning of something, although not quite the something he had thought.

The laugh again, musical, warm. He scanned the deck chairs, saw no one laughing. Most of the passengers there were reading or talking softly, enjoying the maiden voyage of a ship he couldn't even have imagined fifty years before.

The world had changed, so much that at times he barely recognized it.

He scanned until he saw a grouping around one of the iron tables placed on the deck by the crew before dawn. An umbrella shaded the table itself. The women who sat there were not the young creatures he had thought, but elderly, most of them wearing tasteful black gowns. Not the black silk that Mrs. Cunliffe had worn fifty years before, with reams of material over hoops, but long skirts that covered sensible shoes, black lace around the neck, and in the case of one woman, a long strand of pearls that added a bit of brightness.

He was about to turn away when he heard the laugh a third time. It came from the woman wearing the pearls. She had silver hair rolled into a bun at the back of her head, rather like that of an aging Gibson girl. Softly curling tendrils fell along the sides of her narrow face.

The chin wasn't as sharp as it had been and the skin looked papery, like some women's skin got when they aged, but the brown eyes were still sharp, maybe more sharp now that they no longer matched her hair.

He leaned against the rail, feeling sea spray mist him like tears. His breath was in his throat again, his heart racing like a boy's.

It wasn't possible. It couldn't be possible. She had died, drowned as she tried to escape a U.S. naval blockade runner. The rough seas had pulled her under when the lifeboat she'd stolen capsized.

He'd seen the obituary, visited her grave. Clenched his fist on top of the stone and pounded until his skin rubbed away, and his blood stained the rounded edge.

If that were her, if she really lived, it meant she had told yet another lie, and another lie might be more than he could bear.

MAY 20, 1864

Heat already, even though it was barely noon. Flies, on his face, his arms. Too tired to brush them off. Thinner than he'd ever been. The dysentery was bad. Not as bad as some, dying in the middle of the camp, no one noticing until they'd become so covered with flies that they looked like a strange hive. And the stench . . .

A man never got used to the stench.

Garrison sat, arms around his legs. His uniform was all rags, which was good in this heat. It'd been cool when he was captured, over a year ago now. Over a year and he hadn't changed clothes since. Hadn't really bathed except early on, when he didn't know that he shouldn't use his drinking water for washing.

He sat near the edge of the log stockade. Other men were around him, though he barely noticed. He was too weak to notice much. His brain simply hummed as he tried not to think, tried not to think about any of it, from the first awful days.

Ahead of him, the line drawn in the cracked red Georgia clay, harsh now, deeper than it had been last summer—the days of the miserable heat. He'd tried to bury the dead then, had had some strength, but when he'd collapsed, no one had picked him up. No one had helped. He just kept thinking of the bodies and the disease. Less than sixteen acres this camp was, and, some said, more than twenty thousand men here—living men. Who knew how many dead?

Who cared anymore?

Still, he stared at the line. The dead line, they called it. One foot across it and a guard would shoot him, not care if he was only wounded, let him rot in the wretched Georgia sun. Sometimes men cried from out there, whimpered, moaned in pain, and no one dared go help them. No one dared try. Not if he still valued his life.

Garrison sometimes wondered why he did. It would all end so easily. One foot across, maybe two. The perimeter wasn't as well guarded here. There weren't enough guards for all these men. That's why, he guessed, there was a lack of food, the horrible conditions. Keep the men weak and they couldn't run. They wouldn't even try.

But he stared at the line. The dead line. Like he did every day. So easy to end it all. And so hard.

One shot, or, maybe, escape. But to what?

The thoughts were too much and he willed his mind back to the humming. It wasn't going there, rarely did when he contemplated the dead line. For there was nothing left for him. Nothing at all.

No way he could face her. Anyone. No way he could face anyone from his past at all.

A hand on his back, then a crust of bread thrust at him. He looked over, saw Major Tom Winthrop of the New York Zouaves, his gaudy uniform now in tatters, the colors faded and no longer joyful.

Winthrop thrust the bread at him again, and this time Garrison took it. The crust was so dry it crumbled in his hands. He knew how it would feel in his mouth, impossible to swallow without water—and he wouldn't get his ration until that night, if he was lucky enough to survive that long.

Lucky enough. The thought almost made him chuckle.

Still he took a bite, forced himself to chew, swallow, nearly choking on the scratchy stale crust going down. He uttered a weak cough, wiped his mouth with the back of his hand, and then checked it for blood.

None yet. But it was only a matter of time. Only a matter of time.

"New recruits today," Winthrop said, using the term that had once been a joke and wasn't any longer. More prisoners in the already overcrowded space. Raw and green and unable to know what horrors faced them, thinking at that point that they were better off than their fellows—at least they were *alive*. "There's one you should see."

It took Winthrop awhile to make the whole sentence, but it took Garrison awhile to follow it as well. They were well matched, like old men who had said everything they needed to long ago.

"Why?" Garrison asked.

"News. About that woman."

Winthrop knew everything. Down to the ugliest detail, like a father confessor. There had been nothing else to do in here but talk. Even then, Garrison hadn't said much. Only to Winthrop, whose unit had left him for dead, thinking he had betrayed them, when in truth he hadn't. He knew who did, he had said, not that it mattered now. That man was free or dead or in some other camp. Winthrop was concerned with survival here.

"Don't need news," Garrison said.

"This you do." Then Winthrop turned, slowly, like a man underwater, and waved his fingers at someone, beckoning him forward.

Garrison heard the footsteps, the intake of breath, saw a droplet of sweat hit the dry red clay. The man still had enough water in him to waste it in sweat; someday he would think that a luxury.

"My god in heaven, are you all dying?"

Garrison looked up, saw a young man's face, red whiskers sprouting in patches with the growth of a week, hair messy and covered with grime. New recruit, captured nearby. Not a long journey. Not a lot of suffering. Yet.

"Tell Lieutenant Garrison what you told me," Winthrop said.

The boy waited for Winthrop to finish—impatiently, Garrison thought, obviously not used to the pace of life here: the conservation of life, the way energy had to be stored, held, a commodity as precious as water, twice as precious as bread.

"Lieutenant Garrison?" the boy asked. "Not Nathaniel Garrison?"

"Yes," Winthrop said.

Garrison stared at the boy, the green eyes sliding back and forth, the beginnings of a panic that Garrison didn't yet understand.

"I'm sorry, sir." The boy bit his lower lip. "She said you were dead."

"Who?" Garrison's voice was little more than a whisper. The voice of a man not yet dead. But close. Too damn close.

"Your wife."

Garrison's hand snaked out before he could stop it, all bone and sinew, and it caught the boy's wrist, still fat with flesh. The boy looked down, startled, tried to wrench away and couldn't.

"How do you know my wife?" Garrison asked.

"A party, last summer. She held a charity function for the widows-and-orphans campaign." The boy's voice was trembling. "Please, sir, you're hurting me."

"Did you sleep with her?"

"Sir, I—"

"Did you?"

The boy swallowed, his Adam's apple bobbing. Garrison envied him the saliva that made such a movement so simple, so involuntary.

"She said you were dead, sir."

Garrison flung the boy away from him. How many lives this time, then? How many?

"And I suppose you told her everything you knew, figuring it wouldn't hurt."

The boy was rubbing his wrist. He studied Garrison for a moment; then an awful understanding filled his face, an understanding quickly denied. "Sir, I thought she was a loyal officer's widow."

"She was a loyal officer's *wife*." The words caught in Garrison's throat like the bread crust had, and he coughed again, wiping, checking for blood, seeing none. Not yet. "But *she* was not loyal. Not loyal at all."

APRIL 25, 1863

In his own bedroom, the window open, the spring air carrying the faint scents of cherry blossoms on the breeze, Garrison could almost see the future. His wife beside him, naked, her warm body pressed against his, both of them still sticky from lovemaking, the softness of the cotton ticking in the well-stuffed mattress lulling him toward sleep, it wasn't hard to imagine, years from now, the war over, how he would lie here, holding her, trying to make no noise so that the children wouldn't hear.

Perhaps it was a fantasy. There were no children yet, neither of them wanting to bring a child into this horror, this world that was so far from the one he had known. Lincoln's Emancipation Proclamation, only four months old, guaranteed that if the North won—*when* the North won—the world would be a different place from the one Garrison grew up in.

Serena had just been complaining about how difficult it was to keep help anymore. She had grown up in Evangeline Cunliffe's house, where the servants had once been slaves, who had stayed with the family after receiving their freedom—or so the Cunliffes had told Garrison. He doubted even that was true when, after the war began in earnest, the servants vanished one by one, like thieves in the night, stealing their freedom the way their counterparts had done for decades down South.

Serena sighed next to him and he wondered if she was drifting into sleep. They had promised to stay awake together—he only had twenty-four hours until he had to return to hell—but they had not always managed to keep that promise before.

"Where will you be?" she asked him, her voice sleepy. He felt her breath on his chest, and the softness of her hair beneath his hand.

"I don't know for sure," he said, hating to lie to her. The lie spoiled the beauty of the night. The war came back now in all its bloody terror, the stench of mud, the cold, the smell of gunpowder and smoke filling the air.

She raised up on one elbow and looked down at him. Her beauty was greater without the clothes, the way her neck rose out of her shoulders and collarbone, the way her torso tapered into a waist so small he could wrap his hand around it.

"I swear I don't know why General Hooker trusts you as his attaché," she said, that faint teasing look on her face, the one that had entranced him two years before. "Best hope you never have to lie for him, Nathaniel Garrison."

"You know I'm not supposed to tell you," he said, drawing her down.

But she put her other arm on his chest, keeping her face above his. His eyes had adjusted to the dark. He could almost see her expression, could imagine it even though it wasn't completely clear.

"Who am I gonna tell?" she asked. "Evangeline? She disappeared a month ago. The other wives? They're fearing a summer siege on Washington and have gone farther north. There's no one, Nate, no one I'd trust to tell, not and risk your life."

He pulled her down, kissed her, wished he could stay even one more night. "You don't need to know."

"Sure I do. If you die, how'll I know? Silence for months and then a casualty list? At least—"

"You can watch the battle, see the number of dead, and worry that I'm in it?"

She pushed herself up again. "I do that anyway, only now I do that with all of them. Maybe if there was only one—"

"We're trying for Richmond again," he said. She could always get him to tell her; she said it eased her mind. And knowing that she knew eased his. "And this time, I think we'll take it."

"You have a plan."

"I don't," he said. "General Hooker does."

"Is he as good as they say?"

"Better." Garrison liked working with Hooker. So different from the other generals who had led the Army of the Potomac. The men were fed properly and had decent camps. Hooker had worked with the calvary until Garrison believed they could take on Jeb Stuart, and he knew how to use the abundance of men. "He's given us our confidence back."

"Good." She laid her head on him, her hair falling across his face. "Where will you be?"

"Chancellorsville, most likely," he said, "although there's a chance I might be in Fredericksburg."

"You don't know?"

"It's part of the same maneuver," he said. "It just depends on where Hooker puts me. He usually likes me to be in the thick of the action, so that means Chancellorsville."

"You're splitting the army?"

"And hoping Lee heads the wrong way."

She let out a small sigh, and said nothing for the longest time. He stroked her hair, memorizing it, knowing he would keep this memory with him through the worst of the battle—the waiting.

"Why can't you stay here? You delivered your dispatch to the president. They don't need you."

But they did. There were men who relied on him. They listened to him, much to his surprise.

"If I did that, love," he said, "I'd be hunted for a deserter."

"We could live in Michigan, or maybe Canada. Far from all this. Maybe go west. No one would care."

"Except me."

She was silent for a moment, then she said, "It's like a game to you all, isn't it? Diverting Lee, trying to cross into Richmond, getting the capital, like the king in a game of chess."

He hadn't expected the outburst, although he should have. She had done it before. "Chess doesn't cost lives," he said.

He hadn't meant to. He tried to keep most of the reality of the war from her. He put his arm around her and pulled her back close. "Let's not fight. I have to leave in the morning."

She held the rigid posture for another moment, then collapsed against him. And he held her like he always did, as if it was going to be the last time.

He wasn't even sure where he was. Somewhere in Virginia, but nowhere he recognized. His head ached. He had a lump on his forehead the size of a walnut, according to the man he was chained to. They were tied together like plow-horses, expected to eat and move and shit together like animals. He didn't exactly know how he'd been captured, only that it had happened.

His last memories were of his rifle, hot in his hands, the bayonet bloody from the man he'd just stabbed, the morning sun rising, sending light and heat on the battlefield somewhere outside Chancellorsville.

Lee hadn't retreated as Hooker thought he would. Faced with an army of superior size, Lee had charged forward, with strength and courage and fury. Hooker had expected Lee to turn tail and, for some reason, Garrison had thought that would happen, too; even though now, three days after the worst of it, three days after he'd been captured, he had no idea why. Lee was no coward, although some were saying Hooker was. Inept, cowardly, stupid. His plan had backfired. Somehow Lee had seen through the ruse at Fredericksburg, dodged the trap laid over the Rappahanock, and had come to Chancellorsville ready to fight.

And fight he had.

Garrison had lost his horse in the middle of it, the beast screaming and falling beneath him, throwing him clear. He hadn't had time to see if the horse was dead—the momentum of the battle had carried him forward and he'd stabbed and shot and fought hand to hand with more men than he could remember, most of them younger than he was, most of them bloody and thin and filled with a fighting frenzy that seemed almost crazy.

He'd been fighting with his own frenzy, thinking how angry Serena would be if he died, how she would check the casualty lists and see his name, and that had driven him forward, over bodies, dead men, dead horses, and blood slicker than water on the ground. Forward until he heard—felt—a crack so loud that it shook the entire world, and then he had wakened, a day later, chained to other men, men who said they were sure he would die or never wake up because of the lump on his head.

They fed him, shared water with him, happy that he was awake and they wouldn't have to drag his dead weight to wherever it was their guards were taking them.

Right now they sat in the woods, near thin underbrush and a copse of trees, and waited, as they had done before. Their guards were scouting the path ahead, leaving a handful behind to watch the prisoners.

Garrison thought this might be an opportunity, but he wasn't sure what kind of opportunity it was—a wise one, a foolish one. He was chained by the legs and arms to men he didn't know, and he saw no way of escaping without dragging them all with him. That wouldn't work for even the first mile, and even in his most hopeful state, he knew it.

One of the guards, a man nearer to forty than thirty, had been watching Garrison for the last day, a smirk on his face every time he caught Garrison's eye. He was one of the ones left behind, and when he saw Garrison staring at him, he smiled.

"I can get you special favors if you like," the guard said, strolling toward him as if they were at a lawn party instead of in the woods.

Garrison frowned, felt the tug against the bump on his forehead. "Me?"

"You're Nathaniel Garrison, ain't you?" The guard smiled, revealing a gold tooth. He had bars on his gray uniform, gold bars, and tassels, too. He was someone, then.

"What's it to you?"

"Ain't had a chance to thank you."

The men stirred around him. The ones chained to him moved away as if he were tainted. "For what?"

"Our greatest victory. Heard you made it possible, letting General Lee know he was facing a trap."

"Wha—?" the man next to him started, but Garrison raised his right hand, stopping him.

"I haven't spoken to Lee."

"I know that." The guard's smile grew. "You didn't speak to anyone except your wife. She says you was one of the toughest. Most men, they take a bit of tail now and then, but you was all proper, almost like a Southern gentleman, insisting on courtship and love and marriage. And she was willing, seeing what a prize a man like you was. Right-hand man in the Army of Potomac, not to one, but to all of its generals. They liked you, didn't they, Lieutenant?"

He rose, felt the chains hold him, but he stumbled forward anyway, and fell.

"Didn't know that about your wife, now did you? Little Serena Freneau, one of P. G. T. Beauregard's special ladies, doing the work of Rose Greenhow, but doing it better. So much better, landing a prize like you. Do you think she done it so that she could be with Beau after the war? Or do you think it was the glory all along, like she said? The glory and the cause of it—"

Garrison lurched forward, dragging the others with him, reaching for the guard's boots, but the guard stepped out of the way and laughed.

"Don't like the way the lady took you by your testicles and—"

"That's my wife you're lying about."

"Lying?" The guard crouched, just outside of arm's reach. "Lying? Her aunt run to Richmond before they could put her in the Old Capital Prison, didn't you hear? Mrs. Cunliffe's in London now, making sure the English know we need them at our side."

"Don't listen," one of the other prisoners said. "He's just trying to make you do something stupid so that he can shoot you."

But the guard was watching Garrison like he was enjoying the reaction. He didn't look like a man bent on shooting anyone.

"You couldn't know this," Garrison said.

"I'm on Beau's staff," the man said. "I got the report direct from your wife's contact, like I got the others. Then they told me you was here, and I was to come take care of you. Make you an offer, Lieutenant Garrison. You can join our side and stay with your wife, or you can become a prisoner of war like the rest. We could use someone like you, with the knowledge of the Yank force from the inside out."

Garrison stared at him, at the gold tooth that caught the sunlight, dazzling the rest of the man's mouth and making his tobacco-stained teeth seem even dingier by comparison.

"Think on it, Lieutenant. These men here know your traitorous bent. They'll make sure you pay when you get to whatever camp they're sending you to. You can die there or you can come to Richmond, see your wife, spend the rest of your life in relative luxury."

"By becoming an agent for the Confederacy."

The guard nodded. "Now you're thinking."

And he was thinking of it, for just a brief moment. An agent for the Confederacy, getting information and somehow sending it back to Washington. But he needed a network for that, and if the United States Government knew about Serena, they would never trust his information.

Serena. Her face rose in his mind, the foxlike intensity, the way Evangeline Cunliffe had introduced them, the way Serena had smiled at him when she hadn't given time to any of the other men. A setup, even then?

All this time, the warm words, the loving, all a diversion to get information?

Where will you be? she would ask, her voice sleepy, and he would tell her, things he had sworn to tell no one, thinking her an extension of himself, his wife, loyal to him and to all he was loyal to, believing as he did. Living as he did.

His wife.

"No," he said. "I'll never help your cause."

Only the words came out thick and angry, and he wasn't sure if he was talking about the Confederacy or Serena—her cause, not his, taken at the price of his trust.

Why was he believing a greasy guard with a single gold tooth, over the gestures of his wife, the woman he'd pledged to before God?

Because the man knew too much, too many things, and it put all the questions in perspective.

Where will you be?

"Surely, Lieutenant, your life is worth more than that," the guard said.

And Garrison stared at him, out of reach, the anger cold in his stomach. A killing anger that would have rampaged through this small section of woods if he were only free.

Here I was hoping for a measure of freedom, she had said on that first evening.

And he had replied, so blithely, almost flirting, *That seems to be what everyone is hoping for these days.*

"Lieutenant? Are you reconsidering?" the guard asked.

"I gave you my answer," Garrison said.

The guard frowned. "She thought you would do it for her."

Garrison looked up, that last more appalling than anything that had come before. Appalling perhaps because it held some truth. If he hadn't known of the betrayal, he might have joined her in Richmond, might have found a way to continue his marriage without sacrificing too much of his soul.

The thought rocked him to his very essence.

"It seems," he said slowly, "that my wife doesn't know me as well as she thought she did."

It was an affliction they both had suffered from, although it looked, from his new vantage, as if he would suffer more for it.

If he lived.

MAY 20, 1864

"I'm sorry, sir," the boy was saying. "I didn't know."

Of course not. Garrison hadn't known, either. She had been so good at playing parts, not thinking of the consequences.

At least his discussion with the guard so long ago had done one thing. It had saved him from the wrath of the other prisoners. They had seen his face; they had known his betrayal of his own troops had been involuntary.

But he learned in the year to come, through rumor and discussion and the general torment of the guards who had learned who he was, the cost of his midnight confession. Seventeen thousand lives lost, and just on his side. Seventeen thousand in a battle they should have won.

How many other lives, from Shiloh to Fredericksburg, could be laid directly on his love for his wife? How many?

He would never know.

"I didn't bring him here to have him tell you that." Winthrop had his hand on Garrison's arm. He could feel the bones of Winthrop's fingers, the unnatural scaliness of his skin. Winthrop was dying. They were all dying, slowly, and of more diseases than Garrison had thought imaginable. Disease exacerbated by starvation, heat, and the god-awful stench.

Garrison looked away. "He's not the first to tell me he's had her."

It explained why she was so practiced, when he was so inexperienced that he thought her skill normal for a woman of eighteen years. It explained so much.

All those nights he had thought of it, of her, going over the words they exchanged, the secrets, the way she had wheedled things out of him, even while he was discussing, first with Scott, then with Burnside, then Hooker, how to stop the flow of intelligence from the North to the South, how to deal with disloyal women like Rose O'Neal Greenhow, a society woman just like Evangeline Cunliffe, who had created such a stir by being imprisoned early in the war.

"Why, then?" he asked the boy. "Why are you here?"

The boy looked at the log stockade, the men sitting outside it, the dead line. He apparently thought Garrison wanted to know why he had come to Andersonville.

Garrison clarified. "What do you know about my wife?"

The boy winced at the word, but answered. He had more courage than Garrison wanted to acknowledge—or wanted to see. In a place like this, courage could get a man killed.

"Only that she's dead, sir."

That caught him. He saw, for a brief moment, her vivid brown eyes, remembered how, when he had looked in them on his wedding night, he knew she would outlive him. Nothing, he had thought then, could extinguish a flame like hers.

"How?"

"Drowned, sir. Trying to get back into the Confederacy. She'd been in England, and their ship was being pursued near the Carolina shoreline."

"How do you know this?"

The boy looked down, his red whiskers standing out like bristles against the pasty skin. "I saw her, sir."

Garrison frowned, trying to make sense of this. "You're Navy?" They usually didn't house Navy here.

The boy shook his head. "I was called to identify her." He studied his hands. "It was known that I . . ."

Garrison studied his own hands. It would take little for them to wrap around the boy's throat and throttle him. It would actually be merciful, more merciful than living here, or slowly dying here, as they all were.

Instead he clenched his fists, placed them at his side in the baked clay, and asked, "Did the ship go down?"

"There was a storm, sir. She took a lifeboat, afraid their ship would run aground. If they caught her on it, apparently, she was to be hanged."

Winthrop looked at Garrison. Garrison said nothing. So someone had found her out, long before the boy. And the boy, then, had been under suspicion, to see if he sent secrets to the enemy. Perhaps he had. Perhaps he was here because he had betrayed the wrong person.

Garrison didn't care.

He got up, staggered away from the dead line, trying to avoid the men sprawled like corpses in the dirt.

She was dead, then. The light in those eyes gone forever. That dry humor, the softness of her pressed against him in the night. Gone. He wouldn't have to face her, wouldn't have to face that moment he had been certain would come, the one in which he would have to choose between his loyalty for his country and that passion, whatever it was, that he had felt for her.

It had been so easy in the woods. He had just found out; she hadn't been before him. He could still feel the hurt like an open wound.

But what if she had told him? What if she had leaned against him in the night, after their loving, and told him, then said, as she had that last night, *We could live in Michigan, or maybe Canada. Far from all this. Maybe go west. No one would care.*

Except him, he had said.

Except him.

JUNE 17, 1911

He had a choice, he knew. He could walk away, chalk it up to coincidence, his illness, the dazed feeling men sometimes got while at sea.

But he remembered her eyes, their vividness, the way they had held him when she had said her vows, his certainty that she had more life force than he did.

Nothing, not time, not infirmity, not wishful thinking, could keep him away from that table.

He put his walking stick down forcefully, tried not to lean on it too hard, and made his way toward her.

The conversation stopped as he approached, the women staring up at him as if he were a curiosity. He could see only her. Eyes usually faded, got watery, lost their color and intensity with age and time, but hers had not. They still had a fire in them, a life force so intense he could feel it.

"Good afternoon, ladies," he said, bowing as he had done the first time he had seen her. He smiled as he stood, knowing he still had some of the old charm. "Forgive my interruption, but I would like to speak with Serena alone."

She could have denied it, he supposed, and would have tried if she had been alone. But the other women turned toward her, looking surprised, as if they should have known all of her friends.

Her skin seemed paler than it had a moment ago, and up close, he could see the fine wrinkles, like flaws in parchment. "It's all right," she said. There was still a trace of Maryland in her voice. Like home, he used to think. Like home.

The women got up, gave him another glance, and then walked away. The stoutest of them, an imposing matron with the kind of power women of a certain age gained, patted a gloved hand on hers.

"If you need us, my dear, we'll be on the deck chairs." Then the woman looked at him as if warning him of all sorts of dire problems should he assault their friend.

He slipped into the chair the woman had just vacated, and after a moment, she left them alone. He hung his walking stick on the arm, using the movement to think about what he would say, what he would do.

He wondered if he could get the captain to place her under house arrest, if the United States Government would pursue a forty-eight-year-old case. War crimes, perhaps; treason of the highest order. Could he actually prove she had caused all those deaths, done all those things? Most of the witnesses were dead now, but he was still alive. Himself and a handful of others.

She was looking at him as if she couldn't quite place him. He hoped it wasn't an act. He had thought of her daily for the last fifty years. The first two with a love so fierce he thought he would die from it, and the last with a hopelessness that seared him to his very soul.

He had never loved like that again, never trusted anyone again. He had held several women, almost brought two to wife, but could not bear the thought of letting them in his home, in his bed for an entire night. In the end, he had channeled his energies into his businesses, except for the time he made for his nieces and nephews, treating them as if they were his own. She had taken so much from him, more than the war ever could.

"You wished to speak to me?" she said, so impersonal, so formal, as if they had just met.

"Serena Freneau Garrison," he said softly. "I saw your name on a grave in Washington, D.C."

She stared at him for a long time, her eyes running over his face as if she were searching her memory, looking at portraits. Then tears came to her eyes. "Nathaniel."

She said his name as she had when he loved her, half a whisper, filled with promises. His heart lurched again.

"They told me you died at Chancellorsville."

"They told me you betrayed us two days before."

Her eyes widened.

"I know it all," he said. "The way you pulled information from me. The way you sent it all to Beauregard, who then used it to slaughter our men. Tell me, Serena, who died for you that day in 1864? A servant? A life you considered less valuable than your own?"

"It was all a mistake," she said. "And the rumors were so terrible, I decided to let Serena Garrison go. I thought it better—"

He put a finger over her lips and she closed her eyes, the movement of a lover. She tilted her head into his touch ever so slightly, and he remembered how she had let him hold her fingers so improperly that day on Mrs. Cunliffe's lawn fifty years before.

"No more lies, Serena," he said, and let his finger drop.

She opened her eyes. The tears were still in them. "It was a long time ago," she said. "I was young and stupid—"

"Serena. No lies. I spent two years in Andersonville before I got exchanged out. You owe me the truth."

She let out a small breath of air, glanced at the deck chairs where her friends sat. "I asked you to go away with me. I fell in love with you, Nathaniel. I mourned when they told me you were dead."

"By your hand."

She raised her chin slightly. So familiar. The gestures, the movements. He had remembered them perfectly. "We were at war."

"You and I? Funny, I thought we were in love."

A tear fell, glistening like a diamond as it hovered, caught on her cheek. He saw her more clearly now, how she had acted for him as if she were playing a part on the stage. But the young man inside him, the man who had hoped and believed her to be a part of him, he still wanted to believe her.

And the rest of him wanted to carry her to the rail and toss her over, let her drown for real.

This time, he was the one who glanced at her friends. The stout woman was glaring at him, her eyes accusing.

Serena followed his gaze.

"They're making me uncomfortable," he said. "Walk with me."

She rose quicker than he did. He grabbed his walking stick, used it to lever himself up, then switched it to the other hand so that he could offer her his arm. She took it, her hand light and delicate against his coat. He felt absurdly like asking her if she wanted punch or perhaps to waltz.

They walked to the railing. He led her behind one of the lifeboats, roped in and covered at the edge of the deck. He had stopped shaking. He felt stronger than he had in weeks.

This would be his only chance, here, out of the sight of those women. He would still have to lift her, but only a little. And then a toss that might wrench his back and she would be falling, a scream floating up at him before she hit the froth below.

She was studying him, those dark foxlike eyes probably seeing all the emotions on his face.

"There are people who will miss me," she said. "Are you still such a terrible liar, Nathaniel?"

"No," he said.

A small shudder went through her then. She hadn't expected that, although she had seen in his face what he meant to do. He would be able to toss her over and lie about what he had done. Another of her legacies.

Garrison looked over the railing at the gray Atlantic. The vast ocean of nothingness, the place that was supposed to have claimed her, when in fact it hadn't.

"I'm sorry, Nathaniel—" she started, but he didn't let her finish.

He dropped his walking stick, grabbed her waist—not as small as it had once been—and hoisted her up. She didn't scream, but she grabbed the railing and hung on, her body tense.

It wouldn't be easy. Nothing with her was ever easy.

"My husband is a rich man," she said. "We can pay you, Nathaniel. You could be rich."

His hands tightened on her waist. "Who's your husband?" he asked softly, as if he were intrigued by the notion of another man's money.

"Lord Reginald Seton. Please, Nathaniel. Let me down."

He let go so quickly that she nearly fell overboard anyway. Her body collapsed against the rail, her heels kicking against the side. She eased herself down and for a brief moment, he saw fear in her eyes.

"Does he know of your past life?" Garrison asked.

She raised that sharp chin. "I met him in London. During the war."

One of the collaborators. One of the men who had hoped to fund the South.

"And how long have you been married?" Garrison asked.

She stepped away from him, the movement small but noticeable. "I thought you were dead."

Forty-seven years. They had married while Garrison was starving in a camp she had sent him to. The camp she had condemned him to.

She had spent forty-seven years in London society under a different name, and no one had been the wiser. Forty-seven years in a marriage that obviously had worked, with a man who had a reputation to protect. A man, by the very nature of the peerage to which he belonged, could suffer no hint of impropriety.

"Where is he now?" Garrison asked.

"The smoking room, I believe," she said.

"This early in the day?"

"He enjoys cards," she said. And cards offended many of the women. The smoking room had become a replacement for some of the men's clubs.

"Let's go there."

"I can't."

"But I can." He took her arm, dragged her forward, then slipped her hand in his elbow again. "Walk normally," he said softly, "and smile."

She did. They were halfway across the deck when he realized he'd left his walking stick behind. He was functioning on something purer than energy now, something deeper. He would go through with this if it killed him.

Fortunately, they weren't far from the smoking room. He pushed open the doors and saw, as he had hoped, the reporters the White Star Line had hired to glorify the *Olympic*'s first trip.

"Gentlemen," he said, as he dragged Serena forward. "Come with me."

They did, of course. No one said no to Nathaniel Garrison. How ironic that he needed them—them and their scandal sheets—to get the only revenge possible now.

He would destroy her place in society. Once he revealed her identity, everyone would know who she was, who she had been. His story was familiar enough.

It was time to make that story hers as well.

He would ruin her life as she had once ruined his.

Garrison walked across the checked carpet, past rows of empty tables flanked by green leather chairs, to the center of the room.

There Lord Seton was already standing, his cards turned down in his large arthritic hands. He was a big man who did not stoop with age, with a large white mustache that seemed to have stolen all the hair from his head. His eyes were faded, so faded it took Garrison a moment to see their color.

"Serena," Seton said, "what is the meaning of this?"

Garrison glanced at his side, made certain the reporters were there, saw Serena, her eyes wide, the fear evident now.

"Lord Seton," Garrison said, letting Serena's hand drop and placing his own on the small of her back. "My name is Nathaniel Garrison. I've been so looking forward to meeting you. Please allow me to introduce you to my wife."

He paused for a half a moment and saw the horror plain on Seton's face. The reporters gasped. Serena looked as if she was about to faint.

Garrison stared at her one last time, saw how years of good living had softened her, and knew the publicity, the scandal, the trial would be her Andersonville.

He nodded to her once, an acknowledgment that finally the tables had turned. There was nowhere for her to go, no escape possible. She couldn't even handle the lifeboats by herself.

Then he turned and left her there, surrounded by reporters and a scandalized man who had thought he was her only husband for forty-seven years. Garrison, her real husband, left her to face her future alone—her bleak future—as she had once left him.

Fifty years to the day it began, the war was finally over.

Loren D. Estleman has distinguished himself in a number of literary fields including mainstream, western, private eye and thriller. He has been nominated for the Pulitzer Prize and won a couple of shelves of literary awards, including four Western Writers of America Spur awards, three Private Eye Writers of America Shamus awards, and the American Mystery Award. He is the author of more than forty novels, including the Amos Walker detective series, a number of westerns, and his Detroit historical mystery series, which includes *Whiskey River*, *Motown*, *King of the Corner*, and *Thunder City*.

The Civil War was host to roving bands of vigilantes on both sides, men ostensibly charged by the government to hunt down the enemy, but whom often looted and killed more for revenge than for military reasons. Collingwood's Raiders is one such unit. In this tale, lacking the niceties of war, they inflict a swift and harsh punishment on those they call spies.

SOUTH GEORGIA CROSSING

Loren D. Estleman

His brother was the better killer.

At twelve, Oscar was the more accomplished shooter of the pair. His reflexes were faster, and invariably his old side-by-side boomed half a second ahead of Jacob's newer single-barrel, sending a woodcock plummeting in a vertical drop as straight as a blade of wheat. From that point on he deferred to fifteen-year-old Jacob.

When neither the pellets nor the fall managed to kill the unfortunate bird, it became necessary to wring its neck. Oscar was seldom immediately successful; he would hesitate a split second, or fail to exert the force necessary, and the creature's heart would continue to flutter and one of its elliptical eyes would catch his with an expression of accusation and pain, disturbingly human. Jacob would then seize the bird by its head and snap its neck with a single one-handed twirl, like a muleskinner cracking his whip. On those occasions when two birds fell close together and Jacob got to them first, he would do both at once, whirling them above his head with a flourish Oscar thought unnecessary, showing off. The younger Stone disapproved, but he had come to dread that look of silent condemnation between bird and boy so much that he purposely lagged behind in order that Jacob might be first on the scene. They were both aware that Oscar's slowness was deliberate, but the knowledge was never spoken, and so remained a thing of shame between them.

That was in the late Pennsylvania fall, when their father's potatoes were dug and the hay was in the barn. The next year, Jacob ran away to join the Bucktails, to be counted among the fifty thousand dead at Gettysburg, three years later and less than twenty miles from the stone house where he was born. Their father was gone soon after, buried at forty-seven along with his broken dreams of a son in the medical profession. Ernst Stein himself had wanted to be a doctor like his father in Munich, but had never managed more than two dozen words in English, and Oscar, who could not end the misery of an un-thinking bird, had by his comportment in general demonstrated an equal lack of potential to relieve human suffering. He buried his father on a hillside next to his mother, dead eight years of a neglected infection, and three siblings who had expired in swaddling, placed the farm up for sale with the bank in York, and joined the 150th Pennsylvania there. The recruiting sergeant, a veteran since First Manassas with one empty sleeve pinned to his shoulder, never looked up from his sheet to verify Oscar's age; the bloody draw at Gettysburg had rammed a hole through the federal reserves and the recruiters were filling it with old men and children and scarecrows from the fields.

He served for twenty months, including five weeks when he was laid up with a shattered shinbone after falling from a flatbed car on the tracks outside Chattanooga. He was on his feet too soon, so that the bones knitted poorly, and for the rest of his life limped whenever he was tired or forgot himself. The reason he got up was the 150th was pulling out for Atlanta and he didn't want to be left behind by men he'd marched, slept, and eaten with since training. War was less hideous when faced in familiar company.

He missed out anyway. He was hobbling along the Atlanta road on a crutch he'd cut from a forked limb when he heard hoofbeats coming fast behind him and, without turning to look, withdrew into the trees at the side of the road. The area was crawling with Confederate cavalry and bands of guerrillas and ragged deserters who preyed upon stragglers from both armies.

"You! Soldier! What is your regiment?"

The demand was bawled in the honking bray of the East Coast Northerner, and belonged to a corpulent major in a blue uniform corded with gold braid, aboard a fat gray round-muscled horse, a rarity among the gaunt mounts living off that burned-over land. He wore a felt hat with the brim pinned up on one side and a white plume curling out behind. The dozen men he had with him were mounted equally well, in uniforms less elaborate. All were armed with Henry repeaters, the first Oscar had seen, although he had heard all about them from envious fellow troops weary of recharging their muzzleloaders in the sting of battle; and all were aiming at him.

Oscar remained in the shadows, supporting himself against a tree with his Springfield rifle in both hands. But he gave the major the information he wanted.

"The One-fifty is halfway to Savannah by now," said the other. "You'll never catch them. I've a saddle needs filling. Can you ride?"

"Yes, sir." In fact he had been astraddle a horse rarely; his father would not have his plowhorses used for any purpose other than the work to which they'd been broken. However, he was not so anxious to rejoin his regiment that he would pass up an opportunity to relieve his injured leg of its burden.

"Name and rank."

"Oscar Stone, private."

"Squarehead?"

"No, sir, I am American."

"It matters not. Harney."

One of the men at the rear moved out of line and trotted to the front, leading a riderless gray.

"Mount up, Private," said the major. "You're one of Collingwood's Raiders now."

In 1861, John Quincy Adams Collingwood had closed the bank he owned in Rhode Island, had uniforms made for himself and those of his staff who volunteered to follow him, and struck off south to make war on the Confederacy, armed with new Henry rifles ordered to his specifications from the Volcanic Repeating Arms Company in New Haven, Connecticut. He'd had the foresight to invite along a journalist from the Providence paper, who coined the name "Collingwood's Raiders" and wired back dispatches reporting details of daring skirmishes with the Rebel army and enemy courthouses captured. In reality the band wandered along the broad swath carved by the Army of the Potomac, picking off stranded wretches in threadbare gray uniforms and billeting in hotels and mortar-blasted plantation houses while patrols scoured the country around for edible crops and livestock. Below Mason-Dixon the major was best known for his table, maintained by his personal chef from his estate in Newport, and the cases of pre-Revolution wine he had managed to scrounge from abandoned cellars already picked over by the hundreds of troops who had preceded him. This he had done by seeking out the slaves of the departed owners and paying them to tell where the stores had been hidden to await their return; whereupon he would declare those slaves emancipated and leave them to savor the sweet fruit of freedom in the drafty and roofless cabins where he'd made their acquaintance. Regular officers who came to dine with him and proclaim the excellence of the claret were only too happy to report his humanitarian actions to their superiors, who mentioned them in dispatches when there were no new victories to declare. " 'An army travels on its stomach' "—the major was fond of quoting his hero, Napoléon—and his had been growing since Fort Henry. The assistance of a lieutenant was required to hoist him into the saddle, and most days he suffered from gout, which he excused to visitors who found him with his foot elevated and bound as the recurring misery of a saber wound contracted at Fredericksburg.

All this notwithstanding, the Raiders had not found the war to be one gastronomic and vinial excursion through the ruins of the Old South. They had been involved in some running fights with Confederate cavalry, and had lost one man to a sniper on the Atlanta road the day before they encountered Oscar. This was the owner of the horse he now rode.

As the newest member of the company, Oscar spent his camp time washing Major Collingwood's Irish linen tablecloth and napkins and polishing his silver. He contemplated leaving to resume his search for the 150th, but did not think his leg was up yet to a long journey on foot, and he did not want to take the gray and risk being shot for a horse thief. He might be shot either way, if he were captured and the major decided to treat him as a deserter. And so he remained, following the path of Lincoln's army with the others and sneaking out of his bedroll evenings to soothe the burning in his red, chapped hands by smearing them with river mud, until South Georgia Crossing.

A village had existed there when the ferry was still running across the river, but then state engineers had built a covered bridge and when there was no longer money to be made from passage, the population had moved on. Only a boarded-up schoolhouse and a scattering of cabins still stood along with the remains of the dock to mark the spot where a community had thriven. Major Collingwood moved his gear into the schoolhouse for the night while the others sought quarters in those buildings whose roofs had not yet fallen in, or wherever else offered shelter from the rain, which had begun in the morning as a light drizzle and had settled into a steady downpour by late afternoon. As was their custom, they removed what provisions they needed that night and packed the rest in an oilcloth. They then gathered the corners together, tied them, and hauled the waterproof bundle into the upper branches of a sycamore to protect it from bears.

A rifle report awoke Oscar shortly before dawn. The rain had stopped. Leaving his shelter on the sloping bank beneath the bridge, he approached the glowing globe of a lantern and found most of the command, some in stockinged feet with their braces dangling, standing around the sycamore. The oilcloth bundle was gone; a frayed scrap of rope dangled beneath the limb where it had hung.

"There. I knew I hit one of the sons of bitches." Sergeant Harney, fully dressed and wreathed in smoke and the rotten-egg stench of spent powder, pointed with his Henry at a dark spot on the ground that glittered in the lantern light.

"Here's another," sang out Private Wheelock. He was crouched a few yards away, holding a flaming match near the earth.

Major Collingwood joined them, tucking in his shirttail, as they began to follow the trail of bloodstains, led by Harney with his lantern. The trail ended at a shallow ford downriver. The horses were brought, after which they crossed and discovered more blood on the other side. As dawn broke, they found the fugitives, seated beneath a twisted old apple tree around the oilcloth spread out on the ground as at a picnic. One of them was winding a length of dirty rag around the even dirtier bare foot of another, while the rest were too busy gorging themselves on half a roasted chicken and a leg of mutton to hear the riders approaching. Their dirty, emaciated faces showed no surprise when they were surrounded, only exhaustion.

There were four, including an old man of sixty and a boy not much older than twelve. The others were young men, but their unshorn hair, whiskers, and hollow cheeks and eyes made them ancient. One of these was the man with the wounded foot. The group's clothes were a motley mix of faded homespun and Union castoff. Only the old man retained a morsel of the Confederate uniform: a gray kepi, unspeakably filthy, with a broken peak. The boy and the injured man were barefoot. When questioned, the old man revealed that the three adults were all that remained of the Tallapoosa Volunteers, an Alabama company that had been fighting since Fort Sumter. The boy had been with them only six weeks.

The prisoners were disarmed—it was a pitiful arsenal made up of one good navy Colt, a squirrel rifle of 1812 vintage, a shotgun, and a LaMatte pistol whose action was so loose it would have had to be fired with both hands just to keep it from flying apart—and placed under guard while a conference took place.

"The Articles of War are clear in cases such as this," said the major. "Enemy soldiers found in friendly dress are to be hanged as spies."

Wheelock was argumentative. "It's just old rags. They haven't enough between them to make up a complete uniform."

"The Articles say nothing about completeness. In any case, we can't keep them. They will slow us down, and there is no telling when we'll come upon a regiment that will be willing to take them into custody."

Oscar said, "They're just vagabonds. They were only after food."

"Food is life," said the major. "Where do we draw the line before we starve? Gentlemen, let us vote."

The vote was eight-to-six in favor of execution. The prisoners were driven on foot—the injured man leaning upon the man who had bandaged him—to the covered bridge, which had taken several mortar rounds in some forgotten skirmish, leaving most of one side open with shreds of shattered siding dangling from the timbers. Ropes were produced, and the four were lined up on the open edge with nooses around their necks and the other ends slung up over a stringer. Nobody knew how to tie a proper hangman's knot, and so a square hitch was used. The man with the wounded foot cursed from the pain, the other young man spat insults and struggled when his hands were bound behind him, but Private Bending struck him alongside the head with the buttstock of his Henry, dazing him until he was securely trussed. The old man was silent. The boy cried, snuffling snot and whimpering, and his knees buckled, but Corporal Loesser hauled him up by the seat of his britches while Harney secured the noose. Oscar stood out of the way with a lump of ice in the pit of his stomach and watched.

When the last of the ropes was tied fast and the men who had tied them had climbed down, Major Collingwood told Harney to get on with it. The sergeant strode the length of the bridge, pausing just long enough to give each man a one-handed shove from behind.

One neck broke, Oscar thought, possibly two; those of the young men. He heard a sharp crack, and in any case neither of them moved beyond the jerks and twitches of healthy muscles unwilling to surrender their motor functions without a fight. The old man was all bones, a husk, and lacked the weight necessary to snap the spine, and his body writhed and twisted and his throat rattled. The boy's example, however, would stay with Oscar long after he'd forgotten how the old man had died. The young body is built to survive; once it has conquered the many pernicious childhood afflictions, it resists unnatural death in its every grain. So violent were the convulsions that Oscar thought the boy was consciously trying to regain his foothold on the bridge while the fluid cooked in his throat and his tongue slid out and his face went from scarlet to purple to deepest black. Later, an army orderly who was studying to practice medicine would tell Oscar that a body deprived of oxygen begins to expire within three minutes. He did not believe it. In his memory, the boy struggled for the better part of an hour before he swung at last in a balletic half-revolution to the left, his legs drawn up beneath him to form an elongated question-mark four feet above the South Georgia River.

Seeking for someplace to rest other than that congested profile, Oscar's gaze slid to the boy's hands. Below the coarse rope that lashed his wrists they were swollen, with red streaks against the white where the thick veins and arteries had hemorrhaged. The fingers were as fat as sausages.

The prisoners' bowels had released, and the reek sent Oscar to the grassy bank opposite the Raiders' camp to be sick. But he had eaten nothing and could bring nothing up. He stopped trying and sat down with his forehead resting against his knees. The wet grass soaked through his trousers, chilling him. For the rest of his life, the feel of damp clothes against his skin would bring back the war, and with it the sight of the boy's hands, like scarecrow's gloves stained and stuffed with straw.

Primarily known for making the New England countryside come alive in his novels and short stories, Brendan DuBois has written several dozen critically-acclaimed short stories, and has had his work appear in several year's best anthologies. One of his stories, "The Dark Snow," was nominated for the Edgar Award for best short story of 1996. Recent novels include *Shattered Shell*, the third mystery featuring contemporary magazine writer/sleuth, Lewis Cole, and *Resurrection Day*, a techno-thriller extrapolating what might have happened if the Cuban Missile Crisis had turned into a full-fledged war. He lives in Exeter, New Hampshire, where he is working on another novel.

During the Civil War, all kinds of people were pressed into service as spies, including the most unlikely anyone would think of. DuBois has crafted a fine and subtle tale from this premise.

The Invisible Spy

Brendan DuBois

In a campsite near the farthest point of the Union lines outside of Petersburg, Virginia, Colonel Thomas Cabot of the Union army slowly paced the length of his tent. It was nearing dusk and with each passing minute his impatience grew and grew, like an increasing hunger, like being out on a long march with nothing to eat save an old hunk of hardtack. His adjutant, Captain Jacob Shaw, looked up as he polished his boots. "Colonel, this pacing ain't going to help much, you know that," he said.

"I know, Jacob, I know," he said, pausing as he looked out the open tent flap, seeing the lines of canvas tents, as far as one could see, in a farmer's hayfield. "But we have been promised this information, and I in turn have promised the general that we will have it before the evening is out."

The sound of the brush against the leather was almost rhythmic, reminding Cabot of his time as a music teacher, back in Boston. Keeping time, one of the first things he taught. . . . From a teacher of music to a leader of men, and what strange events over the past few years had conspired to take him out of the cool brick buildings of Boston to this hilly and swampy landscape in Virginia, now crisscrossed with trenches and forts.

"Then there is nothing you can do but wait, sir," his adjutant said. "Wait and be patient."

"Wait and be damned," Cabot muttered, looking out again through the tent flaps. "Just a few miles away are the Rebs, and among those damn Rebs is a spy, working for us, who has promised me information tonight, before we go to battle tomorrow. Think of him over there, trying to slip through those

Rebel lines and pickets. I can rightly tell you, Jacob, that he's not thinking of being patient."

Shaw made a dismissive sound as he continued the polishing. "That's a nasty business, spying. Don't rightly hold with it, sir."

Cabot kept on staring out at the parade ground, at the soldiers going through their nightly ritual, preparing for their evening meal, while he continued waiting and looking for the visitor that was promised to him tonight.

"Spying is mentioned in the Bible, I'll remind you, Jacob," Cabot said softly. "And if it's in the Good Book, and can help us defeat the Rebels and free men from bondage, then I don't mind spying, not at all." Cabot crossed his arms, rocked slightly on his heels. "What I do mind, curse it all, is waiting. Just standing here and waiting."

It was dusk, and already it was cold. Corporal Harmon Brewster of the Army of Northern Virginia shivered as he stood at his post, on the Halifax Road outside of Petersburg, just a few miles from the Union lines. Already he could hear the distant thuds of cannon fire, as the damn blue-bellies tossed shells into his regiment and others, still enduring this long siege.

He heard some low talk and laughter, and he looked over to the small rise of land, which rose up to the west. A small fire burned there as his relief sat and warmed up with a handful of others. Their task tonight was to check whatever traffic was going through on this road, making sure all had the correct passes to let them pass through the regiment's lines. A boring task, almost as bad as drilling in camp during those long months of winter when nothing much ever happened, but he found he was nervous as he stood there, rifle in his hands. For tonight he and the others were looking for a spy, a spy that had been giving the Federals details on their forces and their lines.

He shivered again, remembering the warning from Lieutenant Morgan, who was one of the figures up there around the campfire. The lieutenant had gathered them together earlier and said, "Be extra watchful tonight, boys. It's no secret that the Federals are preparing for another assault. Word is that they have spies among our lines, checking the number of regiments and where they're located. This road comes closest to the Union lines. If a spy is going to try to pass through our lines tonight, this'd be a good place as any for him to try."

Harmon had wanted to ask a question of the lieutenant but was too shy to say anything aloud, in front of the other men in the company. He was a corporal but most of the men just ignored him, for they knew he was young, probably the youngest in the regiment, and Harmon was sure they were right. When he had enlisted, more than two years ago, he had been only fifteen. But he had gone to the recruiter and raised his right hand in an oath, saying that he was over eighteen. Of course, what he had done—what many other farm-boys in his county had done—was to scrawl the number 18 on a piece of paper and put it in inside his shoe. That way, he hadn't been lying. He really was "just over eighteen."

On this day he had a couple of questions, and thankfully, some of the other men had spoken up. Sergeant Mortimer had said, "Lieutenant, just what in hell are we lookin' for? We can't expect a fella to approach with a paper signed by that baboon Lincoln, saying he's working for the Federals."

Somebody else spoke up. "Or to have a paper from Mr. Pinkerton, either," and they laughed, knowing how Pinkerton and his crew were working for the Federals, trying desperately to get information about where and how the Virginia regiments would appear.

Lieutenant Morgan—his mustache heavy and flowing to each side—had smiled patiently at their questions and said, "Look, it's simple enough, boys. Anybody and everybody going through on this road tonight gets searched. I don't care if it's the old granny hisself, General Robert E. Lee. We're gonna search everybody who goes through and look for any suspicious papers. Any maps, long letters, or papers that have words on 'em that don't make sense. Like a code. Everybody gets searched, understood?"

Sure, they had all understood, and Harmon had gotten the first watch, and as he came down to his post, somebody called out, "Remember now, Harmon, if it's a whore going through tonight, you can search her petticoats without paying!"

He had flushed at that, and said nothing in reply. Now he was at his post, a small lantern at his feet. While the others were up there, warming themselves around the fire, jawing and smoking, he shivered here, waiting for some damn person to come through. His shoes were frayed and worn, held together by leather straps, and his trousers had worn right through both knees. His shirt was simple cotton but at least he had a wool jacket and a slouch hat, which he had pulled down around his ears.

The task tonight was simple. The road was straight enough at this point that he could hear or see someone approaching from some distance away. When he or somebody else saw someone coming down the road, he would call out a challenge. "Loud enough for them and us to hear," Lieutenant Morgan had said. That way, Morgan had explained, it would give the men around the campfire time enough to come down and help whoever was on guard duty.

Harmon leaned his rifle against his shoulder, rubbed his hands. He looked up at the campfire. Damn it, he was only supposed to be out here an hour before being relieved, and he had a good feeling he had already been out here long enough. But Lieutenant Morgan was the only one among them who had a watch, and he could be forgetful, especially when some good stories were being told.

Damn, it was cold—and then he looked up.

Somebody was coming down the road.

Colonel Thomas Cabot looked over at his adjutant, who was making a show of putting on his boots. Shaw was a rich man's son, from New Hampshire, and he had the best clothing and supplies in the entire regiment. But he wasn't a dandy—no sir—and Cabot had seen him fight as well as any other man during the long months of this bloody Civil War. But what Cabot didn't like was the man's pessimism, his dark way of looking at things, which Shaw had no qualms in displaying.

"You know, Colonel, I know you trust Sergeant Calhoun, and the spy that works with him."

"I trust him with my life and those of the men in my regiment," Cabot said simply.

"Yes, but just because it has worked once, does not mean it will work twice," Shaw observed. "And to tell the general that you will have this information before the evening is out, well . . ."

Cabot looked out again at the parade ground. "I know. I was no doubt too eager. It may be foolish; yet, if it saves the lives of my men during the assault tomorrow, then I do not mind being made a fool."

"A fool, yes, sir, but I pray that the sergeant is not leading us into a trap. I would much rather be a live fool than a dead hero."

Cabot said nothing, continued staring out the open tent flap.

The sound coming down the road was that of a wagon, the clopping of the horse's hooves, the rattling of the wheels, the creaking sound of the leather. Harmon picked up his rifle and called out, "Halt, halt there, I tell you!"

There were suddenly other sounds as well, as the other men came down from the hill, some carrying torches, and by the time they arrived and joined Harmon, someone said, "Oh hell, it's just Garner, that's all."

Harmon swallowed, saw that he was right. It was Jonathan Garner, a local sutler, and he smiled down from his wagon perch as the men with torches and rifles surrounded him. He doffed his cap and shifted his heavy bulk. "Good evening, gentlemen. It truly is an honor to see our troops in such fine order on this cold night."

It was a two-horse wooden wagon, enclosed by canvas. Faded paint on the side announced, GARNER SUTLERS—Dry Goods, Food Supplies—Honest and True. Lieutenant Morgan called out, "And where are you heading tonight?" Garner leaned over. "I've just made a delivery of blankets and camp stools to your regiment's quartermaster, and now I'm returning home."

"Do you have a pass?" the lieutenant asked.

"I do," the fat man replied. "From your own regiment's colonel. And here it is."

From his clothing he produced a scrap of paper, which the lieutenant read by the light of a torch. Harmon stood by the wagon, rifle in hands, mouth watering. If only he had delivered some food, perhaps they could have scrounged something from the man. But blankets and camp stools . . . Nothing worth taking.

Lieutenant Morgan returned the pass, and made a bowing motion with his head. "I must beg your indulgence, sir, but I have my orders. No one is to pass through the lines without a thorough search. If you will be so kind . . ."

Harmon was expecting the sutler to mutter and curse and complain about being delayed, but the fat man surprised them all. He came down from his perch and opened up the rear of the wagon, and even lit a lantern of his own, to assist in the search. Harmon and a private called Tyler looked in the rear of the wagon, which took only a few minutes. While they were searching Harmon said, "You up there by the campfire seem to be enjoying yourselves. When in hell am I going to be relieved?"

Tyler smiled back. "Take it up with the lieutenant, Harmon. He's the big man with the watch."

Soon the search was over and Harmon stood outside with the other men, where there was some low talking. The lieutenant had just searched the sutler's large leather purse, and after pursuing through the receipts and business papers, he had also run a thumb across a thick stack of Confederate dollars. Harmon could feel his eyes bulge out at seeing all that money. Even with the inflation, there was enough money there to buy the two nearest farms to his daddy's place, back home in Centralia.

But the lieutenant was courteous and Garner returned the favor, and within a few minutes the sutler was on his way. A sergeant called Pinkham said loudly, "Did you see how much money was with that fat boy? Did you? Here we are, sweating and eating ground acorns and getting shot at, and he's making a fortune. Damn it, it ain't right."

Lieutenant Morgan said, "It's wartime, Pinkham. Hardly anything's right. Come along, let's get out of the road."

And the group was back up by the campfire before Harmon realized he should have asked to be relieved.

He stamped his feet. Damn, it was cold!

His adjutant had gone out to evening mess, but Colonel Cabot stayed behind in his tent. If Sergeant Calhoun were to show up with the spy, he didn't want to be absent. Oh, it wouldn't take long for Sergeant Calhoun to find him among the officers of the regiment, but Cabot didn't want to leave anything to chance. Too many skirmishes and battles over the past years had been lost due to missed connections, missed messages, the vagaries of chance.

Cabot rubbed at his jaw, lit a small oil lamp in his tent, noted the flickering light against the old canvas. Plus, he didn't want to be at the mess and to face the questions of the general and his staff. He had promised them the information about the Reb lines and their troops. And he had promised it for tonight. Some of the staff members had had sharp looks, and even sharper comments, about amateur soldiers and even more amateur officers, and he didn't want to expose himself to their gibes tonight.

Damn, he thought, looking at the emptiness of the parade ground, it surely did look to be a long night.

It didn't seem much time had passed when Harmon heard the noise of another wagon approaching down the road. He rubbed his hands again and called out, "Halt, halt there!"

Again the men came down from the campfire, and he noted some loud laughs. Someone had probably produced a little flask of something to ward off the chill. And had anyone thought of him, down here alone, with no fire or whiskey to keep him warm? And sure enough, when the other men had crowded about him, he could smell the whiskey on their breath.

Lieutenant Morgan brought along a torch and said laughingly, "Oh, look at this now, will you. Are you sure you can't handle this alone, Harmon?"

The men laughed with the lieutenant and Harmon felt his face flush. He knew why they were laughing at him, but damn it, he had followed his orders. Before them was a simple farm wagon, pulled by a gaunt plowhorse with its ribs showing. Aboard the wagon was an old black man, wearing baggy pants and blouse and a dirty straw hat. Behind him were some young voices, and he turned to hush them. A couple of pickaninnies, huddled back there. The lieutenant went up to the wagon, thrust his torch up to the old slave's face.

"You there, boy!" he called up. "What are you doing out here tonight? Trying to make a break through the lines? Go work for old Father Abraham? Become a piece of contraband?"

The men laughed and the old man slowly nodded. His beard was quite white and he said slowly, "I'm jus' making a delivery to the Monroe plantation, suh. That's all. This ironwork back here. That's all I'm doin'."

"Got a pass, boy? Permission to be out at night?"

"Right here, suh," the old man said, and he passed over a much-folded piece of paper to the lieutenant. A couple of the men muttered and started wandering back up to the hill, and the lieutenant shook his head as he examined the paper. "Harmon, a quick check, if you please."

Harmon went to the rear of the wagon, raised up his lantern. There were farm tools back there, a plow and some rakes and other pieces of worked iron. Huddled in the rear were two black children, a filthy quilt covering their bodies. He was going to leave them both alone but remembered the lieutenant's orders. Everything to be searched. He climbed up on the rear of the wagon and moved forward. The old black man looked back at him and then looked back to the lieutenant. The lieutenant said, "Who do you belong to, boy?"

"The Coulton family, suh. From Sutherland. Master Coulton, he wanted these tools delivered to Master Monroe. He's his cousin, suh."

"And those two pups back there?"

"My grandchildren, suh. That's all."

Harmon listened to the conversation as he went up to the children. He said nothing as he lifted up the quilt, saw some of the patterns and wavy lines on the dirty cloth. The young colored children's eyes were quite wide as they sat there in the straw, dressed practically in rags, and they said nothing. He tossed the quilt back at them and then looked at all the iron tools. No papers, no letters, nothing. He got off the wagon, tired. The other men had gone back up to the hill. Lieutenant Morgan was talking to the old colored man and Harmon rested for a moment, feeling a bit uncomfortable near the young slaves. Growing up, Harmon had hardly ever seen slaves in his county, for most of the farms were small and barely made enough food and money for the families themselves to live on. It was only on the few trips to Richmond that he had seen slaves, working by the warehouses and large stores, and his daddy had whispered to him, "Don't mind what the preacher tells you on Sunday, Harmon.

This bondage is wrong. Wrong for lots of reasons. Mainly 'cause having the colored here makes our lives that much harder."

"I don't understand, Daddy."

"This free labor," he had whispered, "makes it harder for honest white folk to make a livin'."

So Harmon didn't care one way or another about slaves. For all he cared, they could go back to Africa or move up north or go to Canada. All he knew was that despite what a couple of the boys had read from captured Northern newspapers, he and the other troops weren't fighting for the rich men to keep slaves. Nope, they were fighting for their own states, and if their own states wanted to leave the Union and form their own association, then that was just fine. And if the Northern states wanted to pick a fight over leaving the Union, then it was his duty and those of his friends to fight back.

He was jostled some as Lieutenant Morgan said something aloud, and the old colored man pulled the wagon away. Harmon stood there, watching as the wagon went down the road, seeing those two little pickaninnies looking back at him, until they moved out of the reach of the lantern's glow.

Then he realized he was now alone on the road. Lieutenant Morgan was back up at the campfire.

Once again he had not been relieved.

Damn this night, and all officers!

Colonel Cabot ate some of the beef that his adjutant had brought back to him from the mess tent, and he pulled his camp chair close to the flap and stretched out his legs, a thin wool blanket covering him. There was some singing and fiddle playing, and movement out there on the parade ground, but no one was approaching his tent. No Sergeant Calhoun, and definitely no spy carrying the needed information to turn the tide for tomorrow's desperate battle. He folded his arms, knowing that he should be back there in the tent, at his dispatch desk, writing a letter to his fiancée, Miss Molly Hancock, who was a proud descendant of Mr. John Hancock, he of the large signature on the Declaration of Independence.

He wondered what poor Hancock and the others of that time, Franklin and Adams and Washington and Jefferson, what they would have thought if they had lived long enough to see all of the turmoil, all of the bloodshed, all of the hate. A new, young, struggling country, a little beacon of freedom and hope to the rest of the world, a world ruled by emperors and kings and potentates. Those men of the Revolution must have thought themselves blessed and proud, to bring such a country forth, a place of freedom where the rulers were chosen by the people.

And now? Not even eighty years later, after the Constitution was approved, and the nation was tearing itself apart. The little beacon of hope was flickering, was in danger of being extinguished, and he remembered some of the officers' talk around the mess some months ago. One of the officers—Godin, a Frenchman from Maine—had said, "Look what will happen if the Union loses. Then we'll have two countries here where there used to be one. One free, one slave. What will happen when we move farther out west? Won't we continue fighting, over and over again? And what will happen if the Spanish or the British decided to help the South? I'll tell you what will happen, my friends: We will have decades of hate and war and revenge, much more bloodshed, for centuries to come."

One nation free, one slave. One nation based upon freedom, the other upon bondage. It must not be allowed to happen, and he remembered that bright day when he had first enlisted, back in Boston, so true of himself, so true to the cause. He had been an abolitionist for many years, had given what spare funds he could to Mr. Garrison and his newspaper, and had even heard a remarkable freeman speak in Boston, a man named Douglass. When the news came back in 1861 about South Carolina firing upon Fort Sumter, he had joined up, knowing in his heart that the war would be over within a month, and that he could return to his teaching and to his fiancée soon enough.

He crossed his legs and trembled slightly in the cold. Such thoughts, such stupid thoughts. The war had dragged on for long, bloody months, much longer and bloodier than anyone had predicted. And yet he was determined to see it through, to see this war to its end, to see the colored people freed and the Union restored. And if that meant using spies, so be it. A few months ago, his sergeant, Calhoun, had come to him, shyly staring at his feet, haltingly saying that he had contacts on the other side of the lines, a spy who could help. If the colonel would allow it, Sergeant Calhoun had said. Well, at first the colonel had not wanted to allow it, suspecting a trap. He was not sure of Sergeant Calhoun's convictions and had sent him away, but after a bloody week of skirmishing where he and his regiment had lost ground and so many lives, he had sent for Sergeant Calhoun, glad that he had lived through the week. Within a few days the spy had come into camp, had provided information on the Reb lines, and the information had been true, allowing a glorious victory. A small victory nonetheless, but still, one that improved the morale of his boys.

But where was Sergeant Calhoun and that damnable spy tonight, after he had promised the general he would have news about the Rebs before the start of tomorrow's battle?

Colonel Cabot pulled his blanket higher up to his chin, and then sat up. There! A light was approaching, coming to his tent. He stood up from his camp stool and stepped out onto the parade ground. There was a figure there, about the light, and he called out, "Sergeant Calhoun? Is that you?"

"No, Colonel, it is not," said the voice. The lantern came closer, and Colonel Cabot shook his head in dismay. It was Colonel Thompson, adjutant to the general, a tall man with a closely cropped black beard and impeccable uniform. He stepped closer and said, "You know why I am here, don't you, Thomas?"

He felt colder, standing out there in the open, no blanket, no information, filled with disappointment. "That I do, Colonel. That I do."

The adjutant nodded. "Shortly the general will be writing up his orders for tomorrow, orders for the battle. These orders will be issued, no matter what you report. So if there is something to report, something from this spy of yours, then we need it. Quickly."

Colonel Cabot nodded. "I know, sir."

"Is the spy here, then?"

"No, sir. He is not."

"And do you know when he is to arrive?"

"Sometime this evening, that is all."

Colonel Thompson shook his head. "Then the general cannot wait any longer. You know that, don't you?"

He nodded, filled with misery. "That I do."

The adjutant began to leave. "Then it will be a long night for all of us, and a longer day tomorrow for the boys going into battle."

Colonel Cabot said nothing, watching as the adjutant returned to the general's quarters. He stared for what seemed to be a long time at the departing figure, until the tiny light of his lantern could no longer be seen.

Harmon thought back again to the warning about spies as he shivered now in the cold night air. He hated the thought of spies, despised their very existence. The thought of fighting out in the open, out upon the hills, deep in the trees, grappling with the Federals, was bad enough. But at least there was a fairness about it all. Oh, the Federals may have better uniforms and better rifles, but the Virginia boys and the other boys from the other Confederate states had the will, had the spirit. But to think that the Federals had the benefits of spies working for them, men—and maybe even women!—among them here in the defenses, spies who would go and whisper their secrets to the Federals, made him furious. He knew the penalty for spying was death, and he had no doubt he would find it easy to kill a spy, if they found one tonight.

But it was proving to be a long night. Now the men up around the campfire were singing, sometimes quite loudly, and, Harmon thought, if a spy came down this road now, he would have so much warning that all he would have to do would be to slip around him, through the woods, and from there up to the Federal lines. And whose fault would that be? Not his, not Corporal Harmon Brewster. No sir. Blame it on the drunks up there, and especially blame it on Lieutenant Morgan, who had not once sent someone down here to relieve him.

He leaned his rifle against a tree trunk and placed both his hands underneath his armpits, trying to warm up his bare fingers. He thought about how warm it would be at home tonight, with Mother and Father and his two sisters. Going to war at first had seemed so romantic—volunteer for a few months, teach the Federals a bloody lesson or two, and be back in time for summer work on the farm. Hah. He knew he was still a young man, that he had a lot to learn about this world, but he also knew he had grown up a lot since going into town to volunteer, wearing his only pair of shoes and his best clothes. He had seen it all: long marches in the rain and the mud, making do for food by scavenging in the woods, and, worst of all, the battles. The sharp sound of the rifles discharging. The clouds of smoke from the cannon fire. The yells and the shrieks and the blood, always the blood. A few times he had cried after a battle, bawled like a baby, and was embarrassed at acting so like a child until he had seen the tears on the faces of the older men, the ones who had seen and done more than he ever had.

He shivered again, and then grabbed his rifle.

A horseman was approaching.

Captain Jacob Shaw had come into his tent a few minutes earlier, bearing a tin cup of coffee, which Colonel Cabot eagerly drank. The night had grown colder yet he had not moved from his vantage point at the front of his tent. His adjutant had drawn up a stool and sat next to him, not saying anything, until Cabot sighed and said, "Go ahead."

"Sir?"

"Go ahead and speak your piece. I can tell that you wish to say something to me."

His adjutant coughed. "Well, sir, I must beg to report that Sergeant Calhoun is not to be found in camp. During the officers' mess some talk was going about, concerning you and Sergeant Calhoun. I thought it best to find him and to see if he had learned any more about the spy coming here tonight. But he is gone. Sir."

Cabot nodded, feeling the trembles start along his arms and legs. He knew he should go inside. Knew he should lie out on his cot and try to sleep, with an extra blanket to keep him warm. But he also knew he couldn't sleep. Knowing that the general was now writing up his orders for tomorrow's battle. Knowing that the spy had not yet arrived. Knowing that the lives of so many of the boys were resting with him, all because of that impetuous moment when he had guaranteed the general, *guaranteed*—how could he have been so foolish!—that he would have the spy's report in hand before the evening was out.

He shifted his legs. "That Sergeant Calhoun is missing is to be expected, Jacob. I gave the sergeant a pass through the lines. He is to meet with his spy and return here to camp."

"But still, sir . . . It's been so long. Do you really think he will be returning with the spy?"

Cabot stared out, feeling a breeze rise up and make his face grow even colder. "I have no choice, Jacob. I truly don't. I must believe it, or all will be lost."

The sound of the hammering hooves grew louder and louder, almost like the roar of cannon fire, and Harmon leapt out onto the road, the rifle firm in his hands, as he made out the horse and rider before the dim light of his lantern. "Halt!" he yelled out. "Halt, damn you, or I'll shoot!"

The horse reared up and a man aboard the horse yelled something, and then whipped down at Harmon with the flat of his sword. Harmon gasped as his rifle flew from his grasp, and then he grabbed on to the reins. "Let go, you bastard! Let go of my horse!" the rider yelled, but Harmon shouted back and tugged at the horse, as it neighed and moved about, dragging him along the side.

Then a rifle shot blew through the stillness of the night air, and there were suddenly men about him, and Lieutenant Morgan yelled out, "Dismount, rider. Dismount this instant or the next shot will be through your brain."

Harmon stepped back, almost stumbled across his rifle. He quickly picked it up and from the light of the torches and lanterns, saw who he had stopped. The horse was black and magnificent looking, well fed and groomed, nothing at all like the horses hauling the sutler's wagon or the slave wagon. The saddle and reins also looked expensive, as did the clothing of the man who came off the horse with a flourish. He was tall and well built, with a dark beard that extended down to the middle of his chest. He wore the uniform of a Confederate major, but it was nothing like any uniform Harmon had ever seen.

Even from some feet away, Harmon could see the uniform was made of fine cloth, with elaborate threads of gold and scarlet along the sleeves, and a wide belt with gold tassels as well, from which his long sword hung down. His gloves were white and his boots seemed to be of the softest and shiniest leather, extending up to his knees, and fancy silver spurs clinked as he moved about. His wide-brimmed hat had a cockade of some sort extending from its side, and the hat failed to hide the fury in the officer's face.

"Who the devil are you, and by what right do you halt me?" he demanded. "Who's the officer in charge of this rabble?"

"Well, I guess that would be me, Major," came the familiar voice. "Lieutenant Bruce Morgan. At your service. And why might you be traveling on this road at this hour, Major? And where might you be headin' from?"

"That is none of your business, Lieutenant," he snapped. "Make way or you will be in the stockade by this time tomorrow."

Harmon looked at his lieutenant, knowing that the lieutenant—though he might like a good drink or a good story or be remiss in relieving a lowly corporal on picket duty—was a true officer, one who would not allow anyone to talk his way over him. "Well," Morgan said, drawing out the sound of the word. "Truth be, Major, everything on this part of this road happens to be my business tonight. I've got my orders from my captain, and he told me to keep an eye on things. Which means making sure everyone going through here has the proper pass, and has proper business. Now. Beggin' your pardon, Major, mind tellin' me who the hell you are and where you're goin'?"

"And if I refuse?" came the reply, and Harmon recognized the tone of voice, of a proper plantation gentleman, raised among money and privilege and pride, ready to go to battle over a sharp insult, a wounded dignity. Well, to hell with 'im—and that's pretty much what the lieutenant said.

Lieutenant Morgan stepped closer. "Well, if you do refuse, then I guess me and my boys have no choice, seein' how you were tryin' to get through our lines without being properly recognized. Which means we'd shoot you down, right here, and I get myself a new horse. Do you have any other questions? Major?"

The major looked around at the faces of the boys, and Harmon could sense what they were feeling. Who was this rich and mighty officer, to try to bluff and bluster his way through the lines? Had he ever marched in the mud? Had he ever met the elephant, feeling that tight and tense feeling in the chest when the gunfire started? Then the major drew himself up and said, "The name is Major Monroe Krueger. I am on a mission tonight, bringing messages to the general, up on the north part of the lines."

"And do you have a pass, Major Krueger?"

The two men stared at each other, and then the major reached into his pocket, handed over a piece of paper. A private with a torch stepped closer to Lieutenant Morgan, who held up the piece of paper. A moment passed, then he nodded and handed the paper back to the major. "It seems in order, sir. Now, if you please, do you have any other papers on your person?"

The major motioned to a saddlebag on his horse. "Confidential orders. In the saddlebag."

"I'm sorry, sir, but I'm under orders to examine all papers being sent through the road tonight."

The major shook his head. "And I am under orders not to let anyone examine those papers, save the general or his staff. Under pain of death."

Lieutenant Morgan looked around at the men. "Well, Major, I guess that can be easily arranged. That is, if you don't let me examine your papers. But if you let me, and only myself, examine them, then you'll be on your way, quickly."

Harmon looked on as the major stood there, a thumb hooked on his belt. The major looked around at the grim and dirty faces, and then shook his head again. "Look. Look and be damned. And by this time tomorrow, you'll be a private. This I promise."

The lieutenant laughed. "A private! Now, that'd be something! I get to eat the same grub and sleep on the same cold ground, and without botherin' to lead a bunch of men into battle. That'd be the life."

Some of the men laughed a bit, and then Lieutenant Morgan took a lantern and went over to the saddlebag. He opened it up and the horse whinnied some, and he held up some papers to the light. All the other men looked on, but for some reason, Harmon kept his eye on the major. The major was staring at the lieutenant as well, but his stance was odd. His hand was still in his belt, his thumb moving back and forth, like it was rubbing something. Harmon stepped closer, saw a slight bulge under the belt. Something looked strange . . .

The lieutenant put the papers back into the saddlebag, closed it shut. "Major, it does look like—"

"Lieutenant!" Harmon called out. "His sword belt! He's hiding something behind his belt!"

The major stepped back and it looked like he was going to run into the dark woods, when the lieutenant called out, "Pope! Barnum! Hold him tight there!"

Both privates grabbed an arm and the major started struggling, fighting against them. His hat fell off and he shouted, "This is an outrage! Treating an officer like this! I'll have all of you shot for attacking an officer!"

Harmon felt awful, like he was back in school, making a fool of himself, the other children laughing at him. All this trouble was happening because of what he thought he saw. He felt exposed, like he was on a ridgeline by himself, rifle fire rattling in at him, all by his lonesome.

"Let's just take a quick look, then," and the lieutenant reached into the space between the belt and the uniform jacket. It seemed like everyone had stopped moving for a moment as the lieutenant's hand stayed there, and then came out.

In his hand he held a tightly folded wad of paper.

A failure, Colonel Cabot thought. A complete and utter failure. How could he have been so vain, so full of himself, to think that he—a quiet teacher of music—could take part in this great crusade?

He yawned, despite himself, and then shivered from both the cold and the fear. A complete and utter fool, as well. All these men, slumbering in these tents, going into battle in just a few hours. And he thought he could save some of them.

A failure. And a total fool.

And the parade ground was still quiet, and still no lights approached.

So many torches were clustered around the lieutenant that Harmon feared his officer's hat would catch fire. Morgan unfolded the paper, and unfolded it again, and unfolded it thrice. He held up the thin paper and looked at the letters printed on it, and said, "I'm sorry, Major, I've been to a number of years of schoolin', and I can't rightly make out what is said here. Harmon!"

He stepped forward. "Lieutenant?"

"You know how to read, don't you?"

"Yes sir, I do."

The lieutenant smiled, while the major breathed heavily, still in the grasp of Privates Pope and Barnum. "Then come over and take a look. Tell me if you can make it out."

Harmon moved over to the lieutenant, looked at the well-printed phrases and words, and he stared some more. "Lieutenant, I'm sorry, I can't make out a damn thing."

"You're right. 'Cause it's in code, ain't it? Major?"

The men moved in closer around the major. Harmon's heart was thumping so hard that he thought everyone could hear it. Major Krueger's voice didn't seem as strong. "A code? What do you mean, a code?"

Lieutenant Morgan waved the paper underneath the major's face. "We've been warned, Major. All of us on picket duty tonight. To be aware of spies in our midst, spies who've written messages in code, or who have suspicious drawings. Right here, Major, right here I got a message that none of us can read. Plus you were riding hell-for-leather and tried to get through the lines without stopping. That makes it all pretty suspicious, don't you think?"

"You fool," Major Krueger said. "I was riding because I was late. And I didn't stop for your man here, because he looked like a common thief or brigand. That's why."

"And this message? In code, isn't it?"

Major Krueger looked around and started laughing. "Fool. Is English all you know? That's a letter to my fiancée. Written in German. The language of our families. Placed behind my belt because I didn't want it contained in the dispatch papers. That's all. You are all so ignorant, aren't you?"

Someone in the rear muttered a profanity and the lieutenant spoke up. "German, is it? Well, Major. I guess someone other than me will have to prove that, Major, back at regiment headquarters."

"An outrage!" the major yelled. "You are to release me at once, Lieutenant! Understand? At once!"

Then the lieutenant ignored the major and looked over at Harmon, who no longer felt afraid, no longer felt exposed. "Corporal Brewster?"

Harmon was surprised at hearing the question. It wasn't often that the lieutenant called him by his rank.

"Sir?"

"You're the one who halted him, who captured a probable spy. Would you like the honor of escorting him back to headquarters?"

Harmon looked at the faces of the men, their faces now looking at him with respect, something he had never seen before. It was a good feeling.

"Well, sir . . ."

"Yes, Corporal?"

Harmon smiled. "If it's all the same to you, Lieutenant, I'd like to be relieved, sir, and just go up and warm up by that fire. It's so damn cold!"

The lieutenant laughed. "So it is, Corporal. So it is. We'll let somebody else escort the spy."

And the last thing Harmon heard for a while was the shouts of the major announcing his innocence, announcing his intentions to have all of them shot. So what, Harmon thought, walking eagerly to the fire. He had done his duty, better than he had expected, and now it was time to warm up.

Colonel Cabot was so happy he could hardly stop smiling. It had worked, it had worked, and now the spy was here, in his tent, ready to reveal all. His adjutant had run off to the general's quarters, to halt the planning and orders-giving, for now the spy was here. Sergeant Calhoun had arrived a few minutes earlier, out of breath, just barely saluting, saying, "Sorry, sir, sorry it took so long. The Rebel lines were pretty active tonight."

He couldn't speak, he was so overjoyed, and he escorted Sergeant Calhoun and the spy into his tent. The spy kept quiet as Sergeant Calhoun explained what the spy had brought through the lines, and how to recognize the code. Like before, Cabot had a hard time seeing what the sergeant was pointing out, but then, in a flash, he recognized what the sergeant was saying.

Draped over his cot was a dirty quilt, its designs and lines making no sense at all, until Sergeant Calhoun folded it a certain way, and there it was. Triangles and squares marking Rebel units. Jagged lines marking the extent of their breastworks. A map made of cloth, telling a story, a story of what was waiting for his troops in just a few hours, up there beyond the hills. Cabot looked over at the spy, who was not alone this evening. An old colored man, sitting on a chair, eating hardtack, with two young children at his feet. They had shivered without the warmth of the quilt upon them, and Cabot had gently placed his own wool blanket over them.

"This here be old Tom, Colonel," Sergeant Calhoun explained. "Last time, his daughter came through with a map quilt, and this time it was his turn. I knew them both, a year or two ago."

"So you did," Cabot said. "So you did. Tell me, Sergeant . . ."

"Sir?" he said, looking at him, face proud of what had just been accomplished.

Cabot smiled at the sergeant in amazement. "I still can't believe what this old man and his daughter have done. To work with other slaves to create these map quilts, and then to smuggle them out through the Rebel lines, right under the eyes of their pickets. Even though it's happened twice, I still can't believe it's been done."

Sergeant Calhoun looked over at the old man and the two children. "Well, Colonel, sir, it's a pretty easy explanation, if you'd like to hear it."

"I surely would."

Then his adjutant bustled into the tent, breathing hard from his exertion. "Colonel, the general requests your presence. Right now, with that map."

Cabot held up a hand. "Just a moment, Jacob, just a moment. I was waiting for an explanation. Sergeant, if you will."

The sergeant just shrugged his shoulders and then rubbed a finger across his chin, a chin the same skin color of the old man and the children. "It's like this, Colonel. To most of the Rebs over there, we're not people. We're property. They look at us during the day when we work in the fields or on the docks, and they look at us during the night when they put us away in the slave quarters. They look at us all the time, every day and every month, but you know what, Colonel?"

"What's that, Sergeant?"

"They look at us, but they don't see us. It's like we're not there. It's like we're invisible."

From outside the parade ground came shouts, as men in Union blue started to be mustered out in the torchlight, all the men in this regiment, the same skin color as Sergeant Calhoun and the spy.

Cabot reached over and gently slapped the sergeant on the shoulder. He had not slept a wink all during this long night, but it would be all right. Oh, Lord, how it would be all right. "Thanks to you and old Tom, Sergeant," Cabot said softly, "I can guarantee you that the Rebs will see you in a few hours, and will see you quite well. Come, it's time to meet with the general."

James Cobb has lived his entire life within a thirty-mile radius of a major Army post, an Air Force base, and a Navy shipyard. He comments, "Accordingly, it's seemed a natural to become a kind of cut-rate Rudyard Kipling, trying to tell the stories of America's service people." Currently, he's doing the Amanda Garrett techno-thriller series, with three books, *Choosers of the Slain*, *Seastrike*, and *Seafighter* published and a fourth, *Target Lock*, on the way. He's also doing the Kevin Pulaski suspense thrillers for St. Martin's Press. He lives in the Pacific Northwest and, when he's not writing, he indulges in travel, the classic American hot rod, and collecting historic firearms.

Here he applies his attention to detail to this tale of maritime skullduggery and sabotage as a comely Federal spy attempts to stop a threat to the Union blockades offshore of the island paradise of Bermuda.

Monica Van Telflin and the Proper Application of Pressure

James H. Cobb

REPOSE HOUSE, THE SOUTHERN SHORE OF HAMILTON HARBOR, HER MAJESTY'S COLONY OF BERMUDA 11:23 ON THE EVENING OF JULY 19, 1863

During high summer on Bermuda one had to be either a fool or British to wear more than a mosquito bar to one's bed. Monica Van Telflin was neither. Comfortably bare on the island cotton sheets, she drowsed in the hint of sea breeze trickling in through the open balcony doors. She drowsed . . . and then, in an instant, was totally awake.

There had been the faintest of sounds from outside, something beyond the wind rustling in the trees and the calling of the night birds.

Blue eyes snapped open and a slender hand slipped down beside the mattress, seeking for the butt of the Smith and Wesson Model Two revolver she knew would be there. Then the rose trellis that climbed past the balcony creaked and a muffled seaman's oath drifted up from the shadows.

Monica smiled, letting the revolver settle back into the holster strapped to the bed frame. She recognized that curse. Brushing aside the fine mesh of the mosquito bar, she stood in the room's darkness and reached for her silken robe.

Lieutenant Commander George Wilkinson Garrett of the United States Navy threw an arm over the railing and heaved himself onto the bedroom balcony, manfully suppressing a last outburst of profanity as a thorn wreaked lasting havoc on the leg of his blue uniform trousers.

"Blast it and damnation, Monica! Why can't you organize these meetings in some seamen's dive or rank back alley like a respectable spy?"

Monica chuckled, resting her hands on her hips. "Because, my dear George, having a dashing sailor lover climbing onto my balcony in the moonlight merely adds to the rather brisk reputation of the rich Widow Van Telflin. On the other hand, skulking about in the odd dark corner with the Union's Military Attaché to Bermuda could attract the undue attention of our old friend Captain Fairweather, not to mention the rest of Her Majesty's authorities. I can do much better work as a somewhat loose and vapid expatriate socialite then I could as a suspected Federal secret agent."

The devil induced her to preen back her fall of glossy brown hair. "Besides," she continued airily, "there are any number of eligible men on this island who would have no objection whatsoever to being invited to my boudoir on a regular basis."

"And that has absolutely nothing to do with anything," the tall and dark haired Navy man growled, focusing his attention on a thorn puncture rather than on the tenuous fabric of Monica's wrap.

Monica suppressed an impish grin. Beyond her late husband, George had to be one of the most solid, steadfast, and outright honorable men she had ever encountered. Possibly that was why he was so much fun to tease on occasion.

"You said in your drop message that we have a new problem," Garrett continued. "What's happened?"

"This has. Come take a look."

At the other end of the balcony, a powerful mariner's telescope stood atop a tripod. Taking advantage of the vista available from the second story of Repose House, it permitted a very effective reconnaissance of the colony capital of Hamilton and its port facilities a scant mile distant across the harbor.

Monica lined the telescope up on a target and stepped back. "Observe."

Hunkering down slightly, Garrett peered through the eyepiece. The expensive Swiss-made spyglass had excellent light-gathering qualities. He could readily make out the silhouette of a docked ship in the glow from the stars and the town street lamps.

She was a paddlewheel merchant steamer. Schooner-rigged and slim-hulled, her outsized paddle boxes and twin, sharply raked funnels promised an exceptional turn of speed.

"That new British blockade-runner," Garrett grunted, "the *Reindeer*. We've been keeping an eye on her over townside, trying to find out something about her."

"I can tell you more than you want to know, George," Monica paced off a few slipper-footed steps. "I was aboard her today. In fact, I took a cruise on her. And that ship represents a far greater threat then just another blockade runner."

Garrett straightened, frowning. "How so?"

"She could be a harbinger of things to come if a Mr. Titus Greenly has his way."

Garrett's dark brows narrowed. "Greenly? He's listed as the *Reindeer*'s owner, I believe."

"Um-hm, her owner, her creator, her financier, and the driving force behind her. He's a little Midlands industrialist who looks rather like a balding pigeon. He knows absolutely nothing whatsoever about ships or naval warfare. Yet he may represent the greatest threat to our blockade of the Confederacy since the launching of the *Merrimac*."

Garrett scowled. "What do you mean?"

"While our Mr. Greenly is greatly deficient in naval matters, he does have a nose for money. He's aware of the vast profits that can be made running cargo through the blockade into the Confederate ports and he intends to tap those profits on a massive scale."

Monica turned again, facing the attaché. "He intends to form a business syndicate. A syndicate to run contraband into the Confederate states, supported by an entire fleet of fast merchantmen specifically designed for blockade-running."

"Damnation!"

"Indeed. The *Reindeer* is the model the fleet will be built around. That cruise I wangled myself aboard was a demonstration run for some of the Bermuda money. Mr. Greenly is seeking investors for his new enterprise."

"What's she like under way?"

Monica's brows rose. "She's a bundle of pine boards with the beam of a butcher knife. Get her in heavy seas and she'll either capsize like a canoe or come apart like a cigar box. But she's fast, George. Faster than sin. I'll swear they had her up to eighteen knots today and she wasn't even trying. Full out, nothing we have on the blockade could touch her."

Garrett didn't even consider disregarding Monica's judgment. "Did you get a look at her clockworks?"

"Mr. Greenly gave all of his potential investors a bow-to-stern tour. I trailed along and was careful to act suitably awed and ignorant in the right places. She's got a set of Armstrong Whitworth engines worthy of an ironclad ram. Six forced-draft locomotive boilers feeding through a pressure stepdown. Terrific horsepower for the weight."

The naval officer shook his head. "That rig will never stand up for long."

"Nothing about *Reindeer* will stand up for long. She's so overengined for her hull that she'll shake herself to pieces in a matter of months. But in those months she can make numerous very profitable dashes into Charleston."

"I begin to see what you mean," Garrett nodded. "Who cares how long she lasts? It's the money she makes while she's running that matters."

"Exactly. There are huge turnovers in smuggling. The profits from the first run will pay for the ship and the rest will be gravy of a particularly tasty kind for potential investors. One ship like her would be bad enough, but there is an even greater threat involved.

"Something else is very rapid about the *Reindeer,* her construction time. Greenly had her specifically designed so that she could be quickly and cheaply copied. A good British shipyard could slap a sister ship or ships together in a matter of weeks. By the end of the year, we could have a dozen just like her moored across the harbor and Mr. Jefferson Davis would have a marvelous new supply line for a Christmas present."

Garrett scowled, gazing across the harbor at the lights of Hamilton. "God save us, but you're right. This could be considerably more serious than just another blockader. How is Greenly's proposal being received by the island investors?"

"Cautious interest. They know there's money to be made, but the more nautically knowledgeable have doubts about the *Reindeer*'s design and about Greenly's plan for the rapid production of a fleet. I suspect those doubts will dissipate with the first cargo of cotton Greenly brings out of a Southern port."

Garrett bent over and peered through the telescope again. "When is the gentleman going to make his try?"

"Next week," Monica seated herself on the edge of her bed. "They have to complete the transferal of the *Reindeer*'s registry from Great Britain to the Confederate States and they have to load cargo."

"Any word on what she'll be carrying inbound?"

"The usual runner's burden. Low-bulk, high-value luxury goods mostly. But they'll also be loading half a million Enfield percussion caps and a couple of miles of bomb and shell fuse for the Confederate army."

Garrett straightened from the telescope, brushing thoughtfully at his mustache. "Hmm. I daresay that a slab of guncotton and a yard or so of slow fuse in the same hold with those munitions could put a considerable crimp in your Mr. Greenly's prospects."

"Were it but that simple, George. Blowing up one of Her Majesty's merchant ships in one of Her Majesty's harbors would considerably aggravate Her Majesty's Government, even if said ship was false-flagging under the Stars and Bars. Mr. Lincoln doesn't need that complication to his life just now. Besides, simply destroying the ship is inadequate."

Garrett glanced back over his shoulder. "How so?"

Monica crossed her legs and propped her chin in her palm. "Greenly is a clever little chap when it comes to merchandising. He could use the fact that we scuttled his ship as a selling point to his investors. The Federal Government recognizes his blockade-running syndicate as a threat. Ipso facto, his ideas must be valid and workable. Even slipping a touch of hemlock into his afternoon tea would be insufficient. Someone else could pick up his concepts where he left off. It's the concepts themselves that we have to destroy."

"How in blazes do you destroy an idea?" Garrett demanded.

"By publicly discrediting it, my dear George. And I have some ideas along that line."

"What will you need?"

"Five things. Two of which, an invitation to dine aboard the *Reindeer* and a rather special new gown for the occasion, I can provide. The other three items I'll need your assistance with."

"Name them," Garrett replied promptly.

Monica smiled. "Your company for an evening, a fast navy steam frigate, and twenty feet of telegraph wire."

Hooves clopping on coral cobbles, Monica's carriage rolled along Port Hamilton's Front Street. The last trace of the day's light was fading, as was the oppressiveness of its heat. The little port town was coming alive as Bermudans, white and brown alike, roused from the afternoon's torpor to conclude the affairs of the day. Figures occulted the glow of lamp-lit shop windows, mellow voices spoke from the shadows and the sound of a strummed guitar issued from a tavern doorway.

It was a superb evening to go riding with a handsome gentleman, Monica reflected. A pity it had to be wasted on business matters.

"Have we any more word on our warship, George?"

"The dispatch was countersigned by the ambassador and gotten off aboard last week's fast packet inbound for Baltimore. Her skipper had instructions to relay it to the first Federal Navy vessel he spotted. Good Lord willing, somebody will be out there when the *Reindeer* sails tomorrow morning."

"Well, that's the best we can do in that department," Monica replied, patting a lock of her upswept hair back into place. "The rest will be up to us."

"Indeed. I can understand how you were able to wangle an invitation back aboard for the *Reindeer*'s departure dinner, but I'm still amazed that you were able to procure an invitation for a Union naval officer."

"It wasn't all that difficult really. Mr. Greenly, like many Englishmen, doesn't take our Civil War all that seriously. He looks upon it as just another irregularity by those peculiar Americans."

"Hmm. Well, I've had a look at some of the Rebel officers and crew who'll be taking the *Reindeer* across and they take this war very seriously indeed."

"I daresay, George, and you will provide a marvelous distraction for them. While they're keeping an eagle eye on the damn Yankee in their midst, I, sweet, helpless flower that I am, will be able to go about committing barratry to my heart's content."

Garrett responded with a noncommittal grunt, looking out the carriage window.

"Anything wrong, George?"

"I just don't like it," he replied gruffly. "Damn it, Monica, this isn't your place, fighting in a war. It's no place for any woman. If something goes wrong, you could end up in a British prison for years . . . or considerably worse. With me it's different. It's my duty. But for you . . . I just don't like it."

She lightly rested her hand on his blue-clad shoulder. "It's my choice, George. It always has been."

"Damnation, I know it! I just wish . . ."

"I wish a lot of things, too." Monica's voice hardened. "At the beginning of the war, Rebel agents tried to seize my husband's ship for use as a Confederate raider. My husband James stopped them, but he died doing it, defending his quarterdeck.

"A man might have been able to look upon his death as an act of war, but I'm a woman. I take things far more personally. I looked upon his killing as an act of bloody-handed murder. I swore that the secessionists and slavocrats would pay for it, and I intend to see that they do."

"And I'll help you, good Lord willing. Now, any last minute changes to the plan?"

"No. I'll need about fifteen minutes alone forward of the paddle boxes. I'll give you the sign when."

Reindeer lay moored across the T-head of one of the Port Hamilton piers. A number of the local dockside hangers-on carried Monica's coin in their pockets and they had reported to her that precautions were being taken around the blockade-runner.

A pair of police constables paced the length of the pier while, from the darkened waters beyond the ship, there came the thump of rowlocks and the occasional gleam of a bull's-eye lantern. A port picket-boat circled in the night, guarding to seaward.

Two burly seamen also lounged at the foot of the gangway that bridged the gap between the pier and the *Reindeer*'s quarterdeck, while the third mate stood port watch at its head.

As was common with the blockaders, the *Reindeer* was manned by a mixed bag of British, Bermudan, and Confederate seamen with a Confederate captain and mates. By their clothing and accents and from the cold glares aimed at George Garrett, Monica presumed that this night's watch-standers were all Confederate. She also noted that all three men carried British-made Adams revolvers holstered at their belts.

As she and her escort were ushered aboard and below to the main cabin, Monica checked off the key points of her surroundings. No smoke or heat shimmer over the stacks, *Reindeer*'s plant was still cold. All cargo hatches forward of the quarterdeck were battened down and secured for sea. The only topside illumination issued from the watch lantern at the binnacle, the remainder of the blockader's narrow deck being left to the shadows.

Far forward, a dim glow leaked from the open foc'sle hatch, along with a faint murmur of voices. The majority of the crew would be ashore, saying an enthusiastic farewell to Bermuda. Only the port watch replacements and the black gang that would kindle the furnaces and set the steaming watch after midnight remained aboard.

All was well.

As with the crew, a mixed bag of a dinner party awaited them in the *Reindeer*'s cramped main salon. The Confederate contingent consisted of Captain Welden Enoch and his first and second mates. Enoch was of the lean and hungry kind with graying, muttonchop whiskers and pale suspicious eyes. His mates were of the same breed, differing in appearance but not in attitude. The gentlemanly coldness focused upon Commander Garrett was readily apparent.

Another positive check on Monica's list. *Be ready to trail your coat, George,* she thought. *Keep these hounds drawn off.*

The island contingent consisted of the right honorable Harriman De Vere of the Colonial Banking and Trust. A heavyset and intensely solid middle-aged worthy, he likely knew the exact location and status of nine out of ten of the island's pounds and dollars, his advice having been sought in their investment. He would be Greenly's prize this night. Where De Vere led in money matters, others, many others, followed.

Likewise present, a long-jawed and deceptively relaxed individual in the uniform of Her Majesty's Navy, Port Captain Andrew Fairweather, one of the few men in Monica's experience who could actually unsettle her. He was one of the few men she could not effectively "read."

Since her establishment in Bermuda as a Federal agent, she had performed a complex and at times nerve-wracking dance with this gentleman, her affairs brushing close to his on a number of occasions. Monica suspected that Fairweather suspected her true intents. In turn she could only be sure that he did not know for sure. If he ever did learn to a certainty, she'd be peering out through the bars of "King George's Inn" in short order.

Still, as the tall smiling English officer bent over her hand, she had the unnerving feeling that he could peer through her gown to the myriad secrets hidden beneath it.

And there was Titus Greenly himself, small, rounded, enthusiastic, and totally oblivious to the lightning that played around him in the stuffy little cabin.

"I'm so pleased you could join us again this evening, Mrs. Van Telflin," the little man gushed. "Your presence brightened my investors' cruise and it certainly will do the same for our little departure party this evening."

Monica nodded and smiled. "It's most certainly my pleasure, Mr. Greenly. I so enjoyed my voyage with you last week. May I introduce my escort, Commander George Garrett of the United States Navy. I do hope you don't mind the . . . irregularity but George so wanted to have a look at your lovely little vessel."

"Somehow," Captain Fairweather murmured from the background, "that doesn't surprise me."

The dinner proved . . . interesting. The meal was excellent but the atmosphere veered between a cold correctness on the part of George and the Confederates, and an engineered gaiety from Monica and Greenly. Events merely washed over the stolid De Vere, while Fairweather only looked on, that knowing smile of his hovering close to his lips.

As the sole woman present, a withdrawal was not mandated when the brandy, cigars, and business were brought forth at the end of the meal. As

Monica listened, the true intent of the night's entertainment became clear. The banker De Vere had also been a guest aboard *Reindeer* during the investors' cruise and had displayed a degree of interest in Greenly's propositions. Now Greenly was pushing for the kill.

"Every investment has its risk, sir," Greenly pontificated, "but here the risks are calculated and the potential returns magnificent."

"Indeed they are," George commented softly to the rim of his snifter. "All you have to do is not mind the promotion of slavery."

Captain Enoch looked up sharply from the head of the table. "The War of the Rebellion is an affair of states' rights, sir, not of slavery."

"Indeed, sir." Garrett lifted his cigarillo from the saucer at his side. "Unfortunately, the only 'states' right' anyone seems to be in essential disagreement over is the right to buy, own, and sell our fellow human beings like livestock."

Enoch's face flushed and Greenly hastily cut off his captain's retort. "Gentlemen, please. We do have a lady present. Commander Garrett, I most certainly understand your, ah, apathy toward our venture here, but you must understand. We are only businessmen taking advantage of an opportunity. Good business, nothing more. I assure you there is nothing political or personal involved."

Monica kept her face carefully neutral. Nothing personal indeed. Would the families of the Federal soldiers slain by the munitions in the *Reindeer*'s holds view it that way?

George nodded. "As you say, sir," he replied with a degree of irony, "a lady is present and I wouldn't want to disrupt the party."

"Commander, I have a question for you," De Vere interjected. "And for you as well, Fairweather. All politics aside and speaking purely as naval men, what do you think of Mr. Greenly's ship and his proposal?"

Under the table, Monica lightly pressed George's foot with her own. It was time to begin the show.

George produced another puff from his cigarillo. "Speaking God's honest truth, Mr. De Vere," he replied. "I'm not worried by it in the least. You'd have a better chance of getting a cargo into Charleston by heaving it off the end of the pier and hoping that it would drift in the right direction."

The banker held up his hand, heading off Enoch's explosive challenge. "Indeed, Commander. How so?"

George aimed a contemptuous glance at the cheap veneer on the salon bulkheads. "This ship is a cracker box. If she doesn't break up or blow up on her own, she'll go to pieces the first time she gets a real man-of-war on her tail. And that's not a Federal officer talking, that's a sailor."

"Indeed. And your opinion, Captain Fairweather?"

The English officer took a thoughtful sip of his drink. "Well, in the end, I suppose, the proof shall be in the pudding. However, I must agree that within my own experience, when one purchases a cheap ship, one gets a cheap ship—a fact I wish the admiralty would make note of."

Fairweather's calculating gray eyes shifted to Monica. "And what would you say, Mrs. Van Telflin? Your husband was a noted mariner and you've spent as much time at sea as many in this room."

Monica gave a depreciative laugh. "My good captain, you confuse merely riding about on boats with knowing something about them. I would not presume to comment. I'll leave such matters to you gentlemen."

Again she pressed her foot down on George's. *Now.*

"Indeed, I believe that's precisely what I shall do. I feel the need for a breath of fresh air, so I shall withdraw for a few minutes, leaving the field free for a brief discussion of these maritime and financial matters."

The masculine members of the party stood as she took her departure. "Do you require accompaniment, Mrs. Van Telflin?" Garrett inquired, as per their preset script.

"Oh, of course not, George. There's no sense in your missing what promises to be the most interesting discussion of the evening. Indulge yourself and I shall return momentarily."

As the salon door closed behind her, she heard the beginning of both Captain Enoch's angry challenge and Mr. Greenly's hasty counter to George's statements. George's task now would be to keep the kettle boiling briskly as a diversion. Also working in her favor would be a lady's right to privacy while she dealt with certain bodily functions. Still, every second of her free time would be precious.

Pausing at the quarterdeck hatchway, Monica warily scanned the night. Stars glittered brightly in the moonless sky and a hint of salt mist curled low over the water. With the exception of the watch officer, leaning back drowsily against the binnacle and paying no notice to her silent emergence, the steamer's decks were still deserted. Noiselessly she moved forward into the total darkness beneath the bridge between paddle boxes.

Safe within the deepest shadows, Monica began flicking open the buttons of her gown.

She'd had this garment specially made for this evening. High-collared and long-sleeved to conceal the multitude of sins to come, it closed up the front. Likewise, both its buttons and buttonholes were large and easily manipulated and its petticoats were stitched to the inside of the skirt waistband.

Monica Van Telflin and the Proper Application of Pressure ❄ 121

Monica's Bermudan seamstress had only smiled knowingly when she had been presented with the design for the dress. Being far more civilized and understanding in such matters than her English or American counterparts, she could understand why a lady might require a gown that could swiftly and easily be removed and redonned. Only the specific motivation behind this particular garment might have surprised her.

Watered silk whispered to the holystoned deck and Monica stood free in chemise and pantalets.

The voluminous skirts of her gown had also served to conceal the other required items of the night. The length of copper telegraph wire wrapped around her waist. The spare evening gloves, the large silk scarf that she used to shroud and protect her face and hair, and, finally, the coil of light but strong cotton rope with the steel hook at its end and the knots spaced down its length.

Leaving her dress concealed in an out-of-the-way niche behind the forward stack, she stole portside to one of the great deck ventilators that flanked it. Fitting the hook of the climbing-rope onto the lower lip of the ventilator bell, she flipped the line down the duct, the free end whispering away down the sheet-metal lining. Blessing her childhood love of tree-climbing and general tomboyism, she sprang upward, gripping the upper rim of the bell and jack-knifing herself into the airshaft.

A few moments later, she thumped down on the deck in the *Reindeer*'s forward boiler room, silently cursing at the sloppy metalsmith who had left that silk- and skin-shredding rivet protruding from the side of the shaft.

As she had projected, she was in the cramped flue spaces just ahead of the triple row of boilers. The stack ducting and the belt drives of the forced-draft blowers loomed around her, outlined in the faint glow of a single low-trimmed ship's lamp. Squeezing between the boilers, she working her way aft to their rear facings.

During the ten years of her marriage to Captain James Van Telflin, Monica had voyaged with him to all the corners of the world aboard a variety of different vessels, steam and sail alike. And contrary to her statement in the salon, one could learn a great deal about ship handling and marine engineering during a decade at sea. Especially if one was of an instinctively inquisitive turn of mind and had a husband who enjoyed discussing his profession with a knowledgeable and intelligent mate.

Directly over her head, a service gangway ran back between the great cylindrical pressure vessels, a narrow ladder running up to it from the boiler facing. Cautiously, she peered out from between the iron rungs.

The stoke hold was deserted. There would still be an hour or two to go before the steaming watch would be set for the morning's departure. Ignoring her rapid accumulation of soot, engine oil, and coal dust, she squeezed out from behind the ladder and scrambled up it to the overhead gangway. Moving back into the shadowy darkness between the boilers, she found her objective. The safety-valves assemblies.

By touch Monica explored the mechanisms. In structure, a steam-engine safety valve is the essence of simplicity. A massive steel spring, mounted on a threaded stem, forces a metal plug down into a vent in the top of the pressure vessel. The holding strength of the spring is set below the estimated bursting pressure of the boiler. When the internal steam pressure approaches the danger level, the plug lifts and the excess steam is released up a vent pipe.

In theory the system is foolproof. In reality, catastrophic failures were far from unknown.

Monica selected the central boiler. As was usually the case, the sheet-metal vent pipe housing over the valve had not been bolted down, permitting the engineers a rapid access to the critical mechanism. She slid the housing up and off the valve, exposing the spring. A brush of a fingertip across the heavy coils confirmed what she had suspected. The *Reindeer* was already running with tight valves, very tight indeed, for maximum pressure and power output. So much the better.

She unwrapped the lengths of wire looped around her waist, rewinding them between the coils of the safety spring. In maritime insurance circles, this was called "gagging the safety," a favored method of disposing of a vessel that was proving uneconomical to its owners. The binding of wire stiffened the spring to immobility, locking the vent plug in place.

With the safety valve wired, she hastened back to the deck of the stoke hold. From her prior tour of the boiler room, she knew of the tools neatly racked on the rear bulkhead. Selecting a heavy pair of pliers, she returned to the central boiler and very carefully squeezed a pinch into the brass feed line of its pressure gauge, choosing a point just below the gauge fitting where it would be difficult to note. With luck, it would prove enough of a block to make the gauge read low.

Returning the pliers to the exact place she had taken them from, she dunked her hand into the engine wiper's grease bucket. It was hellish treatment for a pair of the best ladies' kid evening gloves, but in exchange for a blockade runner, it was a worthwhile trade.

A dab of the thick lubricant went onto the pressure-gauge line to conceal the mischief there. Then Monica climbed back to the gangway and returned to the doctored safety valve. She slapped the remainder of the grease over the copper gagging wire, concealing it from any cursory examination of the valve mechanism.

The job was done, but she had used up every minute of her time doing it. She had to get back to the salon before suspicions were aroused.

Monica had just finished easing the valve shroud back into place when she heard noises in the passageway leading to the boiler room. Instantly she went prone on the plank gangway, freezing in place. In spite of dank, belowdecks warmth, a shiver rippled down her spine as an extremely large silhouette loomed in the dim light.

Then she heard the mumbled verse of a Caribbean chantey and caught a whiff of alcohol and sour sweat over the sulfur-and-oil background stench of the engine spaces.

It was one of the Bermudan stokers, hired on for the *Reindeer*'s dash to the coast. A towering and muscular Negro seaman, currently with a towering drunk on. A rum bottle glinted in his hand, probably a prize smuggled aboard from an earlier spree. He must have returned from the beach early and was now seeking out a quiet corner to finish his pre-departure binge. Unfortunately for Monica, he'd chosen the forward boiler room as an opportune locale.

The stoker missed Monica's huddled presence deep in the shadows between the boilers, but, mumbling contentedly to himself, he collapsed at the foot of the inspection gangway ladder, his back to the rungs.

Savagely Monica mentalized some of her late husband's extensive vocabulary of seafarers' language. She was pinned up here and she couldn't afford to wait for the stoker to drink himself into oblivion. All too soon Fairweather or one of the *Reindeer*'s officers would start to wonder what had happened to her. It wouldn't take much of a search to find her discarded dress on deck and after that everything would go to pieces.

Monica wasn't sure which would be worse. Failing in her mission and being turned over to the British authorities, or being yarded out of this boiler room clad only in her nether garments and a coat of coal dust.

That consideration spurred up an idea. The silk scarf she had used to protect her hair and face.

Silently unwinding the fine cloth, she twisted it into a tight cord. What had they called it in the Indian Ocean ports, a thuggee's noose? Lifting up onto her hands and knees, she crawled along the splinter-studded gangway until she knelt directly above drunken seaman. Lightly, she rapped on the top rung of the ladder.

The stoker's meandering song broke off.

Not daring to breathe, Monica repeated the rapping.

The stoker cursed and struggled to his feet, blearily looking about. As he stood, his shaven head rose to the level of the inspection gangway.

Monica lunged, looped the corded scarf around the stoker's thick neck. Heaving taut, she hauled back with all her strength, taking the stoker off his feet and adding his own weight to the strain she had on the scarf.

The stoker's rum bottle crashed to the deck. Had he been steady, the big man could have yanked the scarf out of Monica's hands or readily dragged her completely off the gangway. As it was, his drunkenness worked against him. He clawed wildly but ineffectually at his throat, uncomprehending of what was happening. Ten frantic seconds later, the cutoff of blood to his brain had its effect and his legs buckled. Monica released her hold on the scarf as he collapsed to the deck.

She swarmed down the ladder. Kneeling beside the still form of the stoker, she unwound the scarf. A quick examination of his throat verified that the soft cloth had not lifted a welt.

Unfortunately, it also indicated he was no longer breathing.

"Damn! Damn! Damn!" Monica screamed in a whisper. At the moment she was less concerned about the morality of the seaman's death than she was about the presence of his corpse. The discovery of a stoker, sodden drunk and unable to account for what had happened to him would be one thing. A dead body in the boiler room was another. It would almost certainly trigger a minute inspection of the entire plant that would reveal Monica's sabotage.

"God blast it! Breathe!"

With all of her strength, she drove the heels of both hands into the stoker's stomach. Constricted air wheezed from the man's lungs, followed by a long, shuddering inhalation as respiration resumed.

Monica tore off the grease-saturated gloves and wadded them up with the scarf, hurling both through an open furnace door to the rear of the firebox where they would be mistaken for a wad of discarded wiper's rags. She was past having no time left. She had to get out now!

Ducking back into the flue spaces, she groped for and found the knotted climbing-rope she had left dangling out of the ventilator duct. Frantically she swarmed up the rope and up the shaft, striving for the deck. After what seemed an eternity of constricted inching in the metal passage, she could make out the faint glow of starlight beyond the ventilator mouth. Stretching, she curled first one set of fingers and then the other over the rim of the ventilator bell . . . and almost screamed as another pair of hands closed over her wrists.

The owner of those hands heaved and she shot out into the open air, a dark figure hauling her upright on the deck.

"Damnation, Monica! What were you playing at down there?"

"Oh, thank the Lord, George, it's you."

"For the moment," the attaché whispered back. "When your breath of fresh air stretched out to over fifteen minutes, things started to get tight. I headed off both Fairweather and Captain Enoch with the suggestion that I come looking for you, but we've got aroused suspicions."

"Unavoidable delays, George. I'll explain later, just for God's sakes help me get dressed!"

Pristine white gloves were shot on over her grimy hands and forearms, then hastily she stepped back into her gown. The full skirt, long sleeves, and high bodice concealed both the stains and smears accrued belowdecks and the bedraggled ruins of her undergarments.

Monica was just closing the last wrist button when George Garrett's arm came around her waist and she found herself drawn into a sudden fierce embrace and kiss. Surprise paralyzed resistance and the pressure of his lips on hers smothered her startled yip.

Then, over his shoulder she saw another shadow looming on deck behind them. Well played, George, she thought wryly. Then, closing her eyes, she melted into both the kiss and the experience.

When they paused for breath, Captain Fairweather was looking on, amusement showing on his long-lined face. "Ah, Commander, I see you found Mrs. Van Telflin. I do trust all is well?"

Garrett cleared his throat with just the proper amount of awkwardness. "Quite all right, Captain. No problems."

Monica was pleased with the deftness of his acting. The fervor of his embrace also provided both a justification for her somewhat rumpled condition and a reasonable excuse for withdrawal. "Quite so, Captain Fairweather," she replied, coolly brushing back a strayed lock of hair. "I'm quite all right. However, I do seem to have developed a sudden . . . headache. Commander Garrett has offered to escort me home. Could you please offer our regrets to Mr. Greenly and Captain Enoch?"

Fairweather's smile deepened. "Of course, dear lady. It will be my pleasure. I regret that the fresh air didn't help."

Slipping her arm through George's, Monica allowed herself to be led to the gangway and to her waiting carriage. Garrett's swift thinking had definitely saved that situation. But there had also been something else; something in the fervor of that kiss beyond the mere requirements of the service. Lightly she squeezed the strong and supporting arm at her side. That would be a matter for further consideration in due course and at the proper time.

*   *   *

Since the onset of the Civil War, the departure of a blockade-runner had become something of a social event for the Bermudan colonials. The sailing of the *Reindeer*, with her trailing cloak of interest and controversy, was exceptionally so. As dawn flamed along the eastern horizon, an assortment of horsemen and carriages made their way "up the country" to Daniel's Head at the western end of the island to wave Greenly's creation away on her maiden voyage.

Snowy picnic cloths dotted the sun-crisped salt grass on the hillside above land's end and servants served al fresco breakfasts to the interested onlookers. Monica Van Telflin and Commander Garrett were noteworthy in their presence.

"You realize of course that absolutely nothing may happen," Garrett commented as he lugged the telescope tube from the carriage to its deployed tripod mount. "They might not have gotten our message in time to get a ship into position."

"I'm fully cognizant, George," Monica replied, adjusting the chin scarf of her sun hat. "Just as I'm aware that my tampering could have been uncovered or that I might have made a hash out of fouling that safety or that the boiler might simply refuse to blow up out of sheer perversity. I lay awake all last night considering catastrophes. The point is, there's nothing we can do about it now except to look on and await developments."

Garrett eased the telescope into its mounting bracket. "Here comes one even as we speak."

A small group of people approached along the hillcrest. Monica recognized Greenly, Captain Fairweather, and De Vere.

"At least Fairweather doesn't have a squad of marines with him," Monica murmured. "Let's construe that as a positive sign."

She lifted her head and her voice. "Good morning, Mr. Greenly. And you as well, Captain. And Mr. De Vere. It's always a pleasure to see you."

"Good morning, good morning, Mrs. Van Telflin," Greenly caroled as he bustled up. "I'm so sorry you had to leave us so soon last evening. Your charming presence was sorely missed."

"I regret my premature departure as well, sir," she replied with an appropriate smile, "but as a New England girl I still find these warm Bermudan nights somewhat debilitating at times."

"Quite so," Captain Fairweather interjected. The lanky Englishman was maintaining an air of amused sardonicism. "I trust you have recovered from your . . . I believe it was a headache?"

"Fully, Captain. All I required was an opportunity to lie down for a time." Monica met his gaze levelly for a long moment and then returned her attention to Greenly. "I daresay it would be unpatriotic of me to wish you well on your endeavor, Mr. Greenly, but there should be no harm in at least seeing your ship off."

"Frankly, Greenly, I'm here hoping to see your ship on the reef," Garrett growled, coming to stand beside Monica.

"I understand both your feelings fully," the little merchant preened back. "Even yours, Commander. But please remember, there is nothing personal, just good business."

Monica envied George his ability to openly scowl. Her own smile ached on her face.

Someone along the hillside called out. "She's coming!"

A few moments later and the *Reindeer* appeared around Commissioner's Point to the north, clearing the mouth of Great Sound and heading to the west.

Monica had to admit that the little black steamer was a beauty, her rakishness giving the impression of speed even as she hove to for the pilot's yawl. The impression became a reality within a few minutes as, with the pilot clear, she headed out into the open Atlantic, the smoke from good Welsh coal streaming from her stacks and a broad fan of foam whipping from her paddle buckets. Hats and scarves were waved after her as she pulled away toward the dawn-shadowed western horizon.

Monica felt the warmth of George's body as he brushed close past her. "If there's anyone out there," he murmured, "they'll wait until she's well clear of the three-mile limit."

Monica didn't reply. She kept her attention focused on the eyepiece of the telescope, tracking the blockader as she diminished swiftly in the distance.

Had the chief engineer caught on to the fact that one of his safeties wasn't "talking" yet? Or were they still idling along with the taut-set boilers not pushed close to their pressure limits? Had he noted that one of his pressure gauges was underreading, and investigated, or had he ordered his stokers to push the fire in what he thought was a lagging furnace?

Long minutes passed and the *Reindeer* dwindled away to toy size.

"Hoy!" someone called out. "There's another ship out there!"

Field glasses and telescopes, including Monica's, swiveled around. Garrett brushed her aside, taking over the eyepiece.

"She looks to be a Yankee cruiser," Fairweather reported, peering through his binoculars.

"Damn right she is!" Garrett replied fiercely. "The screw steam sloop *Penobscott.*"

Fairweather's brows lifted behind his field glasses. "Bloody convenient, her lurking about out there this morning."

"Quite so, Captain." Garrett grinned back. "Your investment's in a world of trouble, Greenly. The *Penny* is a ship that can go some!"

The British industrialist's customary bland grin faltered and a handkerchief materialized in his hand to blot a sudden outburst of perspiration. The heartiness in his tone was forced as he turned to the Port Hamilton banker who accompanied him.

"A trifle, sir. I assure you. Now you'll have the opportunity to see my *Reindeer* do what she was built to do: show her heels to the Federal Navy."

De Vere only nodded. "As you say, sir."

Monica said nothing. Resuming her place at the telescope, she watched the chase unfold.

The *Penobscott* had been circling well clear of the island, her topmasts stricken to reduce her silhouette and her gray blockade paint merging her into the horizon haze. Now the big Federal sloop-of-war was driving in hard from the southwest, making a run on the *Reindeer,* as a wolf might lunge at a rabbit. White foam boiled beneath her bowsprit, and the dense smoke trail streaming in her wake suggested that her black gang had the coal flying out of her stacks.

It would have been easy enough for the *Reindeer* to reverse course and scurry back into the shelter of Bermudan territorial waters. However, Captain Enoch knew that his owner had investors watching. Instead, he accepted the challenge. The sleek little paddle-steamer paid off to the northwest, her own smoke plume thickening as she piled on speed. Enoch intended to do an end round of his pursuer, leaving her behind by literally sailing a circle around the Federal warship.

A silence fell across the hillside, the chatter and the casual laughter fading, leaving only the excited voices of the glass-holders as they described the developing events to the other onlookers.

In Monica's view, the *Penobscott* was no longer quartering. She was broadside on, due west of the headland, straining to cut across the circle being drawn by her fleet-footed prey. It was futility, though. The Confederate blockader danced on her wheels, pulling away. Burdened by her size and the weight of her guns, the Federal sloop-of-war stood no chance.

But she was making the *Reindeer* run. Right to her limits.

Monica could visualize the blockade-runner's stokeholds, lit by the hellfire glare of the furnaces, the damned souls of her stokers hurling an avalanche of coal onto the white-hot grates. And looming over them, the boilers. One of which was now a bomb ticking down toward detonation.

Monica wondered if "her" stoker had recovered enough to stand to his station. She had no argument with such men, but she would fight to the death, hers and theirs, to stop the cause they served.

Then again, maybe there was nothing to wait for. Maybe her gagging job had been uncovered and the valve freed and Enoch and his crew were laughing on their victorious way to Charleston.

Monica straightened from behind the telescope, looking to George for encouragement. He provided it with a nod and staunch grin.

Thus, neither of them saw it happen.

Exclamations and shouts rippled among the onlookers and Monica whipped back to the telescope. The dark banner streaming back from the *Reindeer*'s funnels was going pale, raw steam mixing with the coal smoke.

"George!"

Garrett took over the eyepiece and studied silently for a moment. "Her stacks are still standing, so she didn't bust a kettle," he said judgmentally. "But she's venting heavily through her deck hatches. She's blown a feed line or I'm a Dutchman. How would you call it, Captain?"

"Hmm," Fairweather nodded. "I'd think that a reasonable assessment, Commander."

With a scalding geyser of live steam erupting belowdecks, the *Reindeer*'s engine spaces would be unlivable. As her black gang abandoned their stations to escape topside, the racing heart of the blockader began to slow, her paddles clanking to a halt.

Amid the billowing clouds of vapor, the *Reindeer*'s auxiliary sails could be seen crawling up her masts. Enoch was frantically trying to get his ship under way again; no doubt in an attempt to beat back to the safety of Crown waters.

Now, though, it was the *Reindeer* that had no chance. The *Penobscot* thundered down upon the crippled blockade-runner like an express train.

A gout of gunsmoke and orange flame spewed from the sloop's bow-chaser and a mast-high jet of whitewater lifted off the paddle steamer's bow, the thud of the one-hundred-pounder Parrott rifle echoing in dully from the sea. The *Reindeer* came about sluggishly, the tiny gray scrap of the Confederate flag sinking to the blockader's deck.

"Well, that's it, then," Fairweather said, recasing his field glasses. He lifted his voice slightly. "It appears Commander Garrett was right. One can't go about slapping a ship together like a packing case and expect to get anything decent out of it."

De Vere shot a cold glance in Greenly's direction. "Words of wisdom, Captain. In the future when dealing with matters of the sea, I'll make it a point to listen to sailors and not shopkeepers. Good day, gentlemen, Mrs. Van Telflin."

The banker stalked away toward a group of Hamilton businessmen caucusing downslope.

Greenly didn't seem to notice. Ghost-pale, he stared out at the horizon, at what had been his ship. "I'm finished," he whispered to no one in particular. "I put everything into this. Everything!"

Monica almost felt sorry for him . . . *almost*. "I'm so sorry, Mr. Greenly. It was such a pretty boat, too."

As George lugged the tripod and telescope tube back up the hill to where Monica's carriage waited, Captain Fairweather lingered.

"Most peculiar how this morning's event came to pass," he mused. "One of your Federal warships ambling by just when Greenly's great enterprise is launched. Then Greenly's ship breaking down just at the most awkward of moments for him. Most peculiar."

"As you say, Captain," Monica tugged at the scarf bow and removed her sun hat, savoring the feel of the freshening sea breeze. In the distance, offshore, two ships were fading from sight over the horizon, the smaller the towed captive of the larger, both now bound for a Northern naval base. "Of course I know little of such matters but it would seem to me that poor Mr. Greenly was stricken by the most dreadfully bad luck."

"Indeed. But, my dear lady, it has been my experience that sometimes such 'bad luck' is manufactured." The port captain's steel-colored eyes hardened. "And mind you, should I ever catch anyone on this island producing any further such 'bad luck,' male or female, civilian or military, that individual can expect to face the fullest wrath of Crown law!"

Monica laughed and held out a hand, its glove concealing the lingering grease and soot stains that two hours in her bath had failed to remove. "My dear captain, could we ever expect anything less of you?"

Fairweather's expression softened back into wryness and his fingers closed around hers. "Now, having said that, might I ask you out to dinner some evening after you colonials finish this little disagreement of yours? I've simply got to find out how you and Garrett pulled this one off."

"You may consider it an engagement, Captain."

Aileen Schumacher is a civil/environmental engineer who resides in Florida with her husband and two children. *Rosewood's Ashes* is the fourth in her Travers/Alvarez mystery series. Visit her Web site at *www.aliken.com/aileen/.*

The famous, or notorious, depending on which side you may have supported, Confederate blockade runner Michael Usina and his equally famous dog, Tinker, make an appearance in the following story, proving that even a man who's been around the world and back can still fall under the spell of a woman.

WORTH A
THOUSAND WORDS

Aileen Schumacher

The irony of finding himself left high and dry in Nassau was not lost on somebody known throughout the Confederate navy as the Boy Captain.

Michael Usina was the youngest man to ever command a Confederate blockade-runner—a man known for his steady nerves, great courage, and wily strategies. He was a deft and daring sailor who had never been captured in spite of the fact that he had more blockade-running missions under his belt than many men twice his age.

Unfortunately, Michael Usina was also a man who was currently incapable of finding one simple vessel to transport him and five of his crew to Bermuda. A new ship awaited him there. He could visualize her, sleek and stripped down for speed, painted gray to blend in with twilight seas, sitting low in the water because her holds were already packed full of supplies desperately needed by the Confederacy. Unfortunately, that particular ship was, for the time being, as far out of Usina's reach as the moon.

He took another look at the address he'd just been given. It was his latest lead regarding a ship which might possibly be available for hire, something Usina was beginning to think was a fantasy in Nassau. Of course, this new destination was a fair distance away from where he now stood, and why should he be surprised at that? Usina had been from one end of the bustling city to the other more times than he could remember during his futile search for transport, so what was one more trip across town? Especially if the alternative was to remain high and dry, something Usina never intended to do while there was breath in his body and a seaworthy ship at his disposal.

Thinking of ships, Usina shaded his eyes against the bright tropical sun and glanced toward the water, at a harbor so crowded with vessels that it seemed there was not room for even one more. Appearances notwithstanding, Usina well knew that by nightfall, additional ships would have joined those already clogging the waterway.

He reflected, and not for the first time, that whatever the outcome of this hellacious War between the States, the Bahamas and Bermuda would emerge victorious. Because of the Northern blockade, most of the profitable trade between Britain and the Southern cotton-growing states was funneled through these islands, resulting in a lip-service allegiance to the Confederacy. In truth, the allegiance Usina most often encountered in the islands was to King Profit. The ports abounded with spies and sympathizers from both sides, in addition to a plethora of seafarers and merchants who were always seeking the highest bid.

Usina turned from looking at the water to contemplate the crowded street in front of him, which held no appeal to a seagoing man. He had sought transport the previous day, all morning and part of the afternoon, and the last thing he wanted to do was trudge across town to one more shipyard. In spite of the fact that Usina was weary and discouraged, his companion remained steadfastly optimistic, hurrying on ahead, pausing only now and then to look back as though to censor the Boy Captain for his lack of enthusiasm regarding their current endeavor.

"Tinker!" A burly sailor with a patch over one eye called out to Usina's companion in a tone of voice usually reserved for infants and sweethearts. "It's good to see you, boy—you're looking fine today. Stop and say hello a moment—I think I've got a bit of something here in my pocket for you."

In a town housing a United States consul and teeming with spies, I am known as the man who owns that dog. I might as well wear a sign that advertises my nickname, the name of the ship awaiting me in Bermuda, and the cargo she holds. In spite of these thoughts and in spite of his weariness, Usina made a point to stop and talk pleasantly to the big sailor who was now squatting down on his heels, scratching the little black-and-white dog named Tinker behind the ears. After all, Usina suspected the only reason he had the current lead in his pocket was because of Tinker's popularity, not his own.

The little rat terrier had been left to him by a dying shipmate who expired at sea. Usina first cherished the dog for his original master's sake, but rapidly became attached to Tinker on his own. The dog was fond of the water and used to living on board a ship, so the two became constant companions. It was then that Usina began to learn about the other amazing benefits of sharing Tinker's company.

The little dog seemed able to sense approaching Yankee ships even before they were sighted, and more than once his restlessness had sent Usina's men scurrying to the lookout. When under fire, he would calmly follow Usina's every step as though confident that the outcome could only be a successful one. A blockade-runner's safety boats were always prepared for potential use before attempting a run, and Tinker seemed not only to inspect these preparations, but to know which was the captain's boat in particular, and to give it special attention.

After passing a few words with the sailor who was counted among Tinker's many admirers, Usina and his dog continued on toward their destination. They hadn't gone far before a woman, modestly dressed but obviously in a hurry, attempted to cross the crowded street right in front of Tinker and tripped over him. Usina, cursing under his breath, hurried to catch up, but the woman recovered her balance on her own and stood frozen for a moment staring down at Tinker.

For his part, the little dog stood and looked steadily up at her, panting, obviously taking no responsibility whatsoever for the mishap. Although he was already rehearsing words of apology, Usina had no chance to use them before the woman scooped Tinker up in her arms and broke into tears, standing right there in the middle of the street.

"Miss, I'm sorry," said Usina immediately when he'd caught up with them. He noted youth, golden hair, and large blue eyes even as he glared at the source of this current problem. Tinker returned his master's accusing look without blinking, seeming perfectly content to be clutched to the young woman's ample bosom. Surely it was Usina's imagination that the dog looked smug. As though he could read Usina's thoughts, Tinker had the audacity to turn away and lick a single tear from the young woman's porcelain cheek. "Are you hurt? Can I help in some way?" asked Usina. He wanted to snatch Tinker and shake him, but he didn't want the young woman thinking she was being accosted in the street, in addition to tripping over a nuisance of a dog.

"This poor little animal is running loose," the young woman told Usina in a tearful voice with a trace of an English accent. "I can't bear it—she looks just like my beloved Muffin that I had to leave behind." Tinker looked somewhat disgusted by this speech—surely that was also Usina's imagination—but he also looked as though he had no intention of leaving his present location anytime soon.

Usina took the young woman's elbow and guided her out of the middle of the street to stand in the shade provided by the awning of a boardinghouse. She was a small slip of a girl, with her head barely coming up to his shoulder, and she followed his lead quietly and without protest.

"The dog may well be running loose," Usina admitted when they were safe from being run down in the middle of the street, "but he's not without an owner. His name is Tinker." Usina felt he'd explained enough, but damned if Tinker didn't look at him expectantly. Usina cleared his throat. "He's a male dog, miss," he added.

"And he belongs to you?" asked the young woman breathlessly, as though this were a miracle equal to turning water into wine. Usina felt as if he'd done something very gallant, although he knew he hadn't. At least she'd stopped crying. "I'm sorry, you must think me very foolish," she continued. "But your Tinker looks exactly like my Muffin." She paused to take a shaky breath before explaining further. "My brother put me on a ship out of Key West when he decided to send me home, and the captain was beastly about Muffin—he simply wouldn't allow any dogs on board. But then I missed my ship here, and I've been stranded in this awful place all week looking for another passage. I can't help but think we could have waited for a ship that would let me take my Muffin with me."

The young woman gave no sign of relinquishing her grip on Tinker, and damned if her lower lip wasn't beginning to quiver again. Thoughts of his mother and her relentless belief in Southern manners came unbidden to Usina's mind.

"I'm Phillip Cassidy," said Usina, using his middle name and making up the Cassidy on the spot. "It's been years since I lived in Florida, but that's where I was born." He felt certain that this statement, true as it was, disclosed no important information. Only a fool assumed that birthplace or geography of residence identified one's allegiance in this hell of a war that pitted brother against brother, father against son, and neighbor against neighbor. Usina gestured to the door of the boardinghouse, which advertised that food was available along with lodging. "Please, let me buy you a cup of tea," he said. "I assure you that I am a gentleman, and it's the least I can do, considering it was my dog you tripped over."

"I'm Amanda Kelly," the young woman said, extending one hand while the other continued to cradle Tinker. She seemed to take a good look at Usina for the first time, and he found himself trying to stand up taller and look respectable. Due to these efforts, or perhaps in spite of them, Amanda Kelly must have been reassured by what she saw. She gave a little nod as though she'd made up her mind. "It would be very nice to sit and have a cup of tea," she told him. "The worst thing about being in this place is the loneliness. I miss my brother and Muffin terribly."

Usina held the door open for her, and soon they were settled at a table, sharing a pot of tea. Tinker was content to lay on Amanda Kelly's lap as though he were accustomed to being there, and as though Usina himself were only a casual acquaintance. *Traitor.* Usina gave Miss Kelly a polite smile and lifted a teacup to his lips.

"What brings you to Nassau, Mr. Cassidy?" asked Amanda Kelly. Usina paused, the cup halfway to his mouth, but Miss Kelly immediately answered her own question. "No, don't tell me—I'm sorry I asked. My brother warns me constantly that my curiosity can be a terrible affliction during wartime. I keep forgetting that these days even the most innocent of questions can make people horribly uncomfortable."

"Why not tell me about yourself?" suggested Usina. After all, his mother had always taught him that it was polite to let other people talk about themselves. It suddenly occurred to him that perhaps he owed his mother at least partial credit for being so good at what he did, an amazing thought which he filed away for later. "You sound as though you're English," Usina continued, refraining from remarking that only an English girl could look the way Amanda Kelly looked. "So there must be a story behind your travels. Key West and Nassau are a fair ways from London."

Miss Kelly wrinkled her nose deprecatingly. It was not an unattractive gesture, Usina noted. "A story there may be, but it's not a very exciting one," she told him. "You're right, I'm from England, from a town south of London called Guildford." Being a frequent visitor to various British ports himself, Usina was quite familiar with English geography, but he made no comment. "My brother and I are missionaries," Miss Kelly explained. "We went to Florida to work with the Seminole Indians, my brother to preach and I to teach. See— we make such a good team that we can even describe our work in rhyme." There was an expression on her face that probably started out to be a smile, but didn't quite make it. She shook her head sadly and looked down at Tinker, seemingly at a loss for words.

"What happened?" asked Usina gently.

"The war," said Miss Kelly. "The war is what happened. At first, we ignored all the talk of secession, thinking it was something political, something that would go away, and that it didn't concern us. Then, when the war really did break out, we thought it would soon be over, and that it would hardly affect us since we were English citizens, and so far from the Northern states. I mean, we thought that if we were nowhere near the fighting, the war could come and go without it affecting our work." Miss Kelly looked quite forlorn again, one hand still absently stroking Tinker. Usina decided it was not his imagination—the little dog definitely looked smug.

"That's what most people thought," he told Miss Kelly. Usina recalled the months he had spent recovering from a leg wound received at the battle of Manassas, and how he had been so young and foolish then that he feared the war would be over before he was fit to see action again. Two scant years older but many battles wiser, how he wished his fears of those past days had been realized.

"And how wrong we all were," said Miss Kelly sadly. "The shortages and deprivations have gotten so bad—you can hardly imagine." Usina felt quite certain that he could, but he didn't argue the point. "The Indians were poor enough when we first came, but now we lack even the most basic food, clothes, and medicine. With the living conditions, the growing unrest, and the ever-increasing number of runaway slaves, my brother decided that I should return to England. He is ten years older and our parents are dead, so he is quite protective." Miss Kelly took a deep breath, and Usina felt quite certain she was giving him the shortened version of how the decision had been reached between her and her brother. "So, Mr. Cassidy, that is how I come to be in Nassau, while my brother and Muffin remain behind in the place that I have come to call home."

Usina could hear a quiver in her voice again. "Perhaps your brother and your dog will soon join you in England, or perhaps the war will come to an end and you can return to them," he said quickly, mentally cursing the emptiness of his words.

"Perhaps," Miss Kelly echoed softly, her head bent down again as she continued to stroke Tinker, who had fallen asleep. Then she suddenly looked up, the merest sparkle in her eyes where there had been tears before. "I am tired of being sad and weepy, Mr. Cassidy, and I thank you for your patience with me. I won't ask you any more questions about yourself, I really do know better than that, but maybe you could tell me a little bit about Tinker. I miss Muffin so much, and I can sense a great bond between you and this dog."

Usina wondered how she could sense a bond when Tinker looked as though he would be content to remain in Miss Kelly's lap for the rest of his natural days, but he didn't argue. If it would cheer up Miss Kelly to hear about Tinker, then hear about Tinker she would. Usina carefully edited his words to give no hint about his allegiance or his work, which was common enough, considering the times and their surroundings.

Usina told Miss Kelly how he had come to own Tinker, and how it was known throughout various seas that the dog had never sailed on a ship which came to be captured. He told her how he had once had occasion to leave a ship midjourney, going by boat to another ship, and how one of the passengers had pleaded with him to leave Tinker behind.

"He didn't care a bit that I was leaving the ship, along with several other able-bodied men. I don't think he would have cared if the captain and the whole crew left the ship. This man only cared that Tinker stay on board," Usina told Miss Kelly, and was rewarded by a musical laugh. "I even scolded the man, saying that I had come to know him somewhat during the voyage, and that I did not take him to be one to harbor ignorant superstitions. He remained adamant in his desire to have Tinker remain with him, and he was quite indignant when I took the dog with me by boat to board the other ship."

"What an influential little fellow you are," Miss Kelly said to Tinker, who briefly opened one eye and then closed it again.

"That's not even the end of the story," Usina protested. "I happened to learn some months later that that very ship was captured two days after Tinker and I left."

"No," said Miss Kelly. "That is too much to believe—you must be teasing me now, Mr. Cassidy."

"I swear upon my honor it is a true story," replied Usina. "And one that others can attest to. Not long after this incident, a merchant, a Captain Green, came to me and offered me five hundred dollars in gold, simply to let him have Tinker for just one voyage."

"Five hundred dollars in gold?" asked Miss Kelly, her eyes widening in amazement. She was a missionary, Usina reminded himself. Perhaps she was thinking about what five hundred dollars in gold could buy for starving Indians. "Whatever did you tell him?" Usina decided that Miss Kelly must be caught up in the excitement of the story, for her voice sounded breathless again.

"I told him, 'Green, there are two fools here, you and I both,' but I did not let him have the dog. Do not think me selfish—there are others who have profited from their association with Tinker."

"And who would those be?" asked Miss Kelly, her blue eyes dancing, which was much preferable to seeing them full of tears. "Seafaring passengers who band together and pay you to travel with them, simply so that they will have the protection of this noble animal?"

"He's not noble enough to avoid a lady's feet, obviously," Usina reminded her. "No, Tinker and I haven't lowered ourselves to profiting from the superstitions of others. But there is a photographer in Bermuda who asked relentlessly for permission to take Tinker's picture, and I finally said yes. I hear that the man has made a fair sum from the sale of the photographs."

Miss Kelly laughed again and Usina felt quite proud of himself. He was so engrossed in their conversation that he didn't notice a man approach their table until he was standing over them. "Shall I take a picture of you and your lady, sir?" the man asked. He was tall and thin and Usina thought he looked quite ghoulish. "It would make a fine souvenir," the man added as Usina stared up at him, momentarily speechless with surprise.

Amanda Kelly turned a becoming shade of red. "We're just friends," said Usina shortly, recovering his powers of speech.

" 'Twould make a fine souvenir of your friendship, in that case," the man persisted.

"Would you really mind so much?" Miss Kelly asked then, surprising Usina even more than the appearance of the cadaverous photographer. "I have nothing to remind me of Muffin, I had to leave so quickly. I have money—" she added, reaching for her bag.

Usina put his hand over hers. Was she really so foolish as to make a remark like that? "Leave us for a minute," he told the photographer.

"As you wish," said the man, and withdrew to a table in the corner. Usina wondered if he had been there when they walked through the door. For the life of him, he could not remember, and it made him angry at himself. A man in his position could not afford to get careless in the practice of observing those around him.

"You must not say things like that in a place like this, about having money on your person," he told Miss Kelly sternly. "No good will come of it." She started to say something but he squeezed her hand to keep her from interrupting. He wanted to get the next part over with. "And although you said you would ask no questions, and although I have greatly enjoyed our conversation together, I must tell you that I am a married man, Miss Kelly."

It was true enough. The dark-haired Camilla had been his friend since childhood and his wife for the last year. She was his one and only true love, but still, right now, she was so very far away. Camilla had a will of her own, and she had not yet yielded to his pleas for her to come and live with family friends in Nassau, that he might see her more often. So it logically followed that it was Camilla who was responsible for the fact that it had been more than two months since Usina had last seen his wife. He hadn't quite reasoned out whether it was also Camilla's fault that he was entranced by Miss Kelly, but he figured that it didn't matter much. He would have to be dead in his grave to be immune to the unconscious charms of the woman sitting across from him, as different from Camilla as night from day.

"And you must not mistake me," said Miss Kelly, speaking low and urgently. "I have left behind everything that I love and hold dear, and you are the one person in this godforsaken place who has taken any interest in me or shown me any kindness. I am soon to make a long sea voyage by myself, and you tell me that Tinker has some lucky charm about him for preventing a ship from being captured. A man believed so much in this that he offered you five hundred dollars in gold for the dog, yet you turned him down. They say that a picture is worth a thousand words. It would please me so to have such a picture to keep me company on my journey, yet I have only one word to offer in return."

"And what would that one word be?" asked Usina, fascinated by the intensity he saw in Miss Kelly's bottomless blue eyes.

"Please," she said simply, and Usina knew that he was lost.

"Very well," he told her, "but only upon one condition—that I pay for the photograph. After all, you seem to keep forgetting that the same animal you hold now is the one who almost caused you to fall in a busy street."

"Tripping over Tinker may be the luckiest thing that has happened to me since I came to Nassau," replied Miss Kelly. "You spoil me, Mr. Cassidy. First a cup of tea and then a photograph. I may have to start looking for other dogs to trip over."

"But then you would have to be the kind of person you are not," said Usina gallantly, motioning to the photographer. He intended to purchase a photograph of Miss Kelly and Tinker only, but somehow they all ended up in the picture together. Miss Kelly was so pleased, she told Usina she felt certain that their meeting meant a change of luck for them both. Usina wrote down the names of some people she could contact regarding passage to London, and they parted amiably a short while later, with Tinker grudgingly giving up his place in Miss Kelly's lap to follow his master. There had been a reversal in roles, for as they walked out onto the street and bade Miss Kelly farewell, it was Tinker who looked discouraged.

When they reached their destination, he began to think that Miss Kelly might be right about a change in his luck. Within the hour he chartered an English schooner to take him and his men to Bermuda the very next morning. Never mind that the captain of the schooner *Royal* was dead drunk before dinnertime, it was the ship itself that mattered. If need be, Usina could captain it himself.

He was to remember these very thoughts sixty miles into their journey, when at daylight one morning, Tinker came to alert and soon after, Usina sighted the Yankee ship-of-war *Shenandoah*. She wasted no time in coming alongside. "What schooner is that, where from and where bound?" called an officer imperiously from the *Shenandoah*'s deck.

The captain of the *Royal* was the one who should be giving the answers, but he was down below, sleeping off the drinks of the previous evening. "This is the schooner *Royal*, bound from Nassau to Bermuda," shouted Usina, careful to stay within the shadows of the upper deck.

"Lower a boat and come on board," the officer ordered.

"I'll see you in hell first," muttered Usina. He told his men to remember that they were passengers and so they damn well better act like passengers. Then he headed below to rouse their worthless captain and get him to raise the English flag. This endeavor took about twenty minutes, the same amount of time it took the *Shenandoah* to bring an armed boat alongside and put four men on board the *Royal*.

A very young lieutenant was in charge, and he made a great show of examining the *Royal*'s papers. He finally proclaimed them to be in order, as Usina knew he must, since he himself had been over them in detail before ever leaving Nassau. The Yankee lieutenant was preparing to depart, but he wasn't going about it very quickly, and Usina couldn't leave well enough alone. He was curious as to why a ship-of-war such as the *Shenandoah* would bother itself with a lowly schooner like the *Royal*.

Usina stepped forward. "I apologize for our captain's lack of manners," he said to the lieutenant. "I am only a passenger on board, but I can offer you a glass of wine in my cabin before you return to your ship."

The young lieutenant looked at Usina a long moment before answering. "I don't suppose I should," he said finally, "but I reckon that I will."

Usina showed the man to his cabin where Tinker now lay watching the proceedings from the berth, giving one low growl to acknowledge the presence of a Yankee. The two men drank mostly in silence for a while, but after a little wine, the young officer became more talkative. "Was it you who answered our hail?" he asked suddenly.

"Yes," Usina admitted, thinking this was a strange question to ask. "Our captain was indisposed at the moment."

The Yankee took another drink of his wine. "I thought it was you," he said.

This seemed a strange response from someone Usina had never met before. "What do you know about me?" he asked.

Again the man paused before answering. "I know enough to surprise you," he said finally.

"That is something no one has ever done yet," replied Usina recklessly. After all, he was on an English ship, and this man had no authority over him.

"Would it surprise you for me to tell you that your name is Michael Usina?" the Yankee officer asked suddenly.

"You are mistaken—my name is Phillip Cassidy," said Usina, the same name he had given Amanda Kelly coming easily to mind.

It was as though Usina had never spoken. "The man sitting on the rail near you when I came on board, he is your man Irvin," continued the Yankee officer. "He is a slave you own and your leadsman. He is devoted to you."

"Does wine usually affect you this way?" asked Usina.

"You know that I am giving it to you straight." The Yankee took care in pronouncing each word.

"You are badly mixed up," said Usina kindly, pouring the man some more wine.

The Yankee emptied his glass again before replying. "Will you still think I am mixed up when I tell you that the little Frenchman on board is John Sassard, your chief engineer, and that the redheaded fellow is Nelson, your chief officer? Two others are your men also, although I don't remember their names at the moment. You are Michael Usina, called the Boy Captain, a master of blockade-running, and you are going to Bermuda to take charge of a new ship."

"Perhaps you had better not have any more wine," Usina told the Yankee, but the man reached out and poured another glass for himself, then looked around the cabin as though in search of something else to identify. "And that," he said, pointing at the berth, "is your dog Tinker." Tinker acknowledged his name with another faint growl. The Yankee then reached into his pocket and produced a photograph of Tinker, Usina, and the lovely Amanda Kelly. "What say you about this, Phillip Cassidy?" the Yankee asked with a sudden grin.

"That is a picture taken with an English missionary returning home—a young woman who was lonely for her brother and the dog she had left behind, a dog that resembled mine," said Usina, falling somewhat short of his goal of sounding indignant.

"Hah!" said the Yankee, starting to laugh. "That's rich, the idea of Liz as a missionary—and I can assure you that she's not missing anyone's company. The photographer who took this picture has been her partner for quite some time, and I understand that he's her lover as well." The officer turned the photograph over on the table right in front of Usina so that he could see his own detailed history written neatly on the back. "Will you acknowledge that I am right, now?"

"What does it matter?" asked Usina. "Even if I am the man you claim me to be, I am under the protection of Her Most Gracious Majesty, and there is nothing you can do about it."

The Yankee narrowed his eyes. "You may be under the protection of Her Most Gracious Majesty right now, but tomorrow is another day. I have come close to you before, closer than you could ever imagine, and I promise to capture you before long."

" 'Close' does not count any more tomorrow than it does today," replied Usina, bidding a private farewell to the memory of a sweet and innocent English missionary.

"We shall see," said the Yankee, still going to great pains to speak carefully. "You can be assured that this picture will adorn the rogues' gallery in Ludlow Street Jail in New York City. There it will stay, until you and the others posted there find yourselves behind bars where you belong."

"So there are copies of this picture?" asked Usina.

"Of course," said the Yankee expansively. "You don't think that we'd go to such pains to get your picture unless we made great use of it, do you? Liz's services don't come cheaply, I can tell you, so we have to have a care about who we send her to find. But don't look so downcast, you are not the first to fall for her schemes. So far, only your Captain Coxetter has resisted her charms and steadfastly refused to have his picture taken."

Usina had never been particularly fond of Coxetter, whom he thought to be too humorless and authoritarian, but his opinion of the man had just risen considerably. "If you have other copies of this picture," said Usina, "then I'd like to buy this one from you."

"Why? Whatever for?" The Yankee looked truly befuddled by Usina's offer.

"I'd like to have it as a souvenir, just like the photographer said when I paid him to take the picture. I'll give you a ten-dollar gold piece for it."

The Yankee seemed to think a moment, then laughed. "I can't see what harm it would do," he said. "If you're thinking to warn your mates about Liz, I can tell you that you'd never recognize her if you saw her again—she's that good." He looked down at the picture one more time. "I certainly have others where this one came from," he said. Usina gave him his gold piece and another glass of wine. They parted on great terms of drunken friendship on the Yankee's part, with the man swearing to treat Usina well when the day came that he captured him, while Usina swore to himself that day would never come.

Worth a Thousand Words ✠ 145

Usina remained in his cabin after the Yankee left, contemplating the picture in front of him. "What happened to your gift for warning me when Yankees are about?" he asked Tinker. The dog looked at him silently. "Are you saying that she's not a Yankee, that she's a free agent hiring out her services? Or are you saying that you were taken in by that blonde hair and those blue eyes when she picked you up off the street?" Tinker, the soul of discretion, did not deign to reply. Usina lifted his wineglass in a solitary farewell toast to the nonexistent Amanda Kelly.

"One can never be too careful in these troubled times," Usina told Tinker. "And to remind me of that, this picture is worth a thousand words."

Tinker gave a mighty sigh in apparent agreement. Then, since there were no longer any Yankees near and no shots were being fired, he closed his eyes and went to sleep, the perfect picture of a loyal companion.

[Note: With the exception of "Amanda Kelly" and her photographer companion, all the characters in this story are historical figures, including Tinker. All the incidents related in the story, with the exception of the meeting with "Amanda Kelly," are based on real events.]

Bill Crider is the author of the Sheriff Dan Rhodes series, the first book of which won the Anthony Award in 1987. Crider's short stories have appeared in numerous anthologies, including *Holmes for the Holidays* and all the books in the celebrated *Cat Crimes* mystery anthology series.

Here he takes a humorous look at how the exploits of one of the Confederacy's most famous and successful spies, Belle Boyd, might have been immortalized on film.

Belle Boyd, the Rebel Spy (A Proposal for a Republic Serial)

Bill Crider

EDITOR'S NOTE: *I am an inveterate buyer of movie memorabilia at online auction houses. When I had a chance to bid on an "uninspected box of movie-related material, c. 1940s," I couldn't resist. The previous bids were low, and there was always the chance of getting a real treasure, a* Casablanca *lobby card, say, or an autographed wedding photo of Carole Lombard and Clark Gable. I won the box, but it turned out to be a disappointment, containing nothing of much interest other than the yellowing typescript reproduced below, a proposal for a Republic serial that appears to be very loosely based on the no-doubt considerably sensationalized memoirs of Belle Boyd, a notorious Confederate spy during the Civil War. I checked numerous reference books in the hope of finding that the serial had actually been produced, thus increasing the paltry value of the anonymous manuscript, but I could find no record of it. I offer it here, then, for whatever historical interest it may have for readers who recall Hollywood's younger days.*

—BILL CRIDER

Belle Boyd: Linda Stirling
Stonewall Jackson: Robert Livingston
General Beauregard: Jack Holt
Major Huckabee: Lionel Atwill
Rogan: Roy Barcroft
The Rattler: ??

ONE

⬒

The Siren of the Shenandoah

ESTABLISHING SHOT: A brick building in Washington, D.C. The
   Capitol is in the distant background. The date 1861 is superimposed
   on the screen.
CUT TO: The interior of the building.

The men in the blue uniforms of the Union army paid little or no attention to
the homely servant woman who was using her mop and pail to clean the room
in which they sat smoking their black cheroots and discussing their plans to
drive the Confederates out of Virginia.

"I believe," said one, smoke wreathing his head, "that we must begin to
march on to Richmond at once. The secessionist army is weak at Bull Run,
and we can easily rout them."

"But General McDowell," said another, a younger man with curling black
hair, "we hadn't planned to begin our advance quite so soon."

"All the more reason to begin now," McDowell said decisively, gesturing
emphatically with his cheroot. "The Confederates will be unprepared, and there
will be no time for them to bring up reinforcements."

"I see," the other man replied. "So we will march on July sixteenth, then."

McDowell nodded, and other heads nodded in wise agreement. No one
took any notice when the serving woman set her pail down in a corner and
stood the mop beside it. They were so engrossed in their conversation and their

grandiose plans that they hardly heard the opening and closing of the door as she left the room.

CUT TO: A woman galloping on horseback along a trail through the woods. The horse's hooves pound hollowly on the trail. A close-up of the rider reveals that it is the serving woman.

She did not see the Union pickets sitting under the tall tree until she was almost upon them.

"Halt!" one of the soldiers cried, leaping to his feet. He was so surprised by the rider's sudden appearance that he failed to pick up his rifle.

The woman didn't stop. Instead she ignored his warnings and put the spurs to her horse's sides, urging it forward at even greater speed.

The soldier scrambled aboard his horse, shouting to his companion, "It's Belle Boyd, the Siren of the Shenandoah! No other woman could ride like that! You must go and tell the general!"

With that, he was away in pursuit of the swiftly vanishing rider. Drawing his Dragoon Colt, he began to fire, with never a thought that it was a woman under his gun. Had he considered her sex at all, he would have dismissed any thoughts of gallantry. From the point of view of the Union, Belle Boyd was the most dangerous woman alive, a spy who, though the war was hardly begun, had already begun to make a reputation for foiling the Union's plans.

The second soldier mounted his horse and rode in the opposite direction, back toward Washington to warn the general that the Siren was on the run. What good that would do, he had no idea, but he knew his duty.

Belle Boyd smiled fiercely as she rode. Once more she was engaged in the kind of action that thrilled her to her marrow. She never felt so alive as when she was pitting herself against the Northern enemy.

A bullet whistled over her head, tearing a branch from a tree.

Belle was only momentarily shocked. She should have known the Yankees would shoot a woman without compunction. They had no sense of chivalry. She, too, had a pistol, but she would not raise it unless she was desperate. That was not likely to happen, she thought.

Just at that moment, however, another soldier appeared, not more than a hundred yards in front of her. There were others with him, though Belle could not tell how many. At least three, she thought. It was not entirely unexpected. She had known the dangers; she knew that she was circling the flank of Mc-Dowell's army, so it was likely there would be pickets set.

She yanked the reins and turned off the trail and into the trees, a dangerous tactic. She gave the mare its head and hoped that it would not run into a tree trunk. She could hear behind her the hammering of hooves as her pursuers followed her into the woods.

All of them must have had pistols, for the bullets fairly filled the air around and above her. The gunshots soon drowned out the sound of hooves, and it was a wonder that she remained untouched. The firing was continuous. It was almost as if the pistols never had to be reloaded.

She leaned close to the mare's neck and whispered endearments into the horse's ear. But the great-hearted animal could go no faster and had already run far. The soldiers were gaining.

Belle raised up and looked over her shoulder. The trees were momentarily screening her from the soldiers' sight, and just ahead of her a thick, low branch hung out over the trail.

With amazing agility, she stood in the saddle. Arriving at the branch, she reached up and grasped it in both hands, holding tightly to it as the mare continued to gallop ahead. With the lithe dexterity of a circus performer, Belle pulled herself up onto the branch and hid herself among the thick leaves just as the soldiers came into sight. They passed rapidly beneath her perch without an upward glance.

Belle sat on the limb with a smile on her face as the horsemen thundered on through the woods. When the sound of their horses had faded into the distance, she gave a whistle, and her mare came walking out of the trees. Belle dropped lightly onto the horse's back and rode calmly back toward the trail she had been following before her journey was so rudely interrupted.

But her calm ride was not to last for long. The Union soldiers had left a man behind them to guard the trail. When Belle emerged from the trees, he kicked his horse into motion and charged after her.

Belle implored the mare to run, and the horse responded. Horse and rider soared over the ground, clods of earth flying up from the mare's hooves.

CUT TO: The bridge over Bull Run. General Beauregard has destroyed most of the bridge; only fragments of it remain, though to anyone approaching rapidly, the balustrades at either end might appear to be intact.

CUT TO: Belle Boyd, riding at full gallop toward the demolished bridge.

Belle knew that if she could get to the other side of the river the Union soldier would be thwarted, unless he wanted to be taken prisoner by the Confederates camped in wait on the other side. She looked back over her shoulder and realized that she had enough of a lead on him to accomplish her goal. Knowing that victory was hers, she smiled.

Her smile changed to a grimace of shock and dismay when she turned and saw the remains of what had once been a fine wooden structure. She thought briefly of hauling back on the reins and trying to stop the racing mare, but if she did, the soldier would have her.

And then it was too late to do anything at all. Her smile returned as she and the horse sailed out into the void.

Two

#

A Watery Grave!

Belle's smile turned to a grimace of shock and dismay when she saw the remains of what had once been a fine wooden bridge across the Bull Run. It was too late to stop the racing mare, and after only a few more hurtling strides, the two of them plunged over the bank and fell through the rushing air.

When she struck the water, Belle sank straight down like a stone. Her dark hair came undone and swirled in the rushing current as she began to fight her way to the surface.

When she broke through, gasping for air, the Union soldier atop the bank began to fire at her. The noise of his rifle gave notice to the Confederate troops that something was amiss, and they ran from their tents to see. It was only a matter of time before they brought their own rifles to bear on their enemy, whose bravery was unquestioned. He stood calmly in the face of their bullets, trying to end the career of Belle Boyd before she betrayed the Union's secrets to secessionist ears yet again.

But his efforts were in vain. Struck by a minié ball, he dropped his rifle, clutched his breast, and pitched over the edge of the chasm and into the waters below.

Belle saw little of this, as she was swimming strongly to the opposite bank. She had hardly reached it before eager hands reached for her and drew her dripping from the fast-flowing stream.

"General Beauregard," Belle said. "I must see him at once."

"Right away, ma'am," a private said.

Belle smiled at him, and he blushed shyly. He could hardly have been more than sixteen.

"Follow me, ma'am," he said, and led the way through the gaping soldiers, as a whisper went through the troops, letting everyone know that they were in the presence of the Siren of the Shenandoah.

The private stopped in front of the general's tent and pulled aside the flap. Belle stepped inside, her riding clothes and her hair already nearly completely dry. She no longer looked like a homely serving woman; in fact, she was quite lovely.

"Hello, General," she said.

General Beauregard and another officer that Belle didn't recognize stood to greet her.

"Hello, Miss Boyd," the courtly Beauregard said. "Allow me to introduce my aide-de-camp, Major Huckabee."

"A pleasure," Huckabee said suavely, bowing over Belle's hand.

In spite of his charming manner, there was something Belle disliked about the major, though he was handsome enough, with a thin mustache and dark eyes.

"You appear to have had a bit of a hard time of it," General Beauregard said.

"Not as hard a time as the Yankees will have on July sixteenth."

The general smiled, knowing that once again Belle had information that would prove useful to him.

"Why that day?" he asked.

"Because that's the day they will march on Manassas."

Huckabee frowned, but the general's smile grew wider.

"Are you certain of that?"

"I'm certain, all right. I heard it from the mouth of General McDowell himself."

"My dear, you are a wonder," Beauregard said. "I know you put your life in great danger, but the information is worth its weight in gold. I'll send for reinforcements right away, and we'll drive the Yankees from the field. They'll never expect us to be prepared for them. The South owes you a great debt, and its sons and daughters should laud you from the rooftops."

Belle smiled. "Fame and fortune mean nothing to me, General. I expect no payment, and I certainly don't need lauding. The Yankees know far too much about me already."

"That part, at least, is true," Beauregard said. "Your exploits have put you at risk even when you aren't engaged in spying. What do you plan to do now?"

Belle looked thoughtful. "I would like to spend a little time with my family, if possible. I want to lull the North into believing that I've retired from the spying trade."

"They may have a hard time believing that, my dear."

"I'll give them every reason to believe it's true, however. Can you furnish me with an escort?"

"Certainly. But I'm afraid I don't have any clothing that would befit your true station."

"I can manage for that later," Belle said. "For now, a good meal would do."

"That," said the general, "can be provided. See to it, Major."

"Yes, sir," Huckabee responded.

CUT TO: Stock footage of a Civil War battle scene. A Confederate private cries out, "Rally around General Jackson, boys! Look at him standing there, like a stone wall!"

CUT TO ESTABLISHING SHOT: The entrance to a cave, partially hidden by trees. It is night.

CUT TO: An interior chamber of the cave, extremely well lit by torches placed in sconces around the walls. There is a wooden table in the center of the chamber, around which are seated five men. Other men are standing around the walls. At the head of the table in a thronelike chair sits the Rattler, wearing a cloth mask that covers his entire face except for eyes and mouth. The figure of a coiled rattler decorates the mask's forehead.

"Belle Boyd must be stopped!" the Rattler exclaimed, striking the table with a gloved fist. "As you know, I plan to own every plantation in the South once the Northern army has conquered it. I can buy them for a pittance. But if Belle Boyd continues to provide information like that which caused the North's terrible defeat at Bull Run, I'll be ruined!"

"What do you want us to do about it, boss?" asked a burly man seated near the Rattler.

"I'll tell you what I want you to do, Rogan," the Rattler said. "I happen to know that she is on her way to Richmond to stay with her family. But she won't get there. Someone informed on her, and she'll be arrested in Front Royal and confined in the private home where General Shields is quartered. I want you to go to Front Royal and burn that house to the ground!"

"But what about the general?" Rogan asked.

"You'll be posing as Rebel raiders. If anything happens to the general or his men, the Northern soldiers will be that much more determined to wipe out the Rebels."

"Pretty smart," Rogan said, stroking his chin and nodding. "But what if Belle Boyd gets out of the house?"

"It's your job to make sure that she doesn't. Understand?"

"I get it," Rogan said, and the other men at the table nodded.

"Good," the Rattler said. "Now get going. And don't fail me!"

CUT TO: Shot of men riding hard from the mouth of the cave.

CUT TO: Shot of men riding along a dark trail.

CUT TO: The interior of a house. Belle Boyd, dressed as a Southern lady, is talking to General Shields.

"I must demand that you detain me here no longer," Belle said. "You must give me a pass through your lines at once, so that I can reach my family in Richmond. My mother is expecting me there."

General Shields, a tall Irishman with a military bearing, smiled at her.

"Ah, sure, and you do not believe that I would give you over to the none-too-tender mercies of General Jackson and his army," he said. "Did you know that they're calling him 'Stonewall' now?"

Belle smiled flirtatiously. "I know what worries you, General. You're afraid I might have heard things from some of the handsome soldiers who've paid me so much kind attention these last few days and that I might reveal what I've heard to General Jackson, in the unlikely event that our paths should happen to cross. But never fear. I would never betray a confidence."

"Of course not!" Shields said with a smile. "Everyone knows that Belle Boyd would never help the Rebels in any way. But those 'handsome soldiers,' as you call them, may have revealed too much. It is easy to see why some call you 'La Belle Rebelle.' "

"Why thank you, General," Belle said, with a mock curtsy.

The general's face sobered. "But even if you could or would tell, it would do you no good. General Jackson will soon be running back to his home, and all his soldiers with him. We have great plans for General 'Stonewall' Jackson."

"And what might those plans be, if I may be so bold as to ask?"

General Shields looked at her and then burst out laughing.

"You are a bold one, all right! You are the boldest woman that I've ever met. To come right out and ask me for my plans like that! No man I know would have dared."

"Then more shame to them," Belle said.

"You have a great heart, Miss Boyd, but you will never help those Rebels again. And now I must ask you to retire to your room. I have a meeting with my subordinates and we will be discussing things not for your ears."

Belle said nothing more. She turned and left the room, going up the stairs to the bedroom set aside for her. As soon as she was inside, she locked the door, then moved swiftly to the closet, where she pushed aside a heavy trunk to reveal a small crack in the floor. Quickly she knelt and looked through the crack. Satisfied with what she saw, she turned to the trunk, opened it, and reached under some clothing to pull out a pencil and paper. She then leaned down to watch and listen at the crack in the floor.

CUT TO: Shot of the room below as seen through the crack in the floor.
General Shields is talking to his officers.

"But how can we prevent General Jackson from taking back the town?" one of the officers asked.

"Simple," Shields said. "We'll blow up the bridges, like McDowell did at Bull Run. We have plenty of time. Jackson knows nothing of our plans."

CUT TO: Shot of Belle writing feverishly on her piece of paper.
CUT TO: Shot of the raiders entering Front Royal, guns blazing. They ride down the street and attack the house where General Shields is quartered. Soldiers pour out of the house and begin returning fire.

"Get those torches lit!" Rogan yelled.

His horse reared up, and he fired a shot into the chest of a Union soldier, who crumpled in the doorway of the house.

Rogan's men began riding around the house, trampling the picket fence in front and the roses growing in the bed. They smashed out windows and put the torches to the curtains, then tossed them inside.

One of the men was shot out of the saddle in the act of throwing his torch to the roof, but another was right behind and succeeded where the other had failed. The wood-shingled roof began to burn immediately. The flames spread so quickly it was as if the entire house was made of tinder.

CUT TO: Belle's bedroom. Smoke is swirling all around and flames are licking around the window. As Belle watches, the window glass cracks like the sound of a pistol shot. Belle puts the paper on which she's been writing into the bosom of her dress and runs to unlock the door.

Belle opened the door. The hallway was full of smoke, and the entire house was burning. The stairway at the end of the hall was the only way out. Belle started toward it and saw through the smoke that someone was trying to climb the stairs to rescue her.

"This way, Miss Boyd," the man called out, but just as he did, the stairway collapsed beneath him, dropping him into the flames below.

Belle took another step forward, even though the stairway was no longer there. As she did, the ceiling near the stairs fell downward in a cloud of flame and smoke.

Shielding her face from the intense heat, Belle backed down the hallway to her room and went inside.

She appeared to be trapped. The stairway was gone, and even if she could reach the window, it was two stories above the ground.

But it was the only way out. As she started toward it, she looked up to see the entire roof of the house disintegrate above her. With a look of horror on her face, she disappeared into the fiery explosion of timbers, ash, and smoke.

THREE

✷

Flaming Doom!

ESTABLISHING SHOT: Armed raiders surround the home where Belle Boyd is being held under house arrest. They are firing at Union soldiers who have come out of the house and are throwing torches through windows. One man throws a torch onto the roof, which bursts into flame.

Belle Boyd placed a piece of paper in the bosom of her dress and looked at the flames licking around the window of her room. The window glass shattered like the sound of a pistol shot. Belle hurried into the hallway, but as she approached the stairway, the ceiling collapsed downward in a cloud of fire and smoke. She backed toward her room, shielding her face with her arm.

Inside the room, she looked around. She appeared to be trapped. The house was two stories tall, and the stairway was gone. The window was her only hope.

As she started toward it, the entire roof of the house crumbled to pieces above her. She did not slow her steps, even as she seemed to vanish into the explosion.

Burning timbers crashed to the floor behind her as she leaped through the window.

Luck favors the bold. One of Rogan's riders was just below the window, and Belle landed behind him on the horse's back, her crinoline skirts billowing all around.

The astonished rider hardly had time to realize what was happening as Belle threw him from the saddle, grabbed up the reins, and assumed his place. She kicked her heels into the horse's side, and it responded by leaping forward, clearing the remains of the picket fence and racing into the street.

Rogan saw the fleeing horse with the woman on its back, and his mouth dropped open in astonishment.

"Get after her, boys!" he yelled, wheeling his horse around. "It's Belle Boyd! We have to stop her!"

The raiders who heard him spun, turned their horses' heads, and galloped off in pursuit of the Siren of the Shenandoah, Rogan in the lead. Though they fired at her repeatedly, their shots all harmlessly passed her by.

As she rode, Belle tore away her crinolines, exposing the lacy bloomers beneath. Modesty was not nearly as important now as escaping from the men whose pistols were blasting away at her from behind.

The raiders trampled her skirts into the dust of the street in their pursuit, but they were getting no closer as Belle passed by houses and stores that seemed to blur with the speed of her horse.

She had begun to pull away when she looked up and saw in front of her a group of Union soldiers, alerted by the shooting. With their rifles at the ready, they completely blocked her passage.

With the soldiers in front and the raiders behind, Belle was trapped between them and appeared to have no hope of escape. Of course the Federals were more interested in the raiders than in her, she was certain, so all she had to do was make sure the two groups had clear shots at each other without her being in between.

She pulled back strongly on the reins, jerking her horse to a stop. Then she turned its head toward a narrow alley, dug her heels into its sides, and dashed away.

The soldiers engaged the raiders in a pitched battle, and the only one to follow Belle into the alley was Rogan, who fired shot after shot at the fleeing Siren, his bullets chipping wood from the buildings all around her but never touching either her or her mount.

When Belle judged she was safely past the Union soldiers, she turned back toward the street, and, when she reached it, she once again made a run for the countryside.

She was almost at the edge of town when her horse stumbled.

Belle flew over the horse's neck, did a somersault in midair, and landed on her feet. Seeing that Rogan was almost upon her, she turned and ran for the nearest building, which appeared to be a barn or livery stable.

Her horse struggled upright and ran away riderless, but Rogan wasn't fooled. He'd seen where Belle had gone, and when he reached the spot, he jumped from his horse and ran in after her.

CUT TO: The darkened interior of the building, where Belle Boyd, dressed in bloomers and top, locates a lantern and matches sitting atop a barrel. When she lights the lantern, the entire scene appears nearly as bright as day, and Belle is astonished to discover that she has by accident stumbled into the very place where General Shields is storing his munitions. There are numerous barrels bearing labels reading *"Gunpowder,"* boxes labeled *"Dynamite,"* and other boxes that clearly hold rifles and ammunition.

Belle set the lantern down on the barrel. Hearing a noise behind her, she turned and looked around. The door of the barn opened, and Rogan entered, his pistol drawn, a smile creasing his rugged face. He looked her over slowly, his eyes moving from her bare shoulders to her narrow waist and on down to her ankles.

"Not bad," he said appreciatively. "For a spy. But it looks like this is the end of the line for the Siren of the Shenandoah."

"Maybe not," Belle said, her hand moving toward a hay hook lying beside the lantern on the barrel. "Look!"

She pointed at the door with her left hand, and Rogan began to turn. He was distracted just long enough for her to reach the hook.

"You can't fool me," Rogan said, whipping his head back around.

When he did, he saw the hook flying toward him, and Belle was sprinting for the ladder that led to the hayloft.

Rogan turned aside, but the hook nevertheless struck him a glancing blow on the side of the face, causing him to fire his pistol into the hard-packed floor.

By the time he recovered, Belle was in the hayloft, reaching for a pitchfork. She snatched it out of the hay and threw it down at Rogan, who sidestepped it neatly, getting off two quick shots that made holes in the roof but didn't come close to Belle.

Rogan straightened and fired two more shots, but Belle was by that time concealed behind bales of hay. The bullets thudded into the bales in front of her, and Rogan started for the ladder.

When he began to climb, Belle came out of concealment.

"The Rattler will be glad to hear I've killed you," Rogan said, pausing midway up the ladder. "You'll never pass another Federal secret to the Southern army."

"The Rattler?" Belle said. "Who's the Rattler?"

"Never mind that. Even if I knew the answer, it wouldn't do you any good. Dead men tell no tales. Dead women, either."

He triggered a shot that barely missed Belle as she made a dive for the ladder. She slid forward on the floor of the loft, and before Rogan could shoot again, Belle pushed the ladder backward. It balanced precariously for a moment, then began to rock as Rogan tried to steady it. But he was unable to do so, and he and the ladder fell to the floor of the barn.

Rogan landed on his back, losing both his breath and his pistol.

Belle jumped for a loosely hanging rope and swung to the floor, landing lightly on her feet near the pistol, which she scooped up.

But she had not counted on Rogan coming to himself so quickly and finding the hay hook so conveniently near him. As she turned to face him, he threw the hook, striking the hand that held the pistol.

Belle dropped the gun and Rogan launched himself toward her, driving his head into her stomach and knocking her backward. She hit the floor hard, her fingers scrabbling for the pistol, though she had no idea where it had fallen.

Rogan knew. He was scooting toward it in a rapid crawl.

Belle flipped to her feet and kicked the pistol out of Rogan's reach. He grabbed her ankle and jerked her feet out from under her.

This time when she fell, she struck the back of her head on the floor and was momentarily dazed.

Rogan stepped over her and reached down for the pistol.

Belle raised her head and saw what he was doing. She planted a foot against his backside and gave a strong push, sending him ankles over elbows. He was brought up short when he hit a stack of rifle boxes.

He appeared stunned, and Belle made a break for the door. If Rogan's horse was outside, she could still get away.

Rogan stood up, shaking his head to clear it. He saw the pistol, picked it up, and fired three rapid shots at Belle's fleeing figure.

"Stop right there," he said, "or I'll ventilate you."

Belle stopped and turned to face him.

"You're a Southerner," she said. "And yet you'd shoot a woman?"

"I'd shoot anybody the Rattler told me to. I wouldn't want the Rattler mad at me. What he'd do would be worse than shooting a woman."

"But why me?"

"You're messing with the Rattler's plans. He wants the South to lose this war. That's all I know, and it's more than you need to know, since you're as good as dead."

"We'll see about that," Belle said.

She broke to her right and used a gunpowder keg as a stepping-stone to reach the top of a row of dynamite boxes. She ran along the boxes with Rogan firing at her all the way.

"Hit this dynamite and we're both dead!" Belle said.

"Better than having the Rattler kill me for letting you get away!" Rogan replied, firing again and again.

As she came to the end of the row, Belle once again saw the rope. She jumped for it, grabbing hold and propelling herself directly at Rogan.

Just before her feet struck him in the face, Rogan got off a lucky shot that parted the rope. He ducked aside as Belle sailed past him and smashed into the barrel where the lantern sat.

The lantern flew into the air and crashed to the floor, sending an oily layer of flames sliding in every direction.

Rogan didn't waste time shooting at Belle. Instead he blasted away at several gunpowder kegs, shattering their sides. The gray gunpowder leaked onto the floor.

When the fire ignited the gunpowder and blew the dynamite, the barn was going to be a hell on Earth. Rogan ran for the door as fast as his legs could pump him.

Belle lay stunned on the floor as the flames licked around her. Her eyes were closed, and she appeared not to see as the flames drew ever closer to the gunpowder.

CUT TO: The street outside the barn. Rogan mounts his horse and begins to ride furiously. Before he has gone far, there is a tremendous explosion behind him. Planking and timbers fly through the air and nothing can be seen of the barn other than fire and black, roiling smoke.

EDITOR'S NOTE: *The manuscript concludes with the above scene. I have no way of knowing how Belle Boyd escaped what appeared to be a certain death, or even if she managed to do so. I suspect, however, that the next chapter, had it been written, would have the Siren alive and well, revealing General Shields's plans for the bridges to General Jackson. That is, in fact, what the real Belle Boyd did, achieving perhaps her finest moment of the war. She continued her spying throughout the conflict, in spite of numerous arrests, even passing information through the prison bars. Near the end of the war, she was deported to Canada by Union authorities. Afterward, she took intermittently to the stage in both the U.S. and England, supporting herself by telling appreciative audiences of her exploits. She died in 1900.*

Robert J. Randisi has had over 375 books published since 1982. He has written in the mystery, western, men's adventure, fantasy, historical, and spy genres. He is the author of the Nick Delvecchio series, the Miles Jacoby series, and is the creator and writer of *The Gunsmith* series, which he writes as J. R. Roberts and which presently numbers 240 books. He is the founder and executive director of the Private Eye Writers of America.

Allan Pinkerton and his already famed detective agency had their hands full during the Civil War spying for the Union. Timothy Webster was one of Allan's top operatives, until he was caught and hung by the Confederacy. But that fateful end is still in his future at the time of this story.

The Knights of Liberty ("The Double Spy," from the Case Files of Timothy Webster)

▓

Robert J. Randisi

One

▓

BALTIMORE, MARYLAND
OCTOBER 1861

"Damn you, Timothy Webster, you're a goddamned spy!" the man shouted. His name was Mike Zigler, and while he was known to some of the men in the saloon, he was not as well liked as good ol' Tim Webster.

"What are you babbling about, Zigler?" one of the others asked.

"This man's a damned Yankee spy!" Zigler shouted. "I saw him in Washington yesterday."

Webster rushed to his own defense with the truth.

"He's right," he said calmly. "I was in Washington yesterday. Many of you know that already."

"Yeah," Zigler said, "but do they know that you were in the company of the chief of the Yankee detectives?"

Now Webster had no choice but to call the man a liar by being one himself.

"You are a liar!" he cried, with as much indignation as he could muster.

"Damn you!" the man shouted, and sprang at him. . . .

When Timothy Webster was summoned by Major E. J. Allen he knew he would once again be placed in danger while performing a service for his country. He had no problem with that. It was the way he preferred to live his life, risking it from time to time. From the time he first went to work as a detective for the major's agency his life had become worth living. Prior to that he'd just been marking time. He'd come to America from England with his parents when he was twelve. They'd lived in Princeton, New Jersey, where he had worked as a mechanic. Eventually, he went to work for the New York City Police Department. It was the kind of work he wanted, but still not enough. So when he met the major and was offered a job to work for him, he jumped at the chance.

Now, five years later, he was working for the major in a different capacity. This time he was a spy for the newly formed secret service, serving President Lincoln and the Union cause. However, it was not so much patriotism that brought him to this work—even though he had adopted the United States as his country—as it was loyalty to the man for whom he'd worked for five years.

When President Lincoln decided there was a need for a "secret" service he went to the one man he thought could head up such an operation. That man was now known as Major E. J. Allen—but, in reality, his name was Allan Pinkerton.

Webster had been a Pinkerton detective for five years, and only recently had he been pressed into service as a secret-service man. Pinkerton had closed his offices and, in accordance with President Lincoln's specifications, had formed his secret service—and many of the men he pressed into service were his own operatives. Of them all, Timothy Webster was the best. This was not vanity on Webster's part, but Pinkerton's own opinion. That was why he summoned Webster for the dangerous job of becoming the country's very first double spy.

"Come in, Tim," Pinkerton said, using a firm handshake to draw the man into his office. As usual Pinkerton was looking prosperous in a tweed three-piece suit, a gold watch fob hanging from a vest pocket. He accepted President

Lincoln's appointment on the condition that he would not have to wear a uniform. He preferred to worry about blue and gray only when talking with his tailor. He proffered a well-fed appearance which he attempted to temper with sideburns and a heavy mustache.

"How are you, my boy?"

"Fine, sir."

"Sufficiently recovered from your last assignment to take another, do you think?"

"I'm ready when you are, sir."

"Good man!" Pinkerton went around behind his desk and indicated the chair located directly in front of it. "Have a seat and let me explain it to you. This one might be extremely dangerous."

Webster was a tall, impressive man, sometimes referred to as "Big" Tim Webster, but it was not his size, nor his courage, which made him an effective double spy. Rather it was his ability to ingratiate himself to anyone, to make friends at a moment's notice. In addition, there was his incredible good luck. It was the sort of luck that Pinkerton, his fellow operatives, and his friends thought could only be brought by a Guardian Angel. Some thought Webster depended too heavily on this luck, took it for granted, and would someday pay the price. Perhaps he would, but that did not stop him from putting it to the test.

This time, explained Pinkerton, it would be put to the test in Baltimore in pursuit of a group of hostile Southern sympathizers known as the Knights of Liberty.

"You would be alone among the enemy, using your uncommon charm to ingratiate yourself to the extent that you will be invited to join this brotherhood of Rebels. Do you think you can do this?"

Webster smiled and said, "It's a challenge I gratefully accept, sir."

"As I knew you would, my boy," Pinkerton said, proudly, "as I knew you would. . . ."

TWO

✠

Baltimore, Maryland, was under a state of martial law when Webster arrived. Southern sympathizers were at work everywhere. Lincoln's administration had arrested people in authority, city officials, newspaper editors, and the like, but some of the Baltimoreans who were also Southerners had formed organizations whose purpose it was to undermine the government at every turn. One such organization was the Knights of Liberty, and it was Webster's assignment to insinuate himself into their service for the purposes of disbanding them and having the members arrested.

Webster had done his double-spy work in the South before, and had also been to Baltimore in the past. For those reasons, when he arrived this time he was recognized by some and greeted as a friend of Dixie. He arrived in grand style, too, as Pinkerton had supplied for him a generous expense account. He took up residence in the Miller Hotel, one of the finer establishments in Baltimore. Not as alone as he might have thought, he made contact with another agent of the North named John Scully, whose assignment it was to assist Webster in any way possible.

"In what way will you establish yourself?" Scully asked during their first meeting. They were sitting in the bar of the Miller Hotel, preferring to be seen in public rather skulking about in private someplace. This way their meeting seemed very innocent, and no one else could hear what they were saying. They sat with a glass of sherry each, and sipped slowly. It would not do for a double spy to become drunk and loose-lipped.

"I have already taken steps to do so," Webster said. "I have railed openly against Union outrages and predicted victory for the Confederacy. Also, I have offered to transport papers, maps, and anything of that sort into Washington for any Southerners who have messages they need delivered."

"And will you deliver them?"

"Oh, yes," Webster said, "but only after we have opened them, copied them and sent them on to Mr. Pinkerton."

Only Lincoln, some of his staff, and the operatives who worked for him knew that "Major E. J. Allen" was actually Allan Pinkerton.

"That is devious," Scully said. "I don't understand how you do it, Tim. Everyone seems to trust you."

"It is a gift," Webster said, "and one I have always used to my best advantage."

"That is why I am glad we are colleagues," Scully said, "and not friends."

Webster understood exactly what his "colleague" meant. You cannot betray a man with whom you are not friends.

"I propose a toast," he said, raising his glass, "to our business relationship."

And so, for the next two weeks Webster worked flawlessly at establishing his identity. He did make trips into Washington, lest anyone check his story closely, and he was able to send Pinkerton copies of many messages sent into the capital city by Southerners—some harmless, some not so. By the end of those weeks no one in Baltimore doubted his veracity, all thought him a fine fellow working for the cause of the South.

But perhaps not all. . . .

Webster had just returned from Washington, a trip which had not yielded very much in the way of information, but still he was in good spirits. Many of the Southerners he had ingratiated himself with were actually fairly good fellows whose company he enjoyed. That would not, however, keep him from doing his job and having them arrested if the need arose. Whenever an arrest took place as a direct result of his actions, he was the one who protested the loudest about the indignity and unfairness of it. This only endeared him that much more to his Southern friends.

On this particular night he was in one of Baltimore's popular saloons with a dozen or more of his "friends" around him. Nowhere in sight was John Scully; it was just Webster and a roomful of Southerners. Suddenly a man appeared, sullen and scowling, and pushed his way through the crowd so he could face Webster nose-to-nose.

This, then, was Mike Zigler, who was presently springing at Webster with very bad intentions. . . .

Before anyone could move, Tim Webster's fist caught the man right in the face and sent him to the floor. He sprang up angrily, a knife in his hand. At this point Webster produced his pistol and pointed it at the man, unwaveringly.

"Get out of here before I kill you."

Zigler glared at Webster, then looked around him and shared the glare with the others.

"You'll get what you deserve if you befriend this man."

"Ah, you're crazy!" someone shouted from the back. "I'd just as soon believe that Jeff Davis hisself was a spy, as ol' Tim here."

Others piped in with their agreement and Zigler had no choice but to skulk from the saloon and melt into the darkness.

Webster holstered his gun and called out, "Drinks for everyone!" which was met with a chorus of cheers. The incident served to bolster Webster's position as a fellow Southerner, but he still had not achieved his ultimate goal— to be invited to join the Knights of Liberty.

He assumed that invitation would require a very special act.

THREE

After the incident in the saloon Webster decided he needed to do something drastic to further cement his position as a true Southerner. He decided that a few secret trips into lower Maryland and Virginia while carrying secret messages would do the trick. He decided to take Scully with him. His admiring Southern friends warned him to be on constant lookout for Union soldiers, because "those Yankees are capable of anything."

Webster and Scully were actually able to move very easily in and out of the areas because they carried secret Union passes. Meanwhile, the messages they were given to carry enabled the Union to connect to the South persons never even previously suspected. These forays into "Union territory," enabled Webster to facilitate the arrest of many Southern sympathizers while also serving to endear him further to his fellow Baltimoreans.

When he returned, he found himself hailed as a Southern hero, and waiting for him was the very invitation he had been waiting for.

He was several days returned from Virginia when a man came up beside him in a saloon and offered to buy him a drink.

"I have one, sir," Webster said, "but I'll gladly take you up on the offer when I've finished."

"No," the man said, "not here."

"Where, then?"

"Are you aware of the Knights of Liberty?"

Webster took a good look at the man now. Slightly built, thinning gray hair, probably in his mid-forties, with just the hint of a Southern accent.

"I certainly am," Webster said.

"They have been watching you," the man said, "and have decided it is time to invite you to be one of us."

Webster looked around and then lowered his voice. "You are a member of the Knights of Liberty?"

"I am," the man said proudly, "and it is my duty to make you one. What say you?"

"What else could I say," Webster asked, "but 'Lead on.' "

"Not now," the man said, lowering his voice even more and glancing about. "We meet at midnight. Meet me here at quarter-to and I will take you there."

"I cannot wait, sir," Webster said. "This is indeed an honor."

"For us as well, Mr. Webster," the man said. "Your exploits are well known to us. No one has risked their life more for the South without actually donning a uniform. Quarter till midnight, sir."

"I'll be here."

The smaller man nodded, and then faded away into the crowded saloon.

Still later, seated at a table together, he made his arrangements with Scully.

"You're going in alone?" the other agent asked.

"I must," Webster said, "tonight and other nights, as well. I must discover all I can before we take steps to disband them. We must know who all their members are, and who their contacts are, as well."

"But I could follow you, see where you go, and then bring troops to take them—"

"Not tonight, Scully," Webster said. "We must wait until the time is right."

"If you have another incident like that night in the saloon with that fellow Zigler—"

"I'll have to take my chances, John," Webster said. "I implore you, do nothing tonight but wait for me to contact you."

Scully worried his bottom lip but finally agreed.

Webster met with the slight man in the saloon as arranged. He was then taken to a deserted street corner where they stopped.

"What's wrong?" he asked.

"You must be blindfolded from here."

"But if I am to be a member, why can I not see where we are going?" Webster asked, contriving to sound confused.

"First you must be accepted as a member," the man said. "That is what tonight is for. Once you have been accepted you may come and go to meetings freely."

Webster wondered if this was a trap. Had they found out who he really was, perhaps from that man Zigler, or someone like him? Was he being blindfolded and led to his death?

He decided he must take the chance. He was so close to his ultimate goal, the disbanding of the Knights of Liberty, that he had to accept the risk.

"Very well," he said. "Blindfold me."

FOUR

▟

Once the blindfold was in place he was led down the street, the slight man—whose name he still did not know—holding him by the arm. They stopped at a gate, where the man gave a proper password, and then they went down a concrete stairway and along an alleyway until they reached a door which was opened only after a second password was uttered. Webster fervently hoped, as he was led down another stairway, this one inside, that when the blindfold was removed he would not be facing cocked pistols and rifles.

Finally they reached a room and stopped. He could sense the others around him, knew he must be in a crowded room full of Southern supporters who, if they knew who he really was, would tear him apart.

"Timothy Webster?" a strange voice said.

"Yes."

"If you are to be a member of the Knights of Liberty," the voice said, "you must take an oath to support the South and to thwart, hate, and violate the Northern abolitionists until you draw your last breath, or until we have won this accursed war. Do you so swear?"

"I swear," Webster said. "With all my heart."

"Remove the blindfold."

Someone did so and Webster had to wait for his eyes to adjust before he could look into the faces of the men who surrounded him. Suddenly they surged forward, closing on him, and after a moment of panic he saw they were smiling. Then they were shaking his hand and patting his back heartily, and just like that he was a Knight of Liberty.

That night he was called on to make a speech and he did so with verve and vigor, denouncing the Yankees and all they stood for. In the end the place exploded with applause and he was truly accepted as a brother.

That night, and for many nights after, Webster attended the meetings and memorized names, and faces, and facts. He learned that they did, indeed, work in direct contact with the Southern army, and that they had branches outside of Baltimore. He stored enough information in his mind to cripple their organization, and yet he still would not allow Scully to close in and round them up.

Then one day Scully said, "I think you should contact Mr. Pinkerton, Tim. Let him decide what to do."

"And if I don't," Webster asked, "you will?"

"The longer you are inside, the more danger you are in. It is my duty to look after you," Scully said, "and that is what I intend to do."

"Very well," Webster said. "I will consult with Mr. Pinkerton."

Scully nodded his thanks and breathed a sigh of relief that the matter had been taken from his hands.

Webster got in touch with Pinkerton who, while he realized that Webster could learn more and more, decided not to take any chances. He told Webster to close the group out at the next meeting.

"Put an end to it, Tim," he said, "and let's be on to something else."

"Is that official, sir?"

"It is."

At the next meeting Webster entered the room and looked around at the other men in attendance. It was actually a good night to close them out, as this was as large a gathering as he had been at since joining. While he recognized many of the faces, there were many more still which he did not. Then he saw a man approaching him with such purpose in his stride that he sought out the man's face, which was familiar to him, but not immediately—and then he knew!

Mike Zigler, the man who had attempted to denounce him in a saloon earlier in the month.

"You!" Zigler shouted, drawing the attention of the others. "You are here, you traitor?"

Webster wondered if he should draw his pistol and shoot the man dead before he could say anything more, but how would he explain it?

"This man is a Yankee spy!" Zigler shouted, frothing at the mouth, such was his anger. He glared at Webster and said, "You are among my people now, Webster, not yours. There's no help for you here."

"What are you saying, Mike?" It was the slight man who had invited Webster to join. Webster had discovered that his name was Rufus Blight. "What do you mean?"

"I mean he is sent among us to spy," Zigler shouted.

"Can you prove this?" another man called out.

"Mike's word is good enough for me," someone else called.

"Me, too."

Zigler's eyes shone as shouts of support continued to pour forth. He looked at Webster and a triumphant glint appeared in his eye, for this night he would have his revenge for the previous humiliation.

Zigler produced his knife, and as Webster went for his pistol his arms were seized and pinioned behind him.

Webster had no time to shout the words which were to have been a signal for Scully and a troop of Union soldiers to break in. He'd finally gotten himself in too deep, as friends and colleagues had said he someday would.

Unless he could talk his way out.

"Listen to me!" he shouted. "Zigler is lying. I am not—"

"None of your silver-tongued oratory will save you now," Zigler said, drowning him out. "Tonight I'll carve me up a spy."

Zigler came forward, his blade held low, and as Webster felt the tip of the blade prick him there was a crashing sound and suddenly men were shouting, pushing and shoving. His arms were released, but someone pushed him and he gasped as Zigler's blade went into his side.

A squad of Union infantry swept into the room and began herding the frightened, surprised Knights of Liberty against the wall.

Webster brought his hand down and clamped it around Mike Zigler's wrist. The knife had gone in barely an inch, but Zigler was trying to push it farther. They were jostled and the knife sliced sideways, opening a gash in Webster's side that bled freely. However, it also brought the knife free of his flesh and now he twisted and, with his great strength, snapped Zigler's wrist so that the man cried out in agony and released the knife.

Suddenly someone grabbed Zigler and pulled him away, pushed him against the wall with the others. Webster, his knees weak from relief and shock, felt his legs go out from under him, felt hands catch him and lower him easily to the floor.

"John?" he said, looking up at Scully.

Scully pressed his hands to Webster's wound and shouted to a Union soldier, "I need a medic, fast!"

"Yes, sir."

"John," Webster said.

"I'm here, Tim," Scully said. "You'll be fine. It's a tear, lots of blood, but you'll be fine."

"No signal . . ." Webster said.

"It took too long," Scully said. "When there was no signal I just had the soldiers break down the door."

"Looking after me?" Webster said, with a weak smile.

Scully nodded to his colleague and said, "Which is just what I am supposed to do."

In the days that followed the word got out that the Knights of Liberty had been captured, with only a few exceptions. Among those who had escaped was Timothy Webster. No one was surprised, for wasn't Webster a true and amazing son of the South, and wasn't he always able to escape the clutches of those damned Yankees?

Jane Haddam is the pseudonym of Orania Papazoglou, who is best known for her series featuring retired F.B.I. agent Gregor Demarkian, who has appeared in more than a dozen novels. She had worked in publishing long before turning to writing fiction, with stints as an editor at *Greek Accent* magazine and writing freelance for *Glamour*, *Mademoiselle*, and *Working Woman*. She has written books under her own name (*Graven Image* and *Arrowheart*) but it is the Demarkian series that continues to garner the most attention.

During the Civil War, men fought for various reasons, honor and their country among them. Women, however, took the war much more personally, for various reasons of their own. Although the character in the following story is fictional, it would be easy to imagine a woman taking matters into her own hands upon uncovering a traitor.

PORT TOBACCO

⊞

Jane Haddam

Sometimes, falling half-asleep in the corner of the carriage while the wheels rattled and jerked against the ruts in the road, Sarah Gilbert Slater wondered how long it would be before this war was over. Not long, she thought. There had been fighting for weeks in Virginia, and not just in Virginia, but right up close to Richmond, right there, so that you could stand on the terrace of the President's house and smell the dead. The smell made her head ache. If she had been another kind of woman, it might have made her faint. She thought of herself in Connecticut, before the talk had started, climbing the big tree in the yard of their house at Hartford. She could hang upside down by her knees for half an hour at a time, high up, when her brothers wouldn't even dare to try it. Then she would climb down and sit on the branch next to her father's "consulting room" window. Those were the days when her father had called himself "doctor" and made patent medicines in the cellar. Women came to him from the better streets in Hartford. Her mother sat in the parlor and sewed samplers as the women went in and out. Sarah could have told her mother the truth, but for some reason she hadn't wanted to. It had felt like a betrayal of her father. She wasn't sure why, but it would have been better if her father had been having his way with those women. Instead, he had sat in his chair against the wall and the women had talked, endlessly, in words Sarah had never been able to make clear. In the branches above her head, the leaves had shivered and hissed. The birds had called to one another. The squirrels had fought it out over nuts and acorns. There had been no smell of the dead.

The carriage shuddered, and rocked, and then hit hard ground: cobblestones or brick. Sarah leaned forward and tried to get a look out the carriage window, but there wasn't much of anything to see. The sun was too high in the sky, too hot and too bright. The women on the wooden walkways in front of the small stores looked as if they had been painted over with dust. If she stayed at the window long enough, she would see the thing that fascinated her the most about Port Tobacco, Maryland. She would see the nuns. What she saw instead was a soldier in Yankee blue with a rifle slung over his shoulder and a piece of fruit in his hands. The fruit looked raw and painful, like something bleeding. She sat back.

"You can't go looking out the windows now," Mr. Corbinson said, from the seat he had taken, facing her, all the way back in Virginia. His voice was high and pinched and hysterical. "You can't go looking at what the women are wearing now. You'll get us all in trouble, my Kate."

"Mrs. Thompson," Sarah said automatically. "My name is Mrs. Thompson."

"Mrs. Thompson," Mr. Corbinson said.

"I was looking for the nuns," Sarah said. "Did you know there were nuns here, in Port Tobacco? Papist nuns."

"You're not looking at nuns. You don't have anything to do with nuns. You have a job to do in Port Tobacco."

"They have a house where they live together. A convent. There are ten of them, in those long black dresses and the white around their faces. I've seen them over and over again. When they walk, they look at the ground."

"You're not looking at nuns," Mr. Corbinson said, looking stubborn.

Sarah gave it up. They were too close to the center of town by now for her to see the nuns. She felt along the edge of her dress until she came to the two stiff folds of paper that had been sewn between the layers of fabric in the sweep of skirt just underneath her waist. Then she put her hands in her lap and folded them, as if she were one of those nuns she had missed, in prayer. Instead, she was kneading the soft pouch of her string bag, feeling the edges of the knife she had put there before she left Richmond. It was a good knife, sharp enough so that she had had to wrap the blade in muslin to keep it from poking through. This time, she had not wanted to feel as if she were out in the world with no way to fight for herself, and only Mr. Corbinson—or Mr. Surratt—to protect her.

On his side of the carriage, Mr. Corbinson looked filthy and tense and afraid. The smell of him filled the carriage, choking and thick. There was dirt crusted into the folds of his skin around his eyes, and dirt under his fingernails. There was so much dirt in his heavy wool coat, it was stiff.

"I don't like Port Tobacco," Mr. Corbinson said. "I don't care if they did want to be on the right side in the war."

"All you need to do is to see me safely into the hands of Mr. Surratt," Sarah said. "Then you can go back to Virginia."

"I'm not going back to Virginia. Ain't none of us going back to Virginia. Don't you know that?"

Sarah put her head back and closed her eyes. She was only twenty-two, and slight. That was what made them think she needed an escort, at least in the South. She hated these endless Mr. Corbinsons, who spent half their time telling her she wasn't capable of doing what she had already done a dozen times before, and the other half gloating about the fact that they were holding all the money. She wondered what was happening now, up in Canada. Then she imagined herself at forty, full-figured and fair. She would be one of those women who ran Charitable Societies and ruled their husbands and sons the way overseers had once ruled slaves. She would be the one who was holding the money.

Somewhere in the trip through the short, pocked streets, she fell asleep. She dreamed of herself standing on a scaffold in a wide prison yard. The ground around her was dry and dead. No matter where she looked, she could see no sign of trees. *If I had only been holding the money,* she thought.

Then the carriage bounced and jerked again, and she was much too wide awake.

For the longest time, the Brawner Hotel in Port Tobacco had been an unofficial outpost of the Confederacy, a place where blockade runners and secret agents met, a place for plotting and sedition. Now it looked oddly empty and dispirited. The wide double-deck front porch seemed to sag in the corners. The rail fence had been replaced on one side by pickets. The front walk was full of grass. The carriage stopped and Mr. Corbinson got out to look around. Sarah wondered what he thought he was looking for. Maybe he expected Yankee soldiers to come marching down the street at them. What struck her was how quiet it all was, dead quiet, as if all the people who had ever lived here had turned to ash and blown away.

I would feel better if I had been able to see the nuns, Sarah thought. Then she smoothed her wide black skirt and prepared to let herself out of the carriage on her own, if only so she wouldn't have to touch Mr. Corbinson's hands. The hoop under her skirt was so stiff, she couldn't force it through the carriage door without crushing it. The material of her dress was brittle and rough. She was always careful to dress as a widow, even though she wasn't one. More women than not were widows these days, or worse, and soldiers didn't stop widows even if they were widows for the other side. It was strange, the way that was. It was as if agreements had been made in secret that couldn't have been made in the bright open air.

Just as she hit the ground, she realized that the cobblestones weren't very well anchored in the dirt. Her soft slippers plowed into sand. Dust rose around her in puffs of half-bleached brown. Mr. Corbinson turned from where he had stopped halfway up the path to the Brawner's front door and rubbed the palms of his hands against the sides of his coat. Dirty hands. Dirty coat. Dirty face. For one frantic moment, Sarah thought she could still smell him, the way she had been smelling him, all those long hours in the carriage. The smell made the air thick. It seemed to pattern and snap.

"Hey there," Mr. Corbinson said. "Are you coming now, Mrs. Thompson? We don't want to keep the carriage man all day."

Sarah felt the papers sewn at her waist again. She adjusted her bonnet on her head. Jumping down from the carriage, she had dislodged it. The stiff edge of its crown was digging into her ear. She wound her hands around her soft string bag and checked automatically for the hard thing inside it.

"Hey there," Mr. Corbinson said again.

Up on the top level of the Brawner's double porch, a man had appeared next to the railing: Jacob Surratt. Sarah caught his eye, and nodded, and then went up the path to where Mr. Corbinson was finally waiting. Maybe the hotel would really be as empty as it appeared to be. Maybe, when the time came to do what she had to do, she would actually be alone.

The Brawner's front door swung open and a colored woman came out, but Sarah didn't notice her. There were colored women everywhere. Nobody paid attention to them.

From the beginning, Sarah Gilbert Slater's job in the war had been exactly what it would always be. She would wait patiently in a boardinghouse in Richmond, until a man would come to tell her she was wanted at the War Department. In Richmond, everybody thought she was the widow of a man who had died in glorious martyrdom. They had no other way to explain why an insignificant child, a half-woman living on her own in a way no respectable woman ever could if she were under the age of forty, was invited so often to Jefferson Davis's house. For her part, Sarah lived quietly and without entertainment. She came down to dinner at the boardinghouse every night and sat in the parlor afterwards, discussing the war news and the blockade runners and how difficult it was to get tea and spices now that the war had gone on for so very long. Sometimes she sat looking at her hands, making a show of grief, so that the other women couldn't see how much they frightened her. They did frighten her, too. All the women she had met in this war scared her silly. The men were fighting out of principle or loyalty or inertia. The women were true fanatics. If you listened to them long enough, you could hear the blood in their voices.

When she got to the War Department, there was always a woman waiting for her, silent and steady, ready to sew her dress. She was not a colored woman—or rather, she was not any more. In the beginning, the seamstresses had always been colored and sullen and stout. Sarah had found herself thinking once or twice that it would take nothing at all to prod them to bloody murder. They seemed to be on the edge of it. Later, it was an older white woman with thick white hair and eyes the color of slate who did the sewing, and when Sarah asked why she only said, "It doesn't hurt to take precautions."

What they sewed into her dress at the War Department were "dispatches," and sometimes other papers that were needed by Friends of the Cause in Montreal. They sent her to Montreal because she could speak French so well, she could claim French citizenship if she were ever caught. None of them ever asked her why she was willing to go. Every time but one it was the same. The papers were sewn into her clothes. She was introduced to her escort, a man who carried twenty gold pieces to see them through the trip and who knew nothing else about it, except that it would help the Confederacy win the war. They traveled North, first to Port Tobacco, then to Washington, then to New York, then to Canada. In Canada there were people waiting for her, who did know what it was all about. She delivered the papers to them, and they did what had to be done. Once, they organized a raid on a small border town in Vermont. They wanted to bring the war home to the Yankees who had up to then been able to fight it as if it weren't happening at all. Once, they paid the Canadian government to release three of their soldiers who had been jailed as spies. The Canadians were supposed to be neutral. When they were faced with the obvious, they had to do what they were expected to do or risk being invaded themselves. Time after time, it was always the same, except for that once. The air got colder and colder the farther North they rode, even in the summer, and her hands got more and more chapped. Sometimes she wondered what they would think of her if they knew why she was doing what she was doing. She didn't care for the Cause at all. She only cared not to be living at home with Mr. Slater, whom she had married because it was the only way she had of holding onto her reputation. She only cared not to know any more of the secrets of the marriage bed.

The one time it was different, she had carried not papers, but gold, and not on her person, but in two big traveling trunks that had been fixed to the top of a carriage bought and outfitted for the purpose. That time, she had been with Mr. Surratt, too, and nothing had been left to chance. There had been no waiting around at inns, hoping for a coach to come in that would carry them on the next leg of their journey. There had been no free afternoons in New York to go shopping, or free evenings in Washington to see a play. There had only been the purpose, stark and unembellished, so that in the end she had not been able to keep herself from looking. Sitting alone in a room on the top floor of Mr. Surratt's mother's boardinghouse in Washington, she had opened the trunks and run her hands over the solid yellow bricks. She had even picked up one in her hands and felt its weight. She wouldn't have believed it before then, but gold had a voice. It sang to you.

Now she let a colored woman show her to the door to what would be her room at the Brawner Hotel. Then she waited, immobile, until the colored porter deposited her bag and left. That one time it was different, she had considered the possibilities. The war would be over one of these days, and it almost didn't matter if she was on the right side or the wrong one. She would be expected to go back home, like any married woman, and to take up life as she had left it in New Bern, North Carolina. Housework. Church. Those awful times in the dark when Mr. Slater reached for her, caring not at all that she hated the sight of him. She was supposed to hate the sight of him in bed. It was expected of her.

Now, she thought there might be something worse. She might not be able to go home, even to the punishment of Mr. Slater, even to New Bern, if there was anything left of it. She had always known the war would end one day, but she had never considered what it would mean—or maybe, if she had, she had assumed the outcome would have nothing to do with her. The smell of the dead had begun to change her mind. There were too many stories around about what the Yankees did when they captured a town and had it under their authority. There were too many rumors about hangings and fires. She went to the window and looked out on the empty stretch of land behind the hotel. A colored woman was feeding chickens in the side yard. A colored man was carrying chamber pots towards a stand of trees far at the back, where the latrines would be.

Sarah went behind the screen that had been put up for her to dress and reached up under her skirt. She tore at the loose stitches along her waist and got out the papers meant for Mr. Surratt and laid them down on the small stool in the corner. Then she went back up under and felt the second set of papers in their pouch, but these were not so easy. The stitching had been made much tighter. She had to pull at it so hard, she was afraid she was going to rip the dress in two. What would they expect her to do then? But of course, they would expect her to do nothing. They would expect her to wait until she got to Canada to get the second set of papers out, and then if her dress was ruined she could just put on a different one.

The second set of papers came out. Sarah came out from behind the screen with both sets of papers in her hand and laid them out on the lumpy feather bed that took up most of the room. The set that had been difficult to retrieve was different than any other she remembered carrying, but she had been expecting that. Most of what she carried were messages. These papers were official, documented, sealed, clotted with wax in some places—the keys that opened the vault where all that gold had gone. She folded them up again and put them up under her skirt, not caring if a maid walked in to find her with her leggings exposed to the air. The papers slipped into the pouch that had been made for them. She let her skirt drop and took the other set of papers into her hand.

Out in the yard, there was what sounded like chickens panicking. Sarah went to the window to look out. There was a nun standing in the dirt with a basket over her arm, talking to a fat white woman Sarah seemed to remember was Mrs. Brawner herself. But maybe not. It was hard for Sarah to see, and suddenly it was hard for her to think. That hadn't been the first time she had had the dream about the wide prison yard. Now she seemed to be having it while she was wide awake. The prison yard was empty of trees, of grass, of anything. There was only the scaffold and the rope. What frightened her most was that she could see nothing else. There were no soldiers. There was no executioner. There was only herself and that scaffold and that rope, as if the entire project was to be carried out by ghosts. But maybe it wouldn't happen like that at all. Maybe it would happen by firing squad, and she wouldn't be able to see anything because her eyes would be covered by a cloth.

Suddenly, there was something wrong with her heart. It pounded and pounded. It felt as if it were coming out of her ears. She closed her eyes and swayed close to the wall, determined not to start fainting now, after all this time. The wall smelled of woodworm and rot. All of Port Tobacco smelled of woodworm and rot. The papers she held in her hands began to crackle under her fingers. The bile rose up in the back of her throat like hot porridge boiling over on an untended stove.

She was sure some poet somewhere had said something beautiful about dying young, but she had never liked poetry, and she did not want to find a fantasy in it now.

Mr. Surratt was waiting for her in the entryway when she came downstairs. As soon as he saw her, he stopped his pacing and held his hat in his hands. He looked drawn and pale—but then, they all did these days, all the men on the Confederate side, because this war was so close to being finished. He held out his hands to her and Sarah took them. His skin was very rough. She had no idea how old he was, but she thought that at some time in his life, he must have worked on a farm. He dropped his arms and looked around the entryway, as if a Yankee spy had to be hiding there somewhere, or a Yankee soldier had to be waiting at the ready with a rifle.

"We should go into the lounge," he said finally. "I could order you something to drink. Lemonade? You drink lemonade."

Sarah thought it would be better if they could go into the tavern, where it would be dark and hard to hear even in the middle of the day, but the tavern was off-limits to her as long as she wanted to remain respectable. She looked around the entryway herself and said, "I'd very much like some lemonade, Mr. Surratt. And someplace to sit. I feel as if my bones have been rattled into pieces. The roads have grown very rough."

"Everything has grown very rough."

"I thought we were going to meet Mr. Corbinson here as well. Or have you already spoken to him?"

"I've spoken to no one but you. I've had a letter from my mother."

"I hope your mother is well."

"My mother is not well, Mrs. Thompson. None of us are well. None of us can be well. Not with the war the way it is."

Sarah let this pass. Mr. Surratt's mother was one of those women, the women who craved blood. It made her nervous every time she had to stay at Mrs. Surratt's boardinghouse. It was a curse that she had to stay there often, since it was one of the few safe places left in the District of Columbia.

She went into the lounge, leaving Mr. Surratt behind her. He was staring at her back, but she didn't turn to look at him. She took a chair near a window that looked out onto the drive at the front of the hotel. She put her string bag in her lap as if she were afraid that sprites would steal it.

"Mrs. Thompson," Mr. Surratt said, coming in after her.

"I've had letters from all my people at home," Sarah said pleasantly, looking at the string bag and not at him. "Come sit with me and I'll catch you up on what's going on at home."

Out on the drive, a pair of men rode up on horses, both of them in uniform. Sarah looked quickly at them and quickly away. They were officers and full of money. They would go to the tavern and play cards until well after dark. They were not looking for her.

Then she opened her string bag and took out the papers, quickly, so that even Mr. Surratt would not be able to see the knife.

It was only after the lemonade had been brought and the colored woman who had brought it had melted away that Sarah got down to business. She found it so hard to accept that she had to pay attention to where the coloreds were and what they were doing before it was safe for her to speak. Mr. Surratt was driving her to distraction. He was always nervous and high-strung. Today he was like a wire pulled tight. Any small noise made him jump, and if she looked straight at him she could see that he was visibly sweating. It was not a good omen.

"I don't trust that Mr. Corbinson," Mr. Surratt said. "I've never seen him before. Is he known to you?"

"No."

"He looks like a drunkard. Or worse. And he's disappeared into thin air. And he's holding the money."

"Is that all the money we have? If Mr. Corbinson runs off with it, will we be unable to go on with our work?"

"No," Mr. Surratt said.

"Well, then." Sarah picked up her papers and looked through them. "These are mostly what you expect them to be. They haven't arrived at any surprises. They only wanted me to ask you if you mean to go through with it."

"Of course I mean to go through with it."

"And your mother, does she mean to go through with it?"

"She lives for nothing else."

"And the others?"

Surratt looked her up and down the way men sometimes did when they realized that she was a young woman underneath all that black, but Sarah could see that there was nothing in him of lust or appreciation for her. Instead, he looked like someone who was drowning and refusing all hope of rescue, as a matter of principle. He looked already dead.

"You know what Mr. Booth is like," he said finally.

"Yes," Sarah said. "I know what Mr. Booth is like."

"You know what my mother is like," Surratt said. "I don't understand the need for this catechism. It's been four years. None of us has ever wavered yet."

"Circumstances have changed," Sarah said carefully. "There's no hope of victory now. This will not turn the tide of the war. And at least some of you are certain to be caught."

"Booth may escape in the confusion."

"He won't."

"I may escape. I've made my plans for escape. Haven't you?"

"I will be well on my way before a single shot is fired," Sarah said. "I have business in Montreal. One last set of dispatches to deliver for the Cause. But your mother will not be well on her way. She's tied to that boardinghouse."

"She's prepared to suffer martyrdom, if that is what is necessary."

Necessary for what? Sarah wanted to say. The Yankee soldiers' horses were tied to the posts outside. There was ammunition tied to the saddles. The soldiers had not worried that it might be stolen, or that it might be used against them, even though Port Tobacco was a city bitter with the hatred of them. Sarah passed the papers into Jacob Surratt's lap.

"You do understand it won't change the outcome of the war," she said. "It isn't a chance to turn the tide. The tide cannot be turned."

"It should have been done long ago. Then it would have changed the outcome of the War."

"It wasn't done long ago. It is being done now. As an act of—retribution, I suppose."

"There's much good in acts of retribution."

" 'Vengeance is mine, saith the Lord.' "

"Sometimes the Lord needs willing helpers to do his work."

"I think too many people have lived the last four years thinking they were doing the Lord's work," Sarah said, but she turned away from it. She let it go. Mr. Surratt was reading, with some difficulty, through the papers she had given him. He ran his finger along under the words to keep his place. The sweat was still running down the sides of his face and into his collar. His eyes were feverish and bright.

"There," he said, passing the papers back to her. "That's uncertain enough."

"We can't settle on the details until we know something about his habits. We can't make a plan until we know the men he has around him."

"We will know something about his habits. My mother will take care of that."

Sarah turned the papers over in her hands. "You're to keep these now. I'm to have nothing to do with them. I'm wanted in Montreal. I can't be in a position to compromise myself. When we get to the District of Columbia, we will discuss details. With your mother."

"With my mother." Mr. Surratt smiled. It was a rictus smile, as if there was really nothing left of him any more except his skeleton. He didn't look dead so much as like a reanimated corpse, moving through the flames of hell and lit up by them. Sarah thought she could feel the heat.

"We should all compromise ourselves," he said. "That is what my mother thinks. We should stand up and be counted, so that they can never believe that they had the loyalty of their own people any more than they had the loyalty of the people of the South. Judgment is coming, Mrs. Thompson, do you believe that?"

"I believe we will all be judged when Christ comes in glory on the last day, Mr. Surratt. The Bible tells us that."

"We'll all be judged sooner than that," Surratt said.

Then he got up out of his chair with the papers in his hands and turned his back to her.

For a long time, Sarah sat by herself in the lounge, listening to the sounds drifting across the entryway from the tavern. When she was finally ready to move, it was beginning to get dark outside, but she hardly noticed it. The Yankee soldiers' horses were still tied to the posts, even though it must have been hours since they had first come. Sarah imagined them stumbling home, dead drunk, a danger to themselves and their animals. Sometimes she listened for other sounds in the hotel: for Mr. Surratt, pacing the wood floors with the hard heels of his boots making drumming noises in the halls; for Mrs. Brawner calling out to the colored women working in the yard; for one of the maids rattling teacups on a tray she was not skilled enough to carry properly upstairs. Sometimes she tried to think, but that was the hardest thing of all. Her mind seemed to have been emptied of words. She had nothing left to her but images. The image that came to her most strongly was not that one of the prison yard, but one of herself, in Canada, free and on her own, without even Jacob Surratt. *And then what will I do with myself?* she wondered—and then that seemed odd, too, because she had never thought of it before. Always before this trip, she had gone to Canada and then come back. She would not be able to do that this time. She put her string bag in her lap and looked at it. She wondered if Mr. Surratt even wanted to get away, after the deed was done. What was it about people that they longed so to be martyrs? Sarah had never had a moment's interest in martyrdom in her life, and she didn't have one now. She tried to picture herself in Canada again, her business done, sitting at a table in a small hotel with one of the men she had gone to before, talking about the glorious Cause—but the glorious Cause was finished, and Canada was a long way away.

It was just about full evening when Mr. Corbinson came in, walking up past the two Yankee horses. The horses seemed to be getting restless and annoyed. They weren't used to being left idle, and tethered, except perhaps at night to sleep. Mr. Corbinson came in the Brawner's front door and slammed it behind him. He made too much noise when he breathed. It was that time of the evening when the guests would come downstairs to wait for dinner. Any moment now, the lounge would be full of people, all of them stiff, all of them expecting her to keep up one end of a conversation. If she waited any longer, Mr. Corbinson would slip into the tavern and be unavailable for her until dinner was called. At dinner, he would be unavailable to her still, seated somewhere out of sight, at the end of the table where the less genteel people sat.

Sarah got out of her seat. She slipped her string bag over her wrist, and the heavy weight of it slapped against her side. It felt heavy, even cushioned by all those layers of taffeta and lace. She went out into the entryway and looked around. Mr. Corbinson was standing by himself, looking at a picture on the wall, a little black and white line drawing Sarah hadn't noticed before. There was, she thought, coming up beside him to look, nothing about it to notice. Three ladies in hoop skirts were sitting around a small round tea table. A gentleman in a long coat and a high collar was standing beside them, holding a cup. Mr. Corbinson smelled, if anything, worse than before. Under the scents of dirt and sweat there was now a scent of liquor.

"Mr. Corbinson," Sarah said.

Mr. Corbinson turned. "You shouldn't creep up like that," he said. "Not in times like these. In times like these, if you creep up, anything could happen."

"I need to speak to you," Sarah said.

"We can go into the lounge."

"I need to speak to you privately."

"We aren't going to be any more private than in the lounge," Mr. Corbinson said. "I can't be seen coming out of your room. You can't be seen coming out of mine."

Sarah thought about it. Her instinct was to ask him to meet her out back at the latrines, but they were much too far away, and dangerous. The yard was full of colored women. A woman in Sarah's position would use the chamber pot in her own room. Anyone who saw her walk across the yard or back again would make note of it. The colored women would talk.

"You want to go into the lounge?" Mr. Corbinson said.

"No," Sarah said. "Is there a pantry, or a root cellar? I want an enclosed space that nobody is likely to enter in the next half hour."

"Why would you want that?"

"Because I want to speak to you privately. And this is not a very private place. There are two Union soldiers in the tavern. There may be others in the hotel I haven't seen."

Mr. Corbinson gave her a long look, suspicious. Then he went to the door of the tavern and stepped inside. A moment later he was back, looking faintly yellowish under the skin.

"They are there," he said.

"I told you they were there."

"You know what women are like. They have their fancies. They have their fears."

"I assure you I have neither fancies nor fears in excess of your own. I need to speak to you privately. I do not want us to be overheard, and it would be for your own safety if we were not. Do you know where the laundry is?"

"No, ma'am."

"Have you ever stayed at this hotel before?"

"No, ma'am."

"I've stayed here a dozen times. I'm sick of the place. The laundry is out back next to the kitchen. You can get there by going all the way to the end of this hall, but I don't want you to go this way. I want you to go out the front door and around the back and in by the back door. When you get around the back I'll be waiting for you."

"Everybody will see you," Mr. Corbinson said. "They'll want to know what you think you're doing."

"I'll tell them I couldn't find a maid and came down to the laundry to see if I could have a dress repaired. Of course, there will be nobody to repair it at this hour of the evening, but it won't matter. I'll just say I didn't think. There are some advantages to having a reputation for stupidity."

"What will I say if they see me?"

"You'll say you were drunk and lost your way. You're drunk enough to make that believable."

"You shouldn't put on that tone and think nobody will mind it," Mr. Corbinson said. "I'm not one of the darkies on your old plantation."

"I'll be at the laundry room in five minutes," Sarah said. "I'll expect you to be there. If you aren't there, I'll find some way to make it clear to those two Union soldiers in the tavern just who and what you are."

"You're the same thing," Mr. Corbinson said. "You're the same thing as me."

"They won't believe it."

Sarah turned her back to him and walked away, down the entryway hall, all the way to the back where the laundry room would be. She could hear him breathing behind her. She couldn't hear him walking. She blocked everything else out of her mind and concentrated on getting to where she was going without seeing anybody on her way. She imagined a stiff cold breeze of Canadian air against the sides of her face. They were all panicking, every one of them, even the ones like Mr. Corbinson who were too stupid to truly understand the magnitude of what was about to happen to them all.

I will not be a martyr to the Cause, she thought, as she closed the laundry room door behind her. Then she stood immobile in the dark, listening to the sounds of the hotel creaking and clanging its way to dinner.

It took Mr. Corbinson a long time to come, so long that Sarah had begun to think she would have to take some other course to get what she had to have. Then she heard a shuffling in the yard and knew, immediately, that it was him. The colored women moved differently. The colored men were nearly silent. She had been sitting on a small stool. She stood up and held her hands in front of her. Her chest hurt when she breathed. Still, she had been right about this place. Nobody was here, and nobody would come here. A laundry room was in use most often at the beginning of the day.

"Mrs. Thompson?" Mr. Corbinson said.

"Don't use my name," Sarah said. "Come inside and be as quiet as you can."

"Some colored woman is going to come in here and catch us."

"Nobody is going to come in here. I've spoken to Mr. Surratt. He said he hadn't seen you. Is that true?"

"I haven't had a chance to get to it. I'll see him tonight at dinner."

"If you haven't seen him, you haven't handed him the money."

"The money is no business of yours. The money is business between me and Jacob Surratt."

"It is if you still have it. I don't think you do. You've been out in the town all afternoon. I think you've been gambling."

"The only gambling I ever did in my life was on the Confederate army."

"And drinking."

"I can drink if I want to. I'm a free man."

"You won't be if that money is gone. Twenty gold pieces. Did you think I didn't know?"

"The money is no business of yours," Mr. Corbinson said, but he wasn't belligerent any more. Sarah could hear the shuffle and the wheedle in his voice. She started to relax.

"Here," she said, pulling the stool out between them. "I want to see it. If you've got it, show it to me. Put it down on this stool so that I can look at it."

"You won't see anything on that stool. It's pitch dark."

"There's light enough so that I can see."

Mr. Corbinson hesitated. Sarah held her breath. It really was dark in here. The only light came from the moon, which was full enough but too far away. Even the yard outside was dark.

Mr. Corbinson reached in under his coat and came out with something not-white and limp—a handkerchief, Sarah thought, as filthy as the rest of him. He put it down on the stool and stepped back, leaving Sarah to open the cloth for herself.

"It's there," he said. "It's all there. I may not be a fool for the Confederacy, but I'm not a thief."

"Yes," Sarah said.

"I'm going to take it back now. I'm not going to give it to you to lose it and get me in trouble with Mr. Surratt."

"You can take it back," Sarah said.

Mr. Corbinson moved in on the stool. Sarah stepped away, into the dark edges of the room. Mr. Corbinson took the handkerchief and folded it around the gold pieces, very carefully, as if he could break them if he handled them with roughness.

Sarah put her hand into her string bag and felt the edges of the knife. The kitchen was just next door, and there was a cacophony of sound rising out of it that she hadn't noticed before. The air was full of noise. She could have let out a full-throated scream without anybody being able to hear. She got the knife out and unwound the cloth she had used to protect the bag. There was enough moonlight so that she could see the edge of it, glinting.

"I'm not a thief," Mr. Corbinson was saying. "They treat you no better than dirt, these people, North and South, it's all the same. They treat the coloreds better than they treat a man like me."

Mr. Corbinson put the handkerchief back inside his coat. He peered into the dark in her direction, but Sarah knew there was nothing he could see.

"I'm not a thief," he said, and then he turned his back.

She had been thinking about it all morning—thinking about it, really, for most of the last two days—what it would take to get the money off him. She had known from the beginning that she wouldn't be able to steal it. She had imagined herself plunging the knife into him. She had thought of herself as emotionless and cool.

Now the knife seemed to have taken on a life of its own. It had possessed her hand, like some kind of malevolent ghost. It had a very long blade, so that she had had to work to make it fit inside her string bag. It was a man's knife, not a woman's, and that had been important to her to. What frightened her was how much she loved the feel of it. She plunged it into his back and saw him reel. She drew it out and felt the stickiness of blood against the side of it. She plunged it in again, and then he began to pivot and reel, rounding on her.

She stepped back just in time. She had no idea what it took to kill a man. She thought a bullet could do it in a single shot, but she hadn't been willing to risk the noise of a gun. He fell on his back and took the knife along with him. She leaned down to roll him over and then stopped. She didn't want to roll him over. She wanted his money. She put her hands inside his coat and felt around. She felt the heavy weight of the gold but no way to get into it. She tore at the fabric until it came apart in her hand.

"Mr. Corbinson?"

He didn't answer. Sarah put her hand down on his chest and felt for his heart. She felt nothing—but that might not mean what she thought it meant. That might not mean anything. She put the handkerchief back down on the stool and opened it up.

"Twenty," she said, counting. She wiped her hands on the handkerchief and took a single gold piece out to leave on its own in the dirt. She could make do with nineteen pieces instead of twenty. The important thing was to make them all believe that Mr. Corbinson had been robbed, and probably by one of the colored men who worked in the yard. It didn't really matter what they thought, as long as they never suspected her.

She opened up her string bag again and let the gold pieces drop inside. She would have to find a couple of handkerchiefs to stop them from clinking against each other, but her carpetbag was full of handkerchiefs. They wouldn't be hard to find. She pressed the toe of her boot against Mr. Corbinson again. He rocked when she pushed him, but he didn't move at all when she stopped.

"Good," she said.

Then she went to the door of the laundry room and looked out into the hall. Nobody had seen her go in. Nobody would see her go out. She thought about all that gold in all those banks, up in Canada, and the papers she had folded in her dress, which were the only way to get to it. It was odd what men were willing to do for money.

Half an hour later, when the dinner bell rang, Sarah came down the long front staircase into the lounge, looking for Jacob Surratt. There were not many people in the hotel, and what few there were looked shabby and tired. The Yankee soldiers had come out of the tavern to join the guests. They would be having dinner, now that they were drunk enough not to care if they made outright fools of themselves.

"They wouldn't behave in that way if they were soldiers of the Confederacy," Mr. Surratt said, but he kept his voice low enough so that he wouldn't be overheard.

Sarah wanted to tell him that they would, most certainly, behave in that way if they were soldiers of the Confederacy. Soldiers behaved like soldiers no matter what army they belonged to. They loved and hated like ordinary men. Their lives depended on women like her, and on men like Mr. Corbinson and Mr. Surratt.

"You'll take me in to dinner," Sarah said, not asking it. Mr. Surratt held out his arm.

It was a wonder, Sarah thought, that she hadn't done something like this before. It was a wonder she hadn't asked herself yet if she would be able to get away with it more than once.

Ray Vukcevich's first novel is *The Man of Maybe Half a Dozen Faces* from St. Martin's Minotaur. His short fiction has appeared in *The Magazine of Fantasy & Science Fiction*, *Asimov's Science Fiction Magazine*, *Rosebud*, *Aboriginal Science Fiction*, *Pulphouse*, *Talebones*, and several anthologies including *Twists of the Tale*, *The Year's Best Fantasy and Horror* (Twelfth Annual Collection), and both volumes of *Imagination Fully Dilated*. His latest book is a collection of short fiction called *Meet Me in the Moon Room*, from Small Beer Press. He is currently working on another novel.

The Swan case, which involved the notorious Confederate spy Rose Greenhow, is another famous Civil War spy case, although the ending in this story is entirely fictional.

THE SWAN

✖

Ray Vukcevich

ONE

✖

I came to Indiana hoping to settle a question that had occupied me for over twenty years. An informant had sent a clipping from the May 12, 1885 *Muncie Daily Monitor* to my New York office.

The grand opening of the Imperial Roller Rink in Muncie will feature a promenade of couples on skates, a Wild West show, barrel races, and a special appearance by Mary Elizabeth Swann, known professionally across the state of Indiana and around the world as "The Swan." Mary is renowned for her unusual aspect and unearthly grace.

I very much wanted to see Mary in regard to the spy Charles Wyatt Swann. I had become involved in the Swann case in 1861 while working under Allan Pinkerton in Washington. Pinkerton had had a tremendous success peeking into the windows of Mrs. Rose O'Neal Greenhow's house on the corner of Thirteenth and I Streets, a fashionable neighborhood not far from the White House.

He was eager to do it again. Mrs. Greenhow was a member of Washington high society and had connections everywhere. Her Confederate sympathies were well known, and it was widely believed she had given Beauregard information about McDowell's forces that resulted in the devastating rout of the Union Army at Bull Run. Pinkerton probably already had all he needed to arrest her, but it would be eight days after his first observations before he closed in. In the meantime, he repeated his bold move of looking in her windows several times.

One afternoon the duty of holding him up so he could see into her parlor windows, which were set quite high up from ground level, fell to me and a man named Will Jones. I did not know Jones well. In fact, I was new to Pinkerton's operation in Washington and didn't know any of his male and female operatives in any but the most superficial ways. A railroad man who had worked with my father in the gold fields of California had arranged for me to meet with Pinkerton in Chicago. I had done some law enforcement work in San Francisco, and I thought I could better aid the Union as a detective than as a soldier. Pinkerton agreed, but with some reservations. It soon became obvious that I would start near the bottom in his operation. He hadn't yet given me a chance to do anything exciting, and I was eager for an opportunity to prove myself.

Pinkerton's success in his first peeking had convinced him to do subsequent observations himself. The front door of Mrs. Greenhow's house was at the center of the building and opened onto the street. Visitors approached it by way of a flight of stairs. We sneaked into the shadows beneath a parlor window to one side of those stairs, and Pinkerton took off his boots. We boosted him to our shoulders so he could see inside.

No one had commented upon the difference in height between Jones and myself, but it soon became apparent that the difference would be a problem. Since I was perhaps a foot shorter than Jones, Pinkerton standing on our shoulders listed badly to one side. In his attempt to straighten up, he was forced to put all of his weight on my shoulder, and that proved to be too much for me. I sagged and Pinkerton fell. He snatched at the sill for a handhold but only managed to slow his fall. He sat down hard in a puddle. Jones and I seized him under the arms, and we had only time to drag him away and hide under the stoop before the blinds were thrust away and Mrs. Greenhow poked her head out.

"I don't see anything," she said to someone in the room. "Perhaps an animal." She pulled the blind back into place. She looked matronly and a little older than I had been led to believe. Stories of her using her female endowments to enchant so many men may have been exaggerated.

Pinkerton had regained his dignity by this time. "The man's name is Charles Wyatt Swann," he said. "This looks like a simple business deal. He's trying to get her interested in his invention which seems to be wheels you put on your boots. He's got them in a box."

"Roller skates?" I asked.

"You've heard of them?"

"I read something about bar girls serving beer in Germany on wheels," I said.

"Well, she doesn't seem interested," Pinkerton said. "If it doesn't have to do with the war, she doesn't want to hear it. I'll bet this one doesn't get a good night kiss."

He retrieved his boots and put them on. I thought we'd be leaving but I was wrong. Later I concluded the reason he did not resume the surveillance himself was that he would be presenting to the street his muddied backside. "Daggett," he said to me, "since you're the expert on wheels for your shoes, get up there and see if they do anything we should know about. Give him a hand, Jones."

When it became clear Jones and I would continue the surveillance on our own, I pulled off my boots. Jones cupped his hands together, and I stepped into them. He boosted me up and I grabbed the windowsill and worked my way around until I was standing on his shoulders. I lifted the sash a little and carefully turned the slats of the blinds and peered inside.

Mrs. Greenhow and Charles Wyatt Swann sat in overstuffed chairs near the fireplace. Both were turned my way and I could hear much of their conversation quite clearly. I lost words only when they turned aside or leaned in to speak in softer tones.

Now that I had leisure to study her, I changed my assessment of Mrs. Greenhow. She was a fine looking woman of perhaps forty, and there was a kind of animal energy about her that made her very attractive.

Swann was a small man with a full black beard. The beard made him look older, but nonetheless, I judged him to be in his mid-twenties, a man no older than myself. His hair was much too long to be fashionable and was tied back with a black ribbon. If I had passed him on the street, I might have thought him a mountain man who had been wedged into a city suit for some special occasion. He held the box Pinkerton had mentioned in his lap. It was wooden and perhaps a foot and a half long and half that wide and deep.

"I don't see how I can help you, Mr. Swann," Rose Greenhow said.

"As I've explained," he said, "I am confident the skates will be granted a patent in the North, but I am concerned about their protection in the Confederacy."

"I think you misunderstand my concerns, Mr. Swann," she said. "This is not a place to negotiate Confederate business propositions."

"I do understand that, Mrs. Greenhow," he said, "but surely you can see the potential of my skates."

"Potential?"

"Someday this will be the ultimate in refined exercise. There will be huge establishments called 'Roller Rinks' where people will come to skate and socialize. Polished wooden floors as large as a city park. Everyone who counts will be doing it."

"I would judge you've not been spending much time with anyone who counts, Mr. Swann," she said and looked him up and down. "What would your father have said?"

He did not reply to her question, but asked one of his own. "Surely we do not want the Confederacy to be denied this opportunity?"

"Frankly, Mr. Swann," she said, "I see this only as an opportunity for you. You want your skates patented on both sides so you win no matter what happens. What do we get out of helping you?"

"Have you considered the military implications of my wheeled skates, Mrs. Greenhow?"

She laughed and her laugh was high and gay. Now it was easy to see why she had power over men. She was laughing at him but in such a way that he could not take offense. It was a captivating laugh.

Strangely, he didn't seem captivated. "I'm not joking," he said.

"Very well," she said, "explain how these wheeled skates of yours will help us win the war."

"Imagine what you could do to unsettle the populations of Northern cities," he said.

I had interviewed liars on more than one occasion, and I realized at once that Swann was inventing military uses for his skates on the spot. It was difficult to tell if Mrs. Greenhow shared my opinion. "Go on," she said.

"Imagine soldiers," he said, "swooping down the streets of New York, for example, faster than the fastest runner, firing pistols and yelling like demons. Surely you can see what a demoralizing effect that would have on the citizenry. Think about it."

She was silent and did seem to be thinking about it. "How long has it been since you've been in New York, Charles?"

The Swan ✠ 197

Her tone had softened and the use of his given name told me she would soon be giving him some bad news.

"I don't remember," Swann said. "Sometime before my father died. I was a child. Years ago really."

"Do you remember the muddy streets? Where in the world do you expect your demoralizing wheeled soldiers with their pistols and demon cries to skate?"

His eyes shifted left and right. "On the sidewalks around certain key buildings," he said loudly. I had to give him credit for thinking on his feet. His gestures became more expansive. "They will work in teams. Yes, and each team will have a carriage and there will be three men. One on skates and two to take him under the arms and rush him across the muddy parts and. . . ."

But she was laughing now, and I was having a hard time remaining silent myself. I lowered the sash and climbed down off Jones.

"What are you grinning about?" Pinkerton asked.

I couldn't answer. I knew if I opened my mouth I would laugh out loud. I shook my head and gestured for them to follow me back under the stoop.

I quickly filled them in on what I'd seen and heard.

"It is astonishing," Pinkerton said, "how little it takes for some men to betray their countries. Now get back up there."

So Jones and I went back to the window. He boosted me up again and I lifted the sash.

They were drinking tea now. Swann looked despondent. Business must be over and he must have failed to convince her to help him, and now she was giving him tea because a civilized woman would not just tell him no and throw him out.

Swann put down his teacup. "Maybe there is something else I could do?"

"I can't imagine what," she said. "Frankly, Charles, you do not have the constitution nor the training for the kind of intrigue involved here. Now if you were a telegraphy expert, or if you had railroad connections or a plausible excuse to travel freely to Richmond . . ."

"I could do that," Swann said. I could see him regrouping, coming up with another plan on the spot. I wondered if it would be any better than the last one.

"If you were to supply me with introductions to certain people influential in the new Confederate patent office," he said, "I might be persuaded to carry other messages as well."

This was the kind of stuff Pinkerton wanted to hear. He suspected Mrs. Greenhow sent as much information as she could by courier. I forgot my mirth and paid close attention.

"And how do you expect to move back and forth across the lines, Charles?"

He put his box down on the table by his tea and stood up in front of her. This meant his back was to me and I couldn't see her and I couldn't see what he was doing.

"Charles?" she sounded a little alarmed.

A moment later she made a sound I can only describe as a squeak.

She recovered quickly and came to her feet. She took his hand. "This way," she said.

She pulled him out of the room.

I waited a few moments, and then got down off Jones.

"She's taken him out of the room," I told Pinkerton. "He's volunteered to carry messages for her."

"How the devil is he going to do that?" Pinkerton asked. "I don't have time for this. Daggett, this one's yours. Follow him to the ends of the Earth if you must."

"To the ends of the Earth?"

"I'll expect reports," he said. "You know the procedures." He stood up.

Jones got up, too. I put my hand on his arm. "Help me watch until he leaves," I said.

Jones looked at Pinkerton. Pinkerton shrugged and nodded and then walked off.

I motioned Jones back to the window, and he boosted me up. I didn't get up on his shoulders once I saw the room was still empty. "Not yet," I said.

I could have told Pinkerton about the strange thing Swann did there at the end, but this was my big chance. Once he'd given the case to me, I didn't want him getting interested and taking it back. I am convinced to this day his decision to assign me to what looked like a trivial case was influenced by his fall backwards into the mud which he no doubt blamed on me.

Jones and I waited there for another half an hour. Every few minutes I got him to boost me up to the window, and finally when I saw them come back into the room I stepped up onto his shoulders.

They were subdued. Swann seemed embarrassed. He was reading something on a piece of paper, but he stole more than a few glances up at Mrs. Greenhow. Fussing with the tea things, she looked both astonished and triumphant.

The talk around the office was that any man she took into the back was probably a spy. If she gave him a goodbye kiss at the top of the stairs, he was certainly a spy.

Swann gathered up his box.

"Do you have it by heart?" Mrs. Greenhow asked.

"Yes," he said. "Of course, I do." He handed her the paper he'd been studying.

"Well, you'd best be off then."

"Yes," he said.

I scrambled down from Jones. "He's about to leave." I grabbed my boots, and we got under the stoop.

Swann had memorized the information Mrs. Greenhow wanted conveyed to the Confederacy. That was becoming more common even early in the war. So I couldn't just nab him with incriminating papers on his person. He would have his introductions to powers who could help him with the patent office. Mrs. Greenhow would probably send word about Charles Wyatt Swann by other means. This was his first mission, after all. She would want to test him. His information might be duplicated by another courier. Pinkerton probably would have done it like that.

The interesting thing about Swann now was the method he would use to get himself across the lines to Richmond. I couldn't guess what that would be, but both he and Mrs. Greenhow seemed confident it would work.

His parting with Rose Greenhow was ambiguous. She detained him at the top of the stairs for a minute. I suppose she might have been looking into his eyes. Finally, she told him to take care. He left and she shut the door.

No kiss. But if he got no goodbye kiss, what had they been doing back there?

"Tell Pinkerton I'm on it," I told Jones. I crawled out from under the stairs and took off after Swann.

The weather the preceding week had been dreadful. Huge rainstorms had made the days dim and cold. It had been a mixed blessing, making the hour-to-hour surveillance miserable and wet, but making following anyone who left the Greenhow house easier because he tended to keep his head down and go directly to his destination. I was not so lucky. The weather had turned that day, and it was a bright afternoon.

I immediately crossed the street so it would not be so obvious that I was following. Swann carried his box in both hands in front for a while then tucked it under his left arm for a few paces then took it in both hands again. He was a slender young man in a black suit that was obviously too big for him and a derby. His full beard and long hair made him easy to keep in sight. He moved easily and walked briskly with the gait of a man in his prime.

Several blocks later, he turned onto another street and our paths crossed. He glanced at me, and I looked away too quickly. I was new at this aspect of the detective trade. My experience had been in the rough and tumble side of things in San Francisco, but I was doing my best. I had not yet met Sara, the woman I would later marry, and was quite without family or connections. I badly wanted to show Pinkerton what I could do.

As I followed Swann deeper into what for me was a strange city, I began to feel both at home and out of place. The neighborhood became shabby and the people looked rougher. I was glad to have the pistol under my coat, but I hoped I wouldn't have to use it. One thing was certain, though: if Swann did not come to his destination soon, he would surely notice me following him. I slowed down until he was in the middle of a block of rundown buildings on both sides of the muddy street, and then I ducked around the corner. I would hurry ahead and pick him up again at the next intersection. From then I would follow him by allowing him to follow me. I thought the ruse quite clever.

I nearly lost him. I came around the block just in time to see him step into a building. If I had been a moment longer, I would have lost him.

I walked to the doorway he had entered and saw that the establishment was a cheap hotel called Wilber's. At least the place matched his ill-fitting clothes. I concluded he must be a man who had fallen on hard times. First, he had spoken to Mrs. Greenhow as an equal and she had not objected. Second, she seemed to have been acquainted with his father.

I decided to give him a chance to settle before I continued. I wanted to make sure I knew all the exits before I went in the front door. There was the possibility he wasn't staying here at all but had spotted me and had walked right through the hotel and out the back way. I walked down the alley to check on that. I found a side entrance, but it was locked. In back, there was a patch of greenery surrounded by wooden fence. I eased open the gate and went in. I hadn't expected a garden. This one had not been tended in years, but I could see that once it might have been a pleasant place to sit and watch the sun go down. Weeds grew up through old wooden furniture, and there was a small empty pond.

I made my way through the weeds to the back door. The steps leading up to it were broken in two places. It was easy to see no one had come this way in years. I checked the door. It was locked. I walked back around to the front.

I took a quick look into the lobby and saw that Swann was not there. I walked on in. The man behind the desk was reading a newspaper and didn't look up at me. A deep rumbling sound echoed down from somewhere above. It sounded like someone was rolling a barrel back and forth across the floor upstairs.

I pulled the register over and turned it my way. I didn't see Swann's name so I flipped the page back and found it. Three days ago Charles Wyatt Swann had checked into Wilber's Hotel.

The man at the desk was now looking at me over his newspaper.

"You looking for a room?"

I flipped the register page back. "Yes," I said. Pinkerton had said to follow Swann to the ends of the Earth. I figured this place probably fell into that category. I didn't see any reason for a false name at this juncture, so I signed my own, John Daggett, and paid for a week's lodging.

"What is that noise?" I asked.

"That would be Mr. Swann in number eleven," he said. "Right over my head. You let me know if you can hear it from your room. He's very good about stopping when someone complains."

That was easy. I had gotten Swann's room number for free.

"What is he doing?" I asked.

His look told me that he had his suspicions, but he said, "I have no idea, sir."

I walked up the stairs. I paused and listened at room eleven and heard the rumbling. From here it was easy to guess what it was. Swann must be using his roller skates in there. It sounded like he was going from one end of the room to the other. I walked on to the room next door, number nine, and knocked. There was no answer. That didn't mean it was empty, but I might be able to get it. I walked on to my own room which was number fourteen on the other side of the hallway. My window faced the street. Knowing my room and Swann's faced different directions was all I needed. I walked back downstairs and asked if I could change to a room that faced away from the street. There were several rooms available but I manipulated my way into number nine.

I would make some modifications that would make surveillance easier if I were given the time. Swann might put his plans into motion immediately in which case I would have to be ready to simply keep following him. On the other hand he might stay a day or two and I might learn something more.

Instead of going on up to my new room, I bought a newspaper and settled into one of the shabby chairs in the hotel lobby and listened to Swann move back and forth on his roller skates. It went on for quite a long time, but finally it did stop. I looked up, and the man at the desk shrugged at me as if to say well maybe it's over for now. A few minutes later Swann himself appeared. He was carrying nothing, so I decided he was not ready to somehow deliver Mrs. Greenhow's message to Richmond. He was probably on his way to dinner. This was my chance to get back to headquarters and equip myself. I might even have time to go to my own lodgings and get a few days worth of clothes and necessities. I watched Swann from my chair until I could no longer see him from the front windows of the hotel. Then I stood up and casually walked to the door and watched him enter a tavern. I tossed down my paper and went out into the street. I had hoped to find a cab quickly, but in this neighborhood I had no luck and had to walk several blocks before I found one.

Then it was a simple matter to get back to headquarters and procure the equipment I needed. I saw neither Pinkerton nor Jones so there were few questions to answer. I had time to get some personal things from my lodgings as well. When I got back to Wilber's Hotel, I once again heard Swann skating up in his room. I smiled at that. He was being very accommodating in letting me know his whereabouts.

I went up to my room and listened to him but learned nothing new. I needed him to leave the room for at least fifteen minutes one more time. It looked like that wouldn't happen until breakfast. When he stopped skating, I listened until I was reasonably sure he had gone to bed and then I turned in myself.

I woke early the next morning and waited until I heard him moving around. I thought maybe he would skate again since that seemed to be all he did in there, but after a short time I heard him leave the room. I peeked out into the hallway and saw him walking down the stairs, still empty handed, probably for breakfast. My own meal could wait. I quickly took up my drill and made several holes in the wall at places that would afford me good views of his room. I put a stick polished for this very purpose in each hole so light would not give them away. Next, I slipped out into the hall, picked the lock on his door, went in, and quickly swept up the wood shavings from my drilling. It was too much of a risk at this point to conduct a search of the room. I saw that he had a large amount of luggage, two big trunks and several suitcases. The skates were on the sideboard. I picked one of them up and spun a wheel. Amazing, I thought. I put it back down in exactly the same place it had been before.

I slipped back into the hallway and locked his door again and then went back into my own room. Everything was ready. I would now simply watch him until he did something that would indicate how he intended to convey his information to the Confederacy. When that happened, I would arrest him. That wouldn't be right away. I probably had time for breakfast.

I found a place to eat up the street. I thought Swann might be eating there, too, but he wasn't. I spotted him again as I walked back to the hotel. He nodded at me as we both entered the lobby and walked toward the stairs. I lingered a little and he was just closing his door when I got to the top of the stairs. I went into my room.

I had carefully drawn the shade to minimize any light that might find its way through a hole when I removed the stick. The holes were very small. Since I had several, they didn't need to be large. I peeked through one of them and saw Swann in his shirt standing over the basin and looking at himself in the mirror. Perhaps he shaved around the edges of his beard. I didn't need to watch him do that.

I replaced the stick in the hole and sat down on my bed. It was very lumpy and uncomfortable. I had not gotten much sleep the night before. I hoped Swann would put his plan into action soon.

Perhaps an hour later I was roused from sleep by the sound of him skating again. I sighed. Falling asleep had not been professional, but Swann was making my job easy. He even woke me up when watching him put me to sleep. I got up and stretched and wandered over to one of my peeping holes, plucked out the stick, and peeked in on him.

The sight amazed me, and I made a small surprised sound. It was not Swann, the young bearded man I had been following, who was skating in there. Instead, I saw a young woman. She was tall and wore a plain long skirt and a blouse that buttoned to her throat. She pushed away from the wall by the door and rolled across the floor toward the window. She was very graceful, and just before she might have crashed into the wall, she did an astonishing turn and in a couple of small strides skated back to the door. As I watched there came a knock on her door.

"Just a moment, please," she called. She sat down on her bed and took off her skates. These she put back into the box I had seen Swann carrying. It was then that I noticed the trunks were packed and closed and pulled up near the door. She got off the bed and opened the door. Two men came inside.

"Yes, thank you, all of those, please."

The men gathered her luggage and took it from the room.

I had to do something quickly. I didn't know what was happening yet. I didn't know who the woman was or where Swann was, but I did know she was leaving and that I should stop her.

I jerked open my own door and ran into the hall. I came to a halt in front of her. Her eyes were pale blue, and her cheeks were very red as if she'd been in a high wind under a harsh sun.

"Mr. Daggett," she said and smiled at me.

Using my name knocked me completely off balance. Her gaze moved from my face to something behind me. I turned quickly and came face to face with a man holding a pistol pointed at my heart.

Two

▓

While I wasn't killed back in Washington in 1861, Mary Swann, although I did not know that was her name at the time, did get away from me. After her man hit me in the head, robbed me, and left me bleeding in the alley to the side of Wilber's Hotel, I reported back to Pinkerton. Based on my information, and I'll admit I did not give him all the details, we now knew to keep an eye out for two Swanns, a woman and a man. Neither was seen in the Union again until after the war. We discovered Swann's father had left a house in Boston, and it was kept under watch, but no one ever came back for it, and creditors eventually took it.

Mary probably did succeed in conveying that first message. In those early days, it was relatively easy for a woman to cross the lines. But she never got a chance to carry another one. If Swann patented his skate in the Confederacy, it proved to be pointless. He never did apply for a patent in the North, so I concluded he was stuck in the Confederacy. James Leonard Plimpton patented a roller skate in New York in 1863 and became known as the father of modern roller-skating.

When McClellan was removed from command in November of 1862, Pinkerton retired from the eastern theater, and I left his company and started my own private investigation office in New York City. I never did tell him that I thought Mary and Charles Swann were the same person. I had many other cases over the years, but I always considered the Swann case to be open until I settled that last question.

Now I was in Muncie, Indiana, with a chance to finally close the case.

Over one thousand people were said to have paid fifteen cents to participate in the grand opening of the Imperial Roller Rink. The rink was a large wooden building, and inside it was essentially one big room. Most of the floor space was given to the polished skating surface. There was railing all the way around and then seating and standing room for spectators. Above, there was a balcony for spectators, too. Both the lower and upper spectators' areas were crowded tonight. The space was bright with electric lights and loud. Sounds echoed and collided. The band had a hard time sounding good.

Men and women skated in an unorganized jumble. It reminded me of formal dancing except that it was too fast and not everyone had partners. Boys in plaid skating caps darted around dangerously. The scene also reminded me of a mob milling and stewing but not yet quite at the point of rioting. You didn't have to watch long to see someone fall down.

Roller-skating was popular all over the country in the eighties, but in Muncie it was phenomenal. People were crazy for it. Everyone was doing it. The papers were always talking about it. Tonight's big event was not the first in Muncie, which was well known among skaters as the home of the Muncie Roller Skate. In fact, there were four or five skate manufacturers in town. I knew none of the patents had Charles Wyatt Swann's name on them (and certainly none had Mary's), but I wondered how much influence her designs had had on Muncie skates.

Finally, the organizers cleared the floor, and the grand promenade of Muncie's finest followed. The Wild West show was next. It was not very exciting. Men in costumes I had never seen on anyone in the real West zoomed out onto the floor. Some wore feathers and others had pistols and exaggerated holsters and decorated chaps and oversized hats. The part I liked best was the horse on wheels which was constructed of two men inside a horse costume. They were a big hit since they fell over more than once.

The Wild West show got a less than unreserved applause. The local barrel racers did a lot better.

Then it was time for the big event. Everyone quieted down, and the band sounded a little better when not competing with so many other noises. They played for a moment and then with a drumroll the Swan glided onto the floor. We all participated in one huge gasp of surprise.

Mary Elizabeth Swann was, as I had long suspected, a bearded woman. She wore a formal ball gown of a cut I had not seen in many years. It seemed to be constructed of many layers of lavender material and there was a big white bow at her waist. The gown was cut low and her shoulders were bare. Her long dark hair flowed behind her as she moved. Her beard was still as black as I remembered it from all those years ago in Mrs. Greenhow's parlor.

If a bearded lady were all the Swan was the crowd would have quickly lost interest, but Mary did much more than simply display herself. She was a roller-skating virtuoso, and these were the days that roller-skating was so popular in the United States that on Sundays church attendance dropped. Her grace and her startling jumps and spins amazed and amused. Her stage name was based more on her stately grace than a simple play on her family name. Everyone loved her. The applause went on for a long time after she'd rolled off the floor.

Mary was the last act. The floor was then opened to the spectators, and pandemonium followed. I could not have hoped for more than what happened next. Mary (probably Charles now) dressed as a man skated onto the floor. He mingled with the others and no one seemed to recognize Mary even though surely many Munsonians must have known it was her. I had not come to Muncie to arrest her. I had only come to confirm my suspicions, but now that I had the chance, I could not resist at least some contact. Would she recognize me?

There was a man just sitting down to affix his skates to his boots. I quickly sat down beside him.

"I've always wanted to try that," I said.

"Oh?" he looked up at me, and I could see some interest in his eyes when he saw the double eagle in my hand.

"Fair deal?" I asked, pointing at his skates with the coin.

"Fair enough," he said and pulled the skates off his boots and gave them to me. I had probably paid ten times what they were worth.

He got up and I, after some puzzlement, got the skates attached to my boots. I grabbed the rail and pulled myself up and then worked my way hand over hand to the opening onto the rink floor. Okay, here we go, I told myself and pushed off. How hard could it be?

My feet flew off like startled geese, and I fell down hard on my backside. A couple of scruffy boys in plaid skating caps zoomed in, took me under the arms, and helped me to my feet.

"You should hold onto the rail until you get the hang of it," one of the boys told me with a satisfied smile on his face.

"Probably good advice, son," I said. "But that wouldn't get me where I want to go. Let me get my balance. Okay, now give me a little push. That way." I pointed in the direction I had last seen Charles.

They laughed and shrugged and gave me a push that wasn't much more than just letting me go. I rolled slowly away from them. They gave me a cheer.

I kept my knees locked. My feet drifted apart, and I made many adjustments to my upright posture by waving my arms in opposite directions. People got out of my way.

As I approached, Charles pushed off to my left, and I thought he had recognized me and was fleeing. I turned my head quickly and nearly fell again. Then he appeared from my right and our paths crossed. He had skated a wide circle around me. He did it again, this time spiraling in closer. There was laughter and applause.

As I neared the center of the skating rink, his circles diminished to nothing, and he stopped in front of me, put out his arm, and stopped me with a hand on my chest.

"Nice catch!" someone shouted.

Up close, I could see there was a little gray in the beard, but not much. The face had filled out, and there were some deep wrinkles. The pale blue eyes were as I remembered them from that last encounter in Wilber's Hotel. I could see Mary and then Charles and then Mary again.

"You may not be quite ready to come all the way out here," Charles said.

"I came out to see you, Mary," I said.

Her eyes narrowed and she studied my face closely, but I don't think she recognized me. That should not have surprised me. She had seen me up close only once and that had been a long time ago. Surely I had changed over the years. I realized that while I had wondered often about her over the years, she might have given me scarcely a thought.

"We've met?"

"John Daggett," I said and held out my hand. "In Washington during the war."

She ignored my hand and moved as gracefully as a fish back a few paces, but she didn't flee. "So, have you been looking for me all this time?"

"Heavens, no," I said. "I worked out the Charles and Mary business years ago. I just wanted to see you one more time. I'm nobody official in Indiana."

"Nobody official." She looked me over again, and then she said suddenly, "Mr. Daggett. Wilber's Hotel!"

"That's it," I said. "What happened to you after that?"

"Many adventures, of course," she said. "How about you?"

"Oh, pretty much the same," I said and we laughed together.

"I was right about all of this." She made a gesture I took to mean the skating rink and perhaps the entire skating phenomenon itself.

"Yes," I said. "I suppose you were."

She smiled and skated away to one side, leaving me stranded. Our interview was apparently over, and I was painfully aware that I did not know how to get off the floor.

I could drop to my hands and knees and crawl, I thought, but before I could put that plan into action, she came up from behind and stopped at my side and took my arm.

"Let's get you safely back among the spectators, Mr. Daggett," she said.

Her grip was firm, and I didn't feel at all unsteady as she set us in motion. As we moved, I understood at last the exhilaration that had driven her to work so hard for all those years on her roller skates.

"I don't always just watch," I said.

"I'm sure you don't." She meant I was protesting too much, and she was right. I watched people and events, and then I wrote reports about them. We came to the railing, and I grabbed on. She let me go and smiled and waved and skated back into the thick of things.

P. G. Nagle has had two novels published, *Glorieta Pass* and *The Guns of Valverde*, both set during the Far Western campaign of the Civil War. She has also been published in *The Magazine of Fantasy & Science Fiction*, *The Williamson Effect*, *Elf Fantastic*, and *An Armory of Swords*. She lives in Albuquerque, New Mexico.

Although emotions ran high during the conflict, there often was no reason to be uncivil to civilians, especially if they had information to reveal. The Judge Lemmik in the following story is based on a real-life spy, Judge Kimmel, who coordinated Union espionage activities around Chambersburg, which proved crucial to the North's movements during the war.

THE COURTSHIP OF CAPTAIN SWENK

⬛

P. G. Nagle

"Where d'you suppose General Lee might be going?" asked Buck McAlexander of his two companions as they strode through a thicket of cedar. A short distance to the east lay the turnpike out of Chambersburg, Pennsylvania, full of Confederate soldiers marching north and stirring up a good deal of dust as they went.

"Idiot," said Henry Ball, pushing a branch out of his way. "That's what we're supposed to find out. Didn't you hear a word the judge said?"

" 'Course I did, and I ain't an idiot, thank you very much," Buck replied, tossing a shank of black hair out of his eyes. "If we don't try to guess where he's going, how're we going to know where to look?"

"Got you there, Henry," said Nathaniel Swenk, their companion and fellow scout. Apparently considering this statement the end of the discussion, Swenk returned to chewing on a blade of barley-grass and gazing over at the column on the pike in a contemplative way. Mr. Ball observed this bovine activity with an expression of distaste.

Captain Swenk, recently returned to town after receiving honorable discharge from the United States Army, was understood to be courting, and was consequently considered by his acquaintances to be not quite in his right mind. If there had been surprise at the captain's failure to reenlist after his two-year term of service had concluded, it had been abated by his popularity among his townfellows, and by curiosity (extending, in some reprehensible cases, to the placing of bets) as to which of the eligible ladies in the vicinity he would select for his bride. He was fairly new in Chambersburg, having moved to town early in 1861 with the announced desire of settling there permanently and starting a family. The commencement of hostilities had preempted this amiable scheme, but since his discharge it had apparently been foremost in his mind, and the little task of ascertaining General Lee's movements seemed not to be interfering overmuch with his prosecution of it.

"And anyway, these fellers aren't with General Lee. They're under D. H. Hill," Buck declared.

"Rodes," said Ball, shaking his head. "Hill has a beard."

"Well, and so he did have a beard when he rode by."

"No, he had a mustache, but no beard."

"It was trimmed close—"

"Hold up, boys," Swenk interrupted.

They came to a stop just inside the end of the grove. Before them was an open oat field, recently relieved of its crop. They gazed across it at the marching Rebels. Buck shifted from foot to foot.

"Over to the creek," Swenk said softly, and struck west toward the Conococheague. The trees growing along the watercourse would afford them cover until another wood could be reached.

The three of them—Swenk, Ball, and McAlexander—had been charged with their important task by Judge Lemmik who, since the twenty-second of June, had sent messages by secret means to General Couch about the activities of the Confederate forces occupying Chambersburg. Getting this information past the net of Confederate pickets surrounding the town was impressive in itself, though Buck, being merely nineteen, had expressed the opinion that the secrecy of Lemmik's operations robbed them of all glory.

Kept from enlisting by the earnest entreaties of his mother, whose husband had been visiting relatives in Tennessee when the war broke out and had not been heard from since, Buck had been overjoyed to receive the judge's invitation to act as an observer, gathering Important Information to send on to the Union army's headquarters. It had sounded more glorious than it had so far turned out.

"We must've walked every danged road in the county," Buck complained. "We know General Lee ain't here. We should be looking out south of town."

"The judge said all enemy movements are important," said Ball.

Buck let out a guffaw. "Only enemy movement worth seeing was that crack-fine fiddle dance Jenkins's cavalry gave last night in your barn, Henry."

Ball's expression grew yet more sour. Captain Swenk, failing to notice,

The Courtship of Captain Swenk ❧ 213

said, "That was a mighty fine dance, indeed. I was surprised at how many of our ladies attended. Miss Kindle is a delightful dancer, don't you think?"

"She wouldn't dance with me," Buck said. "Only had eyes for you, Cap'n."

"And General Jenkins's staff were generous hosts," added Swenk.

"Generous with my beer," Ball replied.

"Didn't they pay you for it?"

"In Confederate scrip. Same worthless stuff they're giving all the merchants in town."

"At least they didn't just break into the shops and help themselves," Swenk remarked.

"Yet," said Ball darkly, and kicked a rock off the bank into the creek. The pike was now obscured from view, but the cloud of dust was plainly visible. They were approaching the neighborhood of Ball's house and farm, which he had only recently purchased, being, like Swenk, a newcomer to Chambersburg. The annoyance he demonstrated at the recent infestation of Confederates was understandable to his companions. His wheat and his animals had been confiscated, Rebel pickets lived in his cornfield, and his house had been taken over by General Jenkins's staff. Mr. Ball had consequently spent a good deal of time in town of late, and was often to be found at Judge Lemmik's when he was not tramping the roads and byways of Franklin County.

The day—a Thursday afternoon late in June—was warm, and birds peeped in desultory tones as the three men walked northward. Captain Swenk was the only one of the trio who seemed at ease with the world. He smiled placidly as they reached a footbridge across the creek just short of where the waterway bent northeastward. The land was a blend of cultivated fields and wild, wooded areas. Mr. Ball's farm occupied the far side of a hill across the creek; the near side was owned by a Mrs. Bannister, a widow, who was one of the ladies Captain Swenk had been courting. Her house, neatly painted white, lay just beneath the crest of the hill and was shaded by a great, ancient live oak.

"I think," Swenk said to his companions, "I shall stop at Widow Bannister's awhile. You go on ahead and I'll catch up."

Buck and Ball exchanged a glance of knowing disapproval. "We are to share the task of counting the Rebels, are we not?" Ball said in a stiff voice. "How are we to divide the work without your presence?"

"You two make your best count, and I'll verify it," Swenk replied. "That way we'll know our information's good." He tipped his hat to them, smiling, and strode off across the bridge toward Bannister's Farm.

"We won't see him for an hour or more," grumbled Ball.

"Hopeless," Buck agreed.

"How such a great stupid ox of a fellow ever got anywhere in the army is beyond me!"

"Come on," Buck said, nodding his head eastward. "Let's go count Rebs."

"Good day to you, Mrs. Bannister," called Captain Swenk, bowing as he removed his hat, his face slightly reddened by the exertion of climbing the hill to the farmhouse.

The widow, not a handsome woman, stood on the step of her tidy home, dressed in a gray gown, modest cap, and stiffly starched apron, and bestowed a smile more of politeness than warmth upon her visitor. "You did not come to feed this morning," she said.

"I beg your pardon," the captain said humbly. "I was unavoidably detained. I hope you sent Will to do it."

"I do not like sending him into the cellar with the animals. One of them might kick and injure him," the widow said, a slight frown creasing her brow.

"He knows better than to expose himself to harm," Swenk replied, smiling.

"I am still not convinced this is the wisest course," the widow complained.

"But, ma'am, do you not wish to keep your horse and cow out of the Confederates' hands? I assure you, they've snabbled up everything on four legs in the county."

"I do not like keeping Dobbin and Daisy underground, and in such close quarters with your mare," she said.

"They will neither of them suffer for it," he assured her. "Have you—"

"Captain Swenk!" cried the big live oak tree that shaded the house and yard.

"Willie! Come down from there this instant!" the widow called to the tree. A rustling of leaves preceded the arrival upon the ground of a grubby ten-year-old boy who immediately flung himself upon Captain Swenk, soiling the sleeve of that gentleman's coat.

"Hello, Will!" the captain said, beaming upon his youthful admirer.

"General Jenkins went out riding this morning!"

"Oh, he did?"

"How could you know that?" demanded the widow.

Will glanced at the captain, then said, "I can see Mr. Ball's place from up there," and pointed to the oak. "The general had a big black hat with a feather in it, and a big long beard."

"Don't point, Willie. It's rude," said his mother in an irritable tone. "I wish you would not climb that tree."

The Courtship of Captain Swenk ✖ 215

"Oh, it's a fine old tree," said Captain Swenk. "Must be one of the oldest in the county. How could he not climb it?"

"His sister has begun to copy him," the widow complained. "I live in fear of her falling and breaking her head."

"Where is little Katie?" asked the captain, smiling as he produced a small box from the depths of his coat pocket. "I've brought her some crayons."

The widow's face relaxed somewhat, and she said, "That was kind of you. I suppose you want some coffee? Well, come inside."

A smile curved up one corner of the captain's mouth, which gave him a somewhat foolish appearance. He looked down at Will and winked, then ruffled his hair, and the two of them followed Widow Bannister into the house.

Judge Lemmik always poured the best beer in Chambersburg, and Buck always strove to do it justice. Henry Ball sat next to him at Lemmik's parlor table with a half-empty tankard before him and a slight frown creasing his brow. The judge, an energetic man who seemed unencumbered by his threescore years, set a full crockery pitcher in the center of the table, closed the parlor door against unwanted intrusion, and seated himself.

"I have some bad news, gentlemen," he said, graciously including Buck in the description.

"Withers was caught?" asked Ball.

The judge nodded. "I've just heard General Jenkins has a new prisoner at his headquarters. I must assume it is he."

Ball grimaced. "I suppose you want me to go home and learn what I can?"

"No, I doubt you'd find out anything more, and we don't want to draw their attention." The judge took off his spectacles and began to polish them. "That makes three couriers captured since Wednesday. Either the Confederate pickets have suddenly become much more efficient—"

"No sign of that," Buck offered, refreshing his tankard from the pitcher.

"Or we're being spied upon," Ball concluded.

"I'm afraid so," the judge said.

Buck looked around at the door, which was shut, and the windows, which looked out onto the judge's peaceful garden, where the last sun was gilding the leaves of the rosebushes. Having concluded this survey without discovering any spies, he returned his attention to the beer.

"Shall I try to get through?" Ball offered.

"No," the judge said. "The news Withers was carrying is stale now. The Rebels are preparing to move, from the looks of it. We'll wait until we have something decisive to send." He poured beer into a small horn cup and took a sip. "What did you learn today?"

"That column kept marching north on the Harrisburg pike," Ball said. "They had artillery, but we don't know how many guns. If Swenk had been with us we might have done more—"

"He went off a-courting again," Buck supplied, swirling his beer around. "Danged if I know what he sees in that Widow Bannister. Got a face like a mule."

"It is admirable in Captain Swenk to pay attention to a widow with children," the judge said kindly. "Not every man would consider courting such."

"Not any man, other'n Swenk," said Buck.

Henry Ball shifted in his seat. "Should we not be discussing our plans?"

"We should indeed," said the judge. "This infantry column—were you able to identify the units?"

"Alabama, we think," said Ball.

"Saw Hill riding with them," said Buck, setting his tankard down and wiping his mouth on his sleeve.

"It was General Rodes, not Hill," Ball said in an annoyed tone.

"I'm pretty sure it was Hill—"

"And how far did they go?" the judge asked.

Buck looked at his partner and shrugged.

"Green Village," Ball said. "Maybe as far as Shippensburg."

Sounds of an arrival in the house penetrated the door, precipitating a pause in the discussion. Buck set down the pitcher and put a hand to the butt of his pistol. All three men tensed as the parlor door opened. Captain Swenk strolled in, smiling benignly. The housekeeper, Mrs. Ellis, cast the judge a wry look behind the captain's back and came in to set about sweeping the hearth.

"Afternoon, Judge. Afternoon, boys," said Swenk. "Say, I never could find you again."

Judge Lemmik got up to fetch the captain a tankard. Swenk made himself comfortable in the judge's armchair by the fireplace, and accepted the beer with a nod of thanks. He stretched out his feet before the empty fireplace, and gave her a kindly smile as she arose from the hearth. She sniffed, and took herself off, closing the door.

"We weren't hard to find," Ball said dryly. "Your afternoon must have been taken up with other business."

"Well, that's true enough, I suppose," said the captain, grinning. He pulled at his beer, set it carefully on the slate hearth, and withdrew a sheet of notepaper from his breast pocket. "Here you are, Judge," he said.

Judge Lemmik perused the page with interest. "Twenty-four regiments under Rodes and Johnson—Third Alabama, Sixth Alabama, Twelfth Alabama—you're sure this is accurate?"

"Should be."

The judge sat down at the table, one finger tapping its polished surface as he read through the notes. "Very good, very good," he murmured.

"Did the Widow Bannister tell you that?" demanded Ball.

"No," said Swenk with a pleasant smile. "She doesn't care for armies. Thinks they're a nuisance."

The judge folded the page. "You've done very well, Captain, but I think we shall wait to see what tomorrow brings. Most of Lee's army is still to the south of us. Perhaps tomorrow we'll learn whether they are headed toward Harrisburg or York."

"The units that passed today went toward Harrisburg," Ball pointed out.

"But they went into bivouac," said Swenk. "They could turn right around tomorrow and head for Gettysburg."

"We must learn where the bulk of the army will go," said the judge. "If it's Harrisburg, we know they'll attack Philadelphia. If Gettysburg, they're after Baltimore and the capital. As soon as we know which, we must get word to Couch's headquarters, and quickly. Tomorrow or the next day should tell."

Swenk finished his beer and stood up. "I'll be going along, then, if you don't need me. I have an invitation to supper."

"We'll meet again in the morning," the judge agreed, shaking the captain's hand. "I'll see you out."

The door closed behind them. Ball stared at it, frowning thoughtfully.

"It was Hill," said Buck, reaching for the beer.

Friday dawned cloudy and quiet. There were few soldiers to be seen in the town, so the three observers struck southward to a hilltop overlooking the road to Green Village. Captain Swenk had brought a pair of field glasses, which he and Mr. Ball passed back and forth like drunkards sharing a flask. Buck sat with his back against an oak, alternately watching his companions and the glowering clouds.

"Could be Heth," Swenk said, handing off the glasses. "We could tell for sure if we got a bit closer."

"Too risky," said Ball. "They're coming this way anyway, might as well wait."

"That's right," Buck said, stifling a yawn. "Judge told us not to take chances, on account of too many men have been caught. He thinks there's a Reb spy in Chambersburg."

Ball shot him a withering glance. "We've had hundreds of Rebels through Chambersburg. A spy would be rather superfluous."

"But he said—"

"It's getting on," Swenk said, putting the glasses away. "I think we've learned what we can for now."

"Good," said Buck, getting to his feet. "I'm ready for breakfast."

They turned their steps northward, back toward town, descending the hill to the road through a meadow of daisies. Captain Swenk delayed them for five minutes while he collected a couple dozen of the bright-eyed flowers, to the disgust of his companions.

"The Reb spy could be setting our men up," Buck told Ball while they watched Swenk's operations. "First they caught Barnes, and then Byrd, and then Withers—"

"Withers went up the railroad tracks," Ball said. "He was caught because he was plain stupid."

"Judge is right to be careful," Buck insisted. "Could be all of us are in terrible danger. Spy could be fixing to capture us all!" His eyes glowed at the thought.

Ball didn't appear to share his enthusiasm. He leaned in to Buck and said in a fierce whisper, "That spy may be closer than you think!" He jerked his head toward Swenk—who strode unconcerned through the daisies—and frowned his young companion into silence.

Buck fixed his gaze on the captain with a look of new appreciation. He whispered back, "Swenk's a spy, and hoodwinked us all? Well, what a stunner!"

Ball put a cautionary finger to his lips. Captain Swenk appeared not to have heard.

"I don't know," Buck added, still whispering. "Fellow who walks about picking daisies with a big, silly smirk on his face—just don't seem right for a spy."

"Won't they be pretty, bound up in a blue ribbon?" Swenk asked, displaying the bouquet as he returned.

"Quite," said Ball in a sour tone. "Shall we go? It's beginning to rain." He strode off without waiting for an answer.

Buck looked at the captain, who was watching Ball's departure with a bemused expression. With a shrug, Buck fell in with his comrade as they hurried back to town.

The Courtship of Captain Swenk ✖ 219

*　　*　　*

By Saturday morning Chambersburg was swarming with Rebels. Captain Swenk and the Widow Bannister stood together atop the courthouse steps among the crowd of citizens who had come out to watch the Rebel army pass. Below them a column of Confederate infantry poured into town from the south, passing through the Diamond at the center of town in a continuous stream. Now and then they raised a cheer of "Hurrah for the Southern Confederacy." The townspeople made no answer, merely watching, exchanging words of apprehension in lowered tones.

"Mrs. McAlexander entertained four of their officers to dinner last night," said Mrs. Bannister, disapproval in her voice.

"She may be trying to ensure her family's safety," said the Reverend Biggs, who stood nearby. "After all, her husband is not at home."

"If she thinks harboring the enemy will ensure her protection she is sadly mistaken," pronounced Mrs. Bannister.

"It is better than being robbed," said the captain with a shrug.

"We will all be robbed sooner or later," complained Dr. Lengham. "They've taken all the sheets from the hotels for their wounded. No doubt they'll want ours next."

Miss Katie Bannister, who had reached all the dignity of six years, tugged at Captain Swenk's trousers. He picked her up, cradling her in powerful arms.

"I drew you another picture," she said, proffering a slightly crumpled page.

Swenk took it, balancing the child on one hip while he admired her artwork. "That's beautiful, Katie. What a pretty flag."

"That one was the prettiest," Katie agreed. "I saw a man with a peg leg," she added.

"A peg leg? Was he a pirate?"

Miss Bannister gravely shook her head. "He was a 'Federate."

"Katie Bannister!" cried her mother, becoming aware of her presence. "Where is your brother?"

"Up there," Katie said, looking up toward the cupola atop the courthouse. The widow, the minister, and Captain Swenk all followed her gaze. Mrs. Bannister emitted a muffled cry of dismay.

"I'll fetch him down, shall I?" the captain offered. He kissed Katie's cheek, gently set her on her feet, and strode into the building.

"A kind and considerate man, Captain Swenk," said the minister, nodding approval.

"He talks too much," the widow told him, "but he is well enough, I suppose. Katie, your apron is smudged."

Buck leaned against the wall of Hoke's store, not quite succeeding at appearing nonchalant. Henry Ball stood nearby with his hands buried deep in his pockets, watching the sea of Rebels continue to wash through the Diamond. Officers on horseback, leading columns of weary infantry, were beginning to give way to artillery and wagons full of supplies. It was not as colorful as the annual Fourth of July parade—which would take place next week and in which Buck, wearing Parson Biggs's second-best wig, was to portray George Washington—but it was much, much bigger.

"Is that General Lee?" Buck whispered in a tone of awe.

Ball looked up at the mounted officer entering the Diamond, a man of erect carriage and silvered beard, wearing a black felt hat and a heavy caped overcoat, and riding a gray horse. "Has to be," he admitted.

The column behind General Lee halted right on the pike while the general moved forward to consult with one of his subordinates. This man, also mounted, had a long, reddish beard and made a crisp salute.

"Who's that he's talking with? Longstreet?" asked Buck.

"I think it's A. P. Hill," said Ball.

"Isn't Hill shorter than that?"

"He's on horseback, it's hard to tell."

The two generals withdrew a bit from the throng. Ball restrained his young friend from trying to get close enough to hear their discussion.

"They'll clap you in irons, you fool!" Ball hissed.

"We mustn't have that," Judge Lemmik remarked, joining his volunteers by Hoke's store. "I believe I'll need you to run that errand today, Buck."

"Right now?" Buck asked, his eyes aglitter with excitement.

"Possibly. Let's see which way the wind blows."

They all looked toward the two Confederate generals. As they watched, a third general joined them, tall in the saddle.

"*That's* Longstreet," said Buck and Ball together.

The judge nodded and softly said, "Don't appear too interested, boys." He ambled a few steps away to talk with some of the other citizens who were out to watch the show.

Ball turned his back to the Confederates, shot Buck a glance full of warning, and proceeded to examine the goods in Hoke's window. Buck took some dice from his pocket and squatted to toss them, but he didn't take his eyes off the Rebel generals.

*   *   *

"Will, your mother doesn't like you being up here," Captain Swenk said from the top step of the stairs. Young Mr. Bannister knelt on the floor of the cupola, peeping over the rail at the crowded town below.

"She wouldn't mind if she came up here and saw it," Will said. "I counted thirty-six flags so far."

"That's excellent," the captain said, placing a hand on Will's shoulder as he joined him to peer down at the Rebels. "But you ought to come down now."

Will looked up at the captain, who wore a slightly strained expression. The boy made no protest, but quietly gathered up his pencils and notebook. Captain Swenk, however, made no move to go.

Below, in the Diamond, the conference of generals had broken up. General Lee rode forward, the column falling in behind him. In the center of the Diamond, the general pulled on his right rein, and his horse turned eastward.

"Gettysburg," the captain murmured.

A frown creased his brow. Below, Buck McAlexander slipped behind Hoke's store and started off swiftly through the alleys, heading north. Henry Ball paused to speak to Judge Lemmik, then followed. The captain's frown deepened.

"Come on, William," he said. "Let's go."

"We should go across-country," Ball said, dabbing at his brow with his handkerchief as he strode along the railroad beside Buck. Insects buzzed in the grasses and the tracks glowed dully under a sun dimmed by thin clouds. A haze hung over the valley ahead.

"This way's faster," Buck said. "Judge said get there as fast as possible."

"Withers was caught on this road."

"We'll slip off if we see any pickets."

"If we see them it'll be too late," Ball said crossly.

"You don't have to come." Buck waved his arm westward. "There's your farm over yonder. Don't you want to see what the Rebs left?"

Ball was silent for a moment, then said, "Wouldn't your mother be alarmed if she knew what you were doing?"

Buck merely grinned. "She knows it's for a good cause."

No more conversation passed between them for some minutes. Mr. Ball glanced from time to time at his house and fields, but did not stray from Buck's side. They walked quickly, and Ball was perspiring quite strongly by the time they reached the shade of an apple grove growing close to the tracks. The rail fence that had once bordered it had been torn apart and used for firewood by the Rebels who had camped in the neighborhood.

"Want to rest?" Buck asked.

"I thought you were anxious to go on," said Ball with asperity.

"Don't want to wear you out," Buck replied kindly. "You set a spell, I'll climb up and look for the enemy."

"Get down!" Ball said, but Buck was already into the branches of an apple tree.

From the south a tall figure was approaching, loping up the tracks. Ball redoubled his entreaties, but Buck refused to budge. Ball turned to face the new arrival, and his expression of displeasure deepened as he recognized Captain Swenk.

"I'm glad I caught up to you boys!" called the captain, huffing cheerily. "You certainly made good time. Come on down, Buck."

"I'm looking for Rebels," Buck announced.

"Well, you won't find any up there," Swenk said. "Come along, I'm going with you."

"Won't three men be rather conspicuous?" said Ball.

"More so than two? I doubt it," said Swenk. He glanced ahead to where the railroad crossed the Conococheague. "There was a picket at that bridge two days ago. We'll be much better off away from the railroad."

"Mighty thoughtful of you to come and warn us," Ball said, still frowning. "Those aren't ripe," he added as Swenk pulled an apple from the tree.

The captain glanced at it, said, "You're right," and tossed it aside.

A rustling and scraping issued from the tree, followed by Buck's emergence. He landed in the road so close to Ball it made him jump. In Buck's hand was his Colt revolver.

"Put that away, you fool, before you hurt yourself," said Ball.

"No, I don't think so," Buck replied, aiming the gun at Swenk.

The captain slowly put his hands in the air. Ball looked from him to Buck with an expression of fury.

"What do you think you're doing?"

"I believe he thinks he's capturing us for the Confederates," said Swenk calmly.

Buck grinned. "You're sharper than you look, Captain. That's exactly right. I'll have your pistol, the one you keep in your pocket. Nice and easy."

Swenk handed over the weapon. Buck relieved Mr. Ball of his own defense—a wicked little knife—then smiled at them both in a friendly way.

"Now, you two walk on up to the bridge there where my friends are waiting. I'll be right behind you, so no tricks. Ain't fired this gun in weeks, and I wouldn't mind some target practice."

Captain Swenk looked at Ball, whose fury had turned his face purple. With a shrug, Swenk obeyed and started toward the bridge, a good quarter-mile away. Ball walked beside him, frowning intently at the ground.

Buck started whistling, which seemed only to increase Ball's rage. Captain Swenk managed after some moments' effort to catch Ball's eye.

"On three," Swenk whispered.

Suddenly alert, Ball faced forward and gave a short nod. A step, another, then he and Swenk turned as one and grappled with Buck, who yelled in surprise. The pistol fired into the air, Swenk having made it his business to grab Buck's arm and direct it skyward. The three of them tumbled to the ground, Buck kicking and squirming. At last Swenk wrested the pistol away and placed the barrel against the traitor's chest, at which Buck lay still. Ball, pinning his legs, looked up at the captain.

"You followed us on purpose. How did you know?" he asked, out of breath.

"I only suspected," Swenk said. "I didn't know until he tried making a present of us to the Rebel pickets."

Buck's eyes narrowed, but then he smiled wickedly. "Tried and succeeded," he said, nodding down the valley.

A half dozen pickets were running toward them from the bridge. The captain frowned, then looked back at Buck.

"Sorry for this," he said, and fired.

Ball flinched at the sound, then gaped at the awful mess the pistol had made of McAlexander's chest. The youth's eyes went blank, and a haze seemed to film them over.

Ball worked his jaws, but only managed to say, "Wh-wh—"

"No time," said Swenk, quickly retrieving his gun and Ball's knife from the spy's pockets. He handed the knife to its owner and dropped the gory pistol by Buck's corpse, pocketing his own gun. "Come on," he said, and with a glance toward the shouting pickets, took off running down the tracks.

They sped along the cinders to the bottom of the hill, then Swenk left the tracks and climbed in loping strides up through the trampled fields of Ball's farm. Ball kept up as best he could, the shouts of the pickets behind them and the occasional whiz of a musket ball serving to speed him.

"Not my house," he shouted to Swenk, gasping for breath.

"I know," called the captain over his shoulder. "The wood."

Ball followed him into a stand of oak that grew uphill of the house. The captain dropped speed, trotting through the wood, still angling uphill. The oaks climbed over the hilltop, affording some cover, at least, to their flight. Shouts came from behind and beside them now; the pickets were splitting up.

At last they reached the crest of the hill and the tall, old oak. Both men picked up speed, the captain running, Ball stumbling downhill toward Mrs. Bannister's house. The captain ran to the cellar doors at the side of the house and flung them open, leaping in. Ball, a hand pressed to his side, halted in the opening, gasping as he peered into the darkness.

"Come on, hurry," the captain's voice called.

Ball took a step down the sloping, earthen ramp. A jingling sound made him pause, then hurry forward.

"Your mare's been here all along?" he cried. "I thought the Rebels had taken her!"

"Here," the captain said, thrusting a bridle into his hands. "That's Dobbin's. I'll get the saddle."

Ball moved to the plowhorse's head and coaxed him to take the bit. "Was it necessary—" he began.

"Yes," Swenk replied, tugging at the girth. "If I'd let him go he'd have betrayed Judge Lemmik and the others, not just you and me."

Ball swallowed, and nodded, passing the reins over Dobbin's head. "Captain Swenk," he said, and paused to clear his throat. "I've been mistaken in you. I've not given you the credit you deserve."

"I thank you, Henry," said Swenk, his grin a pale glow in the darkness. "But we'll sort that out later. You must get to Lemmik's and warn him. Wait two minutes while I lead the pickets off."

"General Couch—" Ball began.

"I'll take care of it," Swenk said, mounting the mare. He had to crouch low in the dark cellar. Clicking his tongue, he eased her toward the light of the open doors. A figure appeared to bar his way, silhouetted by sun.

"Get inside, Will!" the captain called harshly. "Remember what I told you to say if the Rebels come around."

"Yes, sir! I'll close the door for you first," said the boy.

Swenk didn't answer, but urged his mare up the slope. By the time Ball had followed, blinking in the daylight, the captain was galloping over the hilltop.

Dobbin heaved a sigh and began cropping the grass at his feet. Will Bannister stared at the horse and its rider for a moment, then grinned and tossed Mr. Ball a salute before shutting the cellar doors and running for the farmhouse door.

Gunfire sounded from beyond the hilltop. Sparing a glance for the house, where the widow's face peered indignantly from one of the windows, Ball urged his mount forward, riding for Chambersburg.

Two weeks later, on July 10, the only Rebels remaining in town were either residents of the hospital that had been set up in the schoolhouse, or prisoners. News of the mighty battle at Gettysburg, a glorious victory for the Union, had set all the bells in town to ringing, and a huge crowd had gathered to watch the Fourth of July parade despite its having been delayed a week on account of the Rebel occupation. Nearly every person in town was present to view the spectacle. Among the few absent was the grieving Mrs. McAlexander, who remained at home, packing for a visit to her cousin in Clarksville.

Henry Ball sat watching the parade from a place of honor on the reviewing stand in front of the town hall. Beside him sat Judge Lemmik on the one hand and Widow Bannister on the other. Mrs. Bannister, upon receiving Mr. Ball's abject apology for the peremptory borrowing of her horse, had graciously bestowed her favor on him, expressing the belief that, short of losing her children or her home, she could bear any suffering in the cause of the Union. If thoughts of the convenience of joining his farm to the widow's—they were adjacent, after all—had occurred to Mr. Ball, he was gallant enough not to voice them.

"Here they come," he murmured to Mrs. Bannister, who gave him a fleeting smile in return before shifting her gaze to the parade. The grand finale, a hay cart decorated to resemble a rowboat, with men pulling oars through imaginary waters as it passed majestically through the Diamond, boasted the proudly waving figure of Captain Swenk, dashing in the parson's wig and a fancy coat covered in braid. If Washington had not crossed the Delaware in company with two small children—one a young scamp tootling on a fife and wearing a gory bandage about his brow, the other a pretty child in her best Sunday dress— none of the observers seemed to mind. Cheer after cheer rained upon the captain and his two recruits as they were carried through the Diamond.

"He makes a fine George Washington," Henry Ball remarked to the widow.

"He is too broad-shouldered, I believe," said the widow, but she deigned to smile on him nonetheless.

Jane Lindskold grew up in Washington, D.C., and lived for a time in the Blue Ridge Mountains, not far from the Shenandoah Valley where this story is set. The author of over forty short stories and several novels—including *Changer* and *Legends Walking*—she lives in Albuquerque, New Mexico, with her husband, archaeologist Jim Moore. Lindskold is currently at work on another novel.

Mixing history with fiction in her story, she brings to life Captain Sandie Pendleton, Jed Hotchkiss, Howell Brown, and, of course, Thomas "Stonewall" Jackson in this story of feint and counterfeint in Virginia.

THE ROAD TO STONY CREEK

Jane Lindskold

If one of the cows hadn't strayed, Katie Rowland might never have spotted the spies. The girl had been toiling up to the little copse where Princess took herself when she had a mind to be ornery, when she spotted two men on the road below, riding slowly along and talking in low voices.

Immediately Katie hunkered close to the ground, taking shelter in mountain laurels that crowded the edge of the ridge. The ground was wet from recent rain, but even in late March the laurels were covered with dense green leaves that granted her ample cover.

Both of the strangers were mounted, one on a blue roan, the other on a rather faded chestnut. The man on the roan was sitting in the saddle, one leg crossed over the other. He had a notebook and was busily sketching his surroundings as the horse ambled on. Seemingly he trusted the horse to carry him without guidance, for he never touched the reins.

His companion didn't seem as sure of the roan's good sense for he kept a weather eye on the man with the sketch pad, even while doing incomprehensible things like dismounting to test the surface of the road or to measure the distance between two tall oaks at the roadside.

Carefully angling herself so that she could glimpse what the man was drawing without herself being seen, Katie realized that he was making a map. It was odd to recognize in those dark penciled lines the familiar contours of the road, the twisting of the nearby creek, the neighbors' farms.

Now, Katie knew about the battle that had been fought about a week before at Kernstown; knew, too, that the Sesch forces under General Jackson had been routed by the Yankees, that they had retreated south to Rude's Hill, not all that far from her own home. It didn't take a great leap of logic to guess that these two strangers just might be associated with one or the other of the armies.

She tried to guess which side these men were on, but for the life of her she couldn't decide. They wore more gray than blue, but neither wore what she'd call a uniform. The man with the sketch pad didn't even seem to carry a gun, but—given his tendency to cross one leg over the other right there in the saddle to give himself a better desk for drawing—Katie thought he might have trouble carrying one without hurting himself.

The artist's companion carried guns, though: a pistol at his belt and a rifle in the saddle holster. He was more aware of his surroundings, too. A couple of times Katie'd been worried he'd sensed her presence even though she'd made no more noise than a squirrel.

Despite the one man's guns, the pair looked more like civilians than soldiers to her, but, civilians or soldiers, they were too interested in spying out the lay of the land near the Rowland family farm for Katie's comfort.

Like many of her neighbors in Virginia's Shenandoah Valley, Katie Rowland didn't particularly embrace the secessionist cause. Her family didn't own any slaves, not since Mammy had died ten years before when Katie was just five. They didn't really need slaves to farm their acreage on the rolling slopes near the North Fork of the Shenandoah River. Nor did they have any quarrel with the government in Washington except that the men there didn't seem willing to let honest folks get on with their lives without meddling.

But the Rowlands were Virginians born and raised, and when Virginia had sided with the Confederacy the previous April, they had, too. Katie's father and older brother had left home just about at once and ridden north to Winchester to volunteer. Her grandfather probably would have gone with them, but he was old—past sixty—and his right leg below the knee was carved from wood.

These days there were times Katie almost wished that her family did own a slave or two, because as spring came on and there was planting to do and young animals being born—as well as all the routine chores—she felt pulled in just about as many directions as could be.

Last year, when Tod and Father had been newly departed, all the work had seemed more like a game. Katie and her mother had bragged about how they'd show the menfolk they could keep the farm going nearly as well without them. This year neither had much energy for smiles. Tod was dead and they hadn't heard from Father for so long they'd stopped looking for a letter—though they couldn't quite stop hoping.

Katie's younger sister Lorry was delicate and so Mother kept her close to the house. War had cost them Katie's older sister, Beth, for she had gone south to Staunton in order to stay with their aunt who'd been left without any help at all and a baby at the breast when her husband had gone off to war.

Katie's younger brothers, Adam, Nathan, and Robert, tried to help but even ten-year-old Adam might forget to gather eggs or feed the livestock if not reminded. The littler boys were worse.

So Katie was the oldest child left at home. Normally she was fairly responsible. Today, as she peeked down over the hillside at the two mapmakers, she forgot about the strayed cow, forgot about how the neck of the ugly homespun dress Mother made her wear for outside chores scratched her neck, forgot everything except the two spies.

She crept after them—her up on the ridge, them down along the road. She was almost Indian-quiet despite the clumsy brogans—castoffs of her older brother, Tod—she wore since she had no better shoes for mucking outside. They were too big and so she had stuffed the toes with rags. In those shoes there was no way that Katie was particularly graceful, but there'd been rain or snow on and off for more than a week and the wet ground was forgiving.

After a half mile or so, the road bent and Katie came to herself with a shock, realizing that the spies were approaching where the Rowlands' farm road met the public road. She didn't doubt they'd turn down that road. Once upon a time, two men wouldn't have seemed much of a threat, but now, with the farm's only grown man her grandfather, Katie felt suddenly afraid.

She abandoned her watch and sped down the hillside toward the farm. The hill was so steep that she spread her arms out like wings to steady her balance as her feet thudded along almost faster than she could lift her legs.

For a moment, Katie was a child again, running like blazes to try and beat Tod in a race. Tears burnt hot against her cheeks, but whether from grief for the brother who since Manassas would never come home again or just from the wind in her eyes, Katie didn't admit even to herself.

Arriving at the flatter pastureland, Katie spotted her grandfather coming out of the dairy barn. He was shading his eyes with one hand, looking up the slope of the pasture. Katie realized with a sudden flash of guilt that she hadn't brought in the cow, but there was no time for that now.

The spies would be awhile yet getting to the fork that led to the farm road—that is, if they kept ambling along at the pace the artist seemed to demand—but if they turned at the fork, they'd reach the Rowland farm soon enough.

Katie grabbed her grandfather by one arm and practically dragged him into the relative privacy offered by a toolshed. From there she could still keep an eye on the road, but their conference wouldn't be visible to a casual observer.

"Kathleen Ann Rowland . . ." her grandfather began sternly, but Katie gasped, for she was still short of breath:

"Grandpa, I saw spies on the road! I went up for Princess, 'cause she strayed again, and I saw spies. Two of them at least. They were making maps!"

"Down on the road?"

"That's right." Katie tried to talk slowly and carefully so he'd believe her. "Two men on horses. They were drawing maps. I followed them for a bit along the ridge, then I thought I'd better tell you."

"Federal or Confederate army?" Grandpa asked. It was one of his gifts that he didn't waste time telling a child she had too much imagination.

"I don't know," Katie replied. "They didn't look quite like any soldiers I've seen.

"Not," she added honestly, "that I've seen too many."

That was true enough. Though there'd been fighting in the valley since Harper's Ferry, much of it had been farther north, nearer to Winchester and other points so far away that they were just names on the rough map Mother had drawn for the family so they could have a picture against which to imagine the news they got from the newspapers or from neighbors.

"Well, then," Grandpa said slowly, "if you can't guess their allegiance, there's a chance that they're as likely to be friends as enemies. There's even a chance we can make friends of them even if they're inclined to be enemies. Go to the house and tell your mother we may have two more for dinner. Then go get the cow."

"Yes, sir," Katie replied readily enough, but she paused before obeying. "And what are you going to do, Grandpa?"

"Keep an eye open without seeming to do so," he said. "The front gate to the house yard has needed mending for a while. I expect this is a good time to do it."

Katie found Princess, a pretty fawn-colored beast, already halfway down the hillside when she went looking for her. Princess's calf, a wide-eyed, knobby-legged heifer too innocent to be shy, trailed after.

"Got tired of playing coy and wondering why no one came looking for you?" Katie asked, rubbing the cow's soft nose and wishing her own eyelashes were as long and silky. "Come along and get settled in. You're the last."

Princess lowed a reproach but allowed herself to be escorted to the barn. Katie hurried the cow along, for she'd glimpsed the toylike shapes of horses on the farm road. Although she knew eavesdropping was frowned upon, she wanted to get to where she could hear what they said to Grandpa.

Katie managed to slip into the toolshed just before the two riders drew up before the farmyard gate.

"Would you be Dr. Rowland?" asked the one Katie thought of as the artist. His tone was polite and courteous, but Katie couldn't make out his accent. It held notes of Virginia but something else lurked beneath. She stiffened and hoped Grandpa would be careful.

"I am," came the measured reply. "Now, who might you be? You may know my name but I don't fancy I've set eyes on you before."

"We learned it from your neighbor up the road, Mrs. Sally Miller," the artist replied. "I'm Jed Hotchkiss and this is Howell Brown."

Katie pressed her eye to a crack in the toolshed wall and finally got a look at the spies that wasn't distorted by her being above, and them in the shadows below.

Jed Hotchkiss seemed a man of middle years—somewhere around thirty. He was fairly tall; Katie guessed him around six feet in height, but he was not at all bulky. Hotchkiss wore his dark beard long, spilling over his chest, and what she could see of his face was calm and thoughtful.

Howell Brown was another big man, but where Hotchkiss gave the impression of leanness, Brown was strongly made. His beard was more neatly trimmed, too. Whereas Hotchkiss seemed a scholar or artist, Katie thought Brown more a soldier or at least an outdoorsman.

Glancing at her grandfather, Katie saw that Dr. Rowland was inspecting Hotchkiss with the same cool appraisal she'd seen him use on bellyaching patients who weren't confessing all they'd had to eat or drink. The old doctor hadn't uttered a word since Hotchkiss finished his initial introductions, but his very silence seemed to press Hotchkiss to explain further.

"We're with General Jackson," Hotchkiss said, "General Thomas Jackson and the Army of the Valley."

"I know of General Jackson," Dr. Rowland said. "Indeed, last I heard, my son was serving in his army."

Hotchkiss didn't blanch at this. Indeed, he seemed to relax a bit, but Katie wasn't willing to trust him yet.

"I've been trying to decide," Dr. Rowland continued, "whether you gentlemen are civilians or military. Your horses bear the army brand and so does some of your gear, but you are not in uniform, sir, nor did you offer me a rank."

Hotchkiss sighed almost imperceptibly. Katie had the impression that he had answered this question or some form of it many times before.

"I am a civilian, Dr. Rowland, as is my companion, but we are in the employ of General Jackson. Doubtless our commissions will come in time, but I only met the general a few days ago—three days before the battle of Kernstown."

"So you've seen fighting," Grandpa said.

Hotchkiss nodded. "And when the retreat to Rude's Hill was completed, General Jackson sent me right out again to map him the valley."

"All of it?" Grandpa laughed, for the Shenandoah Valley was both long and broad. Katie had never been out of it her entire life.

Hotchkiss shared the laughter, though Brown looked vaguely disapproving.

" 'From Harper's Ferry to Lexington, showing all points of offense and defense,' " Hotchkiss quoted. "Those were General Jackson's orders. I figured he'd be needing to know the lay of the local land first, though. Brown and I have been mapping west of Mount Jackson, for the army has men and supplies there, as well, and it would be good to have a clear picture of what surrounds them."

"And what might you want me to do for you?"

There was steel in the old man's tone and Katie was suddenly very conscious that Grandpa had not yet invited the visitors to step down from their horses.

"A very important thing, Dr. Rowland," Hotchkiss admitted frankly. "No one knows the land like a country doctor. I was hoping you might tell me what to expect in this area. I'd like to know about any fords or bridges, any particularly bad stretches and any particularly good. After all, though the Pike is an admirable road, we may not always be able to rely on it."

"I might be able to help you there," Dr. Rowland said equably. Katie thought he was coming to like Hotchkiss. "Why don't you gentlemen join my family for dinner? We are starved for news and anything you can tell us would be a fair trade for my knowledge of the countryside."

Hotchkiss beamed and the silent Brown smiled his own thanks. When the strangers led their horses around to the stables, Katie slipped out of the toolshed and into the house. As she stepped out of her brogans in the mudroom, she heard Grandpa cautioning the others:

"Let me do the talking over dinner. Hotchkiss and Brown seem polite enough and their gear is more Confederate than not, but we need to be careful."

He spied Katie as she paused at the foot of the stairs.

"That goes double for you, Katie Ann. Best they don't know you were watching them."

"Yes, sir," she said, and scampered barefoot up the smooth wooden steps.

Dinner conversation was absorbing enough that Katie felt no desire to interrupt. Even the little boys were quiet, awed by the presence of strangers. Lorry, who read more than was wise, was frankly starry-eyed, envisioning these two as heroes from some novel.

Dr. Rowland began by asking for news of his son, Michael Rowland, who at last report had been part of the Twenty-seventh Virginia. Katie was aware of her own heart beating faster and saw her mother pause with her fork partway to her lips.

"I'm sorry, but I don't know of him," Hotchkiss replied, looking at the intent faces around the table. "The Twenty-seventh is with Jackson but, as I told you, I joined the army only a few days before Kernstown and then Jackson sent me out again before I had a chance to get to know many of the men. Still, when I report to Jackson, I will make inquiries after your son."

"Thank you," Dr. Rowland said gravely, and politely turned the conversation to other, less personally painful matters.

At his request their guests related the details of the battle of Kernstown. His right hand gesturing widely as if to map the action on the air, Hotchkiss told how General Jackson—misled by reports that the Federal forces had mostly withdrawn from the area—had attempted to take Kernstown; how the Confederate attack, though fierce, had ultimately failed, how Jackson had refused to leave until every one of his wounded could be collected.

"Had the Yankees pressed," Hotchkiss admitted, with the same openness that Katie suspected had won her grandfather over, "it would have been ugly for us, but they didn't, maybe because the light was fading. Even the day after the battle, General Banks didn't venture more than four miles in pursuit. Our men may have failed to take Kernstown, but that battle surely put the fear of Stonewall Jackson into General Banks."

"And now?" Grandpa probed.

"The army's resting at Rude's Hill," Brown said. "It's a natural fort, as you must know, living so close to it."

Grandpa nodded. "The river curls around the hill on two sides. There's only one bridge over the North Fork of the Shenandoah anywhere close and that could easily be burned if pursuit came from the west side of the river."

Hotchkiss grinned, looking as pleased as if he'd invented the position himself.

"And burning the bridge would cut the turnpike, making it harder for the Yankees to pursue. Rude's Hill is gifted with height in addition to that natural moat. As my altimeter read it, it stands some hundred feet over the surrounding countryside."

Katie recalled picnicking on that high hill, looking down over the Shenandoah River and enjoying the view over the relatively clear land. It was hard to imagine the quiet place full of soldiers—harder, too, to believe that her father could be so close to home and yet not get word to them. She began to believe that he must indeed be dead.

While Katie's thoughts wandered, Hotchkiss continued his account of the aftermath of the battle at Kernstown.

"Now, the Federals didn't dally forever. Our commander of cavalry, Colonel Turner Ashby, and his troops slowed them a bit. At last report they were holding the Yankees at a water course . . ."

He paused and Brown, who Katie had already noted tended to be methodical and precise regarding any sort of detail, interjected:

"Tom's Brook."

"Tom's Brook!" Hotchkiss repeated with a nod of thanks to his companion. "The cavalry is holding the Federals at Tom's Brook, but that can't last. Eventually the bluecoats will get the courage up to go wading and then our army will be pressed again. Rude's Hill may be a natural fortress, but you need men to hold a position and Jackson's are tuckered out."

Grandpa pondered, then said slowly, "I may be able to help you there. There's another creek—Stony Creek, we call it—between Mount Jackson and Tom's Brook. It's wide, especially at this time of year when the waters are running high, and its banks are steep. A smaller force could hold off a larger one there even better than at Tom's Brook."

Hotchkiss, who had been looking sleepy as the meal drew to a close, was suddenly alert once more.

"I believe I recall where that creek crosses the turnpike, but that's well out of our way. Surely the creek extends farther west. Could you guide me there overland, sir? I could do a quick survey and pass on the essential information to General Jackson."

Dr. Rowland hesitated, coloring a dark red. Hotchkiss looked confused.

"If it's a matter of payment for your time," the cartographer ventured tentatively.

"No, I . . ."

Katie's mother took mercy on her father-in-law's embarrassment.

"My father cannot ride—not as you would need him to ride," she explained in a soft voice. "He lost his right leg below the knee some years ago. Muscles were damaged as well, so he cannot stay on a horse over rough ground. When he does his rounds, he takes a light gig, but the gig won't reach Stony Creek—not overland, and you need to go overland if time is essential."

"I believe it is," Hotchkiss stated frankly. "Colonel Ashby has been playing cat and mouse with the Yanks for nearly a week. Eventually—even if for no other reason than to save their pride—they must push forward."

Inspired by Hotchkiss's intensity, Katie forgot her grandfather's order to keep silent.

"But I know," she blurted out. "I know how to get to Stony Creek overland."

She blushed as all eyes—most of them quite disapproving—centered on her. At last Grandpa spoke:

"You do indeed, Katie," he said, "and you may be the best chance if we are to help these men buy General Jackson's army the time it needs."

Katie's mother drew in her breath sharply, but the same courage that had allowed her to send both son and husband off to war kept her from protesting.

Brown stated with deliberate politeness and a solemn frown, "We couldn't bring a young lady into dangerous territory, sir."

Dr. Rowland sighed. "Without a local guide, it would take you quite a bit longer to find Stony Creek from here and I have no gift for drawing maps. Let Katie go with you. I trust her good sense."

The two mapmakers fell silent and Katie realized something of the seriousness of the Confederate position in the men's willingness to accept her as a guide.

Her mother broke the silence. "You gentlemen won't want to be heading out tonight—after all, you can't make maps in the dark. We'll bed you down in the parlor and Katie can guide you come dawn."

Hotchkiss smiled and for the first time Katie realized how tired he and Brown must be if they'd fought at Kernstown and then been sent out to make maps as soon as the retreat to Rude's Hill was accomplished.

"Mrs. Rowland, thank you," Hotchkiss said. "I can't say no to a bed, not when it's offered so kindly."

Katie lay awake for what felt like a long time that night, feeling alone despite Lorry's soft breathing from the other bed. She was suddenly afraid of what she'd volunteered for.

At last she convinced herself that the trip wouldn't be a whit more onerous than the picnicking jaunts she'd taken with Tod and Beth before the war had ended such pleasant things forever. Even when she slept, however, her dreams were peopled with men in blue coats.

The rooster's crowing announced the coming of dawn and Katie, conditioned to awaken at that signal, rolled out of bed. Lorry moaned softly and pulled the blanket over her head. Most days Katie would have resented her sister's invalid's privilege, but today she was eager to avoid conversation.

She wondered if Lorry was, too.

The room was chilly, so Katie hurried to dress, waiting until after she had her clothes on to break the thin shell of ice that skimmed the water pitcher and wash her face. Lastly she dragged a comb through her thick, curly black hair, wishing as she did every morning that Beth was there to comb and braid it like she had done as long as Katie could remember.

Lest she wake the little boys, Katie carried her shoes in her hand as she went down the stairs. After some consideration, she'd chosen her boots rather than the useful brogans, for she guessed she'd be riding.

As she slipped past the parlor, she could hear Hotchkiss and Brown moving about inside. In the kitchen, Mother was stirring a pot of grits with one hand and turning thick slabs of bacon with the other.

Her expression was grim and her eyelids were red, as if she'd been crying, but when she heard Katie come in she managed a bright and almost convincing smile.

"Your grandfather will tend the cows," she said, as if this was any other day, "and I'll have the boys take care of the other stock. I know we were going to make butter, but that will wait until you get home."

Mrs. Rowland's brave smile broke for just an instant.

"And do come home, Katie," she added earnestly. "I've given enough of my family to this war. I need you here."

She laughed, the notes just a little high and false. "After all, otherwise Lorry and I will be the only women in this house of men!"

Katie hugged her, squeezing the comfortable roundness of Mrs. Rowland's farmwife's waist.

"I'll be careful," she promised. "Stony Creek isn't far. I may be home early enough that we can still get to the churning."

A discreet throat-clearing at the doorway announced Brown and Hotchkiss. Hotchkiss, ever the spokesman for the two, said:

"Good morning, ma'am, Miss Katie. That smells wonderful."

Mrs. Rowland immediately set the bacon to drain. Katie started dishing out the grits.

"My father," Mrs. Rowland said by way of greeting, "is saddling up the horses and giving them a bite to eat. They'll be ready for you just as soon as you've eaten."

Hotchkiss bowed his thanks and Brown stepped over to carry two bowls to the table.

Hotchkiss cut a bit of butter to top his grits and said conversationally, "I happened to hear that this is churning day. Don't worry, ma'am. We'll not keep your daughter a moment longer than we must."

Mrs. Rowland smiled. "Stony Creek's several miles from here, so I'll cut you some bread and give you the extra bacon, just in case you need a meal."

Dr. Rowland led the horses around as they were scraping their bowls clean. Katie hurried herself into the saddle of the mount her grandfather had chosen for her, a cobby dark gray named Stormshadow. Stormshadow wasn't long on looks but he was as steady as rainfall and could walk—so Grandpa claimed—straight up the side of the Massanutten Mountains if you let him pick his own path.

Leave-taking was brief and matter-of-fact—mostly because Katie was afraid her mother would start crying and Katie knew that if Mother did, Katie wouldn't be able to stop her own frightened tears.

She felt a bit odd when Hotchkiss and Brown hung back, waiting for her to take the lead. Then she urged Stormshadow forward and they were under way.

Late March had brought out the early spring flowers. Snowdrops peeped white and delicate from the shelter of the wet, brown earth. Dogwoods were showing white blossoms. Many of the trees were beginning to leaf out, the pale green of the new growth seeming like a watercolor wash over the grays and browns of winter. The air was chilly, but Katie was used to that and Stormshadow was warm beneath her.

After they had left the familiar buildings of the Rowland farm behind them, paradoxically Katie felt more at ease. Her natural manners asserted herself and she fell into the role of hostess.

"You headed west from Mount Jackson," she said. "We'll be heading back east and somewhat south, but we can't go directly since gullies cut up the land all over. Still, there's a game trail we can take that will give the horses fair footing. Even with slowing down to go through the woods, this way should be faster than if you rode back east to the turnpike and then north some seven miles along the Pike to Stony Creek."

"Sounds like you know this land as well as I know the area around my hometown of Staunton," Hotchkiss said admiringly.

Katie warmed under his praise, enough so she found the courage to ask a question that had been bothering her since she'd first heard Hotchkiss speak.

"Are you from Staunton, Mr. Hotchkiss?"

"I am," he said. "Taught school there—my own Mossy Creek Academy. My wife, Sara Ann, still resides there."

"So you *are* a Virginian," Katie said, and heard the note of doubt in her own voice.

"By residence, yes," Hotchkiss said, "but I was born a Yankee in Windsor, New York. You seem to have guessed."

Katie felt a shiver of fear, but she hid it.

"I heard it in your voice," she said, "or something, anyhow, that didn't sound right."

"Well, rest easy, Miss Katie," Hotchkiss said. "I may have been born a Yankee, but I'm a Virginian now."

"I'm sure," Katie replied stiffly, but she remained uneasy.

As they rode closer to Stony Creek, they saw, or rather Brown and Hotchkiss claimed *they* saw—Katie noticed nothing but some small patches of trampled earth—evidence that at least a few Yankees had crossed Tom's Brook and were scouting ahead of the main force.

"They'll be hunting out a ford," Hotchkiss explained as he remounted his roan after investigating one patch of dirt. "Men and horses can cross where artillery and supplies cannot. They'll never chase Old Jack from Rude's Hill without artillery."

"Could starve him out," the laconic Brown suggested.

"Hard to do with the Shenandoah running round the hill," Hotchkiss objected, "and with our side having the drop on them. And for a siege they'd want artillery."

"True," Brown admitted.

Katie kept her peace. Ever since she'd learned that Hotchkiss was Yankee-born, all her suspicions of the day before had come back. Brown sounded like a Southerner—he claimed in a rare spate of talkativeness to have been a Jefferson County surveyor before the war. Still, there were Southerners who had espoused the Union cause in the conflict. She'd heard that there were whole battalions in the Federal army made up of such traitors.

And hadn't they admitted to being spies? They'd never say right out if they were spying for the Yankees. Hadn't Grandpa needed to sort of force Hotchkiss to say they were with Jackson? Hadn't they admitted they didn't have commissions? What if they were sort of freelance spies, ready to sell their information to the highest bidders?

Still, for now, Katie was committed to her role as guide. She decided that she'd show them Stony Creek, and get away as soon as possible. This plan kept her calm as they rode on through the damp woodlands, but when they reached Stony Creek she found her simple plan foiled by Hotchkiss himself.

"Why don't you stay with us for a bit, Miss Katie?" Hotchkiss suggested, getting his sketch pad out of his saddlebags. "I'm right worried about what might happen if you came across some Union scouts. My thought is that you could stay with us until we've checked out enough of this creek to ready a rough map. Then either Brown or I can ride to Rude's Hill to report and the other can take you home. Or . . ."

He twinkled, just like her uncle did when he was about to offer her a treat.

"Or we could take you along to camp with us and introduce you to the general. Maybe you could ask about your father. Then the general could detail a slightly larger party to escort you back to Rowland Farm."

"If it's just the same to you, sir," Katie said meekly, though the mention of her father sorely tempted her, "I'd rather go home soon as possible." A sudden inspiration hit her. "I did promise Mother I'd help with the churning."

"I'm sure she'd rather have you home safe than soon," Hotchkiss said, "but we can manage both. Lend us a hand taking some measurements and the like and we'll finish all the more quickly."

Katie couldn't very well just ride off, not without giving away her suspicions, so she complied with Hotchkiss's suggestion.

In this way she learned the reasons behind many of Brown's mysterious actions the day before. She discovered that he knew precisely the measurements of his handspan, his forearm, and even the length of his horse's stride. These— and other even more peculiar rulers—were used to provide measurements for the map Hotchkiss began to sketch.

At Brown's request, Katie waded Stormshadow into the bed of the creek at various locations to test both the depth and the texture of the bottom. Whenever they found a promising ford, Hotchkiss would add it to his map. Overall, the banks of Stony Creek were too steep to permit good crossing for wagons and artillery but there were places that could be adapted, perhaps with a bit of digging.

Whenever they found a potential ford, Katie was asked to ride into the creekbed again and see how easily she could spot Brown as he tried out various hiding places from which the defending Confederates might operate. As rolling hills rose sharply about a quarter mile from the creek, several spots proved quite promising for stationing artillery or hiding ambushes.

The mapping process was quite interesting and, since Brown never asked her to ride into water that might be too deep or too dangerous, Katie never even got her bootsoles wet.

Finding Brown when he hid reminded her so much of playing hide-and-seek with Tod and Beth when they were still children that Katie had to fight against enjoying herself.

After a time, Hotchkiss suggested that they halt and enjoy the lunch Mrs. Rowland had packed for them.

"I'll finish some details while we eat," he said to Katie, "and then Brown can take the map to Rude's Hill while I escort you home."

Katie's sense of apprehension returned at these words, but she reminded herself there was nothing to be gained by letting Hotchkiss know she distrusted him.

They were eating thick slabs of her mother's rye bread with cold bacon and onions when Brown suddenly stiffened. He held his finger to his lips when Katie opened her mouth to speak, and cupped his ear. Hotchkiss, who had been absorbed in his drawing, was nearly as surprised as Katie, but, unlike her, he knew his companion and trusted his woods wisdom.

Though she strained her ears, Katie heard nothing. She was just beginning to relax when she realized how odd that "nothing" was. The local birds and small animals had long ago dismissed the three humans as nonthreatening and the forest had resounded with birdsong. Now it was quiet.

Stormshadow lifted his head from the bit of grass he had been lipping and flared his nostrils suspiciously. The roan and the chestnut also seemed uneasy.

Katie felt tension building like a physical thing beneath her breastbone. She was afraid and excited all at once and the desire to do something—*anything*—to relieve the tension was so intense that she thought she must scream if the quiet stretched on a moment longer.

Then a sound broke the silence: a sharp, artificial metallic *click*. Katie had gone hunting and target shooting with Tod. She knew too well the sound of a gun being cocked. Then a voice with a hard, nasal Yankee accent spoke:

"Keep your hands where I can see them. Don't move a muscle or even breathe too hard. I'm a nervous man."

He didn't sound nervous, Katie thought. He sounded just like a cat might when it had a mouse cornered.

"You, the fellow with the short beard," the Yankee went on, "drop the rifle in the water."

Brown did so, moving with careful deliberation.

"Now the pistol," the Yankee ordered.

Brown dropped his hand with the same slow carefulness. Even though Katie was watching with fascinated horror—her mind focusing on Brown's every move so she wouldn't think about what might come after the Yankee had him disarmed—she didn't guess what Brown intended.

His hand unholstered the pistol, but rather than dropping it into the stream, Brown leveled it and shot in the direction of the voice.

Katie saw the little spurt of fire that followed the bullet and heard a second shot so close to the first that the two sounds merged into one loud thunderclap. She saw Brown clap his hand to his side, saw the red that blossomed there, and heard a scream. She was scrabbling on hands and knees toward Brown before she realized he had not been the one who had cried out.

Brown's lips were compressed into a thin, pale line, but even in this moment of shock and pain he didn't make a sound.

She paused, but already Hotchkiss had leapt to his feet and was smashing through the bushes. Katie bent over Brown.

Dr. Rowland had never been one of those men who believed women should be spared the sight of blood. Indeed, he held the very realistic opinion that what with nursing the ill, childbirth, and other such things, the average woman would see far more blood in the course of her life than would the average man. Thus Katie ascertained quite expertly that Brown was badly hurt.

The bullet had sliced into his side, leaving a deep, bloody furrow. Worse yet, his quick intake of breath when Katie pressed gently on his ribs indicated a probable break. There was no blood on his lips or other indication of that a lung had been pierced, but if there was fragmented bone, this would be an all-too-likely complication.

Hotchkiss crashed out of the brush as Katie finished her initial inspection. He held a pistol belt in one hand and an ammunition case in the other.

"Dead," he said of the Yankee, for once as laconic as Brown.

Katie noticed Hotchkiss didn't mention whether the Yankee had been killed by Brown's bullet or in some other fashion, and felt relieved.

"And from his level of confidence in tackling all three of us," Hotchkiss continued, "the Federals won't be sitting on the other side of Tom's Brook very long. How's Howell?"

It took a moment for Katie to recall that this was Brown's given name.

"With care, he'll live," she said, and fancied she saw a look of relief cross her patient's face, "but there is a possibility that his broken ribs could damage a lung and then he'd be in danger of a collapsed lung, pneumonia, or worse."

Hotchkiss didn't question her diagnosis, only crossed to the roan and drew some medical supplies from a saddlebag.

"Can he ride?" he asked.

"He shouldn't," Katie stated bluntly, taking Brown's knife from his belt and using it to cut away his shirt.

"And we shouldn't stay here," Hotchkiss said worriedly. He stood guard while Katie tended to Brown. "Not only might those shots bring the curious, but General Jackson must be told that the Federals are getting bolder."

"What about that Colonel Ashby?" Katie asked. "Shouldn't he be warned?"

An odd frown wrinkled Hotchkiss's brow. Katie got the distinct impression that he was speaking out of turn when he said:

"Frankly, Miss Katie, I'm not sure anyone knows where Turner Ashby is to be found at any given minute. Ashby's men are as devoted to him as you could wish, but if he's not with them, they're not the most organized unit in the army. I'd rather report to the general, give him my map, and let him decide what to do."

"You go," Brown whispered and it was clear that even those two syllables hurt him. He managed one more. "Both."

"You want us both to go," Hotchkiss interpreted angrily, "and leave you?"

"Hide," Brown managed. "Rest."

Katie couldn't help but think that Brown's usual habit of being economical with words had made him a master of saying the most with the least.

Hotchkiss wasn't pleased.

"Miss Katie could stay with you," he suggested tentatively.

Katie interrupted.

"I don't know how to fire a gun, so I'd be less than help if trouble came, but," she continued, so steadily that she amazed herself, "I could ride to General Jackson and deliver your map. We could hide your horses in one of the thickets Mr. Brown and I spied out and you two could stay here."

Hotchkiss stared at her. "You'd ride out to Rude's Hill with Yankees about?"

"They won't take me for anybody," Katie replied with more confidence than she felt. "I'm just a local farmgirl. You two, you stand out."

She managed a weak grin. "After all, I thought you were spies myself."

"What changed your mind?"

Katie pointed to the dead Yankee's gun belt which proclaimed U.S. ARMY in square letters neatly stamped onto the leather.

The Road to Stony Creek ✷ 243

Hotchkiss shook his head. "Lots of Confederates wear U.S. Army gear. The Yanks are our best suppliers."

"They don't," Katie stated firmly, "leave their wives in Staunton."

The matter wasn't settled all at once, but at last Hotchkiss accepted Katie's suggestion. They moved the injured man into cover. At the end of the process, Brown looked quite pale and a slight froth of blood on his lips suggested that despite Katie's best efforts at binding his wounds he might have damaged a lung.

While Katie tacked up Stormshadow, Hotchkiss wrote a note for the general. Then he suggested that she hide both it and the map between her saddle and saddle blanket.

"That way," he said seriously, sealing the packet in oiled cloth, "no one will take *you* for a spy."

Katie accepted a hand up into the saddle then smiled down at the Yankee-turned-Virginian.

"I'll be as quick as I can," she said, "but I'm going to need to double-back some and then cross to the turnpike. I don't want to ride along Stony Creek if the Yanks are scouting it."

Despite the rough ground, Katie pushed Stormshadow hard in her eagerness to get to the turnpike. She thought about stopping at Mount Jackson and seeing if someone would go from there to help the two mapmakers, but feared the delay.

As she had expected, no one bothered a farmgirl riding a shaggy gray horse along a public road, but when Stormshadow clattered across the bridge over the North Fork of the Shenandoah, Katie was aware of the watching pickets. Sure enough, she was stopped as soon as she turned toward Rude's Hill.

"Hotchkiss and Brown" wasn't precisely the password, but the pickets seemed fascinated that an unattended girl would insist on seeing the general, and passed her through to the next level of command. Eventually Katie was handed over to a sharp-featured, beardless young man who looked to be little more than a boy.

Introducing himself as Captain Sandie Pendleton, the general's aide-de-camp, her escort took her to the general's headquarters.

Thomas J. "Stonewall" Jackson came riding in just as Katie's escort was leaving to find him. The general relaxed in the saddle as he listened to Pendleton's brief explanation, giving Katie a moment to study the man who had been indirectly responsible for her brother's—and possibly her father's—deaths.

Stonewall Jackson was mounted on a scrawny sorrel that seemed no more what Katie thought of as a general's horse than Jackson himself seemed like the popular image of a general.

For one thing Jackson's feet were too big. For another, he sucked on a section of lemon all the time he listened to his officer's report. The general's dark hair and beard lacked the cavalier flare favored by so many Virginians; his pale eyes seemed to belong to a preacher rather than a war-leader. Yet he was all military as he accepted this latest twist of fate.

"Unsaddle Miss Rowland's horse," he ordered in a rather high voice as he himself dismounted, "and retrieve the papers the lady has carried here."

When this had been done and Jackson had the papers in hand, the general listened impatiently to Katie's account of the situation.

"Captain Gisiner," he snapped at another soldier, "get a detail together to rescue Brown and Hotchkiss."

"Yes, sir!"

"Miss Rowland . . ."

Katie resisted an impulse to salute as each of the men had done when accepting their orders.

"Yes, General Jackson," she said, dipping a slight curtsy.

"Can you guide a party back to where Hotchkiss and Brown are?"

"Yes, sir." She was worried that as yet he hadn't looked at Hotchkiss's report. Feeling too tired to be tactful, she blurted out, "What are you going to do about Stony Creek?"

She didn't know then that Stonewall Jackson maintained a fetish for secrecy regarding his plans. That would explain the steely, indeed angry, gaze he turned on her. Then, perhaps seeing her exhaustion and realizing that she was little more than a child—a child hard-pressed by the day's events—Jackson replied kindly.

"I will take a moment to look at Mr. Hotchkiss's map," he said, "but I believe his recommendation to be a good one. Colonel Ashby will be ordered to prepare a stand along Stony Creek in the event that our line at Tom's Brook is broken."

"Thank you, sir," Katie said meekly, eager now to be away from that pale preacher's gaze with its hidden ferocity.

"Thank *you*, Miss Rowland," he said. "Captain Pendleton, see that Miss Rowland is given something to drink before she departs and that Captain Gisiner understands that she is to be escorted to her home and that thanks are to be extended to her family."

Then, with an abbreviated bow, General Jackson turned away. Knowing herself dismissed, Katie walked a few steps away to where the boyish Pendleton was pouring coffee for her. Despite the camp noises surrounding her, Katie imagined she could hear the oilcloth packet being opened and the papers being spread out for the general's inspection.

Later Katie would learn that Hotchkiss's maps had reached Colonel Ashby in time for him to prepare against the Federal army's crossing of Tom's Brook. For two more weeks, Ashby's cavalry, reinforced by rotating companies sent by General Jackson, had held the Union forces on the north side of Stony Creek.

Eventually, however, the dashing cavalry commander grew less than attentive to his picket duty. Union troops forded the upper reaches of Stony Creek. Near Columbia Furnace they captured fifty Confederates, their horses and equipment—a stunning setback for Ashby's troop. That defeat was the beginning of the end for the Army of the Valley's tenancy on Rude's Hill.

Some days after the Confederate troops had retreated, Jed Hotchkiss stopped by the farm to inform the Rowland family of the change of affairs and to report that Brown was mending nicely.

"When the Federals crossed Stony Creek," he reported to a rapt audience clustered in the parlor, "General Jackson decided that they might be fronting something bigger than merely Banks's army so he pulled back his vanguard. Good thing, too. The Federals hit Rude's Hill hard. Some say what we managed there was a retreat. I heard Major Harman, the quartermaster, call it a rout and I'd be forced to agree with him. Still, Old Jack got his army out mostly intact."

Dr. Rowland said gruffly, "I'd want to hang Colonel Ashby."

Lorry, who had been collecting stories about the valiant cavalier from the newspapers, looked at her grandfather in horror.

"Ashby isn't a bad man," Hotchkiss said in a conciliatory manner, "just too enamored of glory and too little with dull routine. Sadly, he's not at all a unique element in our army. Rumor says that Jackson will try to clip Ashby's wings, but I fear that if he does so he may end up with a mutiny in the ranks. Ashby is well loved and too many of the men witnessed his heroics during the holding action at Stony Creek."

Dr. Rowland shook his head. "More men should see war from my perspective, then they would prate less about glory—but I apologize. I have interrupted you, sir. Pray, tell us what happened next. We have only heard fragmented accounts of the battle. Some say Colonel Ashby was nearly killed."

"Not even scratched," Hotchkiss assured the wide-eyed Lorry, "though his horse was shot out from under him as he held the rearmost line of our retreat.

It is said that he was so close to the Union army that it looked as if he was leading their charge."

"I can see why the men love him," Dr. Rowland admitted.

Hotchkiss gave a rueful laugh of agreement. "Yet once again General Banks may have been our greatest ally. Just as after Kernstown, he chose not to pursue when he might have. Banks likes a sure thing and a running battle along a wet road isn't his type of fighting at all."

Katie sighed, feeling bitter.

"Then two weeks was all we won for Jackson's army?" she said grimly. "Two weeks, and even that thrown away in the end!"

"It wasn't thrown away," Hotchkiss insisted firmly. "The army had two more weeks of rest and training—two weeks to heal. Old Jack had two weeks to get his staff in order and to send supplies to our Southern bases. He even had a locomotive moved from Mount Jackson. He had two weeks to decide where to go next rather than being forced to retreat blindly with a Yankee army at his back. Indeed, though we gave up the crossing at the North Fork, Conrad's Store is a far better base than Rude's Hill."

Hotchkiss laid a fatherly hand on Katie's shoulder.

"Never think, Miss Katie, that two weeks is nothing. General Jackson didn't. That's one reason I'm here."

He held out to her a neatly folded letter.

"I believe this contains the general's personal thanks for the risks you took in guiding Brown and myself."

Katie was starting to tear General Jackson's note open when Hotchkiss again dipped his hand into his pocket. He took out another packet, this one much fatter, which he handed to Mrs. Rowland.

"And this," he said with a broad grin, "is from your husband. It took us awhile, but Sandie Pendleton and I tracked him down. He's been convalescing at a farmhouse, too feverish to write until recently. Then there was no one to carry a letter. He's on the mend and will be given invalid's leave as soon as he can travel."

Mrs. Rowland shrieked with delight and for a moment looked as if she might faint. Impulsively Katie hugged the bearded cartographer and was surprised to see him blush.

"Thank you, Mr. Hotchkiss! Thank you!"

Hotchkiss bowed. "My pleasure, Miss Katie."

He made his exit while the family clustered around Mrs. Rowland, begging for her to read aloud from the thick sheets of paper crammed in the packet.

The Road to Stony Creek ✖ 247

Listening from the doorway, Katie watched Hotchkiss ride off, waving until the roan carried him out of sight. She held General Jackson's note unopened in her hand, feeling that nothing could add to the joy of this moment.

Her father was coming home.

In her twenty-five years as a writer, editor, and publishing consultant, Janet Berliner has worked with such authors as Peter S. Beagle, David Copperfield, Michael Crichton, and Joyce Carol Oates. Among her most recent books are the anthology *Snapshots: 20th Century Mother-Daughter Fiction*, which she edited with Joyce Carol Oates, and *Children of the Dusk*, the final book of The Madagascar Manifesto, a three-book series coauthored with George Guthridge. Currently Janet divides her time between Las Vegas, where she lives and works, and Grenada, West Indies, where her heart is.

Here she brings her own distinct view to the Civil War, shedding light on a little-known involvement of the Territory of Nevada and the West getting involved in the War between the North and South. The following story is based on true events.

OTHER 1

■

Janet Berliner

FACT: The Territory of Nevada participated in the Civil War.

FACT: Thirty-three of the troops furnished by the Territory of Nevada died while in service. These men were listed as Civil War casualties. One of them, known to inner circles as a spy, was listed only as "Other . . . . 1"

1864

Ulrich Luserke balanced his stein against the railing and watched the flow of traffic on the Rhine. The same barge he watched at the end of each day made its way slowly over the water. The captain was a friend of his. As he did each day in greeting, he lit his lamps and raised a glass in greeting. As the barge passed directly below Ulrich, he whistled melodically.

Tonight he chose "Tales from the Vienna Woods". Ulrich smiled. He was partial to waltzes and had ridden often through the forest with that particular song echoing through his head. He reached into his pocket, pulled out his harmonica, and played an accompaniment, momentarily at peace with the world. How unfortunate, he thought, that this moment could not last, especially during Oktoberfest.

The barge moved out of sight and he turned to view the rising activity in the biergarten. Immediately in front of him, the wooden tables were filling up. Each seated a half a dozen beer drinkers comfortably. As the night wore on, they would become tables for ten, even twelve—this being the most popular drinking place in Karlsruhe.

In the restaurant beyond, a round of applause greeted the arrival of the piano player. Ulrich found a seat at an as-yet-unoccupied table. He watched through the glass door as Gerhard bowed to his audience and sat down at the pianola.

"When Johnny comes marching home again, hurrah, hurrah."

"As if I didn't hear enough of that song in North America, I stop here for beer and wurst and some good German music and what do I hear? *'When Johnny comes marching home again, hurrah, hurrah.'* "

The man who addressed Ulrich was well dressed and alone. "May I join you?" he asked, though he could simply have assumed ownership of the space.

"But of course. Sit." Ulrich took a sip of his beer. He had lived in the small industrial town of Karlsruhe all of thirty or so years, the last several as a journalist for the town's only newspaper. His work had sent him to Vienna and Berlin, once even to Paris, but he had only dreamed of traveling to the other side of the world. To that end, he had chosen to take English lessons at school, had continued his studies afterward, and he had read widely about the New World.

"Ulrich Luserke," he said, putting out his hand. "You have been to the Americas?"

"Ernst Marcus," the stranger said. "And yes, I have just lately returned across the ocean."

"Will you tell me what it is like over there?" Ulrich asked.

Marcus was happy to oblige. As the table filled with other drinkers, he boasted of hitting it rich in the silver fields of Nevada and, as if to prove himself an honest man, bought round after round of drinks. During the course of the evening, he substantiated what had, he said, previously been revealed only in top-secret documents.

"The Confederacy will soon be running out of money for weapons and ammunition and bodies to fight the war," he said, "while the Union seems to have limitless funds. Imagine. While the South starves, the North thinks nothing of giving sums as high as twenty-five thousand dollars for the care and feeding of remote American Indian tribes."

"*Mein Gott*, but that is a fortune," Luserke said.

"Yes. It is." The stranger looked thoughtful. "I think they must be convinced the money they send in that direction will come back to them tenfold from the fruits of the earth."

Neither the Indians nor the stranger were more deserving of riches than he was, Luserke thought. "If I could only find a way to pay for the journey, I would leave home at once," he said, his voice melancholy.

"Go as I went, that is, if you are not too proud," his new friend said.

"And how was that?"

"I took a position as a valet for the journey." He looked contemplative. "As a matter of fact, I but yesterday refused the same position. If I were to recommend you . . ."

So it began, the journey of Ulrich Luserke. With the help of Ernst Marcus's introduction, the small-town journalist and budding opportunist was hired on as a valet to Robert Rabe, formerly underling to the undersecretary to the Kaiser and, now, a spy in the service of the Confederacy.

At first Mr. Rabe, an older man of obvious means and education, kept to himself. He spent his time in his cabin, or on deck in a lounge chair, a book in his hand and a blanket wrapped around his knees. As the journey progressed, he became increasingly more garrulous, until one day, having indulged perhaps in one too many glasses of wine with dinner, he confided in Ulrich.

All but the most optimistic, he said, agreed things were not faring well for the Confederacy. They also agreed that the war with the South was not yet over.

"In North American places as far afield from the battlefront as Nevada, scalps are being removed in the name of the War between the States," he said. "Even in Europe a stance is being taken. Great Britain supports the Confederacy. France, not wanting to be overlooked, allies itself with the Union."

"And what of Germany?" Ulrich asked, pouring the last of the bottle into his employer's glass.

"We have as yet to play an active role, but that is soon to change," Rabe said. He lifted his glass. "To the Kaiser, who has declared himself a moral supporter of the South."

Two things had recently happened simultaneously, Rabe explained. First, the Union Senate, with money to spare, designated large sums for the care of Indians in the Western Territories, messengering as much as $25,000 in cash for that purpose.

Interesting as this was to Ulrich, it merely confirmed what he had already learned from Ernst. What Rabe said next, however, was both fascinating and new to Ulrich. "The South," he said, "entered into a secret exchange of letters with an undersecretary to the Kaiser."

"With you?"

Rabe smiled. "With my immediate superior," he said, "whose English was not quite as good as mine." By way of this correspondence, he explained,

Germany offered its services to the Confederacy. They suggested that, if a suitable amount of money exchanged hands, they would provide armed mercenaries which, clearly, the South sorely needed.

The Confederacy was without funds to pay for such services. Being in desperate need of money, men, and weaponry, it determined that the money designated for Indian assistance was free game and said as much to the undersecretary. He at once took action by way of Robert Rabe, who had often expressed the desire to travel to North America.

With that, Rabe declared himself ready for bed, where he remained for the next several days. At first Ulrich concluded that Rabe was feeling unwell as a result of his overindulgence with Bacchus. As it turned out, however, he appeared to be suffering a serious ailment from which the ship's doctor—called in by Ulrich—did not expect him to recover.

Call what happened next "Fate," call it synchronicity. The fact is that, knowing he would not survive the trip, Robert Rabe decided to place his full trust in Ulrich Luserke.

"I am on a mission for the Kaiser," he said, "a most important mission. God give me the strength to explain it to you, and give you the courage to fulfil it."

Rabe, it appeared, was to journey first by sea, then by train, to Cleveland, Ohio. He was to meet a man named Isaac Stewart, a secret supporter of the Confederacy. Together, under the guise of being miners, they would travel to the Nevada Territory. There, Stewart would join the Nevada Volunteers, who guarded an enormous area extending from the Great Plains to the heights of the Sierras, and from California's Mojave to the Territory of Idaho. Apparently, to their regret, the Volunteers were less involved in the affairs of the great Civil War and more involved in protecting the miners from the thieves, the gamblers from the squatters, and the Piutes, Bannocks, and Shoshones—who outnumbered them five to one—from each other.

The uniform would allow Stewart to move without suspicion around the state. This would simplify contact between the two men and the Indian Agent, who was also secretly a supporter of the Confederacy and who had been instructed to hand over the $25,000 entrusted to him by the government.

This money, delivered personally to the Kaiser's undersecretary, would easily pay for German mercenaries to assist the South.

"For your Kaiser, do this," Rabe pleaded.

Though in truth Luserke didn't care much for the Kaiser, he cared everything for the prospect of holding twenty-five thousand North American dollars

Other . . . . 1 ❖ 253

in his hot little hand. Trying not to show too high a degree of immediate enthusiasm, he agreed to carry out the plan.

Two days later, Robert Rabe was buried at sea.

Ulrich spent much of the remainder of the voyage to New York in Rabe's cabin. When the ship docked in New York, he disembarked with Rabe's possessions, including his identity papers.

Calling himself Robert Rabe, Ulrich boarded the American railroad to Cleveland. The journey, while bumpy and disjointed as the train switched from what he found out was one independently owned segment to another, provided Ulrich with time to admire the seemingly endless forests and hills of America.

He was met at the train by a fairly tall, light-haired, utterly unremarkable fellow who identified himself as Isaac Stewart and took Rabe/Luserke to a bar not unlike the one where he had first heard the story of the $25,000.

"How did you recognize me?" Luserke asked.

Stewart smiled. "In those clothes, you stand out like a silo in a cornfield."

He looked at his clothes, a mixture of his own and some of the finer pieces from Rabe's trunk, then at the other patrons in the bar in their home-sewn, rough-woven garments.

"I wouldn't worry about it none," Stewart continued. "There's plenty of Germans come over here heading west, and a fair enough number heading back again."

The two men paused their conversation while a barmaid brought two mugs of beer to their table. Luserke took a sip, then, appreciatively, a second. "Good."

Again Stewart smiled. "Yes, a few Germans settled near here, too, and one of them knows how to brew good beer."

"So tell me of the plan."

"We're to rendezvous with the Indian Agent who is in possession of the money at some place in Nevada called Walker Lake," Stewart told him.

"How do we know he will come?" Luserke asked.

"He's under threat of exposure for illegally renting Indian lands to white ranchers. He'll come."

"And how do we find this place? This Walker Lake?"

"A good map, an Indian guide—one, the other, or both."

"When is this meeting to take place?"

"In early March."

"Sounds like a simple matter," Luserke said. *Then all I have to do is get rid of you, my stupid, patriotic new friend,* he thought. "This will be a piece of Bavarian pie."

"Yes." Isaac said, laughing. "A piece of pie, indeed. What's more, the world is flocking westward in search of silver. It's said the mines are over-burdened with ore which is there for the taking. When we're done with our ... assignment ... you will have to return at once to your Kaiser. Doubtless he will reward you for your services. No one will reward me, so I intend to stake a claim to a silver mine. I'm sorry you won't be able to stay and mine it with me."

Stewart might want to break his back down below the earth, but that was hardly his idea of a good time, Luserke thought. All he said was, "Things are shaping up well."

Nattee-Tohaquetta hovered around the edge of the sweat pit where his father had spent the better part of three days and nights. As always, this was for him a period of high anxiety. It was his father's frequent habit to undergo this ritual, for purposes, he said, of cleansing himself and communicating with the spirits of his ancestors.

Which was all well and good, except that no one ever quite knew how to predict his mood when he emerged. The only thing they knew for certain was that after bathing, eating, and sleeping, he would tell stories about the journey of his mind and pass on the instructions of his ancestors.

"Nattee-Tohaquetta!" his father bellowed.

The boy froze. Rigid, he watched his father's big head emerge from the pit.

"Nattee-Tohaquetta," his father said, more quietly this time. "I am ready. Come. You are old enough yourself to sweat in the pit. You will sit here and think while I rest and recover. Then we will talk."

Before he knew it, twelve-year-old hunter-gatherer Nattee-Tohaquetta, who was named after the great Chief White Belt, was sitting in the three-day sweat smell of his father, staring up at the blue sky of morning and wondering if he would be allowed out in time for dinner.

"What should I think about, Father?" he asked.

"Think about your spirit guide," his father said. "If he comes to you, you will not have to leave home to search for him."

And then there was silence.

Sitting by himself, with no distractions, Nattee-Tohaquetta tried to think about his spirit guide. He thought of what it was to be a hunter-gatherer, and he thought about what he had learned from the storytellers and from his Paiute father, that the white man's country was embroiled in a Civil War. Though they had explained what that meant, he knew nothing of it from personal experience. It was as far removed from his life in Paradise Valley, Nevada, as wearing shoes or going to school or attending church services.

The day passed more quickly than he could have imagined. At the setting of the sun, his father returned. Handing him a carved pipe and a bag containing the dried fruit of the peyote cactus, he said, "Follow the dreams this brings you. They will lead you to your spirit guide. Do not return until you have found each other."

The boy looked closely at the pipe, ran his fingers over the carvings, put the mouthpiece between his lips and sucked. He heard a tiny whistle of air, a melody almost.

"Your spirit guide will take care of you," his father said.

"I'd rather not go. There are dangers out there," the boy responded, never having been too big on the spirit-guide business.

His father nodded; still, the intractable set of his mouth told Nattee-Tohaquetta that he had no choice but to depart from the bosom of his family.

That night, alone in the darkness, the boy filled the pipe, lit it, and took one short puff. He inhaled and waited, hoping for something to happen that would cancel his father's plans. Nothing happened, not really, except that he lost his fear and began to grow excited at the idea of escaping his father's control.

Early the next morning, the boy crawled out of the pit. He packed a small bag with some eggs and a few other provisions and bade his mother, his father, his sisters, and his uncle farewell. Bravely facing the unknown, he headed through Paradise Valley, northward in the direction of Walker Lake.

That night, after puffing more thoroughly on the peyote, he lay under a cotton tree. Not sure if he was fully awake or asleep, and afraid to find out, he watched an Indian being clubbed with an empty pistol by a white man dressed in the strangest outfit he had never seen. He did not know it then, but he was getting his first view of a Nevada Volunteer.

The Indian died; the white man, angry that the clubbing had ruined his pistol, took the man's scalp. Exacting revenge, the dead Indian's friend killed two white men and left the bodies near the lake. Weeping women, stumbling across the bodies, tied grasses into small bundles which looked as if they were meant to be used as funeral pyres.

Nattee-Tohaquetta was not happy. He puffed again on his pipe and fell asleep, only to be awakened by a conversation between two uniformed white men who sat easily on the other side of the bush that hid him from view.

"Do you miss your wife and family, Colonel McDermit?" the one man asked.

"Indeed I do, Lieutenant," the colonel said, "but the last of this foolishness is near. I am so sure of it that I have written to my wife and told her to fatten the biggest turkey in our stock for my return at the end of this month."

Through a gap in the branches, Nattee-Tohaquetta watched three men approach. They were carrying with them a grotesque trophy. The boy had never seen such a thing before; he felt his stomach heave.

"I know my reputation," the colonel said. "I am considered soft on the Indians, preferring discussion and compromise to battle. That is truly my preference, yet I must say that scalp—a grand French tradition—pleases me immensely."

He leaned forward, almost as if to kiss the bloody object. At that, the boy lost control. Forced to abandon discretion, he vomited up his meager dinner. The sound of his retching was sufficient to draw attention to himself, and he was soon being escorted to the other side of the bush.

"Spying on us, were you?" the colonel said, with apparent anger.

"N-no, sir."

"Then what were you doing?"

"Looking for my spirit guide—"

" 'Sir.' "

"Sir," the boy repeated.

"Well, whatever your name is, go to the lake and clean yourself off," the colonel said. "When you're done, prepare to come with us. We could use an Indian guide for the climb ahead."

"My name is Nattee-Tohaquetta," the boy said.

"Okay, Nate. Go. Do as I said."

Nattee-Tohaquetta glanced at the scalp and did as he was told. When he returned from the lake, two of the three men who had appeared with the scalp had gone. The third was packing the gear that belonged to the two men who were clearly his superiors.

With the boy in the lead and the newcomer trailing, they climbed to about seven hundred feet above the valley before stopping to catch their breath and rest.

"I feel I am climbing straight to the heavens," the lieutenant said. He broke into song:

> *"Soon with angels I'll be marching*
> *With bright laurels on my brow.*

Other . . . . 1 ✠ 257

I have for my country fallen.
Who will care for Mother now?"

Sitting down to rest, the two talked of the glory of God, of love and justice and angels. McDermit, the colonel, spoke of their good fortune in being given the opportunity to serve both God and country, a country which, he pointed out, allowed them to feast on wild currants for breakfast and dine on trout from the stream.

Later, while the men slept, the boy returned to the place where he had left his meager belongings. He rested there for a while, under the cotton tree, with the intention of hastening out of the valley at his earliest opportunity. He awoke to see the third man hovering close by, observing him.

"The colonel and the lieutenant will continue alone. They wish you to take me to Cottonwood Station," he said, when he saw that Nate's eyes were open. "You will be paid for your trouble."

Perhaps he should not take money from a scalper of Indians, Nate thought, but refusing seemed stupid. "Okay," he said, a little tentatively so that it would seem as if he had considered other options.

Nate's days and nights developed a pattern. He led the way, spoke when he was spoken to, shared his food with the Volunteer, who called himself Mr. Stewart, and did not share his pipe. After sundown, when the stars were out and he was far enough from Mr. Stewart to feel some sense of privacy, he used the pipe to warm him. It gave him sleep, but it also brought him ugly dreams of a war where people burned to death and others lost their limbs. He dreamed of digging a rifle pit alongside another Paiute brave and watching soldiers approach, then turning and running as they came upon bloody scalps drying in the morning sun. He walked in his dreams with the Paiute Nation from the Humboldt to the Carson, and grieved for those who stayed behind and, branded hostiles, died.

When the sun shone, he moved on. As he walked, his feet hurt, but they took him to Cottonwood Station where Mr. Stewart immediately availed himself of the telegraph office. He came out with two sheets of paper in his hand. He looked very well pleased with himself.

"These were waiting for me," he said, though he did not explain what "these" were and kept the papers away from the boy's eyes. It wouldn't have mattered had he done otherwise, since Nate did not know how to read. "I must be at Walker Lake by March the fifth to meet with my . . . um . . . friends," he went on. "Will you take me there, Nate?"

Since Nate had intended to spend his birthday at Walker Lake, this suited his purposes. He agreed to help out.

"First, I wish to purchase a horse," Mr. Stewart said. "Wait for me here."

He left Nate to his own devices. When he returned, he was riding a horse of sorts, mangy at best, but equipped with a halfway decent saddle and saddle-bags.

Leading the horse, they left Cottonwood Station. They got as far as Carson Lake before they stopped again. After a few hours' rest, they moved on. Nate kept walking, and listening, and hearing, inside his head, the song whose melody had been just beyond reach the day he first tried out the pipe. The one the colonel had sung at the top of the mountain:

> *I have for my country fallen.*
> *Who will care for Mother now?*

Finally, Nate and his companion reached Walker Lake. They made camp in a sheltered place where they could find easy fodder in the small weirs and dams which diverted the fish from the main lake. Nearby, the boy found an edible grass which contained a seed that was pleasant to chew and, when dried and smoked, induced new and different dreams.

Long and complex dreams were in no way unusual for an Indian boy approaching puberty, but he was supposed to dream about his spirit guide— or maybe about girls.

Neither was the stuff of these dreams.

They were about Paiutes and Shoshones; about soldiers with names like Lieutenant Joel Wolverton and Colonel Charles McDermit; about a second lieutenant by the name of Lansing; and about his tribal chief, Josephius. And new men appeared in his dreams: Lieutenant W. Gibson Overend of the Second Cavalry Volunteers and a Mexican Pack Mule Teamster.

He saw ranchers and men in mine shafts, working hungry side by side. He saw water holes being fenced, hunters coming home empty-handed, he saw forests where piñon nuts had been harvested being turned into timber for the mines.

What he did not see or hear was the voice or form of his spirit guide.

By this time, young Nattee-Tohaquetta was running low on peyote and provisions and high on confusion. Truth to tell, he felt lost and lonely and began to think longingly of his family.

The peyote had also increased his hunger. Thinking to allay his hunger with fish, he moved and made camp behind one of the large scrub bushes that dotted the shores of Walker Lake.

It had been a long day, so Nate chose to sleep first and fish later. Perhaps, he thought, his spirit guide would come to him tonight and he could head for home with the dawn.

His wish was granted, if only in part. When the moon was high in the sky and it was surely after midnight, his birthday dreams were interrupted by the poking head of so strange and hideous an animal that he was sure he had gone mad. What he saw looked like a giant sage-hen, with its legs and neck devoid of plumage and incredibly distended so that it stood well over six feet. The feathers that covered its enormous body were an odd grayish brown color. The good part was the gigantic egg which he could see within his peripheral vision; the bad part was that he could never go home again. He didn't dare lie to his father, nor could he embarrass himself and his family by telling them the truth, that this bizarre-looking creature was his spirit guide. He would have to find a way to circulate a rumor that he had lost his scalp to one of Nevada's Sagebrush Soldiers, so that his family would believe him to be dead.

He pushed at the bird, such being what he presumed it to be. It skittered to one side, but made no attempt to fly. He would have understood if he'd known anything about ostriches. However, he did not, and this remained a puzzlement for years to come.

Satisfied that he was not in any immediate danger from the creature, he started to rise, but the sudden sound of voices floating toward him from the other side of the bush stopped him.

Parting the branches, he saw by the light of the moon a stranger whom Mr. Stewart addressed as Robert.

The man stood a small distance away, unsaddling his horse. He was a few years older than Mr. Stewart, somewhere in his late twenties, though it was difficult for Nate to tell for certain with a white man.

The man called Robert set down the saddle and turned toward the bushes on the opposite side of their camp, his hand resting on the pistol butt at his hip. By the attitude of his body, Nattee-Tohaquetta knew that he listened for something. The Indian boy heard it, too, the sound of a heavy man dismounting from a horse in the darkness.

"I believe I hear him coming," Robert said at last. He spoke with a guttural accent unfamiliar to the boy.

"I hope you're right," Mr. Stewart responded, somewhat irritably. He squatted next to the makings of an unlit fire. "I am not loath to confess that I have even lost my yearning for silver. All I want to do is get this over with and return to Cleveland."

"Cleveland," Nattee-Tohaquetta repeated, under his breath. He liked the sound of it. He would take it as a part of his name. Henceforth, he would be Nattee-Tohaquetta Cleveland.

At that moment, there appeared a large older white man. The boy instantly recognized him as the one Chief Josephius called the Indian Agent, the man who was supposed to help the Paiute, but instead took money from white ranchers to allow their cattle to graze in the Paiute's fields.

"Did you bring the money, Agent?" Mr. Stewart asked.

The newcomer handed him a bulging leather pouch. "That is why I am here," he said, in a surly voice.

Mr. Stewart took the pouch and patted it. Then he walked over to his horse, which he had yet to unsaddle, and stuffed the pouch inside the saddle-bags. "You may leave now," he said.

Without any further exchange of words, the Indian Agent disappeared the way he had come. Nattee-Tohaquetta could hear him mount his horse and ride north very quickly.

Back in the small camp, the man called Robert searched in the saddlebags he had just placed on the ground until he found a bottle. He opened it, drank heartily, and passed it to Mr. Stewart, who shook his head.

"Later," he said. "When we have eaten." Returning to the pile of sticks, he hunkered back down and lit the fire. When the trail of smoke had spread flames to the larger branches, he asked, "How soon until you can get the funds to Germany and your troops arrive?"

Robert, who had been drinking steadily, held the bottle upside down to show that it was empty. "Do what? Come now. You don't really believe that stuff, do you?" he asked.

"Believe it? Of course . . ." He looked up at Robert. "You're drunk," he said. "I'm going to get some water for cooking. We'll talk when you've sobered up."

"This is as sober as I'm going to get for a long time," Robert said, feeling around for another bottle. "Get the water if you like. I'll split the money while you're gone."

"Split it? That's not your money . . . or mine." The expression on the uniformed man's face told the young observer behind the bush that trouble was afoot.

"It's our money now," Robert said, laughing.

"But the mercenaries, the Confederacy—"

"The mercenaries be damned. The Confederacy be damned. I may have told Rabe that I'd come get this money for him, but I don't have his convictions or yours." Robert took another hearty slug of liquor and tossed the bottle aside.

Mr. Stewart looked stunned. "You mean, you're not Robert Rabe?"

The stranger laughed again. "No, you fool. Rabe died in my arms. I'm Ulrich Luserke, adventurer. As of now, *wealthy* adventurer."

"You're not going to have that money," Mr. Stewart said.

If he stepped out there now, Nattee-Tohaquetta Cleveland thought, it was possible his presence alone could prevent the blood from flowing that every instinct told him was about to be shed. But he did not step out, and Mr. Stewart turned toward the rifle that lay resting on the ground behind him, presenting Robert with his back and opportunity.

In what seemed like no time at all and forever, the man who said he was not Robert had his gun in his hand and he had fired. Mr. Stewart jerked once, yelled, gurgled, and keeled over.

Walking perfectly sober and moving fast, the shooter gathered together a few things including the other man's hat. He made sure that the saddlebags that contained the money were secure and, without once looking back, he mounted the other's horse and rode away.

Neither the boy nor the gigantic bird that had awakened him moved. Motionless, they watched as two Paiutes, not much older than Nattee-Tohaquetta, came by and finished off Mr. Stewart, crushing his skull with a rock. Obviously unconcerned about being apprehended, they joked with one another, saying that they had rendered his scalp valueless, and took everything they could carry before they vanished back into the brush.

Nattee-Tohaquetta set off toward Austin, Nevada, where he hoped to find Colonel McDermit, tell him what he had seen, and gain his good graces. He needed temporary employment and a few solid meals. He was closely followed by the ostrich, which had decided that the boy was her master.

It was a time of hardship for Nate. He went hungry often and was not above stealing livestock when his belly growled with hunger. He worked briefly for the *Reese River Reveille* in Austin, in return for food and old copies of newsprint which he used as a blanket. Then he realized how much the newspaper's owner and editor-in-chief detested his people, and he left their employ. He had long run out of peyote, but not out of nightmares in which he heard the crunching of rock against the skull of Mr. Stewart, and the plaintive melody and words about a mother left without anyone to care for her. Mostly, he heard war cries and thunder across the desert he called the Mojave.

And then things changed.

Through a stroke of good fortune, he met a lovely young woman by the name of Dora who took him into her heart and unto her bosom, settling him at her place of employment—the larger of Austin's two whorehouses. There, his ostrich provided the rental ladies with eggs to eat and feathers to refill their beds in exchange for board and lodging for the two of them.

Though he occasionally missed his family and he sometimes suffered nightmares about what he had seen at Walker Lake, the boy settled readily into his new life. In what free time she had, Dora taught him many things, including the skill of reading. Since he would not take lessons from the *Reese River Reveille*, she used as his schoolbook Virginia City's *Territorial Enterprise*.

It was thus, during a reading lesson, that he learned of the death on August 7, 1865, of Colonel McDermit.

The notice in the newspaper read,

On August 7th, 1865, Col. R. C. Drum of San Francisco received the following telegram: "*Col. McDermit was killed yesterday afternoon within half a mile from camp by Indians lying in ambush.*"

The telegram was signed "G. F. Lansing, 2nd Lieut. 1st Inf., Nevada Volunteers."

That night, seated with a variety of house guests at dinner, Nate at last told the story of Robert Rabe, the crooked Indian Agent, and of Isaac Stewart, the turncoat Nevada Volunteer.

By coincidence, one of the guests was none other than William Wright, owner of the *Territorial Enterprise*, and his good friend and colleague, Samuel Clemens.

Mr. Clemens swore that if he ever visited Germany, he would make it his business to find "this murderous Luserke rascal" and recover the $25,000 and return it to the Indians. Mr. Wright, being a much more practical man, immediately resolved to report the story of the death of "Other . . . . 1" in his newspaper and to inform the Nevada Volunteers accordingly.

Since Stewart was dead, Wright did not, in his article, call him a spy, though he was no less.

The money was never retrieved.

NOTE: Colonel McDermit's grandson, Charles, passed along a variety of papers and letters to one Alice Addenbrooke. From there they fell into the hands of Philip Dodd Smith, Jr. who wrote a defining paper about Nevada's Volunteers in the Civil War. The paper, titled *The Sagebrush Soldiers,* was published by the Nevada Historical Society as part of their Civil War Centennial.

FACT: Colonel McDermit was one of 1,080 mostly forgotten men who, for two years, comprised the Nevada Volunteers.

FACT: Twenty-five thousand dollars designated by the Senate for Indian rehabilitation in Nevada reached its destination and disappeared.

Doug Allyn is an accomplished author whose short fiction regularly graces year's best collections. His work has appeared in *Once upon a Crime, Cat Crimes Through Time*, and *The Year's 25 Finest Crime and Mystery Stories*, volumes 3 and 4. His stories of Tallifer, the wandering minstrel, have appeared in *Ellery Queen's Mystery Magazine* and *Murder Most Scottish*. His story "The Dancing Bear," a Tallifer tale, won the Edgar award for short fiction for 1995. His other series character is veterinarian Dr. David Westbrook, whose exploits have recently been collected in the anthology *All Creatures Dark and Dangerous*. He lives with his wife in Montrose, Michigan.

In the following story, he delves not only into American history, but his own family tree, basing the events here on the exploits of his great-uncle Riley Radford, who hid his own herd of horses from both sides during the war.

THE TURNCOAT

Doug Allyn

Gus sensed it before he heard it, something moving outside the ring of firelight, coming closer in the dark. He could feel it between his shoulder blades, sharp as a nudge from a spike bayonet. A ghost walking on his grave?

No. The horses sensed it, too, shifting uneasily in their brush corral at the base of the ridge, raising their heads, tasting the wind. Someone was circling the camp. Definitely. Gus hadn't survived three years in these mountains by ignoring his instincts.

His battered Remington-Jenks carbine was in a rock cleft with his bedroll but the primer tape was so old the gun only fired half the time. And if the intruder meant to harm him, he'd probably be dead already. Best to wait him out and—A twig snapped in the shadows.

Gus rose slowly, keeping his hands in sight. "Come on in," he said quietly. "I've got no weapon and nothin' worth stealin' but I got stew—"

"Shut your mouth. You alone?"

"My son's up in the ridges, hunting. He'll be back in a while."

"Yeah? When did he leave?"

"I don't know, around noon, I guess."

"You're lyin', old man. I been watching you since morning. Nobody's come or gone." The boy stepped out of the shadows. Tall and gawky, he hadn't seen twenty yet, but his weapon was man-sized, a Colt horse pistol, the hammer eared back, muzzle centered on Gus's belly.

His ragged uniform jacket was so grimy and faded it was hard to tell its original color. Union artillery blue? Or Arkansas gray? Didn't matter which side he was on anyway; the boy'd obviously been on the dodge awhile. Face dirty, scraggly beard, cheeks hollow from hunger.

"My name's Gus McKee, son. I give you my word you got nothin' to fear from me. I'm hidin' in these mountains waitin' out the fight the same as you."

"You a soldier?" The boy's eyes flicked around the campsite, edgy as a cat on a cookstove.

"Was once," Gus acknowledged. "Went down to Mexico with Winfield Scott in '46. Killed folks I didn't know in a place I never heard of. Still carry a musket ball in my hip from it. I want no part of this fight."

"If you ain't a deserter, why you hidin' out up here?"

"The wife and I got a little stock ranch west of Reynolds. Raise mostly draft animals, a few saddlebreds. But southern Missouri's sorry country for breedin' horses nowadays. Lyon and his Hessians raided my place on their way to Springfield in '61—"

" 'Hessians'?"

"Germans," Gus explained. "Immigrants just off the boat, all Union. Folks 'round here call 'em Hessians, like them mercenaries the Brits used in the Revolution. Anyways, after Lyon got killed at Wilson's Creek both sides started raidin' our stock, burnin' crops. Between the so'jer boys and runaway slaves headed north we're about picked clean. I brung the last of our animals up into these hills so's my boys have somethin' to come home to when it's over."

"You got boys in the fight? Which side?"

"Both." Gus shrugged. "Oldest run away to sea in '57, stayed with the Union navy when war broke out. Last I heard, he was on the *Hartford*, off Mobile Bay. Second-oldest is with Bedford Forest, two younger boys went off with General Price in '62."

"And which do you favor, Mr. McKee?"

"I favor stayin' alive in a troubled time, same as you. Can I put my hands down? Coffee's 'bout to boil over and it's hard to come by out here. Care for some?"

"I'd appreciate it," the boy said, slowly lowering his pistol as Gus knelt to retrieve the pot from the coals. Pouring two cups of scalding brew, Gus passed one to the youth.

"I didn't catch your name, boy."

"It's Mitchell, Elias Mitchell. I apologize for comin' down on you like this. I been on the run."

"You're Federal." It wasn't a question.

Eli nodded, sipping the coffee. "How'd you know?"

"You never heard of Hessians for one thing. Where you from?"

"Illinois. My folks got a farm near Cairo. I enlisted for a year but my unit got busted up after Perryville and my new outfit drafted us for the duration. I served more'n three years, seen a lot of action. Then I got a letter that said my folks are farin' poorly. I've had enough. I joined up to save the Union and free the slaves but we mostly been burnin' farms and villages, leavin' folks to starve. Couldn't do it no more. Lit out from Vicksburg last month, workin' my way home."

"You're still a ways from Illinois."

"Not as fur as I was. Had a horse for a while but she went lame on me, had to turn her loose."

"Near here?" Gus asked sharply, suddenly wary.

"No, down in Arkansas, two weeks back. Why?"

"These hills may look empty but they ain't. Union patrols are out, foraging, huntin' deserters from both sides. Got a bounty on Union boys, twenty dollars a head."

"Hell, that's more'n we been gettin' paid!"

"Worse than that, it's dead or alive and they ain't fussy about which."

"Man, that's crazy," Eli said, shaking his head. "You're doin' the proper thing stayin' up here, Mr. McKee. There ain't no right side in this fight no more. If there ever was."

"Maybe not. You got any money, boy?"

"Money? No sir. A few Dixie singles for souvenirs, is all. I'm afraid I can't pay you for the coffee. Sorry."

"So am I, especially since I was hopin' to sell you a horse. Is your word any good?"

"Yes sir, I believe it is," Eli said, puzzled. "Why?"

"Because I'm going to loan you a horse, young Mitchell. But I want your word I'll get my animal back when this is over."

"I don't understand."

"Boy, I been shiftin' my little herd around these hills, dodgin' Union and Reb patrols, jayhawkers and outlaws for three years now. But I know every foot of these mountains. You don't. You try walkin' home through the Ozarks, you'll be taken sure as God made green apples. Maybe they'll even track you back to me. Way I see it, the sooner you're long gone from here, the better for both of us. With a horse and some luck you can be home in a week."

"You're taking a hell of a gamble for somebody you hardly know, Mr. McKee. To be honest, I staked you out because I planned to steal a horse. At gunpoint if I had to."

"Is that a fact? More coffee?"

"I'm serious."

"Maybe. But you didn't backshoot me or try to rustle my stock and nowadays that'll pass for righteous. Drink your coffee, boy, have some stew. Come moonrise I'll put you on a jayhawk trail. You can cover eight, ten miles yet tonight."

"I—surely do thank you, Mr. McKee. But it ain't quite that simple."

"No? Why not?"

"Last few days, I been layin' up with a wounded Reb at a spring few miles south. I told him I'd fetch help."

"A creek with cedars around it, end of a long valley?"

"You know it?"

"I know every waterhole for sixty miles around, boy. But I ain't the only one. Yanks scout that valley regular."

"I didn't see any."

"You was lucky. How long's he been there?"

"I don't know. A few days. He's hurt bad. Gutshot."

"A local boy?" Gus asked, swallowing.

"No sir, he's from Arkansas. From what he said, I believe he was a lieutenant with General Price. He's ravin', half out of his head. He won't last long without help."

"Gutshot, he won't last long, period. Your home's the other direction, Mr. Mitchell. Goin' back will only buy trouble for yourself, maybe for him, too."

"But I promised."

"You can't be held to that. There's a war on, for God's sake. He's probably dead already. Tell you what, I'll try to look in on him in a day or two. Will that do?"

"I—guess it will have to. Thank you."

"No need. Bein' a damn fool comes natural to me. Here, have some stew." Dumping a steaming mix of rabbit, wild corn, and a yam onto a metal plate, Gus passed it to Eli. "I don't get much news up here, can you fill me in?"

"Don't know much myself," Eli mumbled around a mouthful. "Nobody tells the infantry nothin', but from what I've seen it's almost over."

"Been hearin' that since '61."

"It's true. Atlanta's fallen, Sherman's marchin' to Savannah burnin' everything for sixty miles around. Richmond's surrounded. Hood's still loose, though, headed for Nashville, they say."

"And General Price?"

"He got whipped bad at Westport in the fall, fell back into Arkansas. I hear his men are havin' hard times, eatin' their horses, livin' on grass themselves. Sorry, you said your sons . . . ?"

"Two of 'em are with Price," Gus spat. "Damned nonsense. I never owned a slave in my life, don't hold with it. But after them Yanks hit us, there was no keepin' my boys back. Went off to fight for the Cause."

"For slavery?"

"For independence, by our lights. To live free without Yanks or Hessians runnin' off our stock. The only slaves I've seen since the Emancipation were runaways grubbin' for food in my fields like animals. Think they're better off than before?"

"Sir, near as I can tell, this war ain't made anybody better off, Negro or white. The slaves we freed had nowhere to go, no food, no land. Like I said, there's no right side to it. I just want to go home."

"I know the feelin'," Gus agreed. "Know it well."

Later, in the moonlight, Gus saddled his own mare with one of his working rigs, Elias Mitchell climbed aboard and Gus sent him north along an old jayhawk trace. Watching the boy move off into the shadows, he felt surprisingly content, considering he'd just given away an animal he'd raised from a colt. The damned war was turning the whole world upside down.

But Gus woke uneasy at first light with a nagging sense of something amiss. Huddled in his blanket beside the dying campfire, he tried to put his finger on it.

Was it something about Mitchell? Something he'd said or done? Didn't seem likely. He'd given the deserter his mare freely. What else could he do? Kill the boy? Drive him off? He had no regrets about his decision.

True, he scarcely knew the boy, but Gus was a stockman who could rank a horse at forty paces and a fair judge of people as well. Young Eli Mitchell struck him as an honest man. He'd promised to return the mare later on and Gus believed he would try to do so. . . .

And that was the rub. Eli would return the mare because he was honest and he'd given Gus his word. But he'd also promised to help a wounded Reb lieutenant. And now he had a fresh horse and some food . . . Damn it!

Cursing his own stupidity, Gus rolled out of his blankets, fetched his rifle from the cache and headed off down the trail at a trot. The mare's tracks were easy to follow in the morning dew. The boy had ridden north just long enough to get out of Gus's sight, then he'd turned south, working his way back to the spring and his wounded friend.

But Gus knew the hills far better. Leaving the trail, he trotted uphill through the aspens at a mile-eating lope. A horse couldn't go directly over the mountain crest but a man could, and it would cut the journey in half. With luck, he'd make the waterhole by noon.

But Gus was running short on luck. And Eli Mitchell's was gone altogether.

As he crested the ridge overlooking the valley, Gus heard a shout, then the thunder of hooves. Threading the mare through the trees at the edge of the valley, Eli Mitchell had been spotted by a Union patrol. Though he was clearly trapped, Eli never hesitated. Wheeling his mount, he raced down the valley toward the mouth. The patrol fanned out to intercept him, cutting him off easily, encircling him before he'd covered half a mile.

Dropping to his belly on the ridge, Gus fumbled in his pouch for the brass-cased Mexican field glass, his only trophy from the war. Snapping it open, he hastily homed in on the meadow below, bringing it into focus. It was already over. The Union patrol had Eli surrounded, the boy with his hands in the air as the troopers closed in, weapons at the ready.

Gus was too far away to make out faces clearly. Didn't recognize the officer in charge—a captain, tall, gaunt, with a Vandyke goatee, a cape, and a French-style kepi forage cap. The troopers? Militia, judging from their mismatched uniforms. Probably Hessians from Saint Lou or Jefferson City. But their civilian scout . . .

Damn! Gus recognized the slouch hat and stooped shoulders even before he zeroed in on the scout's face. Aaron Meachum, a jayhawker renegade who'd been raiding and murdering in Kansas years before the war came, camouflaging his thievery with a smokescreen of abolitionist bushwa. As a Hessian sergeant questioned Eli, Meachum casually circled his mount around behind the boy, looking his mare over.

Would he recognize the animal? Gus searched his memory, trying to recall if Meachum had ever seen the mare. Once, maybe, at the Reynolds County Fair. Meachum had tried to goad Gus's younger son into a fight, backing off when Gus stepped in. Meachum might have seen the horse then, but that was before the war and—

With a single, fluid motion Meachum drew his pistol and shot Eli in the head! His hands still raised, the boy collapsed like a broken puppet, toppling from the saddle to the grass of the valley floor.

"No!" Gus was on his feet, stunned, staring. But too far away to be heard. The other troopers seemed just as surprised. Red-faced, the sergeant was yelling at Meachum, his voice carrying across the valley. Ignoring him, the jayhawker scout dismounted and ran his hands over Eli's horse, stepping across the boy's body without so much as a downward glance.

Satisfied, Meachum unsaddled Eli's mare, tossed the battered work saddle aside, then transferred his own McClellan rig to the mare's back, kicking the wind out of her belly as he yanked the cinch taut.

The troopers watched in silence as Meachum swung into the saddle, then the sergeant muttered something and men dismounted, hoisted Eli's body across the back of Meachum's horse and tied him on. Meachum said something to them, a joke apparently since Gus could read his grin clear across the meadow. None of the others smiled.

Wheeling his horse, the captain led the troop out of the valley by twos with Eli's body bouncing like a saddlebag on the last horse. Gus stayed crouched, watching them vanish into the distance, then waited another hour to be sure they were gone.

And only then did he begin working his way across the ridge crest toward the spring Eli had described, the one he'd led the patrol away from before they rode him down.

Gus wanted the lieutenant to be dead. It would be simpler. He could get back to his camp to think, clear his head of the vision of Eli, falling with his hands still raised. . . .

He heard a soft click. A pistol hammer being eared back.

"Stop where you are. Raise . . ." The voice faded away,

Gus froze. "Lieutenant? My name's McKee. Elias Mitchell sent me to you." No answer, only a muffled cough. Gus could see him now, half concealed in a copse of cedars beside the brook that trickled into the basin. An officer, all right, cadet gray tunic, gilt buttons, yellow cavalry stripe on his trousers. And an army Colt in his fist.

But the gun wasn't aimed directly at Gus. Only in his general direction. And even at that distance Gus caught the sour stench of a suppurating belly wound. Mortification. Gangrene.

Kneeling beside him, Gus gently took the gun from his hand. Doubted the Reb even knew it. The lieutenant's eyes were open but he was gazing into some impossible distance, his face ashen, blood bubbling in the corners of his mouth, his lips red as rouge.

After a time he seemed to drift back, staring up at Gus, faintly puzzled.

"I'm sorry," he said, licking his lips. "I was with my mother . . . do I know you?"

"No, Lieutenant. My name's McKee. Elias Mitchell sent me."

"Who?"

"Elias Mitchell. A boy who stayed with you a few days back?"

"Mitchell, yes. The Yankee. Is he all right?"

"He's . . . fine. He's gone home. To his people."

"I'm glad. He was kind to me. . . ." He swallowed. "I haven't much time, sir. I am Lieutenant James Oliver Neeland, of the First Arkansas. I have family on the White River Valley. Could you write to my father, tell him what happened? Jason Neeland, general delivery, Clarendon."

"I'll see to it. Lieutenant, I have two sons serving with Price, Jared and Levon McKee. Have you . . . ?" But the boy had drifted off again, his lips moving in soundless conversation. Gus waited for what seemed an age. And realized Neeland was staring up at him again.

"I'm sorry I . . . seem to have forgotten your name."

"McKee, Lieutenant. Gus McKee."

"McKee. Of course. And you asked me . . . Was your son Jared McKee? A sergeant with the Missourians?"

"Yes, he and his brother—"

"Sergeant Jared McKee fell at Westport, sir. I'm sorry. I don't recall hearing about his brother. I hope he's well."

Gus looked away, his eyes stinging. It was too much. Eli's death. And now Jared. Dear God.

"Mr. McKee, I'm sorry to trouble you at such a time but I find myself in a . . . quandary. I'm dying. And in truth, I don't mind much. The pain's not so bad now. My mother is . . . May I ask where do you stand, sir? North or South?"

Gus didn't answer. Couldn't. He saw Eli falling, his hands upraised in surrender . . . and Jared. Falling.

Gus shook his head to clear it. "I have sons in gray, Lieutenant," he said hoarsely. "I stand with my sons."

"Good." Neeland closed his eyes. "I was carrying dispatches to General Hood from General Price. I burned them after I was wounded but the message is simple. General Price cannot support Hood at Nashville. We have neither supplies for the march, nor ammunition to fight. Hood must be told."

"But how can I—?"

"There's a letter in my tunic. It will verify that you come from Price. We have a contact at Cape Girardeau, a storekeeper named Groton, Cecil Groton. Show him the letter, relay the message, and he'll forward it. Can you do that for me, Mr. McKee?"

"Lieutenant—"

"Please!" Neeland grasped Gus's forearm desperately, pulling himself up. "For your sons, sir. For the South!"

"All right, son, take it easy. I'll see to it."

"Thank you." Neeland fell back, spent. "The letter is in my blouse. Take it, please."

Gus reached inside the lieutenant's coat, found the envelope, then hesitated. He felt no heartbeat. He glanced at Neeland. His eyes were empty. He was gone. Just like that. Gone.

Rising stiffly, Gus looked over the letter. It appeared harmless enough, a short note identifying the bearer as a friend of Ishmael. Which apparently would mean something to the storekeeper in Cape Girardeau.

Good Lord. Three years in these hills, waiting out the madness, and now that it was nearly over, he'd finally been forced to make a choice. Eli Mitchell said there wasn't any right side to this but he was mistaken. His own death proved it. And Jared's. And this poor bastard who'd kept himself alive long enough to pass his message. Some part of their Cause must be worth dying for. It had to be.

Gus buried Neeland in the forest not far from the creek, said the Lord's Prayer over him, then headed back to his camp to pack up. Right or wrong, he'd just enlisted. Again.

Leaving was risky but the horses had forage enough for a week or so in their blind valley and they were well hidden. A straggler might stumble across them and steal the lot, but there was no help for that.

He chose his mount with care, a swaybacked gray plowhorse named Nell. Six years old, she had a canted jaw, broken by a kick when she was a colt. Her crooked mouth kept her gaunt and her disposition was on the surly side of rabid. But most importantly, her injury made her nearly mute. She seldom whickered or whinnied. An admirable trait in a companion, horse or human.

After rubbing soot between her ribs to accent the bones, he smeared small lumps of bloody suet on her legs to simulate sores. It wasn't perfect but only an expert would spot it. Most stockmen's tricks were to disguise a nag's shortcomings, not make them look worse.

Finished, Gus stepped back to admire his handiwork and nodded. "Nell my girl, you are just about the sorriest-looking animal I've ever seen, too swaybacked to work and too scrawny to eat. Definitely not worth stealing."

Nell didn't reply but her glare was so ferocious Gus couldn't help smiling. The last time he'd gone to war it was in a proud new uniform with brass buttons. This time he hoped to pass for a ragamuffin, pride be damned.

Saddling Nell with his poorest work rig, he lashed his bedroll to the cantle, tossed a few hardtack biscuits and some jerky in a sack, and climbed aboard. He looked over his camp a moment, making sure he'd erased all traces, campfire buried, gear stowed in the rock cleft. He had half a dozen hideouts like this one scattered through the mountains, moving from one to the other as the horses cropped down the canyon grass or patrols got too close.

Hadn't been much of a life these past three years, living like a bandit, seeing his wife and youngest boy a few nights each month during the dark of the moon when he could slink out of the hills without being seen.

A sorry way to live, but it was his only chance to save what little they had left. Now he was risking it all for two dead boys he'd hardly known, boys who'd fought on opposite sides. As his own sons were doing.

It was lunacy and he knew it, yet he'd given his word and couldn't see backing off. Not if he was ever going to look in a shaving mirror again.

But being swept up in the madness of this fight didn't give him leave to be careless. It meant the opposite. For his family to survive he had to come through this. If he could.

He trailed northeast out of the Ozarks, down through the foothills, making a cold camp that night. Nell's bony back and plodding gait made for a damned uncomfortable ride and since she tended to balk in the face of rough cover he'd been forced to lead her through it on foot, walking much of the way.

Dog-tired and sore, he stared up at the silent stars, waiting for sleep that wouldn't come. Seeing Eli fall, his hands raised in surrender; the blood bubbling at the corners of Neeland's mouth. And remembering Jared as a boy, a tow-headed kid with a gap between his front teeth.

His brothers joshed him, claimed he'd miss every other row on a corncob. Jared grinning, sayin' it lasted longer that way. Dead now. Probably thrown in a hole with a dozen others and covered over. Lost in a fight with no right side to it.

Gus rose before dawn, impatient to be gone. On the road to Girardeau he could travel openly. The greatest danger was in the foothills coming out of the mountains. As Eli Mitchell had learned the hard way.

Maintaining a steady pace, he broke out of the hills south of Ellington just before noon. He pointed Nell east but he'd covered barely a mile when a patrol filed out of a copse of poplars, blocking the trail.

Yanks. And his heart sank as he recognized them. The same bunch who'd murdered Eli, half a dozen militia troopers with Aaron Meachum as their scout. No officer with them this time.

No point in hightailing it. Nell couldn't outrun a three-legged stool. So he plodded slowly up to them, feeling the sweat trickle down his back. Where the letter was concealed beneath his shirt.

"Who are you, mister? What you doin' out here?" the sergeant asked, his Hessian accent strong as sauerkraut. Red-faced, stocky. His blue wool uniform coat looked homemade and probably was, but his gray eyes were wary. And dangerous.

"Name's McKee. Got a place over in Reynolds County. Headed east to visit a cousin."

"What cousin would that be?" Aaron Meachum asked. The jayhawker slouched in his saddle, eyeing Gus from beneath the brim of his sagging cavalry cap.

"Keith Stewart, at Buckhorn."

"Didn't know the Stewarts were kin to you, McKee."

"You know this man?" the sergeant asked Meachum.

"Know who he is. Reb sympathizer, got boys in gray. Ain't that right, McKee?"

"Well, he ain't no deserter so he ain't worth no bounty," the sergeant said. "Let's move on."

"Not so fast," Meachum drawled. "He might be carryin' contraband. Step down, McKee."

Gus hesitated.

"Just do like he says, mister," the sergeant sighed. "He likes to kill people, this one."

Forcing his fear back, Gus swung down.

"Step away from that nag and raise your hands. Search him, Dutch."

"Come on, Meachum, he ain't got two pennies to rub together. Let's go."

"The captain left me in charge and I say we search him, Dutch. Now do it!"

Muttering to himself in German, the sergeant swung down, stalked over to Gus, and quickly ran his hands over his body. And felt the letter! No question, Gus heard it rustle as the German's hands passed over it. Their eyes met for a split second, then the sergeant stepped away.

"Nothing," the Hessian said. "I told you."

"Looked like a pretty careless search to me, Dutch. We'd best make sure. Take off your clothes, McKee."

"What?"

"You heard me, old man. Strip. Get 'em off. Let's see your . . . contraband."

Gus swallowed, hard, wanting to rush at Meachum, drag him from his saddle or die trying. But he couldn't. Meachum would kill him, sure as sunup. Gus could see it in his eyes. But if they found the letter, he'd probably die anyway. He could never explain it to this bunch.

"No," he said. "I won't do it."

" 'No'?" Meachum echoed. "Strip him down, Dutch. If he gives you any trouble, kill him. Or I will."

The sergeant turned to Gus, his face a mask. "Don't give me no trouble, mister. He means it."

"Go to hell!" Gus heard a quaver in his voice and hated it.

Grabbing his collar, the sergeant spun Gus around, pulling him close. Gus struggled but could feel the power in the Hessian's arms, knew he hadn't much chance against him—then suddenly he was free.

Thrusting him away, the Hessian stalked back to his horse. He said something in German and the troopers roared with laughter.

"What do you think you're doing?" Meachum said, stiffening. "What did you say?"

"I said now I know why you ain't got no woman, Meachum. You like lookin' at old men's *hinterbacken*." The sergeant reached for his pommel to mount and found himself staring down the muzzle of Meachum's Navy Colt.

"I told you to strip him, Dutch."

"And I say there's no bounty on him and no contraband. Look at him, look at his horse. You waste our time here." He said something else in German, but this time there was no laughter. The others were eyeing Meachum warily.

"What did you say?"

"You don't put that pistol away, you find out." Swinging into the saddle, the Hessian wheeled his mount to the west and kicked her to a trot. He glanced down at Gus as he passed but his face was unreadable. The others fell into line behind him by twos.

All but Meachum. The jayhawker scout considered Gus a moment, cocked pistol in his fist, death in his eyes, then shook his head.

"We'll have another day, McKee. Count on it." Holstering the Colt, he clucked to his horse, trotting off after the troops.

Gus nearly grabbed him as he passed. Needed to drag him off his animal, stomp his brains in for Eli, for Jared—but he didn't. Couldn't. They'd kill him and he had to stay alive.

Or maybe it was just cowardice. Gettin' old, losing heart and makin' excuses. That was the worst of it. Not knowing the truth of it.

Still shaking, Gus hauled himself into the saddle and nudged Nell to a walk, heading east.

He forded the Black at dusk below Clearwater, planning to camp near Muldick Mountain but pushed on through the night instead. Couldn't sleep anyway and Nell paced so sluggishly that the long march didn't seem to tax her.

Kept thinking of the Hessian sergeant. The man had felt the envelope when he searched him, Gus saw it in his eyes. Yet he deliberately misled Meachum about it. He was likely strong for the Union, all the Germans were. So why had he let it pass?

The best Gus could come up with was that the sergeant had seen enough dead men in the road. Amen to that, Hessian or not.

Dawn overtook him on the post road west of Marble Hill and by mid-afternoon Nell was plodding through the outskirts of Cape Girardeau.

After three years in the hills any town would have seemed strange but Cape Girardeau, with the Mississippi as a main street, its houses and citizens more French than Missourian, felt as alien to Gus as Mexico City had all those years ago.

Even the folk on the streets looked foreign, men in spats and five-button suits, veiled ladies carrying parasols, carriages with uniformed footmen. Union troops in spotless uniforms were casually strolling the boardwalks, window-shopping or chatting up the town girls.

Most were infantry but some were cavalry, and a few were Union sailors from the gunboats in the river. Not a one of them looked like he'd ever heard a shot fired, or expected to.

The merchandise in the store windows was fairy-tale fanciful, racks of bright silk blouses, open barrels of pickles and peaches. One shop was filled with musical instruments, banjos, mandolins, gleaming brass trumpets, and other larger horns whose voices Gus couldn't even imagine.

Blacks were everywhere, clerks waiting on Union officers and their ladies or wheeling stock down the crowded streets on barrows, better dressed and fed than any Missourian Gus had seen in years.

Eli was right. The fight would end soon. The ladies of Girardeau were picking out parasols to match their dresses while Price's men were eating horsemeat and boiling hooves for broth.

Plodding through the town, Gus felt like his own ghost. His tattered clothes and scrofulous mount made him invisible to the locals. No one paid him any mind. Which was just as well.

A few inquiries led him to Groton's Emporium, a run-down dry-goods store on the waterfront, wine shop on one side, ramshackle warehouse on the other. Leaving Nell at the hitching rail, Gus trudged warily into the store. The place stank of the river behind it, coils of tarred rope hung on the walls amid slickers, lanterns, and suchlike.

Two poorly dressed Negros were stacking sacks of meal against the far wall while another was wiping down leather harness straps with neat's-foot oil. The only white man in the place was behind the counter, a balding, barrel-shaped merchant in a soiled apron, his face reddened by whiskey, a cigar clamped between stained teeth.

"He'p you?"

"I'm looking for Mr. Groton. Cecil Groton?"

"I'm Groton but if you need work—"

"I've got a letter for you." Gus laid the crumpled envelope on the counter. Groton made no move to pick it up.

"I don't know you."

"Don't know you, neither. The letter's supposed to explain that. Young fella from Arkansas asked me to deliver it to you."

"I see," Groton said nervously. "Way things are, I didn't expect to have any more truck with this business—Boy! What the hell are you doin' sneakin' around here?" One of the Negros who'd been stacking feed sacks was standing behind Gus. Big fella in faded coveralls; wide shoulders, tribal scars on his cheeks, curly hair powdered gray from the meal dust.

"You said see you when we finished, suh. We finished."

"I'll see you when I'm good and ready! Now get your ass out front and see to this man's horse. Move, damn you!"

"Which horse, suh?"

"Don't you sass me," Groton growled, starting around the counter—Gus grabbed his bicep, stopping him.

"No need for that. She's the sorry-lookin' draft animal at the hitchrail, son. If you'd give her some grain I'd appreciate it."

The Negro was big enough to break Groton in half but as he nodded and turned away Gus caught the roil of fear and resentment in his eyes. And recognized it. The man was tasting the same dirt Gus swallowed facing Meachum in the road.

"Uppity bastard," Groton said, pulling free of Gus's grip. "Before the war I had twenty slaves on my pier. Knew their jobs, knew their place. Time was, I'd beat a man half to death for talkin' back like that but these damned runaway field hands are all I can get nowadays. Raise a hand to 'em, they quit on you. No gratitude—"

"You gonna read that letter?"

Groton opened it, gave it a quick glance, then carefully touched his cigar to a corner, setting it alight, and dropped it on the counter. "All right, what's the rest of it?"

Gus stared at Groton as if he hadn't heard, seeing Eli fall, and Jared. And the look in the Negro's eyes.

"Well?" Groton prompted.

"No," Gus said slowly.

"No what?"

"No message."

"What the hell are you saying? Have you forgotten it?"

"I've forgotten a lot of things lately but they're comin' back to me. Like why I stayed out of this mess in the first place. Wars never settle nothin', not in Mexico nor here, either. I was a fool to think any different. I got no message for you, mister. Forget I ever came."

"The hell I will! You're a damned yellow dog turncoat, old man, traitor to your own people—"

Lunging across the counter, Gus seized Groton by the vest, hauling him close, their faces inches apart.

"You ain't my people, mister. A couple days back a boy told me there was no right side in this fight. But there's definitely a wrong one and you're it. You and the politicians and the jayhawkers start the killin' and the rest of us get caught in the crossfire. And the worst is knowin' boys are still dyin' for cheapjacks like you—" Gus swallowed hard, couldn't go on.

He thrust Groton away, sending the grocer stumbling back into a rack of peach preserves, toppling the display, jars smashing on the floor around him as he went down.

Gus was already headed for the door. Needed to be away from this place, from this town, back to the hills.

"Go on, run like a rat, old man!" Groton shouted after him. "You can't hide! A day of reckonin' will—"

He was still raving when Gus slammed the shop door so hard the glass shattered, exploding onto the boardwalk.

The Negro Groton had cussed out was standing by Nell's head, feeding her oats out of his callused hand. If he was startled by the racket, he didn't show it.

"You were kinda rough on that door, mister," he observed. "Anythin' wrong?"

"Just about everything," Gus groaned as he climbed stiffly into the saddle. "Thanks for seein' to my animal, son."

"No trouble. Them suet lumps you stuck on her legs? They look bloodier if you wet 'em with berry juice. Keeps the flies down, too."

"You know 'bout horses?"

"I was a stockman down in Clarksdale 'til the Yanks burnt us out. I come up here, thought it might be better."

"Is it?"

"Work ain't easy to come by but I'm free now. Free's better."

"Yeah," Gus nodded. "I expect it is. My name's McKee. Got me a stock ranch over in Reynolds County. Expect I'll be shorthanded when this fight's over. Think you might want to work with horses again?"

"Depends. I thought you favored Mr. Groton's side of things."

"Son, from here on out the only side I'm takin' is my own." He clucked to Nell, turning her into the street. "If you want a job, you come see me now, hear?"

"Yessir. Maybe I will, at that."

Ed Gorman is a Midwesterner, born in Iowa in 1941, growing up in Minneapolis, Minnesota, and Marion, Iowa, and finally settling down in Cedar Rapids, Iowa. While primarily a suspense novelist, he has written half a dozen western novels and published a collection of western stories. His novel *Wolf Moon* was a Spur nominee for Best Paperback Original. About his western novels, *Publishers Weekly* said, "Gorman writes westerns for grown-ups," which the author says he took as a high compliment, and was indeed his goal in writing his books. "The Face" won the 1996 Spur Award for best short fiction.

There were several assassination attempts planned for Lincoln and members of his staff during the war, and this story may have actually happened, and been lost to the mists of time.

A SMALL AND
PRIVATE WAR

⠶

Ed Gorman

His nightmares once again woke her. She held his sweaty, trembling body until he eased once more into the embrace of sleep.

At breakfast, the maid Irene fed the two youngsters first. They were scheduled to be at Harvey Claybourne's all day. It was master Harvey's seventh birthday and festivities were to be daylong.

Aggie Monroe came down later than usual. She was a pretty, slender woman but this morning she looked pale and tired. She'd hoped to be fresh today. Needed to be. This was the day she was to follow her secretive husband and find out what he was up to. And Irene played a role in it.

Aggie was finishing her eggs when Sam came into the dining room. She noted that he'd stopped by the study and brought in a large bourbon glass three-quarters filled. She'd never seen him drink in the morning before. He came to her, kissed her on the forehead, seated himself across from her.

Before saying a word, he picked up the *Tribune* and scanned the front page. The Confederates had recently been routed near the Rio Grande. He sipped his whiskey. The second story he read dealt with President Lincoln sending an emissary here to speak the night before the election, the day after tomorrow. Lincoln wanted to make sure that only pro-war and pro-Northern candidates were elected. There was a small but ferocious band of Copperheads in Chicago, Northerners who sympathized with the South. They'd already shot a number of policemen, set a library on fire, and tried to smuggle arms into a prisoner-of-war camp not far from the city's outskirts. Jefferson Davis had already declared that the South could not win the war without the consistent help of the Copperheads.

Aggie said, touching his hand, "You had the nightmare again last night."

He nodded. "That's why I hope you'll excuse the bourbon. I was pretty scared when I woke up."

"Bourbon won't help you, dear." She hesitated. "You need to tell me what's going on. You need a confidante."

He smiled. "You and your theory that something's going on. *Nothing's* going on. I'm just having nightmares about my brother dying, Aggie, that's all."

The Monroe family was from Virginia. Sam had come up here after graduating from Vanderbilt. He hadn't any choice. He'd met the fetching Aggie at a governor's ball—the Monroe family owned a construction company in Illinois, and contributed to the governor's coffers—and since she was a self-described "unreconstructed Yankee," he had no choice but to move north, buy himself a small bank with a loan from his father, and set about starting a family with this woman who so obsessed him.

Then, six months ago, his older brother was killed in a battle in Kentucky; he'd died in the uniform of the South. Sam had felt guilty ever since. He couldn't even make love all the time anymore. He felt unmanned by his beloved brother's death. But worst of all were the nightmares. He'd described them to her. How he hovered just behind his brother, trying to warn him to hit the dirt before the bullet took him in the forehead. *Hit the dirt, Richard! Hit the dirt!* But in the nightmares, Richard never heard him. He always stood straight up, aiming his rifle as the bluecoats came streaming over a hill. Stood straight up. Angry that so many of his friends had fallen. Stood straight up. As if daring the bluecoats to kill him.

Irene poured him more coffee.

When she was gone, Aggie said, "The way you stay out nights these days, I'd swear you had a mistress."

This time he didn't smile. Nothing funny about taking a mistress. Aggie was the only woman he'd ever been with, the only woman he'd *ever* be with. He conveyed this to her by getting up and crossing over to where she sat and taking her hand and saying, "Never say anything like that again, Aggie. You're my wife and the mother of my children."

Aggie felt properly admonished. She could see how she'd inadvertently hurt him. Southern men thought of themselves as men of honor and principle.

A Small and Private War ✠ 285

A Northern man might joke about having a mistress. But not a Southern one. Not an honorable one, anyway.

He drank very little of his bourbon and ate all of his breakfast. A very good sign as far as Aggie was concerned.

When he was finished, he came to her again and kissed her. "I need to get to the bank, Aggie."

"On Saturday morning?"

"Yes," he said gently. "On Saturday mornings when I've got all this work on my desk. I'll be home by evening."

She knew there was no point arguing. She'd argued with him many nights about him being gone. It was a dance they did now. Him saying he was sorry he had to go, her questioning *why* he had to go.

In ten minutes, dressed in a suit and the kind of heavy coat called a Benjamin, his slicked-down hair smelling of perfumed macassar oil, he once again kissed her good-bye and set off.

He didn't go to the bank. He drove his horse-drawn carriage to a small business building on State Street. He stayed there two hours, got into his buggy and drove to an isolated spot over by the packing houses and tanneries. Nearby were the tenements and small pine shacks where the workers lived. The stench of the packing-houses and tanneries was suffocating; the cries of the dying animals even worse. Chicago was a fine place to be rich in—a place to rival the infamous Calcutta if you were poor.

He had a Henry. He went to a clearing next to a wooded area and spent the rest of the day practicing on targets he affixed to trees.

He was quite good. Again and again he hit the bull's-eye.

He shot with feverish intent. He did not stop except to reload. The Henry was a breech-loading sixteen-shot rifle. The Union army was justifiably proud when they introduced it only a month ago.

He spent the afternoon this way. Then he got into his carriage and returned to the same small business building on State Street.

Cawthorne said, "Have you ever met Jim McReedy?"

Sam Monroe had been wondering who was sitting with Big Mike Cawthorne in Cawthorne's office.

McReedy, whose clothes were worn and whose expression combined anxiety and contempt, put forth a bony but strong hand. He and Sam shook.

Big Mike Cawthorne said, "McReedy here is my personal spy. I use him to make sure everybody in our little group is staying in line."

"I'm not sure I like that, Mike," Sam said.

"I don't like it, either," Big Mike said in his expansive way. Despite his 250-pound bulk, he was still a dashing figure. He wore custom-tailored clothes and moved with great strength and style. "But I'm not naïve, Sam. Our little cell has to worry about being infiltrated. Or having a double agent. Jim here just checks people out for me."

In every major Northern city there was a half dozen or so Copperhead cells. It had been decided that cells of six or seven were safer than one large one, each operating independently. This gave the Copperheads a stronger chance of surviving.

Sam had known Cawthorne long before his brother's death in Kentucky. They did a lot of banking business together. Cawthorne was in real estate. One drunken night Sam confessed to Cawthorne that he secretly favored the South in the war. Within days, Cawthorne had introduced him to the six other members of the Copperhead cell. Sam joined eagerly.

Cawthorne said, "Tell him, Jim."

"Today when you were practicing with your Henry?"

"Yes," Sam said.

"Somebody was following you."

"What? That's impossible. I would've noticed." His vanity was hurt. How could he have not known he was being followed?

"If Jim says you were being followed, you were being followed," Cawthorne said.

"Who was following me?"

"I don't know. A man. I didn't get a good look at his face. He wore this hat with a snap brim and very heavy clothes."

Cawthorne said, "This is serious."

Sam couldn't argue with that. "You think they're on to us?"

"Somebody's on to *you*, anyway," McReedy said.

"I don't like your tone," Sam snapped.

Cawthorne said, "Let's stick to the problem, all right?" His disgust with both of them was obvious on his face. McReedy liked to play the expert. Sam, with his money, education, and good looks, was all male vanity. "Jim has a solution."

McReedy was pleased he got to play the expert again. "You're going to go home right now and I'm going to follow you again. But this time I'm going to find out who's in the buggy behind you. I can run him off the road now that it's dark. In the daytime too many people could see and I could get arrested." And that, of course, could lead the police directly to Cawthorne's Copperhead cell.

Sam figured McReedy was probably getting a lot of pleasure out of this. A lower-class man like this getting to act superior to his social better.

Yet Sam didn't have much choice but to listen and go along.

Sam set off in his buggy. In the darkest of late afternoon on of November 1, there was a half-moon brilliant in its luminosity. It almost made the 28-degree temperature tolerable.

He could smell the slums on the carriage. He'd have to have one of the servants give it a good brushing and washing. When you were near slaughter-houses that big, you couldn't get the stench off for days.

He drove self-consciously, aware now he was being followed. He'd been stupid not to have noticed this earlier in the day. And behind, his follower, Jim McReedy, no doubt gloating. Waiting his chance.

He went ten blocks on Dearborn before the mansions and the wide estates began appearing. His neighborhood. His house was only six blocks away. He wondered when McReedy would make his move.

He passed estates from which he could hear wonderful music, a party in progress, wondrous European chandeliers casting starlight out upon the autumn-frosted lawns. Good brandy and jokes and—Or so it had once been, anyway, before the death of his brother, before the death at the hands of the Union army had reminded Sam about who he really was in his heart and soul. South-ern. Very much in agreement with his own people and their traditions. By rights he should've been fighting right alongside his brother. Before, he could get along with Yankees, almost convince himself that he belonged here and was one of them. But now—

McReedy made his move.

He pulled his buggy up sharply behind the follower and then lurched right up alongside of him, swerving into the follower's vehicle as he did so. Horses crying in fear and anger; wooden wheels clashing against each other. Shouts, oaths. Sam half expected gunfire.

The paralleling buggies went on this way for half a block, McReedy finally forcing the follower's buggy up against the plank sidewalk.

McReedy pulled his own rig ahead of the follower's, then jumped down. The estate homes were far enough back from the street that nobody inside would see or hear any of this.

Sam, who had been watching this by leaning out of his own buggy, steered his horse over to the side of the road and hopped out. He was frightened. At this point in his life he had but one matter he wanted to take care of and he didn't want anything—or anybody—to interfere. He hoped this follower, whoever he was, could be dealt with.

McReedy had his Navy Colt pulled and was pointing it directly at the man in the buggy. The follower's face was lost in shadow. He said nothing.

"I want your name," McReedy said. "I'm a private investigator and I know you've been following this man all day. I want to know why."

At least McReedy had his lies down, Sam thought. He sounded very imposing. He just hoped he scared the follower.

"Your name," McReedy said again as Sam came up to him.

Sam looked at the man. He was lost in an inverness cape soiled and worn by time, a large theatrical-style hat with an enormous, floppy brim covering his face. He wore tanned gloves on his hands. If he had any weapon, it was concealed somewhere within the folds of his coat.

It was cold and dark here on the street. Fresh horse-droppings scented the evening; a distant violin sang sweetly and sadly.

And McReedy, an obstinate little rat-terrier of a man, said, "Get down from there, and I mean now."

But the follower said nothing. Nor moved.

McReedy waited no longer. He lunged up the buddy step and seized on to the arm of the follower, yanking the man out of the vehicle with strength that startled Sam.

The man might as well have been a rag doll, the way he was jerked from the buggy and flung to the street without much resistance at all.

He lay at the feet of the men, his hat, remarkably, still on, his face still hidden. "Stand up," McReedy said.

But the man wouldn't cooperate even now.

McReedy didn't wait.

He leaned down and tore the hat away from the man's head.

All Sam could do was stammer. "My god, Aggie. Why're you following me?"

"You don't think I have a right to know?" Aggie said.

"I've told you, Aggie. It's just a gun club I belong to."

It was past dinnertime. They'd been arguing in the downstairs study for nearly two hours.

He said, "Do you know how embarrassing it is, having your own wife follow you around?"

A Small and Private War ✼ 289

"I only did it because I'm worried about you. You haven't been the same since your brother died."

"Not 'died.' Was killed. There's a difference."

"You seem to forget," Aggie said, "your side killed *my* brother. You aren't the only one who's lost somebody in this war."

She sank down on one of the French Victorian chairs. David's face came to her, fresh as it had ever been. Three years younger, he'd been. A long and distinguished career in law ahead of him, everybody said. Then the train car he'd been on had been dynamited by Confederate soldiers.

But Sam wasn't listening. He was lost in his own troubles. "How do I explain it to them? My own wife following me around."

"I'm worried about you and our family, Sam. And all you care about is losing face with some stupid gun club." She looked at him. "If that's what's really going on." She made her remark sound as suspicious as possible. "Maybe I'll have to start following you again if I want to find out the real truth."

"Oh, God, don't say that, Aggie. Promise me you won't follow me around anymore. Promise me." Instead of rage, her threat had inspired only a kind of half-pathetic pleading. She'd never seen her husband like this. His pleading was especially worrisome. Sam wasn't the kind of man who pleaded with anyone. When he wanted something, he simply took it. "Promise me, Aggie. Promise me."

What choice did she have? He looked so lost and miserable. She said, quietly, "All right, Sam. I won't follow you anymore."

But she had her suspicions, and she knew that she'd be following him again very soon.

When Sam returned later that evening, there was a stranger in Big Mike Cawthorne's office when Sam walked in. McReedy was there also.

"I'm sorry about your troubles earlier," Cawthorne said. "There's nothing like a nosy wife. And believe me, I know what I'm talking about from personal experience."

"A fine-looking woman, though," McReedy said. "Mighty fine."

Sam didn't like the lurid implications in McReedy's voice. This man just didn't seem to understand his station in life, talking about a true gentleman's wife in this sordid way.

There was some more chatter during which Big Mike was his usual expansive self. He offered brandy and cigars and everybody partook. Sam noticed that he had yet to introduce the stranger.

The man was short, blond, goateed. His clothes were several cuts above those of McReedy's—especially the velvet vest—but he still gave an impression of the streets. Perhaps it was the feral quality of his blue eyes—an unsettling mixture of subservience and arrogance.

Big Mike Cawthorne, all blather at this point, suddenly looked uncomfortable. He glanced anxiously at the stranger and then at Sam. "Sam, this is Lawrence Dodd." He looked nervous. "He's going to take your place."

There. He'd said it. It was over. There would be anger and complaining but it was over. You could read all this on Big Mike's face.

"Take my place? You mean assassinating Kimble?"

"Yes, I'm afraid so."

"But why? I've been shooting every day. I've looked over the site several times. I know just how I'll get in and just how I'll get out."

McReedy said, "Your wife knows."

"She doesn't know anything," Sam snapped.

Cawthorne said, quietly, "She may not *know* anything, Sam. But she suspects something and that's enough."

"No, it's not enough!" Sam said. "And what's more, it's not fair. Not after all the work I've done."

The only way I'll ever be able to pay my brother back for deserting him the way I did. The only way I'll ever be able to do my duty the way he did his. And now they're trying to take it away from me. Dammit, Aggie, why did you have to follow me yesterday?

Cawthorne was his usual slick self again. His nerves were under control. The subject had been broached. "She's a Yankee, Sam."

"You think I don't know that?"

"One of her uncles back in New Hampshire is a colonel in the Union army."

"And," McReedy added, "her brother was killed by some of our people."

"No telling what she might do," Cawthorne said, "her loyalties being what they are. Mr. Dodd here—well, there won't be that trouble."

Sam was sure his name wasn't Lawrence Dodd. He'd been borrowed from some other cell. Probably from out of town, though not far away. He'd been summoned overnight. From here on out, Sam would be told as little as possible about things. His longtime fear that Aggie's Yankee loyalties would hurt him, had come true. Big Mike saying he was no longer quite trustworthy. Sam had seen this happen before, cell members who were suddenly seen as suspicious in some way being subtly pushed out of the cell. Big Mike knew they'd never go over to the other side. Everybody in this cell had a personal reason for being part of it. They'd never betray the South. But that didn't mean Big Mike and the others would trust them with the inner workings of the cell.

But that isn't the worst of it. The worst of it is that I put everything into this. Killing Lincoln's man is the only way I'll ever be able to make things up to my brother. Why can't you people see that? To you, it's just one more killing. To me, it's my honor.

"I'm sorry, Sam," Big Mike said, "I really am."

"She's a fine-looking woman," McReedy said, who must have known he was irritating Sam.

"I'll try to do as good a job as you would have, Mr. Monroe," the man whose name wasn't really Lawrence Dodd said. "I really will."

Aggie didn't have much trouble finding what she needed. She almost smiled when she found it because it was so sloppy of Sam to keep it in the bottom drawer of his desk. Where anybody, including the police, could easily find it.

Several clipped newspaper stories about a Mr. Harper Kimble, Esquire. Arriving by train in Chicago the day before the election to give a rousing public speech about why it was so important to vote—and to vote for those politicians who supported President Lincoln's handling of the war. Several references to the large ballroom in the Courier-Arms Hotel—one of the city's finest—were underlined. Then there was a hand-drawn map showing the front steps of the hotel—and a hotel room directly across the street. And a circle on the steps inside of which appeared the word *Kimble*.

The secretiveness. The target practice. The newspaper stories. Aggie might not be a genius but she was smart enough to figure out what Sam was up to. She cursed the Union soldier who had killed Sam's older brother. Because in a very real sense he'd taken Sam's life, too. He no longer cared about his wife and children. His only reality was avenging his brother's death. And now she knew how he planned to do it.

Sam came home drunk. Not falling-down drunk but in-control, angry drunk. He stormed into the living room where she was sitting by the fireplace with their two daughters and said, "It's way past their bedtime—put them to bed! I want to talk to you!"

She had never seen him so angry. The girls, four and five, were terrified of the man who had once been their loving, congenial father. He stank of the streets. His eyes rolled wildly. His clothes were soiled. His right hand was clenched in a constant fist. "And I mean now!"

"What's wrong with Daddy?" said the youngest, Courtney, as their mother hauled them up to bed, one under each arm.

"He's pickled," said Jenny, the eldest. She loved words and picked up new ones constantly.

"Is he pickled, Mommy?" Courtney said, without having the slightest idea what the word meant.

Sam leaned against the fireplace, a cigar in one hand, a brandy glass in the other. He didn't look up when Aggie came back in. He said, "Sit down."

She knew better than to argue with him.

She sat in a Hepplewhite chair she'd had as a girl, entwined hearts carved on the chair back. All the time she was growing up she had wondered whose heart would be entwined with hers. Sam's, of course. She'd fallen in love with him the very first night she'd met him, even though she didn't realize it until a month or so later. Entwined hearts . . . and they *had* been entwined, until he'd lost his brother in the war. . . .

After a time, he spoke. He said: "They don't want me. They say they can't trust me anymore."

She wasn't sure exactly who "they" were. But she sensed that all this had to do with the newspaper stories she'd found in his drawer.

"So they're not going to let me do it. They got somebody else." For the first time, he looked at her: "And do you know why, dear wife? Because of you! Because you just *had* to follow me around! And because you're a filthy Yankee!"

He had never called her a "filthy" anything before and the word stunned her—shocked her, hurt her as he'd never hurt her before. A bond of faith was broken in that moment and they both knew it.

But she fought against her pain and anger and rose solemnly from the chair as she heard him begin to cry. Not even in all the early months of following his brother's death had he ever wept. But he wept now.

She went to him and tried to take him in her arms. He wouldn't let her. He jerked away like an angry child. But finally, finally, he needed her strength and solace and so he came within her arms and she comforted him.

"I know what you were planning to do," she said after a time, "but you would've destroyed our whole family, Sam. Think of what the girls would have to go through all their lives. Now you don't have to do it. Now we can be a family again and you can forget all this. The girls need you, Sam, need you the way you used to be. And so do I."

An hour later, in the gentle darkness of their bed, they made love with fresh ardor and succoring passion.

A Small and Private War

*   *   *

Sam slept in. He ate a late, good breakfast and then got up. It was a Sunday and he spent the entire afternoon playing with the girls in the living room, reading them stories, playing their favorite games, telling them about all the wonderful things winter would soon bring, including snowmen and ice-skating. It was as if he had survived a terrible fever that had not—thank God—killed him but had somehow burned itself out. He was the Sam of old.

He was that evening, too. He took Aggie out to dine. They took the fancy carriage with the liveried driver, and took in a show following dinner. Nothing about his friends at "the gun club" was mentioned. Nor was the war referred to in any way. When they went to bed, they made long and leisurely love.

On Monday, the day upon which Mr. Kimble, Esquire, was to arrive from Washington, D.C., Sam went to the bank and spent a busy morning catching up on the work he'd been neglecting.

At home, Aggie got the girls off to school and then went out in her buggy for some things she'd been needing at the store. She was only a block away from home when she realized she was being followed.

She went to the store, tied the reins of her buggy to a hitching-post and hurried inside. She wanted to make sure she was indeed being followed. Maybe her suspicions had gotten away from her.

But no. There he was. He'd pulled up to a hitching-post a quarter block away. He jumped down from his buggy and was now standing there and rolling himself a cigarette. Waiting for her to return.

Her boldness surprised her. She bolted the store and hurried back outside into the winds that lacerated everything on this drab, overcast day. There wasn't even any snow to make it pretty.

She walked right up to him. "I want to know why you're following me, sir."

He smiled. "It's people like you who make my work hard for me, Mrs. Monroe."

"Why are you following me?"

Her voice was sharp enough to attract the attention of people walking along the plank sidewalk. This was a block of shops and offices of various kinds, from a saddlery to a doctor and a dentist.

"Just had to make sure you didn't go see the police," he said in a quiet voice. "I've been watching you for three days now. You haven't left the house without Sam. We just wanted to make sure you didn't talk to anybody about what was going to happen."

She hated them all. And for one of the first times, they formed a monolith in her mind: *Southerners*. Devious, violent.

"Well, you can take this message back to your friends," she said. "He doesn't want any part of you anymore."

This time the smile was a smirk. "He's gonna be a good little boy, huh?"

She turned and stalked away.

She told Sam about all this before dinner but he only cupped her face in his hands and kissed her and said, "Let's just have a nice family dinner."

And so they did. Wind lashed the windows and made her thankful for the warmth and beauty of her home. How tall and proud it stood against the most furious of nights. The girls, too, seemed affected by this same sense of melancholy. Not only did they manage to look prettier than ever in the flickering lamplight, they also sat very close to each other and even gave each other hugs from time to time. Sometimes they fought angrily. But not tonight.

She watched Sam watching this. He seemed moved by everything. She even thought for a moment that she saw his eyes dampen with tears. It was one of those moments—so sweet, so peaceful, so tranquil. It seemed that nothing could possibly be wrong anywhere in God's world.

And then he was helping her up to bed. It was so odd. She'd been sitting at the table talking to the girls about snow—it had become their obsession—and then . . . And then Sam had to help her up the stairs. So queer. As if the wine for dinner had suddenly made her very, very drunk . . . sleepy. But she'd had less than half a glass.

And then she was in bed . . . sleeping . . .

Wind.

Panic: disorientation. *Where am I? What happened?*

Headache.

Dry mouth.

Drugs . . . yes.

Her inclination had been to think of the dinner wine. There was the culprit. She wasn't much of a drinker.

But no . . . this was more like the aftereffects of the sleeping-potion the doctors had given her after Courtney's birth. The grogginess . . . the slight feeling of nausea . . .

Wind again.

All she wanted to do was relieve her bladder and sink deep into sleep again.

He drugged me. Sam drugged me. But why?

Even through the blind, numbed, disoriented feeling of the moment the realization of it made her fight her way to wakefulness.

Have to wake up. Find Sam.

Walking was almost impossible. She kept slumping against chairs and bureaus and walls as she took one small step at a time. She found the pull cord for Irene the maid. Then she staggered on into her private toilet and began soaking her face in water standing in the basin.

Irene came quickly. And departed quickly, headed downstairs to make coffee, and a lot of it. . . .

Aggie found the letter in the study. Her name was on the front of it. She was just awake enough for it to make terrifying sense. . . .

Lawrence Dodd got to the hotel room a little early. He was always early. It was part of his professionalism. He'd assassinated seven men since the start of the war and he hadn't yet come even close to getting caught.

He kept the lamp off. He knelt by the window. It was cold enough for frost to rime the glass along the window casing.

He kept studying the place where Kimble would come out around nine, following his speech, on his way to the mayor's house where a reception was to be held. A carriage would pull up. Kimble would start down the front steps. And then Dodd would kill him. . . . that simple.

An hour after he'd gone to the window, there was a knock on the door, startling him. Who the hell would be knocking? Who knew he was in here? He had a bad stomach. Acid immediately began scouring it.

The knock again. A soft knock. As if the caller didn't want to be heard beyond this one door.

Maybe something has happened. Maybe the police have learned about tonight. Maybe I'm not supposed to go through with it.

So many thoughts, doubts, suppositions prompted by the knocking.

Shit. He had to go to the door. Find out what was going on. For now, he had to hide the Sharps.

He looked around in the dim light from the street.

Another soft knock.

The closet. He'd put the Sharps in the closet.

He brought his Colt with him to the door but even with that, the other man didn't have any trouble slashing the barrel of his own handgun down across Dodds's face and knocking him back into the room. Nor any trouble knocking him out.

Nor any trouble tying him up and gagging him.

The buggy ride helped considerably. The harsh, cold weather completed the job of waking her up. The coffee had helped. The cold air was even better.

Downtown was crowded with vehicles of every kind. Police were everywhere. Bands could be heard in a variety of hotels. Both political parties were anticipating victory—or pretending to, anyway. She hitched her buggy, took her bag, and walked the remaining two blocks to the hotel. This was as close as she could get. Gunshots could be heard as she walked. The frontier mentality was still with them: when you were happy, you shot off guns. The police could arrest you but they had to catch you first.

The lobby was packed. Men in muttonchops and vast bellies stood about with huge glasses of whiskey in their fat pampered hands. Their women were almost elegant in gowns that displayed their bosoms to best advantage. The six-piece orchestra played one raucous tune after another.

Nobody noticed her. Just one more person. Pretty as she was, she was still unremarkable in this crowd.

Sam had been helpful enough to put the room number on the map he'd drawn. She had little trouble convincing the desk clerk that she was to meet her husband here. He gave her the spare key.

The hotel had emptied downward. All the rooms seemed to be empty. As she walked along the sconce-decorated halls, she heard nothing but the pounding music from the lobby. Not even New Year's Eve could be noisier than this.

When she reached the room, she paused. Took a deep breath. Said a hasty prayer.

For the first time, she was thankful for all the noise. It allowed her to slip the key in the lock and turn it without being heard.

The gun was in her hand as she walked inside.

A man was on the bed. Bound and gagged. Sam was just turning to her now. He sat in a chair at the window. A Sharps leaned against the wall. He'd have a good, clean shot from here. And in the clamor downstairs, he'd have an easy time getting away out one of the rear exits.

He'd planned well.

She shut the door. "I'm taking you home, Sam."

As she spoke, she thought of the words in the letter he'd left.

Dear darling Aggie:

I wanted to give you and the girls a good memory of me. The last few days have been wonderful. But now I have to be a man of honor and avenge my brother. Avenge my country which is, and will always be, the South. I don't expect you to understand—even though you, too, have lost a brother, you have not lost honor. I should've worn the gray just as he did. This is my only chance to make up for what I failed to do. All my love to you and the girls

—Sam, forever.

"Go home, Aggie," Sam said gently. "Take care of the girls."

"I'd rather kill you myself than have you disgrace your daughters this way. They'll pay for this the rest of their lives, Sam. You don't seem to care how it'll be for them to have a traitor as a father."

"Traitor!" he said. "I'm not a traitor. I'm a patriot."

"You live in the North, Sam. Your girls are Yankees. And they always will be."

He stood up. "I have to do this, Aggie. I have to."

But she stood unwavering. The gun pointed right at him. "Don't fool yourself, Sam. I came here prepared to kill you if I had to."

"You kill me here, the police'll know what happened anyway."

"Not if I take the Sharps and let that man on the bed go. I take it he's your replacement."

Sam started walking toward her. "You won't be able to kill me, Aggie. I know you. You're not violent. And besides, you love me."

"Just stay there, Sam."

But he kept coming, obviously sure of what he was saying. "You won't be able to do it. So why not just hand me the gun and leave? I'm going to do this no matter what."

She raised the gun so that it pointed directly at his chest. "Stay back, Sam. Stay back."

And then he lunged for her.

Overpowering her was easy. Getting the gun away was another matter. As they wrestled for it on the floor, she kept it tucked under herself so that his fingers couldn't quite reach it. He offered her no mercy. He hit her as hard as he would a man he disliked.

Then the gun sounded, muffled by the fact that he was lying on top of her when the weapon discharged. He knew almost at once that she was dead. The death spasm had been unmistakable. And now she moved not at all.

He pulled himself away from her. Felt her pulse. None. The gun had fired just as the band music had swelled. The sound of the firing easily would have been lost.

He stood up. Stared down at her. Wife. Mother of his children. He knew that he loved her but at the moment it was an abstract feeling, one far less vivid than the hatred he bore. Someday he would revile himself for what had just happened on this hotel-room floor. But for now, there was the task at hand. Kimble should be leaving the hotel in less than ten minutes.

He grabbed his Sharps and went to the window. He thought of his dead brother and his own disgrace.

Soon now, he thought. *Soon now*.

Marie Jakober's love affair with Civil War history began as a teenager on a remote farm in northern Canada, from books acquired through a mail order library. She is drawn to the subject not only for its drama and historical importance, but also for the unique quality of its documentary materials. "It was the first major war in which most participants could write, and the last in which they were allowed to write what they really said, or thought, or felt, unhindered by military censorship or public opinion. Their frankness was probably unwise on occasion, but today, a hundred and forty years later, it's pure gold for the storyteller."

Ms. Jakober writes both speculative and historical fiction. She has published five novels, most recently *The Black Chalice*. Her sixth, dealing with the Union underground in Richmond, will be published next year by Forge. She is presently dotting the i's and crossing the t's of a seventh, set in Baltimore during the summer of 1862. Ms. Jakober lives in Calgary, Canada.

Though fictionalized in many respects, including names, "Slither" is based on an actual incident from Richmond's Libby prison, related in his memoirs by Union captain Bernhard Domschke.

SLITHER

❖

Marie Jakober

*Sometimes the best way to go undercover
is to hide in plain sight. . . .*

A great many things can make life miserable when you're living as a prisoner
of war, but the worst of them is discovering that you can't trust your own
comrades. It was a discovery I desperately avoided making—which was why
I didn't want to talk with Colonel Thiessen that day, and why I still wish I
hadn't. I happened to glance up across the faded cover of the dime novel I was
reading, and saw him heading in my general direction. I ducked my head again,
fast, as if all six feet of me could disappear behind one small, battered book.

"Afternoon, Mackie," he said, right by my shoulder.

There was no help for it. I laid my reading aside. "Good afternoon, sir."

"Were you enjoying your book?" he asked, settling down beside me.

"No," I said, truthfully. It was a stupid story, and I didn't like reading
anyway. But you had to do something in Libby Prison to make the time
go by.

Thiessen chatted at me for a while, about all sorts of things I no longer
remember. He'd been a lawyer in Connecticut before the war, and he could
talk a man's ears right off his head. He was somewhere in his forties, older
than most of us, and he'd taken it upon himself to be father confessor to the
whole prison, and the general watchdog of our well-being and morale. Needless
to say, it was a task beyond the competence of any ordinary man.

"You know, Mackie," he said finally, getting down to the real business of our little visit, "I'm a bit worried about your friend. Captain Slater. He seems to be . . . he's getting rather too friendly with the Rebels."

"Oh," I said. "I hadn't really noticed."

Thiessen cocked an eyebrow at me. *Do you really expect me to believe that?* "Have you talked to him about it?" he persisted.

"No, I haven't." I glanced around and saw that several of the men seemed to be paying us more than casual attention. They weren't obvious about it. They played cards. They read the battered *Richmond Examiner* for the seventeenth time. They stared at the window, where a gray afternoon descended on a gray, gray city. But I'd been around groups of men long enough to know when they were watching someone and when they weren't. I lowered my voice.

"Look," I said. "It's just the way Jeremy is, that's all. He's . . . he's *practical*. And he's never been tough, like some of us. Hell, I remember when we were kids, he was always getting hurt. Always catching something; I think he got himself every sickness known to man—"

"You've been friends that long?"

"We went to school together. But . . ." I faltered, reluctant to say more. We weren't friends in our school days, Jeremy Slater and I. I suppose it would be truthful to say we weren't really friends even now, not deep down. We were far too different for that. But I defended him to Colonel Thiessen. I had to, partly because I really thought I trusted him. And partly because I'd misjudged him so harshly once before.

"He doesn't mean any harm, sir. He's just . . . He's just trying to get by. Like we all are."

"Get by, yes, but at what price? Fraternizing with the enemy is a dangerous game . . . quite apart from the rotten example he sets for others. It's bad on morale, what he's doing. Especially for the younger men. And the Rebels aren't stupid; they're likely to raise the stakes. What happens when they ask him for something bigger than mending a trouser leg or sewing on a button?"

"He'll say no."

"I hope so. Some of the men think he won't. They think his backbone's made of taffy."

"Well, they can damn well think different, sir. I fought with Slater. Ball's Bluff, the whole damn peninsula, Bull Run, Antietam. I've seen him on a firing line, men in pieces around him, and him as calm as Moses waggling his hand at the ocean—"

"Yes," Thiessen said, so heavily and so wisely that I stopped still and stared at him.

"That sort of thing," he went on, "isn't always courage. Sometimes it's just fatalism. A man decides there's a minié ball out there with his name on it, or there isn't, and there's nothing he can do about it. So he becomes . . . methodical, I suppose you could say. He just doesn't think about it. Any of it. Real courage—the moral kind—is very different."

He stood up. "I'm not judging the man. Not yet. But I think you should have a talk with him."

It was like a bad headache, that stuff Thiessen said to me—one of those headaches that start at the back of your eyes and go deep into your brain and stay there for days. I couldn't stop thinking about it. I couldn't stop remembering all the things I knew about Jeremy Slater, things I thought didn't matter anymore.

You see, when we were boys together, I had no use for him at all. He was the gold-plated sissy of Springfield, Massachusetts. He couldn't run, couldn't fight, couldn't hit a baseball with a barn door—and to make matters worse, he was twice too smart for his own good. We picked on him, of course, as big, roughneck boys will do, and he'd slink off home with his nose bloody and his head down, thinking hard on how to get us back. And he managed it more than once, always in some sneaky, underhanded way. We all disliked the little grub, but I was the one who gave him the nickname he never outgrew. I called him Jeremy Slither.

So it was a shock for me, marching proudly up to a wooden table in the town hall to put my name down for the new Eighth Massachusetts Regiment, and seeing Jeremy Slater's name on the same piece of paper. This was nothing, however, to the shock I received by the end of the day, when I discovered that I was only a sergeant, and he was a second lieutenant.

I thought I knew everything that went on in my town, but he had friends I knew nothing about. For half a dozen years, while I and most of my old schoolmates were working at the armory, making those famous rifles for the frontier cavalry, and spending our free time in the streets and the taverns, Jeremy Slater was learning how to be a gentleman. He got all his schooling, and quietly cultivated friends among what was called "the better people." So when some fancy lawyer's son said he thought Jeremy Slater was "officer material," Slater was voted in as a second lieutenant. That was right at the start of the war, of course, when a lot of regiments were electing their own officers. The army brass had to come along with a big broom afterward, and sweep out the rubbish. That's when Slater got to be a first lieutenant.

The night we all signed up, though, we thought it was a wonderful joke—

little Jeremy with shoulder pips, ha ha. The whole lot of us having to call him "sir," well, that wasn't quite so funny. That hurt a bit, but we comforted ourselves by wagering how long he'd last. Then, bit by bit, he surprised the howling daylights out of us. He never got over being a sissy; he hated the cold, he hated the rain, he absolutely detested army rations, and most of all, I think, he detested army discipline. But after a while we stopped caring, because he was good at everything that mattered. Like I told Colonel Thiessen, he was steady as a rock when the shooting started, and he had a splendid eye. It came from his trade, I guess. His family were tailors, and had been for three or four generations. After we got to be friendly, he told me it was his dream someday to move to Boston, to the very best part of Boston, and have himself a fancy shop with a fancy sign in the window: J. N. SLATER, ESQUIRE: FINE TAILORING FOR GENTLEMEN. You wouldn't think tailoring had anything to do with war, but it did. Young Jeremy could look at a man and know right off what he ought to be wearing. He could see the shapes of a garment in his head, all the pieces and what they would look like and what he had to cut differently each time, to make each one exactly right. And he could do the same thing with a company of men and a gulley and a patch of trees; he could see all the shapes of the landscape, and how the pieces fit, and how they didn't. Through the whole damn war, the little grub always ranked me. He made captain in the spring of '62, a week before I did. And I have to give him credit: he wore his authority well. If he held it against me, how I'd treated him when we were boys, he never gave a sign.

So we followed the Army of the Potomac from battle to battle, from disaster to disaster, and somewhere in all the violence and boredom and bad food and nights of black fear, somewhere between the town hall of Springfield and the mud of Marye's Heights, I forgot all about Slither. The quick, scrawny boy with the quick, sneaky mind went clear out of my thoughts. Now, in the gray misery of a January day in Libby Prison, I didn't much like Colonel Thiessen bringing him back.

Back he was, nonetheless. He came out of the stairwell into the second-floor quarters, quiet as a footpad, with his hand in his pocket. He was still small, barely five-seven in his ratty socks. He'd been nice-looking as a boy, in a dark-haired, street-urchin sort of way, and he had grown up the same: his face sharp and proudly chiseled, with fine, high cheekbones; his hands as slender and graceful as a girl's. I watched him pick his way through the other prisoners, walking carefully around the pair who'd set up a homemade chessboard on the floor. He was always extraordinarily polite.

Or, perhaps, just giving himself airs . . . ?

Damn Colonel Thiessen anyway.

"Hullo," Slater said, and sat down beside me. We had no chairs, of course, in Libby. No furniture at all. Old wooden crates served for everything—tables and chairs and gaming boards and altars for the Sunday service. He pulled a muffin out of his pocket and broke it in half. "Here."

My mouth watered unbearably, but I didn't move. "Where'd you get that, Jeremy?"

"Dobbin," he said, biting into his piece without hesitation. "He had a nice waistcoat that doesn't fit him anymore. He asked me to cut it down for his boy."

"He should live on our rations for a while. Then his waistcoat would fit him just fine."

Slater laughed. "Sure you don't want this?" he asked, waggling the rest of the muffin. "I'm not going to leave it hanging about."

"Jeremy . . ."

"Dobbin's really a decent fellow," he went on, ignoring my faltering attempt to speak. "He talked to Major Cluny for me, and Cluny says I can help out in the hospital, starting tomorrow."

"What do you mean, 'help out'?"

"Scrub the floors, mostly, I guess. Move stuff."

"Nigger work."

"Doesn't matter to me."

"Jeremy . . ." Suddenly I wanted to curse him, to call him names, to yell at him until something registered in his self-centered little head: *Damn it to hell, man, can't you see what you're doing?*

"You shouldn't be doing stuff like that. It's helping the Rebs."

"Last time I looked, it was our boys in that hospital. Are you saying we should leave the floors dirty?"

"Don't be an idiot. If you do that stuff, a slave doesn't have to. He can do something else instead. Like work on their fortifications, maybe. Use your damned head, Slater."

He looked at me, and he looked away. There was a last little scrap of muffin in his hand. He put it in his mouth, quickly. Like it shamed him, I thought.

"We don't get half-enough food," he said bitterly, "and half of what we get is rubbish. We have no blankets. We sleep on the floor with the wind blowing snow on our heads. We're dying here, Robert, one of us, two of us, every single day—!"

"I know all that."

"I'm not doing any harm, damn it. I'm just trying to survive. Scrubbing a floor or two isn't going to change the outcome of the war."

"First it was just a bit of mending. Now it's scrubbing a floor or two. What's it going to be next week?"

"Oh, go preach at somebody else," he said, and left me.

I sat like a block of wood for a long time, after he was gone. I thought about the things Colonel Thiessen had said. I thought about Springfield, and the times we had waylaid Slither on some quiet street and pummeled him with snowballs. I thought about what it had been like when the Rebels dragged us here to Libby. I felt so sorry for him, those first few days—most of all the night he kept talking about the windows. It was dead of winter, probably the worst winter in the history of Virginia. We were hungry to the toes of our unshod feet, and both so cold we were shivering. The prisoners who had coats or blankets wrapped themselves up like mummies. A few paced endlessly, back and forth, trying to stay warm. The wind was howling to make you want to scream, and snow was gathering in small ridges on the floor around the windows. And I wondered if they got it wrong, in the Bible—if hell wasn't a hot place at all, but wet and windy and icy as a grave. Libby Prison was as close to hell as I ever wanted to get.

Libby Prison, you see, wasn't really a prison at all, not a proper one. It was a big, ugly slab of a warehouse on the edge of the James River, where they used to store cargo from the docks. There was no glass on the windows. There weren't even shutters. That day, for the third day running, the Rebel guards hadn't given us any coal, so we ate our meager offerings of cornmeal raw, mixed in a bit of ice water.

But the worst thing of all was that we had no decent clothing. On his last furlough home, Jeremy Slater had sewn himself a thick, beautiful greatcoat. It wasn't made of the shoddy stuff the army suppliers gave us, but of the finest, softest wool. Every man in the regiment envied Slater his coat. The Rebels stole it, of course, when we were captured, along with everything else of ours they could use, including our shoes.

I still remember how he sat one night, huddled against a pillar, dark-souled like I'd never seen him. He wrapped his arms around his knees and curled himself into a tight little ball, and I knew he was thinking about his precious coat, thinking how it was tucked around some ruffian it probably didn't even fit, chasing General Burnside through the mud. He looked just like a little boy again, bullied out of his treasures on a playground: *But it was mine, you dirty rat, it was MINE . . . !*

A vicious gust of wind hammered against the walls, ruffled his hair, and left a few white snowflakes briefly on his sleeve.

"How can people be so uncivilized?" he muttered. "Any idiot could put shutters on those windows."

"A guard I talked to says they don't have any supplies. Says it's our own fault; we blockaded their ports."

Slater's scowl merely grew darker. "Wouldn't have to be proper shutters," he said. "Any slab of junk wood would do it. A couple of nails, a piece of old harness for a hinge. They don't care, that's all. Uncivilized, the whole howling lot of them."

Uncivilized. It was one of Slater's purest insults. It was his gripe against the whole war. He wasn't an idiot; he hadn't expected the war to be easy, the way some of us had. But he thought it would be . . . "sensible," he told me once. Sane. The horrors would be unavoidable things, like getting blown to pieces in a battle. He hadn't expected raw hate. He hadn't expected generals with porridge for brains. And he hadn't expected anything like Libby.

"We'll be exchanged soon," I said.

He burrowed his chin even deeper into his knees. "Maybe," he said. "Or maybe we'll just die. Maybe we'll just lie down one night and wake up dead, stiff and straight as icicles."

That was the first time I wondered if Jeremy Slater might be scared witless. Really witless, I mean—the way men got before their rifles fell out of their hands and they started blubbering. It was an unworthy thought, and I put it clear out of my head. Then Lieutenant Kramer died—the only other officer from the Eighth who'd been captured with us. He was a big, strapping fellow, twenty-one years old and solid as a tree. He had a bit of the grippe when we got to Richmond. Then he got a bad fever, and they took him down to the hospital on the ground floor. The next morning they came and told us he was dead. Pneumonia, they said. Just like that.

For three days or so Slater hunkered down inside himself like a cat who'd been chewed silly by a dog. He hadn't known Kramer well, so it wasn't a personal thing. It wasn't grief. It was pure, naked panic. Shock, one prisoner called it; a lot of men reacted that way, he told me, when they found themselves inside a prisoner-of-war camp for the first time. Most of them got over it.

So it was all I wanted, at first. I wanted Slater to get over it. When he started talking friendly to the Rebel guards, I didn't worry about it at all. I was just glad he was talking to somebody. I was glad to hear him laughing again. When he started doing favors for them, and getting extra food and little privileges, I still didn't worry about it. I knew he was a little desperate, and I wasn't going to judge him. After all, I'd judged him wrong once before.

It was all about courage, I suppose. Courage is the measure of a man in an army, and every time I saw him cozying up to the Rebs, I remembered how he was on the battlefield, scared of nothing that lived, and I told myself he'd be fine. A man like Slater would never sell out to the enemy. He might tell a joke or two, trade a favor even, but nothing serious, nothing that really mattered. He'd die in Libby first.

Talking to Thiessen changed everything. What if what I had thought was courage, was only fatalism all along, like the colonel said? What if there was no substance inside the man, just the same weak, wet-nosed boy we'd sent scurrying for shelter more times than we could count? What if it was only Slither with us, after all?

I started paying more attention to him after that. I noticed how he moved around among us, so quietly, like he was watching us even more than we were watching him. I noticed that he got up sometimes in the middle of the night, as if he were going to relieve himself, and then didn't come back for upward of an hour. Mornings, of course, he went down to the hospital, where he did chores for the Rebels. And I saw how they won him over, bit by bit, just like Thiessen feared they would. The Rebel doctor, Major Cluny, was one of those sterling gentlemen, the kind Slater admired so much, the kind who talked like dictionaries and knew the difference between seventeen different kinds of spoons. Slater would come back and tell me what a fine man Cluny was, and how he was trying to do the best for the sick prisoners, he really was. It was "Cluny did this" and "Cluny said that," until one day I had enough of it, and told Slater where he could put his Major Cluny, along with the entire Confederate States of America and its armies. After that we didn't talk much anymore.

I didn't really turn on him, though, until the day he got the boots. They weren't new boots, of course. Even by the start of '63, a pair of new boots was worth a fortune in Virginia. But they were still in decent shape, and they fit his small feet extremely well. The whole room stopped what it was doing and turned to stare at him as he walked in.

"Hey, look at that, boys," somebody hooted. "Goody Two-shoes has got himself some shoes."

"What's up, Slater?" shouted another. "We all going dancing?"

There was more joshing, all of it somewhat barbed, but none of it really malicious until Lieutenant Sprague joined in. Sprague was a Pennsylvanian, a farm boy with a sharp eye and a mean, mean temper. The sort you said a prayer over every night, thanking the good Lord he was in your own army and not on the other side.

"So what do you think, boys? Which of our friends is lying barefoot on his deathbed down there?"

The silence was sudden and ugly. Slater looked from one to the other, slowly. There were seventy-odd men in the room, ordinary decent men, most of them, but soldiers nonetheless—killers, really, when you looked at it straight; killing was our reason for being—and I think Slater made the connection the same moment I did.

"Do you think I'd steal from my own comrades?" he said, very quietly.

"I don't think you know who your comrades are," Sprague flung back.

Then Slater made a tactical mistake—one of the few I'd ever seen him make. He sat on a crate and lifted his feet. "Look at those boots," he said. "Do they look like ours?"

They didn't, of course. They had no right or left feet. They were Southern-made boots.

Sprague jumped like a cat on the opening. "Well, I'll be damned. He does know who his comrades are. Tell us, Slater, when you going to get yourself a nice gray outfit to go with your new shoes?"

"You're out of line, Lieutenant."

"And what are you going to do about it . . . *Captain?*"

I never thought an officer's rank could sound like an insult, but in Sprague's snarling voice, it truly did. Heaven knows what might have happened then, but Sprague's own company commander was there in a breath, moving between them. "All right, men, let's just get on about our own affairs, shall we?"

Slither made himself scarce with no further urging, and stayed out of sight for the rest of the day.

That was when I told them—the whole of Libby Prison—I told them what we had called him back in Springfield. I told them what a sissy he had been and how he never fought back when we pushed him, but used tricks and traps on us instead. I told them how I found a dead mouse in my lunch one day, all rank and smelly, lying right on my chicken sandwich. It was the day of a championship ball game, so I had to play empty as a beggar, and didn't get a scrap to eat till I got home after dark. I told them how my cousin John had arrived one night at a big country wedding dance, with Mariana Kopke on his arm and a great spreading stain of brown glue all over the backside of his trousers, thanks to a booby-trapped buggy seat. Of course, no one could ever prove who was responsible, any more than we could ever prove where the dead mouse had come from. But there was Slither at the dance, entirely alone, with nothing to do but rescue the beautiful, neglected Mariana, and dance with her the whole night long, while poor John smoked and sizzled in the yard.

I told them everything I remembered—or most of it, anyway—and if you want to know the truth, I felt a little guilty doing it, because I was grown up now, and had a bit more sense than I had as a boy, and I knew a lot of what he did to us we damn well had coming. It was the *method* which seemed to matter now, the sneakiness, the absolute lack of scruples. He didn't care if our school lost the ball game because I couldn't play my best, or if he broke up a courtship which might have ended in a good marriage.

So we talked it around, and looked at all the parallels, then and now, and there was a general agreement that the man could not be trusted. A few, however, had their doubts—including Captain Deihl, the Pennsylvanian, Sprague's company commander.

"So which of them did Mariana Kopke marry in the end?" he asked, all out of the blue.

"Neither of them," I said. "She went back to Cambridge and married her cousin."

Deihl laughed. "I think, gentlemen, you are all making a mountain out of a molehill." And he got up, rather pointedly, and walked away.

I knew what he was thinking. He was remembering all the things I'd said before, about Slater's competence and courage in the war, and he was weighing it alongside my list of youthful pranks, and the pranks didn't count for piffle in the balance.

I wondered what he thought about it all the next day, when the prison commander himself marched into the second-floor quarters, flanked by a dozen armed guards, and dragged Captain Deihl away to the dungeon.

We were in the cook room when it happened, our mess and three others, the last of the day. It was an utterly vile afternoon, gray and cold, and all we'd had to eat was a watery broth no self-respecting beggar would have called soup, and two small spoonfuls of beans. But at least it was hot; and after several shifts of men had made their meals, the cook room was actually warm. So we lingered in it, huddled around the table nearest to the stove.

Every time I went down there I thought of home: my mother's big roaring stove and all the food we used to have—chickens and hams and sweet brandied puddings in sacks; prune cakes and buttermilk muffins and every kind of bread; fat chunks of cheese; raisins and oranges and slabs of pie drowning in cream ... It was unbearable sometimes, sitting in that bare cook room, hungrier than ever for having eaten just a mouthful, remembering the laden tables of home. Yet we all did it. We couldn't help ourselves. We even talked about it. If we could go to the Astor House in New York for supper tonight, what would we order? And every man would mention his favorites, and we'd ache over them, and laugh over them, and swear we'd go there one day, and eat everything in the place, and send the bill to Jeff Davis. . . .

After a while the men grew melancholy and drifted away, one by one, and there were only half a dozen of my own mess left, Slither among them. Nobody had asked him what he'd eat at the Astor House, and he never said. He scarcely said anything at all. He looked like a man with way too much on his mind, and I had a fair idea what some of it might be. His girl back in Springfield, for one thing. She was from one of those 'forty-eighter families, refugees from the troubles in Europe. They were poor as mice, he told me once, but very patriotic—all for the Union and liberty, as passionate about it as any native-born American. I knew he was utterly, hopelessly, in love with her. He would take out the small daguerreotype he had, fondle it like a jewel and run a finger very gently around the frame, as though he could touch her so, and his face would turn all soft and hungry. How would he explain himself, I wondered, when all of this got back to Springfield? How would he tell *her* what a nice gentleman Major Cluny was, and how he, Slater, was just trying to survive?

There was a clatter of feet on the stairs, and we all looked up in dismay, expecting the prison guards, wondering what new and unexpected misery they would inflict on us. But it was Lieutenant Sprague who came storming in, followed by a small horde of his friends.

"You dirty rat!" he cried, and swore—the longest, vilest string of cuss words I'd ever heard a man use, all of them flung at Jeremy Slater. He was still swearing when he got to the table and hauled the captain out of his chair. Some of us were shouting, too, by then: *What's going on? What happened?*

Sprague was a bigger man even than me. He towered over Slither, and shook him like a rat, still calling him names. It took three of us to calm him down enough to make sense.

"He told! The dirty bastard told! That's how he got his boots!" There was another flood of cuss words, and Slither's voice somewhere in the midst of them, protesting: he didn't know what Sprague was talking about, and whatever it was, he didn't do it. Sprague hit him in the stomach, and Slither folded like a wet towel.

"Told *what*, damn it," I demanded. "What the devil's going on?"

"Our escape! Captain Deihl had it all planned, and this son of a bitch gave it away! The Rebs just came in, a couple of minutes ago, and they went right to the place. Right to the window. We had the bar almost worked loose; the captain figured a couple more days would have done it. He had a rope hid away, made out of scraps of blanket, and they went straight for that, too. Pulled up the floorboard and there it was. How the hell did they know if he didn't tell them?"

I looked at Slither, still bent over, trying to get his breath. I felt sick all through. Still, I stood up for him . . . one more time.

"Did he even know about it?" I asked.

"Of course he did. He come in on us once, just when we were putting the stuff away. You all know he's sneaking around all the time. Everybody else was gathering for roll call an' he was busy spying on us. And then he made a big show of seeing nothing. But I know he saw it. And I know he told."

". . . Didn't . . ." Slater muttered, between gulps of pain.

"Oh, you didn't, huh?" Sprague grabbed hold of his hair and yanked his head up. "All right, then. You tell us what you gave the Rebels for those boots, and maybe we'll believe you. *Maybe*."

"It was for helping . . . in the hospital. Back off, Sprague . . . damn you. . . . I never told them anything. I—"

"Hospital, my ass!" With another string of curses, Sprague smashed the captain back across the table. "You get all sorts of things for helping in the hospital. They gave you extra food. They gave you a blanket. They didn't goddamn give you boots, too. You tell us what you did for them or I'll break your scummy arm off!"

"Sprague . . ." somebody cautioned.

Sprague wasn't listening. He had Slither's right arm pinned hard against the sharp edge of the wooden table. *One quick snap*, I thought, and shuddered.

Slither looked straight at me. "I never betrayed anyone! For Christ's sake, Rob, you know me! Tell them!"

You know me. . . . For a moment I stood irresolute, my officer's training and my Christian conscience—such as they both were—pushing me in one direction, and fifteen years of memories pushing me in the other—those fifteen years he had just drawn to my attention. It was the worst wrong thing he could have done, reminding me how well I knew him, how thoroughly I remembered his weaseling, underhanded ways.

I drew a deep breath, and turned away. *You got yourself into this mess, Slither; you get yourself out. . . .*

I started walking, too numb to think, and almost plowed headlong into Colonel Thiessen. I don't believe he even saw me. He was in full flight, and he looked like Jehovah on the morning of the flood. Even Sprague must have wilted at the sound of his voice—not a loud voice, but so dangerous it could have splintered a tree.

"That will be enough, gentlemen! That will be *quite* enough!"

Sprague hesitated, but only for a second. Then he cursed and flung Slither's arm aside. The captain eased himself upright, with considerably more dignity than I expected. He looked straight at Sprague.

"Lieutenant, next time you say your prayers, ask the good Lord to fetch you up some brains. He missed you the first time around."

"Get out of here, Slater," Thiessen said grimly.

"Yes, sir."

Thiessen barely waited till the little grub was gone, and then he tore into us. This was not—and he repeated—*not* the sort of behavior he expected from officers of the United States Army. We were a disgrace to our uniforms. We were an embarrassment to our country. What the *devil* did we think we were doing, anyway?

"You were the one who said he was getting too friendly with the Rebels, sir," I pointed out.

"I told you to have a talk with him, damn it. I didn't tell you to lynch him."

"He sold Deihl to the Rebels!" Sprague cried savagely. "For a goddamn pair of boots!"

"Maybe he did. And maybe he didn't. What evidence do you have? I mean *facts*, Lieutenant Sprague. Not hunches, not suspicion, not prejudice, not a pile of goddamn schoolyard nonsense. *Evidence.* Something that would stand up for one minute, somewhere, in at least one shabby backwoods excuse for a courtroom. . . . What do you have, Sprague? Or have any of you men ever heard of due process?"

"And what due process is Deihl going to get, down in that hole with the rats?"

"So we lower ourselves to the level of our jailers? Is that it?"

For this we had no answer. And though Thiessen and Sprague went on arguing, mostly about the question of what Slither knew, and who else might or might not have known it, I pretty much stopped listening. I felt ashamed in a part of myself, because Thiessen was right: we'd behaved like thugs. And in another part of myself I was mad as hell, because Slither had got the best of us again. Used our own best man and our own best principles against us, and walked away with a jaunty insult on his lips: *Get the Lord to fetch you up some brains, Sprague. . . .*

Evidence. *Fair enough, Thiessen. You want evidence, you'll get it . . . if it's the last thing I ever do!*

I thought it would be a long wait, getting something solid on the little grub. It took all of three days. They must have been hard days for Slater. Hardly anyone would talk to him, except maybe to call him Slither to his face, or to make soft hissing noises and small, snaky wiggles with their hands as he walked by. He went about quiet as a mouse, and spent as much time in the hospital as he could, with the Rebels.

I almost never let him out of my sight. I kept myself awake at night for hours, but if he snuck out on us, I never caught him at it.

Every morning around nine o'clock, and every afternoon around four, we had to gather in the central room of the second-floor quarters, where we lined up in rows to be counted. Immediately after this, on the third afternoon, Slither disappeared. I suppose I blinked, because I never saw him leave. I simply looked around the room for him, and he was no longer there. I searched the rest of our quarters, quickly, and then, as a last resort, I went down to the cook room. I didn't expect him to be there; he had made a point of going nowhere by himself, except to the hospital. Most especially he stayed away from places where he might be cornered and attacked.

The cook room was empty, too. Just a long, dismal stretch of wooden tables and high gloomy windows. Even the stove had grown cold.

I heard the voice of a Rebel guard behind me, very soft.

"Well, Mackie, what do you think? Do I make a passable Virginian?"

I spun around, utterly bewildered. And for ten or twenty seconds—perhaps for even longer—I almost didn't recognize him. Because he was perfect. The drawl. The uniform. Even the stance, polished and easy and master of all he surveyed. A Southern gentleman born and bred. Oh, yes, he was a passable Virginian.

The uniform was spanking new, and bore the insignia of a Confederate major.

"Where the devil did you get that?" I whispered.

"Major Cluny ordered up a new one. Standard military issue, so of course it didn't fit. He's a man who likes to look dashing, and heaven knows I'm the best tailor in Richmond. And the cheapest. He even gave me a day off to work on it. I had to shorten the legs quite a bit; he's taller than I am. But it's rather becoming, don't you think? A nice gray outfit to go with my new shoes?"

"You planned this all along, didn't you?" I felt like an idiot. And I felt small, too, unbearably small, because it had never crossed my mind that he might be planning anything. "You should have told us. Goddamn it, man, you might've got your arm broke to splinters."

"Yes, that was a near thing." He didn't look at me, saying it, and I felt smaller still. "I had to do it right, Rob, or not at all."

I had no business questioning him further, but I did it anyway. Because I knew Sprague was correct about one thing: the blanket and the extra food the Rebels gave him were all he was likely to have received for his work in the hospital. And Cluny, naive though he was, probably hadn't rewarded him before the work on his uniform was done.

"How *did* you get the boots, Jeremy?"

"I did nothing to harm any of you. And that, Captain Mackie, is all you need to know." And then he looked me hard in the eye. Dead on. It was the same look I'd seen on his face once or twice before, when the whole world was blowing up around us. "I couldn't walk out of here without them, now could I?"

I said nothing. I remembered the nights he slipped away and didn't come back for hours. I remembered Colonel Thiessen and his talk about courage. Moral courage. The real kind. *Right.*

There was a small bundle lying on the table. Slater's fading blue uniform, a few personal trifles. He handed it to me. "If I don't make it, I'd appreciate getting these back. Otherwise they're yours. Now, if you'll wish me Godspeed, I'm going to slither on out of here."

We shook hands. I told him I was sorry, and I wished him luck. He accepted my friendliness with a small smile, but I don't think it mattered to him very much. It came three full days too late.

What he did next we learned in bits and pieces from the guards. He walked calmly into the prison administrative offices next door, paused at the desk of a clerk, and asked if he would be so kind as to tell him where he might find Mr. So-and-so, a minor official who had an office in a building a small way down the street. The clerk politely accompanied him to the door, past the guard who didn't bother to challenge them, since the guard knew the clerk and the clerk appeared to know the stranger—they were, after all, chatting so nicely together.

And finally I understood what he had done, cozying up to the Rebels all those weeks. He hadn't simply been earning their trust. He'd been learning how to talk and how Libby was run and where everything was located and what names he ought to be dropping as he drawled his way out. . . . Oh, it was Slither, all right—Slither at his very best.

I told Colonel Thiessen what had happened, quietly, and we covered for him at the next day's roll calls. The Rebels didn't miss him till around suppertime, when Major Cluny came looking for his uniform. Somebody thought Slither had gone upstairs. No? Then he must still be in the hospital. Gosh, he hadn't gone there at all today? Well, then, he must be in the cook room. Or maybe he had the trots, and was holed up in the sinks . . . ? The more we tried to help Cluny, the sicker he began to look. When he left he was rigid, his mouth as thin as a saber's edge and his face as gray as his Rebel garb. I almost felt sorry for him.

The weeks went by, but we learned nothing of Slater's fate. Every time a batch of new prisoners was brought in, I was scared he might be with them. I knew he'd pay hard for his tricks if they ever caught him. Finally, late in February, I received a battered letter from the North, from a cousin who didn't exist. I had to read it twice before I understood that "Uncle John" referred to our regimental colonel, and Colonel Thiessen had to tell me that "ophidians" were snakes. The rest was clear enough.

Dear Cousin Robert,

I hope you are all right. I thought it would be nice to go home for my birthday. It's a miserable journey in the wintertime, as you might expect. When I got there, Uncle John said the only thing I looked to be good for was a coatrack. So he sent me to Springfield for three weeks. I bought Karin a ring, and we are now formally engaged. I went to see your folks. They are well but very worried about you and they send you all their prayers and good wishes. I'm heading back to Uncle John's place tomorrow; he has a lot of work to do. Good luck to you all. Your obedient servant and ophidian cousin,

Jay N Taylor.

Jeremy Slater and I will never really be friends; we're too different for that. Though he's never blamed me for the times I wronged him, I don't suppose he will ever quite forget. But if we both survive the war, I mean to go to Boston once a year, every summer, to the very best part of Boston, where

I'll find a fancy shop with a fancy sign in the window: J. N. SLATER, ESQUIRE: FINE TAILORING FOR GENTLEMEN. And I'll buy myself something fine—the finest I can afford—as a way of saying what I think of him.

Once every summer. For as long as I live.

ABOUT THE EDITOR

Ed Gorman, winner of the Shamus Award, has been nominated for the Edgar and Bram Stoker Awards. He is the author of more than twenty novels ranging from mystery and suspense to western and historical fiction. He's also had dozens of short stories published in many magazines and anthologies. Editor of *Mystery Scene Magazine,* he lives with his wife, author Carol Gorman, in Cedar Rapids, Iowa.

CIVIL WAR HEROES

BEHIND ENEMY LINES